VIKING
Odinn's Child

Also by Tim Severin

NON-FICTION

The Brendan Voyage

The Sindbad Voyage

The Jason Voyage

The Ulysses Voyage

Crusader

In Search of Genghis Khan

The China Voyage

The Spice Island Voyage

In Search of Moby Dick

Seeking Robinson Crusoe

TIM SEVERIN

VIKING
Odinn's Child

MACMILLAN

First published 2005 by Macmillan
an imprint of Pan Macmillan Ltd
Pan Macmillan, 20 New Wharf Road, London N1 9RR
Basingstoke and Oxford
Associated companies throughout the world
www.panmacmillan.com

ISBN 1 4050 4112 9 (HB)
ISBN 1 4050 4113 7 (TPB)

The extract on page 308 from *A Celtic Miscellany: Translations from the Celtic Literatures* by Kenneth Hurlstone Jackson, first published 1951, is reproduced courtesy of Routledge.

5 7 9 8 6

A CIP catalogue record for this book is available from
the British Library.

Typeset by SetSystems Ltd, Saffron Walden, Essex
Printed and bound in Great Britain by
Mackays of Chatham plc, Chatham, Kent

MAPS

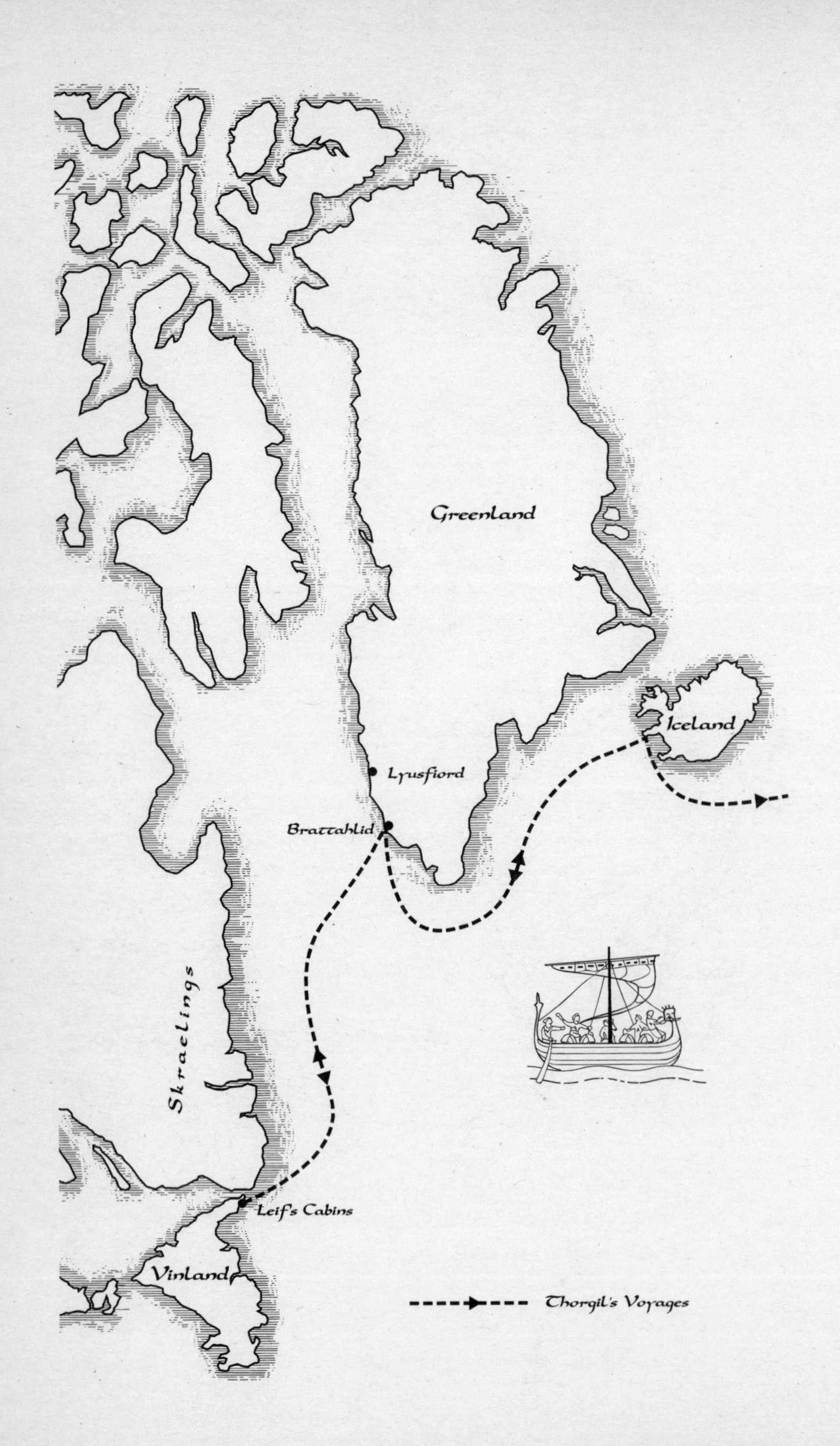
Greenland
Iceland
Lysfiord
Brattahlid
Skraelings
Leif's Cabins
Vinland
Thorgil's Voyages

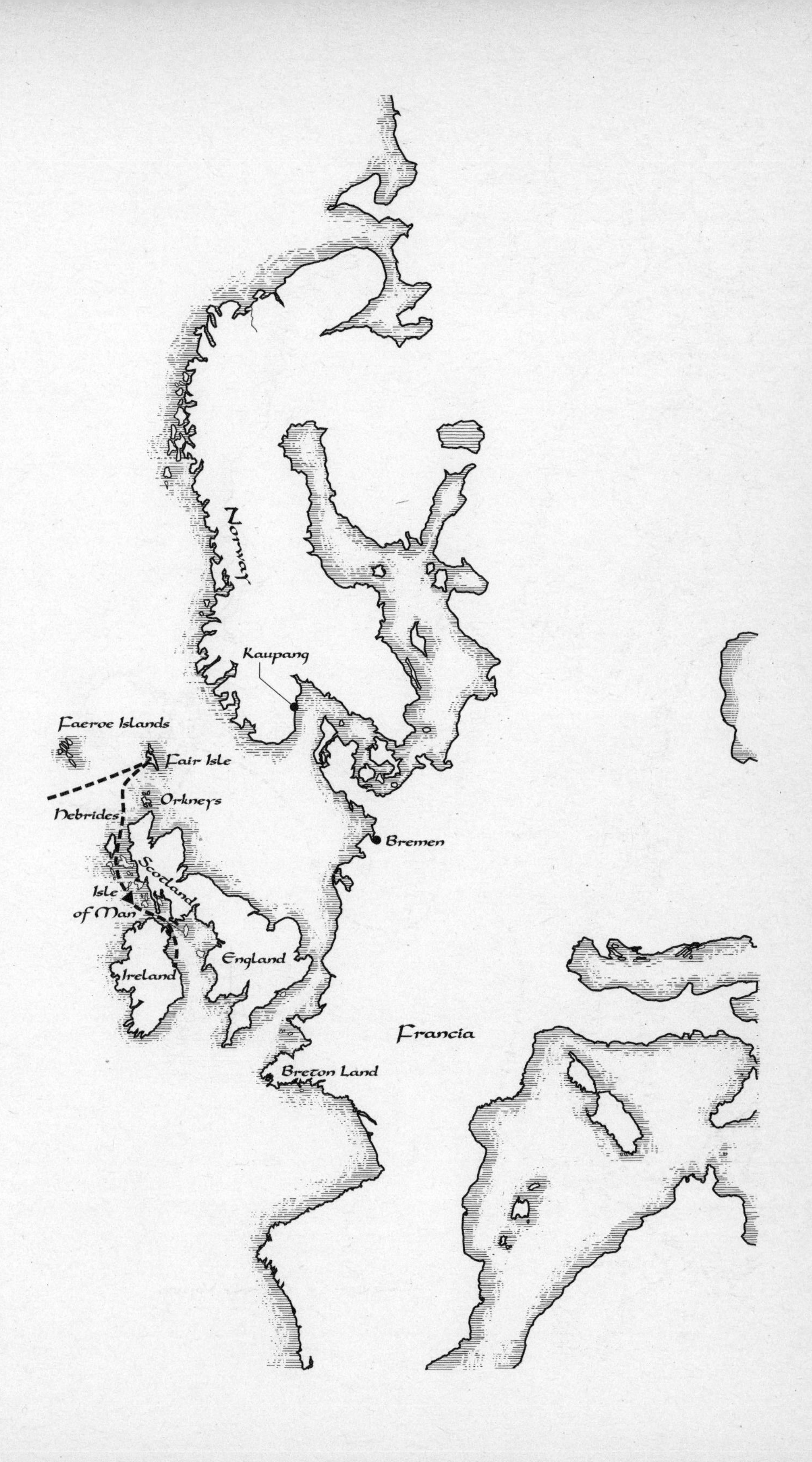
Norway
Kaupang
Faeroe Islands
Fair Isle
Orkneys
Hebrides
Scotland
Isle of Man
Ireland
England
Bremen
Francia
Breton Land

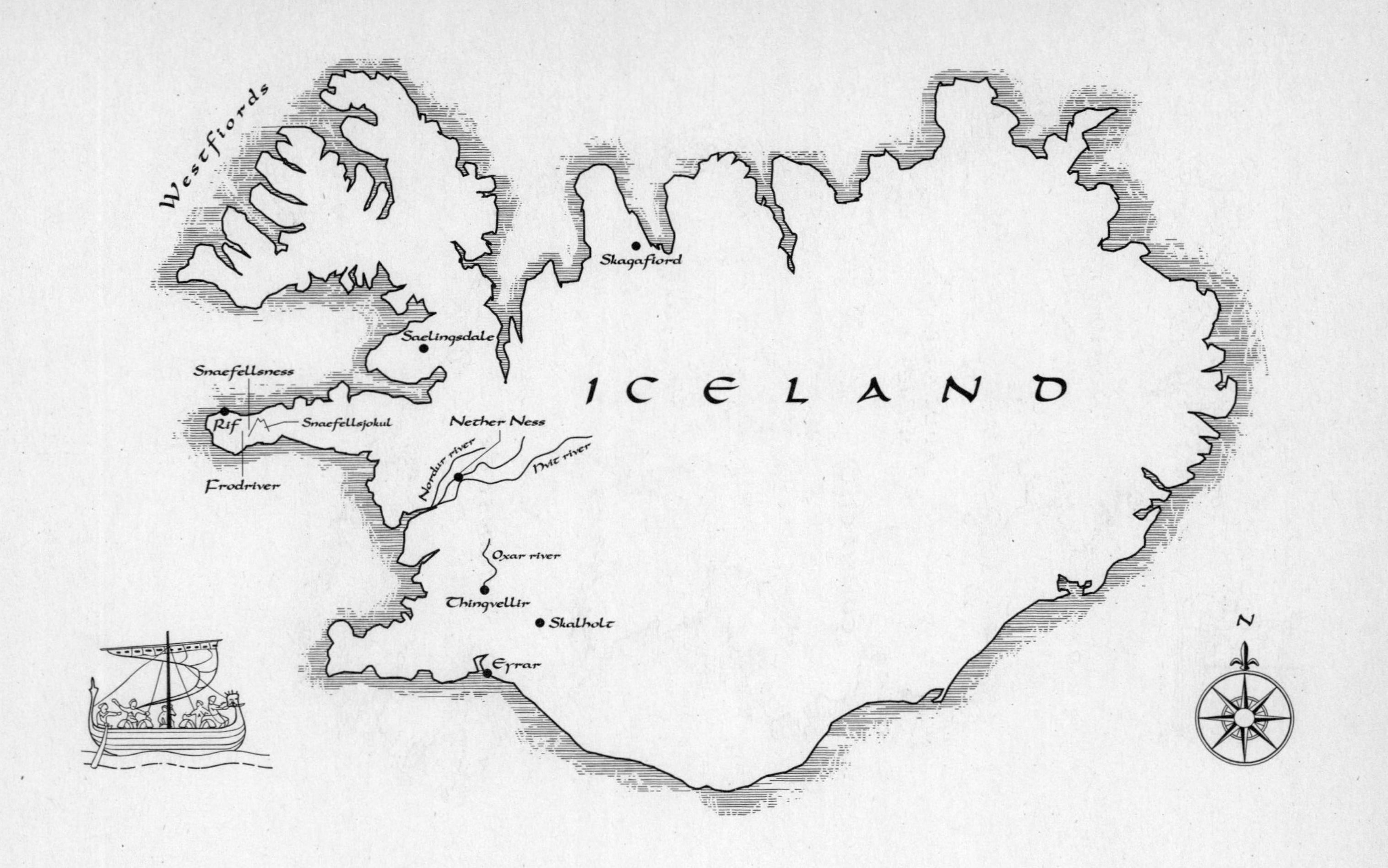
Westfiords
Skagafiord
Saelingsdale
Snaefellsness
Rif
Snaefellsjokul
Frodriver
Nether Ness
Nordur river
Hvit river
ICELAND
Oxar river
Thingvellir
Skalholt
Eyrar
N

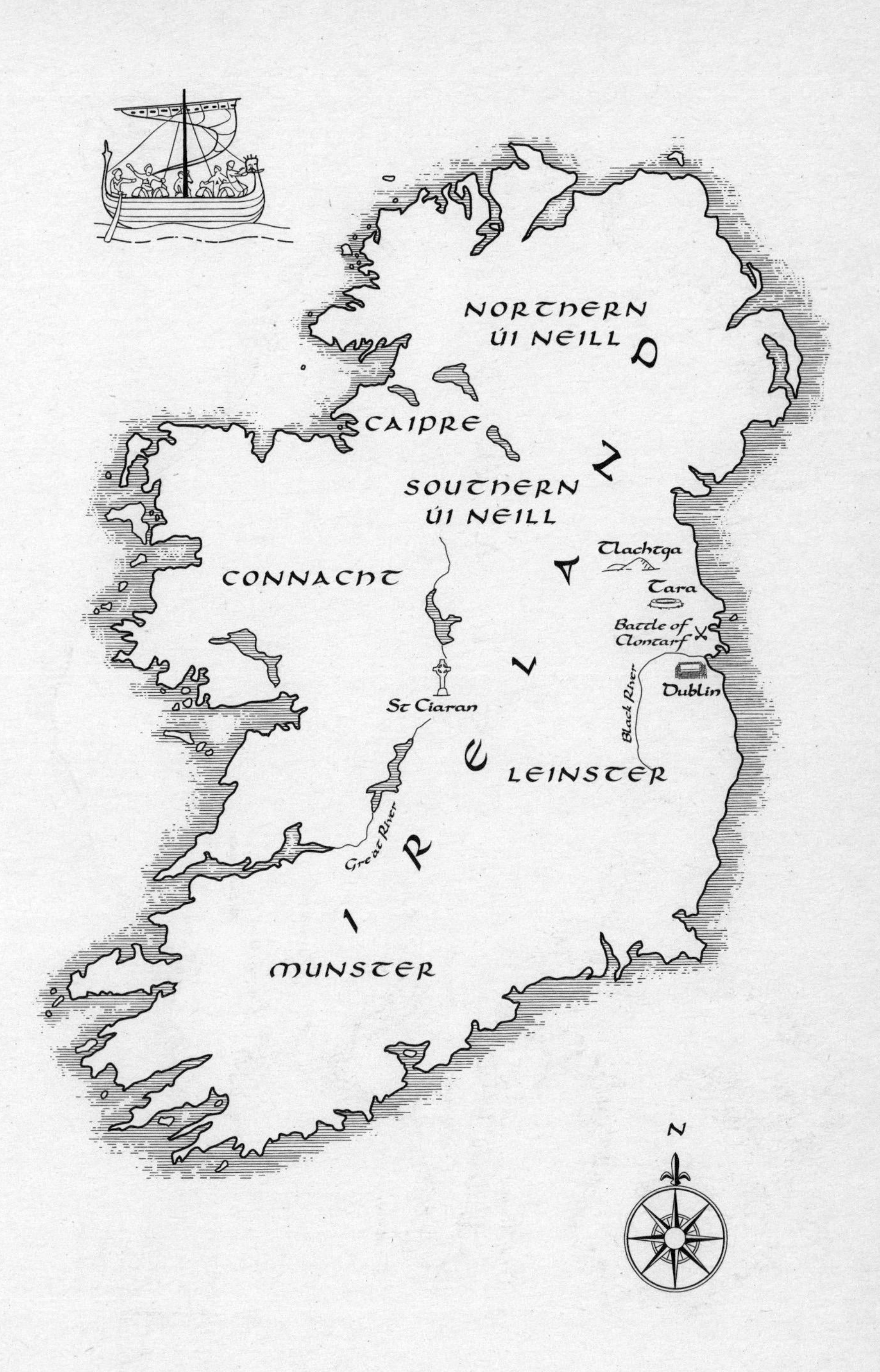

NORTHERN
ÚI NEILL
CAIPRE
SOUTHERN
ÚI NEILL
CONNACHT
IRELAND
Tlachtga
Tara
Battle of
Clontarf
Dublin
Black River
St Ciaran
LEINSTER
Great River
MUNSTER
N

⁂

To my holy and blessed master, Abbot Geraldus, it is with much doubt and self-questioning that I pen this note for your private attention, laying before you certain disturbing details which until now have been hidden, so that I may humbly seek your advice. In choosing this course I am ever mindful how the works of the devil, with their thousand sharp thorns and snares, lie in wait for the feet of the unwary, and that only His mercy will save us from error and the manifold pitfalls of wickedness. Yet, as you read the appended document, you will understand why I have been unable to consult with others of our community lest I sow among them dismay and disillusion. For it seems that a viper has been nurtured in our bosom, and our presumed brother in Christ, the supposed monk called Thangbrand, was an impostor and a fount of true wickedness.

You will recall, my revered master, that you requested of your unworthy servant a full and true inventory of all documents and writings now in our abbey's keeping. As librarian of our community, I began this task in dutiful compliance with your wishes, and during this labour discovered the above-mentioned document where it lay unremarked among the other volumes in our collection of sacred writings. It bears no identifying mark and the script is well formed, the work of a trained penman, so – may I be forgiven if I have committed the sin of presumption – I began to read, imagining to find recorded therein a life of one of those saints such as Wilfred of most blessed memory, whose shining and glorious example was so ably recorded by our most learned predecessor, the monk Eddius Stephanus.

But such is the mystery of His ways that I have found instead a tale which often substitutes hypocrisy for truth, depravity in place of abstinence, pagan doubt for true faith. Much I do not comprehend, part I can comprehend dimly and by prayer and fasting strive to expunge from my mind. Yet other – and this is what troubles me – contains notice of many distant lands where surely the seed of truth will flourish on fertile soil if it is broadcast by the faithful, trusting only in God and his sublime grace.

Of the identity of the author of the work there can be little doubt. He is remembered by several of the older members of our congregation, and by subtle enquiry I have been able to confirm that he came to us already an old man, sorely hurt and in need of succour. His learning and demeanour led all our congregation to suppose he was in holy orders. Yet this was but the skill of the arch-deceiver, for this present work reveals the unswerving error of his ways and the falsity of his heart. Truly it is said that it is difficult for a man who has fallen deeply into temptation to emerge from the wallow of his sin save with the grace of our Lord.

Also I have learned how this false Thangbrand spent long hours alone in the scriptorium in quiet and arduous labour. Writing materials were supplied, for he was a gifted copyist and possessed of many artistic skills despite advancing years and fading eyesight. Indeed, his posture, hunched close over his pages, shielded his work from others' gaze and rendered it difficult to overlook what he was writing. But Satan nerved his fingers, for instead of sacred text he was engaged in preparing this dark and secret record. Naturally I have instructed that henceforward no writing materials be provided to anyone without due justification. But whether what has now been written is a blasphemy I have neither the intellect nor learning to judge. Nor do I know whether this work should be destroyed or whether it should be retained for the strange and curious information it contains. For is it not written that 'A much travelled man knows many things, and a man of great experience will talk sound sense'?

Regrettably, two further volumes I hold in safe keeping, presuming them to be a continuation of this blasphemous and wicked memorial. Neither volume have I investigated, pending your instruction. Holy father, be reassured that no further particle of the reprobate's writing exists. I have searched the library most attentively for any other trace left by this pretended monk, who departed unexpectedly and secretly from our community, and I found nothing. Indeed, until these documents were discovered, it was presumed that this pretended monk had wandered away from us, confused in his senility, and we expected for him to be returned by the charitable or to hear that he had departed this life. But such has not happened, and it is evident from this account that this would not be the first occasion on which he has absconded like a thief in the night from the company of his trusting and devout companions. May his sins be forgiven.

On behalf of our community, beloved master, I pray for your inspired guidance and that the Almighty Lord may keep you securely in bliss. Amen.

Æthelred
Sacristan and Librarian
Written in the month of October in the Year of our Lord One Thousand and Seventy

ONE

I SMILE SECRETLY at the refectory gossip. There is a monk in Bremen across the North Sea who has been charged with collecting information for the Bishop of Bremen-Hamburg. His name is Adam, and he has been set the task of finding out everything he can about the farthest places and peoples of our world so that he may compile a complete survey of all the lands known, however dimly, to the Christian Church, perhaps with a view to converting them later. He interviews travellers and sailors, interrogates returned pilgrims and foreign diplomats, makes notes and sends out lists of questions, travels for himself and observes. If only he knew . . . right here in this monkish backwater is someone who could tell him as much about strange places and odd events as any of the witnesses whom he is cross-examining so diligently.

Had I not heard about this assiduous German, I would be content to spin out the last years of my life in the numbing calm of this place where I now find myself in my seventieth year. I would continue to copy out sacred texts and embellish the initial letters with those intricate interlacings which my colleagues believe I do for the greater glory of God, though the truth is that I take a secret delight in knowing that these curlicues and intricate patterns derive from the heathen past they condemn as idolatrous. Instead, their refectory tittle-tattle has provoked me to find a corner seat in our quiet scriptorium and take up my pen to begin this secret history of my life and travels. How would my colleagues react, I wonder, if they discovered that living quietly among them is one of that feared breed of northmen 'barbarians', whose memory still sends shivers down their spines. If they knew that a man from the longships wears the cowl and cassock beside them it would, I think, give a new edge to that plea which recently I found penned in the margin of one of their older annals – 'From the fury of the foreigner O Lord preserve us.'

Writing down my memories will also help pass the time for an old man, who otherwise would watch the play of sunshine and shadow moving across the edge of the page while the other copyists hunch over the desks behind me. And as this secret work is to keep me from boredom, then I will begin briskly – as my mentor the brithem, once drummed into my young head more than half a century ago – and of course at the very beginning.

My birth was a double near-miss. First, I failed by a few months to be born on the millennium, that cataclysmic year foretold by those who anticipated, often with relish, the end of the world as we knew it and the great Armageddon prophesied by the gloomy Church Fathers of the Christians. Second, I only just missed being the first of our far-flung race to be born in that land far distant across the western ocean, scarcely known even now except in mists and swirling wisps of rumour. It was, at that time, dubbed Vinland the Good. As luck would have it, my foster brother had the distinction to be the original and perhaps only fair-skinned child to come into this world on those distant shores. However, I can claim that the three years I spent there are about as long a span of time in that place as anyone from our people can boast, and because I was still so young they have left their mark. I still recall vividly those huge, silent forests, the dark water of bog streams lit by the glint of silver salmon, the odd striding pace of the wide-antlered deer, and those strange native peoples we called the Skraelings, with their slant eyes and striking ugliness, who ultimately drove us away.

My own birthplace was a land on a far smaller scale: Birsay, an insignificant, dune-rippled island in the windswept archipelago off the north coast of Scotland which the monk-geographers call the Orcades. When I first drew breath there, Birsay was home to no more than a couple of hundred inhabitants, living in half a dozen longhouses and sod-walled huts randomly placed around the only large structure – a great long hall shaped like an upturned boat, a design I was to grow very familiar with in later years and in some strange settings. It was the main residence of the earls of Orkney, and the widow of the previous earl, Jarl Haakon, told me of the circumstances of my birth when I visited that same long hall some fifteen years later, seeking to trace my mother, who had disposed of me waif-like when I was barely able to take my first infant steps.

My mother, according to the earl mother, was a massive woman, big-boned, muscular and not a little fearsome. She had green-brown eyes set in narrow sockets under very dark and well-marked eyebrows, and her one glory was a cascade of beautiful brown hair. She was also running to fat. Her family was part Norse and part Irish, and I have no doubt whatever that the Celtic side predominated in her, for she was to leave behind an awesome reputation for possessing strange and uneasy gifts of the sort which trouble, yet fascinate, men and women who come in contact with them. What is more, some of her character passed on to me and has accounted for most of the unusual events of my life.

The earl mother told me that my birth was not an occasion for rejoicing because my mother had disgraced herself. I was illegitimate. Thorgunna, my mother, had suddenly appeared at Birsay in the summer of the previous year, arriving from Dublin aboard a trading ship and bringing with her an impressive quantity of personal luggage, but without parents or a husband or any explanation for her journey. Her obvious wealth and self-confident style meant she was well received by Jarl Haakon and his family, and they gave her a place in their household. The rumour soon arose that my mother was the ill-favoured offspring of one of our opportunist Norse chieftains, who had gone to try his luck in

Ireland and married the daughter of a minor Irish king. This speculation, according to the earl mother, was largely based on Thorgunna's aloof manner and the fact that Ireland abounds with kinglets and chieftains with high pretensions and few means, a situation I was to experience for myself in my slave days.

THORGUNNA LIVED WITH the earl's entourage through the autumn and winter and was treated as a member of the family, though with respect for her size and strength of character rather than with any close fondness. And then, in the early spring of the pre-millennium year, it became obvious that she was with child. This was a sensation. No one had ever considered that Thorgunna was still of child-bearing age. Like most women, she said as little as possible about her age and she was far too fearsome a woman for anyone to enquire, however discreetly. By her appearance it had been presumed that she was in her mid-fifties, barren, and had probably always been so. Indeed she was such a broadly built woman that not until the sixth month was her condition noticeable, and that made the sensation all the more spectacular. The immediate reaction after the first stunned disbelief was to confirm what the sharper tongues had been saying all winter: Thorgunna employed sorcery. How else could a woman of her age be able to carry a child inside her, and how else – and this was the crux of the matter – had she been able to seduce the father so utterly?

'There was never the least doubt who your father was,' the earl mother told me. 'Indeed there was a great deal of jealousy and spitefulness from the other women of the household on the subject. He was such a dashing and good-looking man, and so much younger than your mother. People were hard put to explain how he had fallen under her spell. They said she had brewed up a love potion and slipped it into his food, or that she had cast a foreign charm over him, or that she had him under the effect of the evil eye.' Apparently what infuriated the critics even more was that neither Thorgunna nor her lover tried to conceal their affair. They sat together, gazed at one another, and in the evenings ostentatiously went off to their own corner of the long hall and slept beneath the same cloak. 'What puzzled people even more was how your father became so besotted with your mother less than a week after he arrived. He had barely set foot in Birsay when she carried him off. Someone remarked that he looked like a good-looking toy being seized to comfort the giantess.'

Who was this glamorous traveller, my natural father? He was a well-to-do farmer and fisherman whose ship had sailed into Birsay's small anchorage in the autumn while en route from the farthest of the Norse lands, Greenland. Indeed he was the second son of the founder of the small and rather struggling colony in that ice-shrouded place. His father's name was Eirik rauda or 'Erik the Red' (I shall try to insert an translation wherever appropriate as my wanderings have given me a smattering of many languages and a near fluency in several) and his own was Leif, though in later years I would find that more people had heard of him as Leif the Lucky than as Leif Eriksson. He, like most of his family, was a rather wilful, dour man with a marked sense of independence. Tall and strong, he had tremendous stamina, which is a useful attribute for any frontier colonist if combined with a capacity for hard work. His face was rather thin (a feature which I have inherited) with a broad forehead, pale blue eyes and a prominent nose that had been broken at some stage and never set straight. He was, people seemed to find, a man whom it was difficult to argue with, and I would agree with them. Once he had made up his mind, he was almost impossible to be persuaded, and though he was capable of retreating behind a series of gruff, blunt refusals, his usual manner was courteous and reserved. So he was certainly respected and, in many ways, very popular.

Leif had not intended to stop in at Birsay. He was on his way from Greenland to Norway, sailing on the direct run which normally passes south of the Sheep Islands, which our Norsemen call the Faeroes. But an unseasonal bout of fog, followed by a couple of days of easterly headwinds, had pushed his course too far to the south, and he had made a premature landfall in the Orkneys. He did not want to dawdle at Birsay, for he was on an important errand for his father. He had some Greenland products to sell – the usual stuff such as sealskins, walrus hides, walrus-skin ropes, a bit of homespun cloth, several barrels of whale oil and the like – but the main reason for his journey was to represent his father at the Norwegian court before King Olaf Tryggvason, who was then at the height of his mania for converting everyone to the religion whose drab uniform I now wear.

Christianity, I have noted in my seventy years of lifetime, boasts how humility and peace will overcome all obstacles and the word of the Lord is to be spread by example and suffering. Yet I have observed that in practice most of our northern people were converted to this so-called peaceful belief by the threat of the sword and our best-loved weapon, the bearded axe. Of course, there were genuine martyrs for the White Christ faith as our people first called it. A few foolhardy priests had their tonsured heads lopped off by uncouth farmers in the backlands. But that was in an excess of drunken belligerence rather than pagan zeal, and their victims were a handful compared to the martyrs of the Old Ways, who were cajoled, threatened, bullied and executed by King Olaf either because they refused to convert or were too slow to do so. For them the word of the Lord arrived in a welter of blood, so there is little wonder that the prophesied violence of the millennial cataclysm was easy to explain.

But I digress: Erik had sent his son Leif off to Norway to forestall trouble. Even in faraway Greenland the menacing rattle of King Olaf's religious zeal had been heard. The king had already sent messengers to the Icelanders demanding that they adopt the new faith, even though they were not really Norwegian subjects. The Icelanders were worried that King Olaf would next send a missionary fleet equipped with rather more persuasive weapons than croziers. With Iceland subdued, fledgling Greenland would have been a mere trifle. A couple of boatloads of royal mercenaries would have overrun the tiny colony, dispossessed Erik's family, installed a new king's man, and Greenland would have been swallowed up as a Norwegian fief under the pretext of making it a colony for the White Christ. So Leif's job was to appear suitably eager to hear details of the new religion – a complete hypocrisy on Erik's part in fact, as he was to remain staunch to the Old Ways all his life – and even to ask for a priest to be sent out to Greenland to convert the colonists. I suspect that, if a priest *had* been found for the job, Leif had secret instructions from his father to abandon the meddling creature on the nearest beach at the first opportunity.

Erik also instructed his son to raise with King Olaf the delicate matter of Erik's outlawry. Erik was a proscribed man in Iceland – a hangover from some earlier troubles when he had been prone to settling disputes with sharp-edged weapons – and he was hoping that the king's protection would mean that certain aggrieved Icelanders would think twice about pursuing their blood feud with him. So, all in all, Leif had a rather delicate task set for him. To help his son, Erik devised what he thought could be a master stroke: a gift to catch the royal eye – a genuine Greenland polar bear to be presented to the royal menagerie.

The poor creature was a youngster which some of Erik's people had found, half-starved, on a melting floe of drift ice the previous spring. The floe must have been separated from the main pack by a back eddy and carried too far out to sea for the polar bear to swim to shore. By the time the animal was rescued it was too weak to put up a struggle and the hunters – they were out looking for seals – bagged it in a net and brought it home with them. Erik saw a use for the castaway and six months later the unhappy beast was again in a net and stowed in the bilges of Leif's embassy boat. By the time Birsay was sighted, the polar bear was so sickly that the crew thought it would die. The creature provided Leif with a first-rate excuse to dally away most of the winter on Birsay, allegedly to give the bear a chance to recuperate on a steady diet of fresh herring. Unfortunately this led to unkind jests that the bear and my mother Thorgunna were alike not only in character and gait, but in appetite as well.

That next April, when a favourable west wind had set in and looked as if it would stay steady for a few days, Leif and his men were eagerly loading up their ship, thanking the earl for his hospitality, and getting ready to head on for Norway when Thorgunna took Leif on one side and suggested that she go aboard with him. It was not an idea that appealed to Leif, for he had failed to mention to Thorgunna that he already had a wife in Greenland who would not look kindly on his foreign import. 'Then perhaps the alternative is going to be even less attractive,' Thorgunna continued. 'I am due to have your baby. And the child is going to be a boy.' Leif was wondering how Thorgunna could be so sure of her baby's sex, when she went on, 'At the first opportunity I will be sending him on to you.' According to Leif, who told me of this conversation when I was in my eleventh year and living with him in Greenland, my mother made the statement about sending me away from her with no more emotion than if she were telling Leif that she had been sewing a new shirt and would deliver it to him when it was ready. But then she softened and added, 'Eventually, if I have the chance, I intend to travel on to Greenland myself and find you.'

Under the circumstances my father behaved really very decently. On the evening before he set sail, he presented his formidable mistress with a fine waterproof Greenlandic sea cloak, a quantity of cash, a thin bracelet of almost pure gold and a belt of Greenland ivory made from the teeth of walrus. It was a very handsome gesture, and another speck in the eye for those hags who were saying that Thorgunna was being left in the lurch and was no better than she deserved. Anyhow, Leif then sailed off on his interrupted journey for Norway, making both a good passage and an excellent impression. King Olaf welcomed him at the Norwegian court, listened politely to what he had to say, and after keeping him hanging around the royal household for almost the whole summer, let him sail back to Greenland on the westerly winds of early autumn. As for the wretched polar bear, it was a temporary sensation. It was admired and petted, and then sent off to the royal kennels, where it was conveniently forgotten. Soon afterwards it picked up distemper from the dogs and died.

I was born into this world at about the same time that the polar bear departed it. Later in my life, a shaman of the forest peoples in Permia, up in the frozen zones, was to tell me that the spirit of the dying bear transferred itself to me by a sort of spiritual migration at the moment of my birth. I was reluctant to believe it, of course, but the shaman affirmed it as fact and as a result treated me with respect bordering on awe because the Permians worship the bear as the most powerful spirit of all. Whatever the truth about the transmigration of souls, I was born with a minimum of fuss and commotion on a summer's day in the year my present colleagues, sitting so piously around me, would describe as the year of our Lord, 999.

TWO

SHE CALLED ME Thorgils. It is a common enough Norse name and honours their favourite red-haired God. But then so do at least forty other boy's names from plain Thor through Thorstein to Thorvald, and half that number for girls, including my mother's own, Thorgunna. Perhaps Thorgils was her father's name. I simply have no idea, though later, when I wondered why she did not pick a more Irish-sounding name to honour her mother's people, I realised she was preparing me to grow up in my father's household. To live among the Norsemen with an Irish name would have led people to think that I was slave-born because there are many in Iceland and elsewhere whose Irish names, like Kormak and Njal, indicate that they are descended from Irish captives brought back when men went a-viking.

Thorgunna gave me my Norse name in the formal manner with the sprinkling of water. It might surprise my Christian brethren here in the scriptorium to know that there is nothing new in their splashing drops of water on the infant's head at baptism. The pagan northmen do the same when they name a child and it would be interesting to ask my cleric neighbours whether this deed provides any salvation for the innocent infant soul, even when done by heathen custom.

The year following my birth was the year that the Althing, the general assembly of Icelanders, chose to adopt Christianity as their religion, a decision which led to much dissension as I shall later have reason to describe. So, having been born on the cusp of the new millennium, I was named as a pagan at a time when the tide of the White Christ was beginning its inexorable rise. Like Cnut, the king in England whom I later served as an apprentice court poet, I soon knew that a rising tide is unstoppable, but I resolved that I would try to keep my head above it.

My mother had no intention of keeping me around her a moment longer than necessary. She proceeded to carry out her plans with a massive certainty, even with a squawling baby in tow. The money that Leif had given her meant that she was able to pay for a wet nurse and, within three months of my birth, she began to look around for an opportunity to leave Birsay and move on to Iceland.

She arrived in the early winter, and the trading ship which brought her dropped anchor off Snaefellsness, the long promontory which projects from Iceland's west coast. Most of the crew were from the Orkneys and Ireland and they had no particular family links among the Icelanders to determine their final port of call, so the crew decided to wait in the anchorage until news of their arrival had spread among the farmers of the region, then shift to the ripest harbour for trading to begin. Iceland has always been a country starved of foreign luxuries. There is not a single town or decent-sized village on the whole vast island, or a proper market. Its people are stock herders who set up their homesteads around the fringes of that rugged land wherever there was pasture for their cattle. In summer they send their herds inland to the high meadows, and in winter bring them back to their byres next to the house and feed them hay. Their own food is mostly gruel, sour milk and curds, with meat or fish or bird flesh when they can get it. It is a basic life. They dress in simple homespun clothes and, though they are excellent craftsmen, they lack the raw materials to work. With no forests on the island, their ships are mostly imported ready built from Norway. Little wonder that the Icelanders tend to join viking expeditions and loot the luxuries they do not have at home. Their viking raids also provide a channel for their chronic pugnacity, which otherwise turns inward and leads to those deadly quarrels and bloody feuds which I was to find it impossible to avoid.

Here I feel that I should try to clear up a misunderstanding among outsiders over what is meant by 'viking'. I have heard it said, for example, that the description is applied to men who come from the viks, the creeks and inlets of the north country, particularly of Norway. But this is incorrect. When the Norse people call someone a vikingr because he goes viking they mean a person who goes to sea to fight or harry, perhaps as a warrior on an expedition, perhaps as an outright brigand. Victims of such raids would readily translate the word as 'pirate', and indeed some Norse do see their vikingr in this light. Most Norsemen, however, regard those who go viking in a more positive light. In their eyes a vikingr is a bold fellow who sets out to make his fortune, takes his chance as a sea raider, and hopes to come home with great wealth and the honour which he has won by his personal bravery and audacity.

The arrival of a trading ship at Snaefellsness – moored in the little anchorage at Rif – was just the sort of news which spread rapidly among these rural farmers. Many of them made plans to row out to the anchored ship, hoping to be the first to look over the cargo in her hold and make an offer to buy or barter for the choicest items. They quickly brought back word that a mysterious and apparently rich woman from Orkney was aboard the ship, though nothing was said about her babe in arms. Naturally, among the farmers' wives along the coast this was a subject of great curiosity. What was her destination? Did she dress in a new fashion? Was she related to anyone in Iceland? What were her intentions? The person who took it upon herself to answer these riddles was almost as formidable as my mother – Thurid Barkadottir, wife of a well-to-do farmer, Thorodd Skattkaupandi, and half-sister to one of the most influential and devious men in Iceland, Snorri Godi, a man so supple that he was managing to be a follower of Thor and the White Christ at the same time and who, more than once, was to shape the course of my life. Indeed it was Snorri who many years later told me of the relationship between Thurid Barkadottir and my mother, how it began with a confrontation, developed into a wary truce and ended in events that became part of local folk memory and scandal.

Thurid's extravagant taste was known to everyone in the area of Frodriver, close by Rif, where she and Thorodd ran their large farm. She was an extremely vain woman who liked to dress as showily as possible. She had a large wardrobe and an eye-catching collection of jewellery, which she did not hesitate to display to her neighbours. Under the pretence of being a good housekeeper, she was the sort of woman who likes to acquire costly furnishings for her house – the best available wall hangings, the handsomest tableware and so forth – and invite as many guests as possible to show them off. In short, she was a self-centred, ostentatious woman who considered herself a cut above her neighbours. Being half-sister to Snorri Godi was another encouragement for her to preen herself. Snorri was one of the leading men of the region, indeed in the whole of Iceland. His family were among the earliest settlers and he exercised the powers of a godi, a local chieftain-by-election, though in Snorri's case the title was hereditary in all but name. His farmlands were large and well favoured, which made him a rich man, and they contained also the site of an important temple to the God Thor. Thurid felt that, with such illustrious and powerful kin, she was not bound by normal conventions. She was notorious for her long-running affair with a neighbouring farmer – Bjorn Breidvikingakappi. Indeed it was confidently rumoured that Bjorn was father to one of Thurid's sons. But Thurid ignored the local gossip, and in this respect, as in several others, there was a marked resemblance between the two women who now met on the deck of the trading ship – Thurid and my mother.

My mother came off best. Thurid clambered aboard from the small rowing boat which had brought her out to the ship. Scrambling up the side of a vessel from a small rowing boat usually places the newcomer at a temporary disadvantage. The newcomer pauses to catch breath, straightens up, finds something to hold on to so as not to topple back overboard or into the ship, and then looks around. Thurid was disconcerted to find my mother sitting impassively on a large chest on the stern deck, regarding her with flat disinterest as she balanced unsteadily on the edge of the vessel. Thorgunna made no effort to come forward to greet her or to help. My mother's lack of response piqued Thurid, and as soon as she had composed herself she came straight to the point and made the mistake of treating my mother as an itinerant pedlar.

'I would like to see your wares,' she announced. 'If you have anything decent to sell, I would consider paying you a good price.'

My mother's calm expression scarcely changed. She rose to her full height, giving Thurid ample time to note the expensive cloth of her well-cut cloak of scarlet and the fine Irish enamelwork on the brooch.

'I'm not in the business of buying and selling,' she replied coolly, 'but you are welcome to see some of my wardrobe if that would be of interest here in Iceland.' Her disdain implied that the Icelandic women were out of touch with current fashion.

My mother then stepped aside and opened the chest on which she had been sitting. She riffled through a high-quality selection of bodices and embroidered skirts, a couple of very fine wool cloaks, some lengths of silk, and several pairs of elegant leather slippers – though it must be admitted that they were not dainty, my mother's feet being exceptionally large. The colours and quality of the garments – my mother particularly liked dark blues and a carmine red made from an expensive dye – put to shame the more drab clothing which Thurid was wearing. Thurid's eyes lit up. She was not so much jealous of my mother's wardrobe as covetous. She would have loved to obtain some of it for herself, and no one else on Iceland, particularly in the locality of Frodriver, was going to get the chance to buy it.

'Do you have anywhere to stay during your visit to our country?' she asked as sweetly as she could manage.

'No,' replied my mother, who was quick to discern Thurid's motives. 'It would be nice to spend a little time ashore, and have a chance to wear something a little more elegant than these sea clothes, though I may be a little over-dressed for provincial life. I assembled my wardrobe with banquets and grand occasions in mind rather than for wearing aboard ship or going on local shore visits.'

Thurid's mind was made up. If my mother would not sell her clothes, then at least she could wear them in Thurid's farmhouse for all visitors to see, and maybe in time this haughty stranger could be manoeuvred into selling some of her finery to her hostess.

'Why don't you come and stay on my farm at Frodriver?' she asked my mother. 'There's plenty of room, and you would be most welcome.'

My mother was, however, too clever to run the risk of being drawn into Thurid's debt as her invited guest, and she neatly side-stepped the trap. 'I would be delighted to accept your invitation,' she replied, 'but only on condition that I earn my keep. I would be quite happy to help you out with the farm work in return for decent board and lodging.'

At this point, I gather, I let out a squawl. Unperturbed, my mother glanced across at the bundle of blanket which hid me and continued, 'I'll be sending on my child to live with his father, so the infant will not disturb your household for very long.'

Thorgunna's clothes chest was snapped shut and fastened. A second, even bulkier coffer was hoisted out of stowage and man-handled into the rowboat, and the two women – and me – were carefully rowed to the beach, where Thurid's servants and horses were waiting to carry us back to the farm. I should add here that the horses of Iceland are a special breed, tough little animals, rather shaggy and often cantankerous but capable of carrying substantial loads at an impressive pace and finding their way over the moorlands and through the treacherous bogs which separate the farms. And some of the farms on Iceland can be very large. Their grazing lands extend a day's journey inland, and a successful farmer like Thurid's cuckolded husband Thorodd might employ as many as thirty or forty men and women, both thralls and freemen.

Thus my mother came to Frodriver under her own terms – as a working house guest, which was nothing unusual as everyone on an Icelandic farm is expected to help with the chores. Even Thurid would put off her fine clothes and pick up a hay rake with the rest of the labourers or go to the byres to milk the cattle, though this was more normally the work of thrallwomen and the wives of the poorer farmers, who hired out their labour. However, my mother was not expected to sleep in the main hall, where the majority of the farm workers settle down for the night among the bales of straw which serve as seats by day. My mother requested, and was given, a corner of the inner room, adjacent to the bedchamber where Thurid and her husband slept. When Thorgunna unpacked her large chest next day, Thurid, who had thought my mother wanted her own quiet corner so she could be alone with her baby, understood the real reason. My mother brought out from their wrappings a splendid pair of English-made sheets of linen, delicately embroidered with blue flowers, and matching pillow covers, also a magnificent quilt and a fine coverlet. She then asked Thurid if the farm carpenter could fashion a special bed with a high frame around it. When this was done Thorgunna produced a set of embroidered hangings to surround the bed, and even – wonders of wonders – a canopy to erect over the bed itself. A four-poster bed arrayed like this was something that Thurid had never seen before, and she was overwhelmed. She could not stop herself from asking my mother if perhaps, possibly, she would consider selling these magnificent furnishings. Once again my mother refused, this time even more bluntly, telling her hostess that she did not intend to sleep on straw. It was the last time Thurid ever asked Thorgunna to sell her anything, and Thurid had to be content, when Thorgunna was out working in the fields, with taking her visitors to give them surreptitious glances at these wonderful furnishings.

My mother, as I have indicated, had a predatory attitude towards the opposite sex. It was the story of Birsay all over again, or almost. At Frodriver she rapidly took a fancy to a much younger man, scarcely more than a boy. He was Kjartan, the son of one of the lesser farmers working for Thurid. Fourteen years old, he was physically well developed, particularly between the legs, and the lad was so embarrassed by Thorgunna's frequent advances that he would flee whenever she came close to him. In fact the neighbours spent a great deal of time speculating whether my mother had managed to seduce him, and they had a lot of fun chuckling over their comparisons of Thurid with her lover Bjorn, and Thorgunna in chase of young Kjartan. Perhaps because of their shared enthusiasm for sexual adventures, Thurid and Thorgunna eventually got along quite well. Certainly Thurid had no reason to complain of my mother's contribution to the farm's work. In the nearly two years that Thorgunna stayed at the Skattkaupandi farm, she regularly took her turn at the great loom at one end of the house where the women endlessly wove long strips of wadmal, the narrow woollen cloth which serves the Icelanders as everything from clothing to saddle blankets and the raw material for ships' sails when the strips are sewn side by side.

Thorgunna also pulled her weight – which was considerable – in the outside work, particularly when it came to haymaking. This is the crucial time in the Icelandic farming year, when the grass must be cut and turned and gathered and stacked for winter fodder for the animals, who will shortly be brought back from the outlying pastures where they have been spending the summer. My mother even had the carpenter make her own hay rake. It was longer, heavier and wider than most, and she would not let anyone else touch it.

Then came the day – it was late in heyannir, the haymaking season which occurs at the end of August in the second year of Thorgunna's stay – which the Frodriver people will never forget. The day was ideal for drying – hot with a light breeze. Thorodd mobilised the entire household, except for a few herders who were away looking after the sheep and cattle in the high pasture, to be out in the home meadow turning the hay. They were widely scattered, when just before noon the sky began to cloud over rapidly. It was a sinister sort of cloud – dark and ominous and heavy with rain. This cloud spread rapidly from the north-east and people began to glance up at it nervously, hoping that it would hold off and not spoil the haymaking. The cloud deepened and darkened until it was almost like night, and it was obvious that there would soon be a torrential downpour. Thorodd instructed the haymakers to stack their sections of hay to protect them from the rain, and was puzzled when Thorgunna ignored him. She seemed to be in a trance.

Then the rain started to pelt down and there was little point in staying outside, so Thorodd called in the workers for their midday break, to eat coarse bread and cheese in the main house. But Thorgunna again ignored Thorodd's instructions, nor did she pay any attention to the other workers as they trudged past her and back toward the farm. She kept on working, turning the hay with the wide slow powerful sweeps of her special rake. Thorodd called again, but it was as if Thorgunna was deaf. She kept working even as the rainstorm swept in, and everyone ran for shelter. It was a most unusual rainstorm. It fell on Frodriver, and only on Frodriver. All the other farms escaped the downpour and their hay was saved. But the Skattkaupandi farm was saturated. That in itself is not so strange. Any farmer has seen the same phenomenon when a summer cloudburst releases a torrent of rain which seems to drop vertically and strike just one small area. Then suddenly the rain ceases, the sun comes out and the ground begins to steam with the heat. But what was startling about the rainstorm at Frodriver was that it was not rain which fell from the cloud, but blood.

I know that sounds absurd. Yet it is no more fantastic than the contention that I have heard from apparently wise and learned men that fire and brimstone will pour from the sky in the great apocalypse. Certainly the people of Frodriver and the locality swear that the drops which hurtled from the sky were not rain, but dark red blood. It stained red the cut hay, it left pools of blood in the dips and hollows, and it drenched Thorgunna in blood. When she returned to the farmhouse, still as if in a daze and not saying a word, her clothes were saturated. When the garments were squeezed, blood ran out of them.

Thorodd asked her what was meant by the thunderstorm. Was it an omen? If so, of what? Thorgunna was slow in recovering from her confused state and did not reply. It seemed to Thorodd that she had been absent from her physical body and was not yet fully returned to it, and that something otherworldly was involved. His opinion was confirmed when the entire haymaking team went back into the field. The sun had re-emerged and the cut hay was steaming in the heat. All except one patch. It was the area where Thorgunna had been working. Here the hay still lay sodden, a dark blotch on the hillside, and though Thorgunna went back to work, turning the hay steadily, the workers noticed that the hay never dried out. It clung flat and damp on the ground, gave off a rank smell and the heavy handle of Thorgunna's hay rake stayed wet.

That evening Thorodd repeated his question. 'Was that strange thunderstorm an omen, Thorgunna?' he asked.

'Yes,' my mother replied. 'It was an omen for one of us.'

'Who is that?' asked Thorodd.

'For me,' came Thorgunna's calm reply. 'I expect I will shortly be leaving you.'

She went off to her splendid bed, walking stiffly as though her muscles were aching. In the morning she did not appear at breakfast to join the other workers before they returned to the haymaking, and Thorodd went to see her. He coughed discreetly outside the hanging drapes of the four-poster bed until Thorgunna called on him to enter. Immediately he noted that she was sweating heavily and her pillows were drenched. He began to make a few mumbled enquiries as to how she felt, but Thorgunna in her usual brusque fashion interrupted him.

'Please pay attention,' she said. 'I am not long for this world, and you are the only person around here who has the sense to carry out my last wishes. If you fail to do so, then you and your household will suffer.' Her voice was throaty and she was clearly finding it an effort to speak. 'When I die, as I soon will, you are to arrange for me to be buried at Skalhot, not here on this out-of-the-way farm. One day Skalhot will achieve renown. Just as important, I want you to burn all my bedding; I repeat, all of it.'

Thorodd must have looked puzzled, for Thorgunna went on, 'I know that your wife would love to get her hands on it. She has been hankering after the sheets and pillows, and all the rest of it from the very first day I got here. But I repeat: burn all of it. Thurid can have my scarlet cloak – that too she has been coveting since I first arrived and it ought to keep her happy. As for the rest of my possessions you can sell off my clothes to those who want them, deduct my burial costs from the money, and give the rest of the money to the church, including this gold ring,' and she removed the gold ring which she had been wearing since the day she arrived and handed it to Thorodd.

A few days later she died. One of the house women drew back the curtain and found her sitting up in bed, her jaw hanging slack. It took three strong men to lift her corpse and carry it out to the shed, where she was wrapped in a shroud of unstitched linen, and the same carpenter who had made her special bed nailed together a coffin large enough to contain her body.

Thorodd genuinely tried to carry out Thorgunna's last wishes. He had the bed frame knocked apart, and the pieces and the mattress and all the furnishings carried out to the yard. The carpenter took an axe to the bed frame and its four posts and made kindling, and the bonfire was ready. At that point Thurid intervened. She told her husband that it was a wanton waste to destroy such beautiful items, which could never be replaced. There would never be another chance to acquire such exotic goods. Thorodd reminded her of Thorgunna's express last wishes, but Thurid sulked, then threw her arms around him and wheedled. Eventually the poor man compromised. The eiderdown and pillows and the coverlet would be thrown on the flames; she could keep the rest.

Thurid did not lose a second in seizing the sheets and hangings and the embroidered canopy, and rushed them into the house. When she came back out, Thorodd had already left the yard and was walking away across the fields, so Thurid darted over to the fire and managed to salvage the coverlet before it was scorched, though it was some time before she dared to produce it before her husband.

Up to this point there seems to be an explanation for what happened in the events leading up to my mother's sudden death, including the red rain: she had caught a bad chill when she stayed out in the thunderstorm, then failed to change into dry clothes, and the chill developed into a mortal fever. Her insistence that her bedding was burned may have been because she feared that she had caught some sort of a plague and – if she had the medical knowledge that I was later to find among the priests and brithemain in Ireland – it was normal practice to burn the bedclothes of the deceased to prevent the illness spreading. As for the red rain, I observed when I was in the lands of the Byzantine emperor how on certain days the raindrops had a pinkish tinge and contained so many grains of fine sand that if you turned your face to the sky and opened your mouth the rain drops tasted gritty and did not slake your thirst. Or again, when I was employed at Knut's court in London, a south wind once brought a red rain which left red splotches on the ground like dried blood, as if the sky had spat from bleeding gums. Also I have heard how, in countries where the earth belches fire and smoke, there can be a red rain from the sky – and, Adam of Bremen should note, there are places in Iceland where holes and cracks in the ground vomit fire and smoke and steam, and even exude a bright crimson sludge. Yet the people of Frodriver will swear on any oath, whether Christian or pagan, that genuine blood, not tinted water, fell on them from the sky that day. They also affirm that in some mysterious way Thorgunna and the red rain were linked. My mother came from the Orcades, they point out, and as far as the Icelanders are concerned any woman who comes from there – in particular one as mysterious and taciturn as my mother – is likely to be a volva. And what is a volva? It is a witch.

Perhaps witch is not quite the right word. Neither Saxon English nor Latin nor the Norman's French, the three languages most used here in the scriptorium, convey the precise meaning of the word volva as the pagan Norse use it. Latin comes closest, with the notion of the Sibyl who can look into the future, or a seeress in English. Yet neither of these terms entirely encompasses what a volva is. A volva is a woman who practises seidr, the rite of magic. She knows incantation, divination, mysticism, trance – all of these things and more, and builds up a relationship with the supernatural. There are men who practise seidr, the seidrmanna, but there are not nearly so many men as there are women who have the knowledge and the art, and for the men the word magician would apply. When a volva or seidrman is about to die, there are signs and portents, and the red rain at Frodriver is a surer sign that my mother had seidr powers than any silly stories about love potions she used on my father.

And this is confirmed by what happened next.

Early the following morning my mother's coffin was lashed to the pack saddle on the back of the biggest horse in Thorodd's stables, and a little procession set out for Skalhot, where my mother had asked to be buried. Thorodd stayed behind on the farm as he had to oversee the rest of the haymaking, but he sent four of the farm labourers to manage the pack train. They took the usual route southward over the moorland. The going was quite easy as the moor was dried out at the end of summer and the usually boggy patches could carry the weight of the horses, so they made good progress. The only delays were caused when my mother's coffin kept slipping sideways and threatening to tumble to the ground. A coffin is an awkward load to attach to a pack saddle. If slung on one side like an enormous wooden pannier, you need a counterweight on the opposite side of the horse to keep the load in balance. The men did not have a sufficiently heavy counterweight to balance my mother's coffin, and in the first half-hour the saddle itself kept slipping sideways, forcing the escort to tighten the girth straps until the poor pack horse could scarcely breathe. In desperation the men were on the point of hauling my mother's body out of its wooden box and draping it sideways across the pack saddle in its shroud, as it should have been in the first place. But they were far too fearful. They were already muttering amongst themselves that Thorgunna was a volva who would come to haunt them if they disturbed her. So they kept on as best they could, stopping every so often to tighten the lashings, and at noontime shifted the coffin to one of the spare pack horses as the first animal was on the point of collapse.

As the makeshift cortege climbed onto the higher ground, the weather got worse. It became squally with showers of rain and sleet, and by the time they reached the ford on the Nordur River the water was rising and the ford was deep. They waded across cautiously and late in the afternoon reached a small farm at a place called Nether Ness. At this point the man in charge, a steady farm worker called Hrolf, decided that it would be wise to call a halt for the day. Ahead lay the ford across the Hvit River, and Hrolf did not fancy trying to cross it in the dark, especially if the water was running high. He asked the farmer if they could stay the night. The farmer said they could bed down in the main hall, but it was late and as he had had no warning of their arrival, he would not be able to feed them. It was a churlish reply, but the Frodriver men were glad to get some sort of shelter even if they went to sleep hungry. So they unloaded my mother's coffin, stored it in an outhouse, fed and watered their horses and put them in a paddock near the farm, and brought their saddle bags into the hall.

The household settled down for the night, and the travellers were making themselves reasonably comfortable among the straw bales, which served as seats running the length of the main hall, when an odd sound was heard. It came from the larder. Going to investigate, one of the farm servants found my mother, stark naked, standing in the larder, preparing a meal. The unfortunate servant was too shocked even to scream. She rushed to the bed closet, where the farmer and his wife were just dropping off to sleep, and blurted out that she had seen a burly nude woman, her skin a deathly white, standing in the larder and reaching to take bread from the shelves, with a full pitcher of milk already beside her on the work table. The farmer's wife went to see, and there indeed was Thorgunna, calmly slicing thin strips off a leg of dried lamb, and arranging the slices on a wooden board. The farmer's wife did not know what to do. She had never met my mother, so did not recognise her, and she was utterly at a loss at this strange apparition. At this stage the corpse-bearers from Frodriver, awakened by the commotion, appeared. They, of course, recognised Thorgunna at once, or so they later claimed. Hrolf whispered to the farmer's wife that the apparition was Thorgunna's fetch or spirit, and it would be dangerous to interfere. He suggested that the farmer's wife should clear off the main dining table so that Thorgunna could set the table. Then the farmer himself invited the men to sit and take their missing evening meal. As soon as they had sat themselves at the farm table, Thorgunna in her usual taciturn way served them, placing down the food without a word and walking ponderously out of the room. She then vanished.

The Frodriver men remained at the table, taking care to make the sign of the cross over the food, and ate their delayed supper while the farmer hurriedly found some holy water and began sprinkling it in every corner of the building. Nothing was too much trouble for the farmer's wife now. She gave the travellers dry clothes and hung up their wet ones to dry, brought out blankets and pillows so they could sleep more comfortably and generally made as much fuss of them as possible.

Was the apparition of Thorgunna an elaborate hoax? Did the supper-less Frodriver men arrange for someone to play the part of Thorgunna? It was dark and gloomy in the farm building, and the candles were not lit until after Thorgunna had served the meal and withdrawn, so a substitution and a bit of play-acting might just have succeeded. The nudity was a nice touch as most people are too shy to look closely at someone stark naked. On the other hand, who did the Frodriver men persuade to act the role of Thorgunna? A local farm woman would have been recognised at once, and the band of corpse-bearers were all male. Yet it is suspicious that her apparition was such a bonus for the corpse-bearers on the rest of their journey to Skalholt, where they delivered the coffin to the Christian priest at the brand-new church there, and handed over the money from Thorgunna's bequest. They lost no opportunity to recount the strange events of their evening at Nether Ness, and every farm they passed invited them in for a meal, for beer, for shelter if they needed it.

Do I believe that my mother's fetch appeared at Nether Ness? If I told that same story here in the scriptorium and changed the details, saying that she had reappeared emitting a strange glow and holding a copy of the Bible, my colleagues would accept my version of events without hesitation. So why would not the farmers of Snaefells be just as convinced that she had reappeared? Farmers can be as credulous as priests. There is hardly a soul in that remote farming community who doubts that Thorgunna came back to haunt the stingy farmer at Nether Ness, and while there might be an earthly explanation for the happenings at Nether Ness, until this explanation is supplied I am prepared to accept the supernatural. During my lifetime of travels I was to see many odd sights that defy conventional explanation. Within a few years of my mother's death I too encountered a fetch, and on the eve of a great battle I had strange and vivid forebodings which proved to be accurate. Often I've witnessed events which somehow I know that I have seen before, and sometimes my dreams at night recall events that are in the past, but sometimes they also bring me into the future. The facility for seidr is improved by apprenticeship to a practitioner, but there must be a natural talent in the first place, which is nearly always a question of descent. Volva and seidrmanna come from the same families down through the generations, and this is why I have spent so much time writing of the strange circumstances of Thorgunna's departure from this life and the hauntings: my mother gave me neither affection nor care, but she did bequeath to me a strange and disturbing gift – a power of second sight, which occasionally overwhelms me and over which I have no control.

THREE

On her death bed Thorgunna made no mention of her son because she already had sent me off to join my real father. I was just two years old. I bear my mother no grudge on this score. Handing on a two-year-old child like a parcel may seem harsh, but there was nothing unusual about this. Among the Norsemen it is common practice for young children to be fostered out by their natural parents, who send them off to neighbouring families to be raised and educated. It binds the two families together, and this can be very useful when it comes to conducting local politics and intrigues among the Icelanders. Almost every family has its foster sons and daughters, foster brothers and sisters, and the attachments built up between them can be just as strong as between natural siblings. Besides, everyone at Frodriver had heard the rumour that my father was Leif Eriksson. So I was not being fostered, but merely sent to him where he lived with his father Erik the Red in Greenland. Indeed it turned out to be the kindest thing that my mother ever did for me because this second sea journey of my infancy placed me in the care of the woman who became more a mother to me than my own. Gudrid Thorbjornsdottir was everything that her reputation claims – she was kind, thoughtful, clever, hard-working, beautiful and generous of spirit.

Gudrid was travelling with her husband, the merchant Thorir, known as the Easterner, just at the time my mother at Frodriver was looking for someone to take her small child off to Greenland as she had long ago promised my father. And perhaps, too, my mother had a premonition of her own death. Thorir was pioneering a regular trading run between Iceland and Greenland, so when his ship called in at Snaefellsness Thorgunna put her request to Gudrid, and it was Gudrid who agreed to take me to my father.

Thorir's merchant ship was not one of the longships which have entered the sinister folklore of sheltered priests. The longships are warships, expensive to build, not particularly seaworthy and unsuitable for trading. At twenty paces' length, a longship offers barely four or five paces in the beam and, being like a shallow dish amidships, has little room for cargo. Worse, from a merchant's point of view, she needs a large crew to handle her under oars and even when she is sailing – which is how any sensible mariner makes progress – a longship must have a lively crew because these vessels have a treacherous habit of suddenly running themselves under or capsizing when under press of sail. Nor was Thorir's vessel one of those dumpy little coasters that farmers use when they creep round the Icelandic shore in fair weather, or to go out to the islands where they graze their sheep and cattle. His ship was a knorr, a well-found, full-bellied ship which is the most advanced of our deep-sea trading designs. She can carry a dozen cattle in pens in the central hold, has a single mast rigged with a broad rectangular sail of wadmal, and can cross from Iceland to Greenland in six dogur – a day's sailing – the standard length by which such voyages are calculated (Adam in Bremen might have difficulty in translating that distance onto a map, if that is what he proposes to do). Her chief cargo on that particular voyage was not cattle, but Norwegian timber. And that cargo of timber was about to save our lives.

Any sensible person who embarks on the voyage from Iceland to Greenland keeps the fate of the second settlement fleet in mind. Seventeen ships set out, nearly all of them knorrs. Less than half the ships managed to reach their destination. The others were either beaten back by adverse winds and limped into Iceland, or were simply lost at sea and no one ever heard of them again. As an experienced mariner, Thorir knew the risks better than most. The open water between Iceland and Greenland can be horrendous in bad weather, when a fierce gale from the south kicks up mountainous seas over the current that runs against it. Even the stoutest vessel can be overwhelmed in these conditions, and although the knorr is the most seaworthy ship that floats, she is just as much a plaything of the elements as any other vessel. Caught in heavy weather, a knorr has a fair chance of survival, but the crew must forget any idea of keeping a course. They spend their time frantically baling out the water that breaks aboard the ship, stopping leaks in the hull if they can, and preventing the cargo from being tossed about and bursting the planks, while the helmsmen struggle to keep the vessel at the safest angle to the advancing waves. If a storm continues for three or four days, the ship is often blown so far off course that no one has any idea of where they are, and it is a matter of guessing the most likely direction of land, then sailing there to try to identify the place.

Thorir had talked with men who had already sailed between Iceland and Greenland, so he knew the safest, shortest route. He had been advised to keep the tall white peak of Snaefellsjokul directly astern for as long as it was visible. If he was fortunate, he would see the high mountains of Greenland ahead before Snaefellsjokul had dipped below the horizon behind him. At worst he had only one or two days of open ocean between the landmarks until he had Greenland's huge white mass of ice in plain view and could steer larboard to skirt the southern tip of that huge and forbidding land. Then he planned to head north along the coast until he would arrive at Brattahlid, the centre of Greenland's most prosperous settlement and home of Erik the Red.

Thorir's knorr was well handled. She crossed the open straits and when she came in sight of Greenland's southern cape, it seemed that the ocean crossing had gone flawlessly. The vessel turned the southern cape and was heading for the fjord at Brattahlid, when as luck would have it she encountered a thick, clammy fog. Now a normal fog is associated with calm seas, perhaps a low swell. When the wind begins to blow, it clears away the fog. But a Greenland fog is different. Off Greenland there can be a dense fog and a full gale at the same time, and the fog stays impenetrable and dangerously confusing while the battering wind drives a vessel off course. This is what put paid to Thorir's ship. Running before the gale in bad visibility, trying to follow the coast, indeed almost within sight of Brattahlid if the weather had been kinder, the heavily laden knorr ran onto a reef with a crunching impact. She slid up on the rocks of a small skerry or chain of islands, the bottom tore out of her, and she was wrecked. Had the cargo been anything other than timber she would have filled and sunk. But the wedged mass of planks and logs turned her into a makeshift life raft. Her crew and passengers, sixteen including myself, were lucky to escape with their lives. As the waves eased, they scrambled up through the surf and spray and onto the skerry, with the shattered remnants of the knorr lurching and grinding on the rocks behind them until the tide dropped and the hulk lay stuck in an untidy heap. The castaways cautiously waded back aboard to retrieve planks and spars and enough wadmal to rig a scrap of tent. They collected some cooking utensils and food, and made a rough camp on a patch of windswept turf. With enough fresh water saved from the ship to last them several days, and a good chance of collecting rainfall later, they knew they would not die of thirst or hunger. But that was the limit of their hopes. They had been wrecked in one of the emptiest parts of the known world (indeed I wonder if Adam of Bremen knows about it at all) and their chances of rescue, as opposed to mere survival, were very bleak.

They were saved by a man's phenomenally keen eyesight.

Even now I can write this with a sense of pride because the man who possessed that remarkable eyesight was my father, Leif. I used to boast about it when I was a child, saying that I had inherited that gift of acute vision from him – as opposed to the second sight, which I possess through my mother and about which

I am far more reticent. But to explain how that remarkable rescue took place, I need to go back briefly to a voyage fourteen years earlier which had gone astray in another of those typical Greenland fog-cum-gales.

On that occasion a navigator named Bjarni Herjolfsson had overshot his destination at Brattahlid, and after several days in poor visibility and strong winds he was in that anxious condition the Norse sailors call hafvilla – he had lost his way at sea. When the fog lifted he saw a broad, rocky coastline ahead of him. It was well wooded but deserted and completely unfamiliar. Bjarni had kept track of his knorr's gyrations in the storm. He made a shrewd guess as to which way Greenland lay, put his ship about and after sailing along the unknown coast for several dogr eventually came back to Brattahlid, bringing news of those alluring woodlands. About the time my mother was thinking of sending me to my father, Leif had decided to sail to that unknown land and explore. Believing in the sea tradition that a vessel which had already brought her crew safely home would do so again, he purchased Bjarni's ship for the voyage.

By a remarkable coincidence he was on his way back from that trip even as Thorir's knorr shattered on the skerry. He was at the helm, battling a headwind and steering so hard on the wind that one of his crew, drenched by the resulting spray, complained, 'Can't we steer more broad?' Leif was peering ahead for his first glimpse of the Greenland coastline. 'There's a current from the north setting us more southerly than I like,' he replied. 'We'll keep this course for a little longer. We can ease the sheets once we are closer to land.'

Some time later another crew member called out a warning that he could see skerries ahead. 'I know,' Leif replied, relying on that phenomenal eyesight. 'I've been watching them for a while now and there seems to be something on one of the islands.' The rest of his crew, who had been curled up on deck to keep out of the wind, scrambled to their feet and peered forward. They could see the low black humps of the islands, but no one else could make out the tiny dark patch that my father could already discern. It was the roof of our makeshift shelter. My father, as I have said, was a hard man to dissuade, and the crew knew better than to try to make him alter course. So the ship headed onwards towards the skerry, and half an hour later everyone aboard could make out the little band of castaways, standing up and waving scraps of cloth tied to sticks. To them it seemed a miracle, and if the story was not told to me hundreds of times when I was growing up in Brattahlid, I would scarcely believe the coincidence – a shipwreck in the path of a vessel commanded by a man with remarkable eyesight and sailing on a track not used for fourteen years. It was this good fortune which earned Leif his nickname 'Heppni', the 'Lucky', though it was really the sixteen castaways who were the lucky ones.

Expertly Leif brought his vessel into the lee of the skerry, dropped anchor and launched the small rowboat from the deck. The man who jumped into the little boat to help row was to have a significant part in my later life – Tyrkir the German – and I think it was because he was my rescuer that Tyrkir kept such a close eye on me as I grew up. Tyrkir was to become my first, and in some ways most important, tutor in the Old Ways, and it was under Tyrkir's guidance that I made my first steps along the path that would eventually lead me to my devotion to Odinn the All-Father. But I will come to that later.

'Who are you and where are you from?' Leif shouted as he and Tyrkir rowed closer to the bedraggled band of castaways standing on the edge of the rocks. They backed water with the oars, keeping a safe distance. The last thing my father wanted was to take aboard a band of desperate ruffians who, having lost their ship, might seize his own.

'We're from Norway, out of Iceland, and were headed for Brattahlid when we ran on this reef,' Thorir called back. 'My name is Thorir and I'm the captain as well as the owner. I am a peaceful trader.' Tyrkir and Leif relaxed. Thorir's name was known and he was considered to be an honest man.

'Then I invite you to my ship,' called Leif, 'and afterwards to my home, where you will be taken good care of.' He and Tyrkir spun the little rowing boat around and brought her stern first toward the rocks. The first person to scramble aboard was Gudrid and tucked under one arm was the two-year-old boy child she had promised Thorgunna she would deliver to his father. So it happened that Leif the Lucky unwittingly rescued his own illegitimate son.

FOUR

LEIF'S WIFE, GYDA, was not at all pleased to learn that the toddler Thorgils, saved from the sea, was the result of a brief affair between her husband and some middle-aged Orcadian woman. She refused to take me under her roof. She already had the example of her father-in-law's bastard child as a warning. My aunt Freydis, then in her late teens, was the illegitimate daughter of Erik and lived with the Erikssons. She was an evil-tempered troublemaker who, as it turned out, was to play a gruesome part in my story, though at the time she seemed to be no more than a quarrelsome and vindictive young woman always quarrelling with her relations. As Gyda did not want another cuckoo in her house, she arranged to have me fostered out, a real fostering this time. And this is how I came to spend my childhood not with my father but with Gudrid, who lived nearby. Gudrid, I suppose, felt responsible for me as she had brought me to Greenland in the first place. Also, I believe, she was a little lonely because soon after her arrival in Greenland she lost her husband, Thorir. He was in Eriksfjord for only a few weeks after his rescue before he went down with a severe fever. The illness must have arrived with his ship because Thorir and most of his crew were the first to begin coughing, spitting blood, and having bouts of dizziness. By the time the illness had run its course, eighteen people had died, among them Thorir and – finally – that old warhorse, my grandfather Erik the Red.

The gossips said that Gudrid took me in as a substitute for the child her body had failed to give her when she was Thorir's woman. I suspect these critics were jealous and only looking for a flaw to compensate for Gudrid's astonishing good looks – she possessed a loveliness of the type that endures throughout a woman's life. I remember her as having a pale translucent skin, long blonde hair, and grey eyes in a face of perfect, gentle symmetry with a well-defined nose over a delicious-looking mouth and a chin that had just the suggestion of a dimple exactly in the middle of it. At any rate I am sure that the young widow Gudrid would have taken me in even if she had children of her own. She was one of the kindest women imaginable. She was always ready to give help, whether bringing food to a sick neighbour, loaning out kitchen utensils to someone planning a feast and then doing half the cooking herself, or scolding children who were behaving as bullies and comforting their victims. Everyone in Brattahlid had a high opinion of her and I worshipped her. Never having known my real mother, I accepted Gudrid in that vital role as entirely normal, and I suspect that Gudrid made a far better job of it than gruff Thorgunna would have done. Gudrid seemed to have endless patience when it came to dealing with children. I and the other dozen or so youngsters of the same age made Gudrid's house the centre of our universe. When we played in the meadows or scrambled along the beach looking for fish and skipping stones on the cold water of the fjord, we usually finished by saying, 'Race you to Gudrid's!' and would go pelting across the rough ground like hares, bursting in through the side door which led to the kitchen, and arriving in a great clatter. Gudrid would wait till the last of us had arrived, then haul down a great pitcher of sour milk and pour out our drinks as we perched on the tall wooden benches.

Brattahlid was, for a child, an idyllic spot. The settlement lies at the head of a long fjord reaching deep inland. Erik had chosen the site on his first visit and chosen shrewdly. The length of the fjord offers protection from the cold foggy weather outside, and it is the most sheltered and fertile place to set up a farm in the area, if not the whole of Greenland. The anchorage is safe and the beach rises to low, undulating meadowland dotted with clumps of dwarf willow and birch. Here Erik and his followers built their turf-roofed houses on the drier hillocks, fenced in the home paddocks, and generally established replicas of their former farms in Iceland. There are no more than three or four hundred Greenlanders, and so there is plenty of room for all those who are hardy enough to settle there. Life is even simpler than in Iceland. At the onset of winter we brought the cattle in from the meadowland and kept them indoors, feeding them the hay we had prepared in the summer. We ourselves existed on sour milk, dried fish, smoked or salted meat and whatever else we had managed to preserve from the summer months. As a result everything carried a rancid flavour, particularly the lumps of whale and shark meat we buried in earth pits for storage, then dug up, semi-putrid. The long, idle, dark hours were spent with story-telling, sleeping, doing odd repair jobs, playing backgammon and other games. In Greenland we still played the older version of chess – a single king in the centre of the board with his troops arranged against a crowd of opponents who were spread around the edge. Not until I returned as a youth to Iceland did I see the two-king style of chess, and I had to learn the rules all over again.

Every youngster, almost from the time he or she could walk, helped with day-to-day work and it made us feel valued. On land we graduated from running errands and cleaning out the byres to learning how to skin and butcher the beasts and salt down the meat. On water we began by baling out the bilges of the small rowing boats, then we were allowed to bait fishing lines and help haul nets, until finally we were handling the sails and pulling on an oar as the boats were rowed back to the landing place. We had very little schooling, though Erik's widow, Thjodhild, did attempt to teach us our alphabet and some rudimentary writing. We were not enthusiastic pupils. Thjodhild's character was embittered by a long-running disagreement with her husband. What irked her was that Erik had refused to become a Christian and this had set an example to many of his followers. Thjodhild was one of the earliest and most enthusiastic converts to the creed of the White Christ, and she was one of those querulous Christians who was always seeking to impose her beliefs on the rest of the community. But Erik was a dyed-in-the-wool pagan, and the more she nagged at him, the more stubborn he became. He had not left Iceland, he said, to bring with him in his baggage the newfangled religion. He had offered a sacrifice to Thor before he sailed to Greenland and, in return, Thor had looked after the colony very well. Erik told his wife in no uncertain terms that he was not about to abandon the Old Gods and the Old Ways. Eventually matters became so bad between the two of them that Thjodhild announced she would have as little as possible to do with him. They still had to live under the same roof, but she had a Christian chapel built for herself, very prominently, on a hillock near the farm just where Erik was sure to see it every time he left his front door. However, Erik refused to let his wife have much timber for the structure so the chapel remained a tiny building, no more than a couple of arm spans wide in any direction. It was the first Christian church in Greenland, and so small that no more than eight people could fit inside at once. We children called it the White Rabbit Hutch for the White Christ.

Halfway through the fifth summer of my life I learned that my foster mother was to marry again. After the hay gathering, the wedding was to be celebrated between the young widow Gudrid Thorbjornsdottir and another of Erik's sons, Thorstein. I was neither jealous nor resentful. Instead I was delighted. Thorstein was my father's youngest brother and it meant that my adored Gudrid was now to be a genuine relation. I felt that the marriage would bind her even more closely to me, and was only worried that after the wedding I would have to go to live in the main Eriksson household, which would put me in range of my detestable aunt Freydis. She had grown into a strapping young woman, broad shouldered and fleshy, with a freckled skin and a snub nose, so that she attracted men in a rather over-ripe way. She was also full of spite. She was always hatching plots with her girlfriends to get others into trouble and she was usually successful. On the few occasions I spent any time in my father's house I tried to stay clear of Freydis. Sixteen years older than me, she regarded me as a pest, and would think nothing of shoving me roughly into the darkness of the root cellar and locking me in there for hours, going off and not telling anyone. Luckily old Thorbjorn, Gudrid's father, who was still alive though weakly, was so pleased with the match that he agreed to let the newly-weds share his house, which was a short walk from the Eriksson home.

The wedding was a huge success. To satisfy grumpy old Thjodhild there was a brief Christian ceremony at the White Rabbit Hutch, but the main event was the exchange of ceremonial gifts, heavy beer drinking, raucous music and stamping dances which are the mark of the old-style weddings.

My next distinct memory of Greenland is a bright spring morning with the ice floes still drifting silently in our fjord. The glaring white fragments, so luminous on grey-blue water, made my eyes hurt as I stared at a little ship edging slowly towards us. She was a knorr, battered and seaworn, her planks grey with age. Some men were rowing, others handling the ropes as they tried to swing the rectangular sail to catch the cold breath of the faint wind that came from the north, skirting the great glacier behind us that is the heart of Greenland. I still recall how, from time to time, the oarsmen stood up to push with their blades against the floes, using the oars as poles to punt their way through the obstacles, and how slowly the boat seemed to approach. A crowd began to gather on the beach. Each person on the shore was counting the number of the crew and searching their faces to see who was aboard and if they had changed from the images we had been holding in our memories since the day they had gone to explore the mysterious land west across the sea, which Bjarni had first seen, and my father Leif had been the last person to visit. Then the keel grated on the shingle, and one by one her crew leapfrogged the upper strake and splashed ashore, ankle deep in the water. The crowd greeted them in near silence. We had already noticed that a man was missing, and the helmsman was not the skipper they had expected.

'Where's Thorvald?' someone in the crowd called out.

'Dead,' grunted one of the seamen. 'Killed by Skraelings.'

'What's a Skraeling?' I whispered to one of my friends, Eyvind. The two of us had wriggled our way through to the front of the crowd and were standing right at the water's edge, the wavelets soaking our shoes. Eyvind was two years older than me and I expected him to know everything.

'I don't know for sure,' he whispered back. 'I think it means someone who is weak and foreign and we don't like.'

Thorvald Eriksson, the second uncle of my tale, I remember only vaguely as a jovial, heavy-set man with large hands and a wheezing laugh, who often smelled of drink. Thorvald and his crew had departed westward eighteen months earlier to pick up where my father Leif had left off. My father had described an iron-bound low vista of slab-like grey rocks, long white-sand beaches extending back into boggy marshes and swamps, enormous still forests of dark pine trees whose scent the sailors could smell from a day's sail out to sea. Now Thorvald wanted to know whether anyone lived there, and if they did whether they had anything of value for trade or taking. If the place was truly deserted, then he would reoccupy the camp Leif had established on the Vinland coast and use it as a base to explore the adjoining territory. He would search for pasture, timber, fishing grounds, animals with fur.

Thorvald had taken with him a strong crew of twenty-five men and had the loan of my father's knorr, the same vessel which had plucked me off the rocks. He was a good navigator and several of his men had sailed with my father and were competent pilots, so his track brought him directly to the spot where Leif had overwintered four years before. There the Brattahlid men reoccupied the turf-and-timber huts that my father had built, and settled in for the winter. The following spring Thorvald sent the ship's small boat farther west along the coast on a voyage of enquiry. They found their journey very wearisome. The coast was a vast web of islands and inlets and shallows where they often lost their way. Yet the farther they went, the more the land improved. The wild grass grew taller, and there were strange trees which bled sweet juice when cut, or produced edible nuts whose buttery taste no one had encountered before. Despite the fertility of the land, they found no people and no trace of human habitation except at the farthest end of their exploration. There, at the back of a beach, they came across a ragged structure made of long, thin wooden poles which seemed to have been fashioned by man. The poles were fastened together with cords made from twisted tree roots and appeared to be a temporary shelter. Our men assumed that whoever had made the structure was living off the land, like our hunters in Greenland when they went north in summer to trap caribou. They found no tools, no relics, nothing else, but it made them nervous. They wondered if their presence had been noted by unseen watchers and feared an ambush.

Meanwhile Thorvald had spent the summer improving Leifsbodir, 'Leif's cabins' as everyone called them. His men felled timber to carry back to Greenland, and caught and dried fish as food for future expeditions. The quantity of fish was prodigious. The shore in front of the cabins had a very gentle slope, and low tide exposed an expanse of sand shallows runnelled with small gulleys. The men found that if they built fish traps of stakes across the gulleys, the fish – cod mostly – were trapped by the retreating tide and lay flapping helplessly. The fishermen had only to stroll across the sand and pick up the fish by hand.

After a second winter spent snug in the cabins, Thorvald decided to explore in the opposite direction – to the east and north, where the land was more like the Greenland coast, with rocky headlands, long inlets and the occasional landing beach. But the tides ran more powerfully there and this caught Thorvald out. One day the knorr swirled into a tide race and slammed against rocks beneath a headland. The impact was enough to break off the forward ten feet of her false keel and loosen several of the lower strakes. Luckily there was a beach nearby where the crew could land their craft safely, and with so much timber around it was a simple matter to replace the damaged keel with a fine clean length of pine. Thorvald found a use for the broken-keel section. He had the piece carried to the top of the headland and set vertically in a cairn of stones, where it was visible from far out to sea. If strangers came to contest the Greenlanders' discovery, it would be proof that the Erikssons had been there before them.

This was the story of Thorvald's expedition as it emerged from the reports of the returned crew that evening. Everyone in Brattahlid crammed into the hall of the Eriksson longhouse to hear the details. We were listening with rapt attention. My father was sitting in the place of seniority, midway down the hall on the right-hand side. My uncle Thorstein sat beside him. 'And what about Thorvald? Tell us exactly what happened to him,' my father asked. He put his question directly to Tyrkir, the same man who had been rowing the small boat that rescued Gudrid and myself from the skerries, and who had gone with Thorvald as his guide.

AT THIS POINT I should say something about Tyrkir. As a young man he had been captured on the coast of Germany and put up for sale at the slave market in Kaupang in Norway. There he had been bought by my grandfather, Erik the Red, on one of his eastward trips, and proved to be an exceptionally good purchase. Tyrkir was hard working and tireless and grew to be intensely loyal to my grandfather. He became fluent in our Norse language, the donsk tunga, finding that it is not so far removed from his mother tongue of German. But he never shed his thick accent, speaking from the back of his throat, and whenever he got excited or angry he tended to revert to the language of his own people. Eventually Erik trusted Tyrkir so completely that, while my father Leif was growing up, Tyrkir had the task of watching over him and teaching him all sorts of useful skills, for Tyrkir was one of those people who has gifted hands. He knew how to tie complicated knots for different purposes, how to chop down a tree so that it fell in a certain direction, how to make a fishing spear from a straight branch, and how to scoop out a lump of soapstone so that it made a cooking pot. Above all he possessed a skill so vital and wondrous that it is closely associated with the Gods themselves – he could shape metal in all its forms, whether smelting coarse iron from a raw lump of ore or fusing the steel edge to an axe and then hammering a pattern of silver wire into the flat of the blade.

We boys found the German rather frightening. To us he seemed ancient, though he was probably in his late fifties. He was short and puny, almost troll like, with a shock of black hair and a ferocious scowl emphasised by a bulging, prominent forehead under which his eyes looked distinctly shifty. Yet physically he was very brave, and during Leif's earlier voyage to the unknown land it was Tyrkir who volunteered for the scouting missions. His German tribe had been a forest-dwelling people, and Tyrkir thought nothing of tramping through the woodlands, wading across swamps, living off berries and a handful of dried food. He drank from puddles if he could find no clean running water, slept on the ground and seemed impervious to cold or heat or damp. It was Tyrkir who had first come across the wild grapes that some believe gave Vinland its name. He came back into Leif's camp one day carrying a bunch of the fruit, and so excited that he was rolling his eyes and muttering in German until Leif thought he was drunk or hallucinating, but Tyrkir was merely revelling in his discovery. He had not seen fresh grapes since he had been a lad in Germany and indeed, if he had not recognised the wild fruit, it is doubtful whether my father and his companions would have known what they were. But the moment Tyrkir explained what a fresh grape is, my father realised the significance of the moment. Here was evidence that the new-found country had such a benign climate that grapes – an exotic plant for Norsemen – actually grew wild. So he gave the land the name Vinland, though of course there were cynics when he got home who said that he was as big a liar as his father. To call a wilderness by a name that evoked sunshine and strong drink was as misleading as to call a land of glaciers and rock Greenland. My father was canny enough to have an answer for that accusation too. He would reply that when calling the place Vinland he did not mean the land of grape vines but the land of pastures, for 'vin' in Norse means a meadow.

'TEN DAYS AFTER repairing the broken keel,' Tyrkir said in answer to my father's question about Thorvald, 'we came across the entry to a broad sound guarded by two headlands. It was an inviting-looking place, so we turned in to investigate. We found that the inlet divided around a tongue of land densely covered with mature trees. The place looked perfect for a settlement, and Thorvald made a casual joke to us that it was the ideal place, where he could imagine spending the rest of his life.' Tyrkir paused. 'He should never have said that. It was tempting the Gods.

'We put a scouting party ashore,' he went on, 'and when the scouts returned, they reported that on the far side of the little peninsula was a landing beach, and on it were three black hump-like objects. At first they thought that these black blobs were walruses, or perhaps the carcasses of small whales which had drifted ashore. Then someone recognised them as boats made of skin. Many years earlier he had been on a raiding voyage to plunder the Irish, and on the west coast he had seen similar craft, light enough to be carried on land and turned upside down.'

Here I should explain that the idea that these boats belonged to the wild Irish was not so incredible as it might seem. When the Norse first came to Iceland they found a handful of ascetic Irish monks living in caves and small huts laboriously built of stones. These monks had managed to cross from Scotland and Ireland aboard their flimsy skin boats, so perhaps they had also spread even farther. Thorvald, however, doubted that. Tyrkir described how Thorvald sent him with a dozen armed men to creep up on the strange boats from the landward side, while Thorvald himself and most of the others rowed quietly round the coast to approach from the sea. They achieved a complete surprise. There were nine strangers dozing under their upturned boats. They must have been a hunting or fishing party because they were equipped with bows and arrows, hunting knives and light throwing lances. When they heard the creak of oars they sprang to their feet and grabbed their weapons. Some of them made threatening gestures, drawing back their bows and aiming at the incoming Norse. Others tried to launch their light boats into the water and escape. But it was too late. Tyrkir's shore party burst out of the treeline, and in a short scuffle all the strangers were overpowered, except for one. He managed to flee in the smallest of the skin boats. 'I've never seen a boat travel so fast,' said Tyrkir. 'It seemed to skim across the water and there was no possibility that our ship's boat would have caught up. So we let him go.'

The eight Skraelings our men had captured were certainly not Irish. According to Tyrkir, they looked more like ski-running people from the north of Norway. Short, they had broad faces with a dark yellow skin and narrow eyes. Their hair was black and long and straggly, and they spoke a language full of high sharp sounds, which was like the chattering alarm call of a jay. They were dressed entirely in skins: skin trousers, skin jackets with tails, skin boots. Any part of their bodies not covered in these clothes was smeared with grease or soot. They were human in form, but as squat and dark as if they had emerged from underground. They squirmed and fought in the clutch of the Norsemen and tried to bite and scratch them.

Tyrkir's story now took a grim turn. One of the captive Skraelings wriggled out of the grip of the man holding him, produced a bone harpoon head which he had hidden inside the front of his loose jacket, and jabbed the point of the weapon deep into his captor's thigh. The Greenlander roared with pain and rage. He slammed the man's head against a rock, knocking him unconscious, and then in a fury plunged his short sword into the victim's body. His action triggered a massacre. Thorvald's men fell on the

Skraelings, hacking and stabbing as if they were dispatching vermin, and did not stop until the last one of them was dead. Then Thorvald's men disabled the two remaining skin boats by gashing the hulls to shreds with their axes, and climbed through the woodland up to the top of the peninsula while the ship's boat rowed back to the knorr.

'On the highest point of the land we sat down to rest,' Tyrkir recalled. 'Thorvald intended to allow us only a few moments' breathing space, and we threw ourselves on the ground, and for some strange reason all of us fell asleep as if we were bewitched. About two hours later I was roused by a great voice howling, "Get back to the ship! If you are to save your lives, get back to your ship." '

At this point in Tyrkir's tale, several members of his audience exchanged sceptical glances. Everyone knew Tyrkir's other quirk: besides his quaint accent and bizarre appearance, he had a habit of mental wandering. From time to time he would slip off into some imaginary world where he heard voices and met strangers. On such occasions Tyrkir's face took on a glazed look and he would ramble off into long conversations with himself, invariably in German. It was a harmless habit, and everyone who knew him would look at one another and raise their eyebrows as if to say, 'There goes Tyrkir again, wool-gathering in his wits. What do you expect of a German winkled out of the woodlands?'

But that evening in Brattahlid Tyrkir insisted that he had been wakened from his drowsiness following the Skraeling deaths by a great bellowing voice. It had a strange reverberating rhythm. At times it seemed to come from far off, then from very close. It was impossible to tell from which direction. It appeared to fall from the sky or to come from all directions at once.

Even if Thorvald did not hear the mysterious voice, he must have realised that he and his men had been very foolish. He sent a man to a rocky vantage point where he could look across the fjord, and the sentry called down that a whole flotilla of skin boats was paddling towards them. Obviously the Skraelings were coming to seek their revenge. The shore party scrambled down the rocky slope, catching at the bushes to keep their balance and grabbing at trees as they bolted for their ship. The moment they were aboard, they unmoored and began to row, heading out of the bay and hoping for a wind to get them clear. Even the most lubberly among them knew that there was no way the knorr would out-row the pursuing skin boats.

There must have been at least thirty boats and each one contained three Skraelings. As soon as they were within range, two of the men stowed their paddles, took up light bows and began shooting arrows at the Norsemen. The third man paddled, keeping pace with the knorr and manoeuvring to give his companions the best angle for their shots. Thorvald and a couple of the sailors leapt up on their oar benches waving their swords and axes, challenging the Skraelings to come closer and fight hand to hand. But the natives kept their distance. To them the Norsemen must have seemed like giants. The Skraeling archers kept up a steady barrage. Slowly the knorr wallowed towards the mouth of the sound, where they could hoist sail. The natives kept abreast of them. Arrows hissed overhead, occasionally hitting with a thunk into the woodwork of the boat. The Skraeling archers stayed seated in their skin boats while they worked their bows, so they were lower to the water than their opponents on the higher-sided knorr, and at a disadvantage. Most of the arrows angled upwards and flew overhead harmlessly. A few rapped into the sail and stuck there like hedgehog quills.

After half an hour the natives broke off the attack. They were running out of arrows and they could see that the Norsemen were in full flight. The skin boats turned back one by one and the knorr was left to sail out to sea.

'It was only then,' Tyrkir told my father, 'that we realised that your brother Thorvald was wounded. A Skraeling arrow had found the gap between the topmost plank and his shield and hit him in the left armpit. It was scarcely more than a dart, but buried so deep that only an inch or two of the shaft was showing. Thorvald reached to pull out the arrow. But the arrow was designed for hunting seal and had triple barbs. He had to twist and tug violently to pull it and when it finally came free, there was a strong jet of dark red blood, and flesh stuck to the barbs. Thorvald gave one of his booming laughs – "That's my heart's fat there," he joked. "I said I would like to spend the rest of my days in this place, and I think that's what is going to happen. I doubt I will survive this wound. If I die I want to be buried here, up on that headland where every passing sailor will know my grave."

'I wish we could have done exactly what Thorvald wanted,' Tyrkir concluded in his thick accent. 'There was not much time. We buried Thorvald on the headland as best we could. We feared that the Skraelings would come back, so we could do little more than scrape out a shallow grave and pile a heap of stones over the corpse. Then we set course for Leif's huts to spend the winter – keeping a sharp lookout for Skraelings as soon as the weather improved.'

My uncle Thorstein spoke up. He was looking distressed. 'Leif,' he said, 'we can't leave Thorvald's body there. There's every chance that the Skraelings will find his body, dig it up and defile it. He deserves better. It's only a three-week sail to the spot, and I would like to take a crew of volunteers, sail to Thorvald's cairn, and recover the body so that we can have a proper burial here in Greenland. Your ship, which has just returned, isn't up to the job. She needs to be pulled ashore and recaulked, but my father-in-law Thorbjorn still has the knorr which brought him and his people from Iceland, and she could be ready to sail in two days' time. I'm sure that Thorbjorn will agree to loan her to me for the mission.'

Of course, both my father and old Thorbjorn, who was in the hall listening to the returnees, had to agree. This was a matter of family honour, and if there is one thing which the Norse are fanatical about it is the question of their honour. To a true Norseman his honour is something he places before all else. He will defend it or seek to enhance it by whatever means available, and that includes raiding for booty, exacting revenge for an insult, and lying or cheating to gain the advantage.

FIVE

DESPITE THEIR ORIGINAL plans, it was a full month before my uncle Thorstein set sail for Vinland. It seemed a pity to go all that distance and not bring back a cargo of timber and fish, so his expedition expanded into more than just a trip to recover Thorvald's body. There was equipment to gather, men to be summoned from the pastures, where they had gone with the cattle, stores to be loaded. Then someone suggested that it might be a good idea to leave a small group to overwinter at Leif's cabins, and this scheme delayed matters still further. When old Thorbjorn's knorr did finally set sail she looked more like an emigrant vessel than an expedition ship. There were six cows and several sheep standing in the hold, bales of hay to feed them, piles of farming gear, and on board were several women, including Gudrid, who had asked to accompany her husband. I, meanwhile, would stay behind with her father.

And by the time the preparations were all made it was too late. Thorstein Eriksson had a fine sense of family honour, but he lacked a sense of urgency and that essential gift of all good sea captains – weather luck. Intending for Vinland, he and his crew set out from Brattahlid but encountered such strong headwinds that they spent most of the summer beating uselessly about the ocean. At one stage they were in sight of Iceland and on another occasion glimpsed birds which they judged came from the Irish coast. At the end of the sailing season, without ever having set foot in Vinland, they limped back to Greenland. Simple-minded folk claim that a ship or boat has a mind and a spirit of its own. They believe that a vessel can 'see' its way back home like a domestic cat or dog that has been lost, or a horse to its stable, and that it can retrace the same routes that it has previously sailed. This is nonsense, the dreaming of landlubbers. Vessels which make several repeat journeys usually do so because they are in the hands of the same experienced crew members or there is some characteristic of the particular vessel – shallow draught, ability to sail to windward, or whatever – which makes it best suited to the task in hand. Seamanship and weather luck make for a successful second or third voyage along a particular track, not a boat's own acquired knowledge. Thorstein's failure to fetch back his brother's bones goes to prove this very well.

They eventually made their Greenland landfall not at Brattahlid but at Lyusfjord some three days' sail to the north-west. Here a small group of Norse had already established a few coastal farms, and Thorstein struck up a friendship with a namesake, who invited him to stay and help him work the land, which was plentiful. Perhaps my uncle was ashamed to return to Brattahlid with so little accomplished and without Thorvald's body, so he accepted the offer. That autumn a small coaster came down from Lyusfjord with a message. My uncle was asking for his share of the family's cattle herd and other stores to be sent to Lyusfjord, and – in a note added by Gudrid – there was an invitation to send me along as well. It seemed that I was still high in Gudrid's affections and her substitute child.

My uncle's new-found partner was remarkably swarthy for a Norseman, hence his nickname Thorstein the Black. This giving of a nickname which identified him from all the other Thorsteins, including my uncle, is a sensible Norse custom. Most Norse derive their names, simply enough, from the parents. Thus, I am Thorgils Leifsson, being the son of Leif Eriksson, who is the son of Erik. But with so many Leifs, Eriks, Grimms, Odds and others to choose from, it is helpful to have the extra defining adjective. The easiest way is to say where he or she comes from – not in my own case, though – or refer to some particular characteristic of the individual. Thus my grandfather Erik the Red's hair was a striking strawberry red when he was young and, as we have seen, Leif the Lucky was extraordinarily fortunate in his early career, always seeming to be in the right place at the right time. During my time in Iceland I was to meet Thorkel the Bald, Gizur the White and Halfdan the Black, and heard tales of Thorgrimma Witchface, who was married to Thorodd Twistfoot, and how Olaf was called the Peacock because he was always so vain about to his clothing, and Gunnlaug Serpent Tongue had a subtle and venomous way with words.

To return to Thorstein the Black: he had done remarkably well in the five or six years that he had been farming at Lyusfjord. He had cleared a large area of scrubland, built a sizeable longhouse and several barns, fenced in his home pasture, and employed half a dozen labourers. Part of his success was due to his wife, an energetic, practical woman by the name of Grimhild. She ran the household very competently, and this left Thorstein the Black free to get on with overseeing the farming and the local fishery. Their farmhouse was easily large enough to accommodate my uncle Thorstein and Gudrid, so rather than waste time and effort building their own home my uncle and aunt moved in with them. By the time I arrived, I found the two families sharing the same building amicably.

So I now come to an event which makes me believe that the mysterious hauntings which accompanied my own mother's death were not as implausible as they might seem. That winter the plague came back to the Greenland settlements for the second time in less than five years. It was the same recurring illness which was the curse of our existence. Where it came from, we could not tell. We knew only that it flared up suddenly, caused great suffering and then died away just as rapidly. Perhaps it is significant that both times these plagues visited us in autumn and early winter when we were all living cooped up, close together in the longhouses, with little light, no fresh air and a tremendous fug. The first person to contract the illness in Lyusfjord this time around was the overseer on the farm, a man named Gardi. Frankly, no one was too sorry. Gardi was a brute, untrustworthy and with a vicious streak. He could be civil enough when he was sober, but turned nasty when he was drunk, and was even worse the following morning when he had a hangover. In fact, when he first fell sick, everyone thought that he was suffering from yet another drinking binge until he began to show all the signs of the fever – a pasty skin, sunken eyes, difficulty in breathing, a dry tongue, and a rash of purple-red spots beginning to blotch his body. When, after a short illness, he died there was very little mourning. Instead the settlers around Lyusfjord began to wonder who would be afflicted next. The illness always picked its victims randomly. It might attack a man but leave his wife unscathed, or it would carry off two children from a brood of five, and the other three siblings never even had a sniffle. My uncle Thorstein contracted the sickness, but Gudrid escaped. Thorstein the Black was spared, yet his wife, Grimhild, succumbed. The progress of the sickness was as erratic as its selection was unpredictable. Sometimes the patient lingered for weeks. Others died within twenty-four hours of showing the first pustules.

Grimhild was one of the rapid victims. One day she was complaining of headaches and dizziness, the next she could hardly walk. She was so unsteady on her feet that by evening she could barely get to the outside privy a few steps away from the main farmhouse. Gudrid offered to accompany Grimhild in case she needed help and, as I was nearby, beckoned to me to assist. I took my place beside Grimhild so she could put her arm over my shoulder. Gudrid was on the other side with her arm around Grimhild's waist. The three of us then made our way slowly out of the door, and we were not halfway across the farmyard when Grimhild came to an abrupt halt. She was deathly pale and swaying on her feet so that Gudrid and I had to hold her from falling. It was bitterly cold and Gudrid wanted to get Grimhild across to the privy as fast as possible, then bring her back into the warmth. But

Grimhild stood rigid. Her arm was tense and trembling along my shoulders, and the hair rose on the back of my neck.

'Come on,' urged Gudrid, 'we can't stand out here in this cold. It will only make your fever worse.'

But Grimhild would not move. 'I can see Gardi,' she whispered in horror. 'He's over there by the door and he has a whip in his hand.' Gudrid tried to coax Grimhild to take a step forward. But Grimhild was petrified. 'Gardi is standing there, not five paces away,' she muttered with panic in her voice. 'He's using the whip to flog several of the farmhands, and near him I can see your husband. I can see myself in the group as well. How can I be there and yet here, and what about Thorstein? We all look so grey and strange,' She was about to faint.

'Here, let me take you back inside, out of the cold,' said Gudrid, half-lifting the delirious woman so that the three of us could turn in our tracks and stumble back into the main hall. We helped Grimhild into the bed closet, which had been turned into a makeshift sanatorium. My uncle Thorstein was already lying there. Fever-struck for the past week he had been shivering and slipping into occasional bouts of delirium.

Grimhild died the same night, and by dawn the farm carpenter was already planing the boards for her coffin. Our burial customs were very brusque. Under normal circumstances a wealthy farmer or his wife, particularly if they followed the Old Ways, might merit a funeral feast and be interred under a small burial mound on some prominent spot like a hillside or favourite beach. But in times of plague no one bothered with such niceties. People believed that the sooner the corpses were got out of the house and put underground, the quicker their wandering spirits would vacate the premises. Even the Christians received short shrift. They were buried in a hastily dug grave, a stake was driven into the ground above the corpse's heart, and when a priest next visited the settlement a few prayers were said, the stake was wrenched out and a bowl of holy water was emptied down the hole. Occasionally a small gravestone was erected, but not often.

That same morning Grimhild's husband went about the day-to-day chores of the farm as if nothing had happened. It was his way of coping with the shock of his wife's sudden death. He told four farmhands to go to the landing place where we kept our small boats and be ready to do a day's fishing. Trying to make myself useful and not wanting to stay in the same house as Grimhild's corpse, I accompanied the men as they headed to the beach to begin preparing the nets and fishing lines. We had loaded up the fishing gear into the two small skiffs, and were just about to push off for the fishing grounds when a runner came stumbling down from the farmhouse. In a lather of sweat and fear, he told Thorstein the Black to come quickly, something very odd was happening in the sick room. Thorstein dropped the sculls he was about to put into the boat and ran, clumping back up the narrow track to the farm. The rest of us stood there and stared at one another.

'What's happening in the farm?' someone asked the messenger, who was not at all in a hurry to get back to the longhouse.

'Grimhild's corpse started to move,' he replied. 'She sat up in bed, slid her feet to the floor and was trying to stand. I didn't see it myself, but one of the women came running out of the bed closet screaming.'

'Better stay away for a while,' said one of the farmhands. 'Let Grimhild's husband sort it out, if the story's true. I've heard about corpses coming alive, and no good ever comes of it. Come on, let's shove off the boats and go fishing. We'll find out what's happened soon enough.'

But it was difficult to concentrate on the fishing that day. Everyone in the two boats kept glancing back at the farmhouse, which could be seen in the distance. They were very subdued. I had gone along in one of the boats, helping bail out the bilges with a wooden scoop when I wasn't baiting hooks – my fingers were small and deft – but every time I caught sight of one of the men looking back at the farmhouse, I shivered with apprehension.

By mid-afternoon we were back on the beach, and had cleaned and split the few cod and saithe that we had caught, and hung them up in the drying house. I walked very slowly back to the house, staying at the rear of the group as we tramped up the path. When we came to the front door, no one would go in. The farmhands held back, fidgeted and looked at me meaningfully. I was just a boy, but they thought of me as a member of their employer's family, and therefore I was the one who should enter the house first. I pushed open the heavy wooden door and found the long hall strangely deserted. At the far end three or four of the workers' wives were huddled together on benches, looking very troubled. One of them was sobbing quietly. I tiptoed to the door of the bed closet and peered in. Thorstein the Black was sitting on the earth floor, his knees drawn up to his chest and his head bowed. He was staring at the ground. On the bed in front of him lay the corpse of his wife. A hatchet was buried in her chest, the haft stuck up in the air. To my left, Gudrid was seated on the side of the bed where her husband lay. Thorstein Eriksson was propped up on a pillow, but looked very odd. I ran to Gudrid and threw my arms around her waist. She was deathly calm.

'What's happened?' I croaked.

'Grimhild was on her feet. Her fetch must have come back and entered her body,' Gudrid replied. 'She was stumbling slowly round the room. Knocking into the walls like a blind person. She was bumping and fumbling. That was when I sent for her husband. I feared she would do harm. When her husband came into the room, he thought that Gudrid was possessed. That she had been turned into a ghoul. He picked up the hatchet and sank it into her. To put an end to her. She has not moved since.'

Gudrid pulled me closer. 'Your uncle Thorstein is dead as well,' she said quietly. 'He stopped breathing during the afternoon and I thought he had passed away. But then he did come back to us briefly. He called me over to him and told me that he knew he was about to die, and that he did not want to be buried here, but back in Brattahlid. I promised him that would be done. Then he told me not to forget the volva's prophecy about my own future. He said he was not the man who had been promised to me. It was the last thing he said. Then he fell back and did not stir again.'

I was half-kneeling beside Gudrid with my head on her lap. 'Don't worry,' I told Gudrid, trying to console her. 'Everything will be all right now. You will not die from the plague. Nor will Thorstein the Black. Only old Amundi is going to die, and Sverting, who was with me in the boat this afternoon. That's all the people who were with Gardi last night in the yard.'

She put her hand under my chin, and gently turned my face so she could look into my eyes. 'How do you know?' she said softly.

'Because I saw them too, just as Grimhild did, all of them were there with Gardi and his whip. Last night, in the yard,' I answered.

'I see,' said Gudrid, and let her hand fall as she looked away.

I was too confused and frightened to make any sense of what was happening. I had never intended to tell anyone that I too had seen the group of fetches in the darkness of the farmyard. It was something which I did not understand. If I could see them, what did it mean about me and my responses to the spirit world? I had heard the rumours about my real mother Thorgunna and the ominous circumstances of her death. Would I see her fetch next? It was a terrifying prospect. But had I glanced up and seen Gudrid's expression when I made my confession, I would have been reassured. I would have realised that Gudrid too had seen the not-yet-dead, and that she had the gift of seidr, far more than me.

SIX

SEVEN-YEAR-OLDS are remarkably quick to adapt. Naturally enough, the farm workers at Lyusfjord refused to spend the winter cooped up in a building where such supernatural events had occurred, so our household moved back to Brattahlid, and within days I was back into the normal routines of childhood, playing with the other children. There were more of them than there had been at Lyusfjord so our games were more complicated and rowdy. I was smaller in stature than most of my contemporaries, but I made up for my lack of brawn with clever invention and quickness of thought. I also found I had a talent for mimicry and an imagination more vivid than most of my friends. So in our group I was the one who tended to invent new games or embellish the existing games with variants. When spring came and the days lengthened, we children moved out of doors to play the more boisterous games that the adults had forbidden indoors during the winter months. Most of our games involved a lot of play-acting with loud shouts, makeshift wooden shields and blunt wood swords. It was only natural that one we invented was based on my uncle Thorvald's voyage. Of course Thorvald's heroic death was a central feature of the make-believe. The oldest, strongest boy – his name was Hrafn as I remember – would play the leading role, staggering around the yard, clutching his armpit dramatically and pretending to pull out an arrow. 'The Skraelings have shot me,' he would yell. 'I'm dying. I will never see home again, but die a warrior's death in a far land.' Then he would spin round, throw out his arms and drop in fake death on the dirt and the rest of us would pretend to pile up a cairn of stones around his body. My own contribution came when we all boarded an imaginary boat and rowed and sailed along the unknown coast. I invented a great whirlpool which nearly sucked us down and a slimy sea monster whose tentacles tried to drag us overboard. My friends pretended to scan the beaches and called out what they saw – ravening wolves, huge bears, dragon-snakes and so forth. One day I created for them a monster-man who, I said, was grimacing at us from the beach. He was a troll with just one foot and that as big as a large dish. He was bounding along the strand, taking great leaps to keep pace with us and – to demonstrate – I left my companions to one side, and hopped along, both feet together until I was out of breath and gave up the pretence.

It was a harmless bit of play-acting, which was to draw attention to me in a way that I could never have anticipated.

The following day I got a really bad scare. I was walking past the open door to the main cattle shed when a thin arm reached out of the darkness, and seized me by the shoulder. I was yanked inside, and in the gloom found myself staring close up at the sinister face of Tyrkir. I was convinced he was about to batter me for some fault, and I went numb with fear as he briskly hefted me to the back of the cow byre and twisted me round to face him. He was still gripping my shoulder and it hurt. 'Who told you about the uniped?' he demanded in his heavy accent. 'Did you speak with any of the crew about it?'

'Turn the boy so I can look at his eyes,' said a voice with a deep rumble, and I saw another man, seated on the hay at the back of the byre. I had not noticed him before, but even without looking at his face I knew who he was, and my fright only increased. He was Thorvall, known as 'the Hunter'.

Of all the men in Brattahlid Thorvall was the one we boys

most feared and respected. He was the odd man out in our community of farmers and fishermen. A huge, weatherbeaten man now in his late fifties but still as fit and tough as a twenty-year-old, he was disfigured by a scar which ran from the corner of his left eye back towards his ear. The ear had been partly torn away and healed with a ragged edge so that Thorvall looked like a tattered tomcat that had been in numerous fights. The injury was the result of a hunting accident in which Thorvall had been mauled by a young polar bear. Standing in front of him in the cowshed, I tried to keep my glance away from that terrible scar, while I thought to myself that Thorvall had been lucky not to lose the eye itself. As it was, the lid of his left eye drooped, and I wondered if it affected his vision when he was drawing his hunting bow.

Thorvall was dressed in his usual hunting clothes, heavy leggings bound with thongs, stout shoes and a jerkin with a hood. I had never seen him wear anything else, and to be frank the clothes did smell strongly even over the stench of the cow byre. Thorvall had no one to look after his laundry. He was a bachelor who lived by himself in a small house on the edge of the settlement and he came and went as he pleased. His only personal ornament was a necklace made of the teeth of polar bears he had killed. At that moment, he was looking at me steadily and I felt I was being scanned by some sort of predatory bird.

'Maybe the woman told him. She has the sight and knows a good deal of the ways,' he said.

Tyrkir was still gripping my shoulder in case I made a dash for the open door behind me. 'We know about her qualities, but she's only his foster mother. Besides she wasn't there either. I think the boy saw the uniped himself. They say that Leif's Orcades woman had seidr powers. More likely the boy has his abilities from her.' He gave me a slight shake as if to check whether these mysterious 'abilities' would somehow clank together inside me.

'You'll only scare him more if you rattle him around. Let him speak for himself.'

Tyrkir relaxed his grip slightly, but did not release my arm. 'Have you talked with Gudrid about the uniped?' he asked.

I was puzzled. I had no idea what a uniped was.

'That creature who hopped along on just one foot.'

I now realised what this interrogation was about, but was completely baffled why Tyrkir and Thorvall would be interested in my childish antics. Surely I had done nothing wrong.

'What else do you see? Do you have any strange dreams?' Tyrkir was asking the question so intently that his German accent was all the more obvious. I did not know how to reply. Of course I had dreams, I thought to myself, but so did everyone else. I had nightmares of being drowned, or pursued by monsters, or that the room was squeezing in on me, all the usual terrors. In fact I was rather ashamed of my nightmares and never spoke about them to anyone. I had no idea where my vision of the so-called uniped had come from. It was not something I had dreamed in the night. The image had simply popped into my head at the time when I was playing with the other children and I had acted it out. I was still too scared to speak.

'Anything else unusual in your head, any odd sights from time to time?' Tyrkir rephrased his question, trying to adopt a more soothing tone.

My mind stayed a blank. I wanted desperately to answer, just to save myself, but I couldn't recall a single dream out of the ordinary. But I was beginning to understand that these two gruff men meant me no harm. With a child's acuteness of observation I was becoming aware that in some mysterious way they needed me. There was an undercurrent of respect, and of something else – of awe – in their attitude to me. Clamped in the rough grip of Tyrkir, and faced by the scarred face of Thorvall, I realised that the two men were expecting me to supply something they could not achieve, and it was something to do with the way I saw things.

'I can't remember any of my dreams,' I stammered. I had the good sense to look straight at Thorvall. A deliberately level gaze is a great help in persuading an interlocutor that one is telling the truth, even if one isn't.

Thorvall grunted. 'Have you talked about the uniped or any other dream like that with your foster mother?'

I again shook my head, still trying to understand why the two men were so interested in Gudrid's role.

'Do you know what this is?' Tyrkir suddenly brought his free hand in front of my face, and showed me what he had been holding in his palm. It was a small metal pendant, squat and T-shaped. The creases and lines on his hand, I noticed, were deeply ingrained with soot and grime.

'Mjollnir—' I ventured.

'Do you know what Thor uses it for?'

'Sort of,' I murmured.

'He uses his hammer to crack the heads of those who disobey him, and to obliterate his enemies. He'll use it on you, if you tell anyone about our little talk.'

'Let the boy go,' said Thorvall, and then, looking at me, he asked in a matter-of-fact tone, 'how would you like to know more about Thor and the other Gods? Would that interest you?'

I felt strangely drawn to his suggestion. I had now controlled my fear and nodded my agreement. 'All right, then,' said Tyrkir, 'Thorvall and I will teach you when we have time. But you don't tell anyone else about it, and we want you also to describe us any other dreams that you have. Now go on your way.'

Looking back on that little episode so long ago when two grown men trapped and questioned a frightened small boy in the cattle byre, I can see what Tyrkir and Thorvall were trying to achieve, and why they behaved in the odd way they did. They feared that knowledge of the Old Ways was fading from Greenland, and had been jolted into action when they detected in me someone who might possess the seidr power. They may even have heard about Christian missionaries rounding up the schoolchildren and the women and preaching at them. By imitation Thorvall and Tyrkir must have been thinking that they should do the same, but in a secret and select fashion, picking a child who seemed to have special powers and was therefore already gifted with seidr ability by the Gods. Then they would teach him what they knew of the old wisdom so that the knowledge and practice of the Old Ways would survive. If that is how they felt, at least a part of my subsequent life would have been their justification, though they would be scornful to see me now, skulking here in a Christian monastery pretending to be one of the faithful.

The uniped, Tyrkir told me in one of my first lessons, was the creature he had seen during the trip with Thorvald Eriksson to Vinland. The uniped had been skulking at the edge of the woods, close to the beach, as their ship sailed by. It looked exactly as I had described it to the other children – a bizarre, hunched body of a man standing on a single thick leg, which ended in a single broad foot. It had hopped along the strand, just as I had done in my childish game, keeping pace with the Norsemen and their boat. But when the visitors turned their vessel and began to make for shore, intending to land and capture the uniped – whether it was beast or man they could not tell – it abruptly swerved away, and had gone leaping off into the undergrowth until it had vanished underground, or so it seemed from a distance.

The sighting of the uniped was curious and inexplicable. Perhaps it was just one of Tyrkir's eccentricities, and he was citing another of his hallucinations. But several of the crew also claimed they had seen the strange creature, though not as clearly as Tyrkir. Nor could they describe it in such detail. None of them had mentioned the incident when they got back to Brattahlid for fear of being considered foolish. So my imitation of the creature – even the exact way it had kept pace with the knorr – had led both Tyrkir and Thorvall to think that somehow my other-spirit had been on that exploring ship off the coast of Vinland, and yet back at home in Brattahlid at the same time, and – as every Old Believer knows – the ability to be in two places at once is a true mark of seidr power. A seidr-gifted person is born with this trick of spirit flying through the air, invisible and at supernatural speed to places far distant and then returning to the mortal body. Judging by what happened to me in Vinland soon afterwards, Thorvall and Tyrkir were right in detecting a spirit link between me and that unknown land in the west. On the other hand, I have to admit that it could have been pure coincidence that I imitated a hopping One Foot in the children's game because no one ever saw a uniped ever again.

But that doesn't mean that unipeds do not exist. Recently I came across one here in the monastery's library. I was preparing a sheet of vellum, scraping off the old ink before washing the page. Vellum is so scarce that we reuse the pages when their writings are too faded or blurred, or the content of the text is out of date or unimportant. This particular page was from Ezekiel, on the demons Gog and Magog, and had become detached from its original book. As I removed the old writing, I noticed a small, simple drawing in the margin. It was rather crudely done, but it caught my attention at once. It was a uniped, just as Tyrkir had described it to me in that cattle shed sixty years ago, except that the creature in the margin was drawn with giant, flapping ears as well as a giant foot. And, instead of hopping, it was lying on the ground on its back with the single large foot held up in the air. I could just make out the faint word '. . . ped sheltering . . .' and then the rest of the caption was a blur. What the uniped was sheltering from was not clear. If it was a Vinland uniped then it might have been the snow and rain. But there was nothing in the adjacent text to explain the mystery.

Over the next months Thorvall or Tyrkir frequently picked on me for some chore or other, ostensibly because they wanted me to help them, but in fact they were looking for opportunities to tell me something of their beliefs out of earshot of the others. Neither of my tutors were learned men and Tyrkir in particular was very artless. But they both possessed the enormous advantage that they were not in the least hypocritical in their beliefs. Their genuine conviction made a stronger impression on me than all the sophistry imaginable. And the pagan world of the Old Ways was so easy to imagine, so logical, so attractive, and so apt to our situation on the remote shore of Greenland, backed by its immense and mysterious hinterland of ice and mountains, that it would have been a very dull student who failed to respond.

Tyrkir told me of the Aesir, the race of heroes who migrated out of the east long ago and established their capital at Asgard, with Odinn as their chief. With the twin ravens Hugin and Munin – Thought and Memory – perched on his shoulders, Odinn was – and is, so Tyrkir insisted to me – cunning and ruthless, a true king. Dedicated to the pursuit of advantageous knowledge, even sacrificing the sight of one eye so he could drink a draught of water from the well of wisdom, he still treads the world in a variety of disguises, always seeking more and more information. But his role is doomed, for in his wisdom he knows he is leading the other Aesir in the ultimately hopeless task of defending the world against the powers of darkness, the frost giants and mountain giants and other grim monsters who will finally crush them, to the hideous baying of the monstrous hound, Gorm. In his palace at Valholl Odinn entertains the departed heroes of our human race, proven warriors who are provided with feasting and drinking and the company of splendid women, until they will be summoned forth for the last, fatal battle at Ragnarok. Then they and all the Gods will be overwhelmed.

There is no doubt in my mind that Tyrkir's eerie tales of Odinn and his deeds were the original inspiration for my later devotion to the All-Father, as Tyrkir always called him. To a seven-year-old there was a morbid fascination in how Odinn interviewed the dead or sat beside men hanging on the gallows to learn their final secrets or consorted with the maimed. His skill as a shape-shifter was no less beguiling, and I easily imagined the Father of the Gods as he changed himself into a bird of prey, a worm, a snake, a sacrificial victim, according to whatever stratagem he had in mind. Being still a youngster I had no inkling of his darker side – that he can trick and cheat and deceive, and that his name means 'Frenzy'.

Thorvall's hero, unsurprisingly given his own name, was red-haired Thor, Odinn's son, who rides across the sky in his goat-drawn chariot, his passage marked by rolls of thunder and flashes of lightning, hurling thunderbolts, controlling the sea, and laying about him with Mjollnir, his famous hammer. Thorvall was an ardent member of the Thor cult, and once he got started on one of his favourite Thor-stories, he became very animated. I recall the day he told me how Thor went fishing for the Midgard serpent, using an oxhead for bait, and when the serpent took the hook Thor pulled so hard on the line that his foot broke through the planking of the boat. At that point in his story Thorvall stood up and, as we were in the cattle shed at the time, put his foot against one of the stalls and heaved back to imitate his hero. But the stall was poorly made, and collapsed in a cloud of dust and splinters. I can still hear Thorvall's great bellowing laugh and his triumphant cry of 'Just like that!'

Despite Thorvall's enthusiasm for Thor – and my boyhood respect for the tough hunter – I still preferred Odinn. I savoured the idea of creeping about in disguise, picking up intelligence, observing and manipulating. Like all children, I liked to eavesdrop on the adults and try to learn their secrets, and when I did so and stood hidden behind a door or a pillar, I would close one eye in imitation of my one-eyed hero God. Also, if my foster mother had searched under my mattress she would have found a square of cloth I had hidden there. I was pretending it was *Skidbladnir*, Odinn's magic ship, which received a favourable wind whenever it was launched and could carry all the Aesir, fully armed, yet when Odinn no longer needed it, he could fold it up and tuck it in his pocket.

Several years later, when I was in my teens, it slowly dawned on me that I myself might be a part of Odinn's grand design. By then it seemed that the path of my life was increasingly directed by the All-Father's whim, and whenever possible I paid him homage, not only by prayer and secret sacrifice, but also by imitation. That is one reason why, as a callow youth, I sought to become a poet, because it was Odinn, disguised as an eagle, who stole the mead of poetry from its guardian Suttung. More important, my growing devotion to Odinn was in harmony with my natural wanderlust. Whenever I have set out on any journey I have done so in the knowledge that the All-Father is the greatest of all far-farers, and that he is watching over me. In that regard, he never played me false, for I have survived when many of my travelling companions fell.

TYRKIR ALSO TAUGHT me the details of the mysterious prophecy which Gudrid had mentioned on that dismal day in Lyusfjord when she sat beside Thorstein's deathbed, and I had let slip that I had seen the fetches of the not-yet-dead. Tyrkir had been delayed late in his workshop, where he made and repaired the metal tools essential to our farming. Gudrid had sent me to take the little German his supper. 'She's a good woman, your foster mother,' Tykir said as he set aside the empty bowl and licked his fingers. 'Far too good to fall under the influence of those crazy White Christ fanatics. No one else can sing the warlock's songs so well.'

'What do you mean, the warlock's songs?' I asked. 'What are they?'

Tyrkir looked at me from under his bulging forehead, a momentary gleam of suspicion in his eyes. 'You mean to say that your foster mother hasn't told you about her and the Little Sibyl?'

'No, I've never even heard of the Little Sibyl. Who was she?'

'The old woman Thorbjorg. She was the Little Sibyl, the volva. She died four years ago, so you really never knew her. But plenty still do, and they all remember the night when Gudrid Thorbjornsdottir revealed herself.'

Tyrkir settled himself on the low stool near his anvil, and pointed for me to make myself comfortable on a pile of sacks that had held charcoal for his simple furnace. It was obvious that his story would be a long one, but he considered it important that I know the details about my foster mother. Anything which concerned my adored Gudrid was important to me, and I listened so attentively that I still remember every detail of Tyrkir's explanation.

THE LITTLE SIBYL, Tyrkir began, had come to Greenland in the earliest days of the colony to avoid the turbulent White Christ followers who were causing such ructions in Iceland by insisting that everyone should follow their one true God. She was the last of nine sisters, all of whom had possessed the seidr skills, and being the ninth she had more of the gift than all the others. She could foretell the weather, so farmers planned their activities according to her advice. Their wives asked her about the propitious names they should give their babies and the health and prospects of their growing children. Young women quietly enquired about their love lives; and mariners timed their voyages to begin on the auspicious days the Little Sibyl selected. Thorbjorg knew the correct offerings to the Gods, the right prayers, the proper rituals, all according to the Old Ways.

It was in the autumn of the year that my foster mother Gudrid first arrived in Greenland that a black famine had gripped the colony. After a meagre hay harvest the hunters, who had gone inland or along the coast looking for seals and deer, came back with little to show for their efforts. Two of them failed to come back at all. As the cheerless winter months wore on, our people began to die of starvation. The situation became so bad that a leading farmer, a man named Herjolf, decided he should consult the Little Sibyl to ask whether there was any action that the settlers could take to bring the famine to an end. Herjolf arranged a feast to honour the Little Sibyl and, through her, the spirit world she would have to enter if she was to answer their plea for advice. Also, consuming their last reserves of food in such a feast was a signal to the Gods that the people placed their trust in them.

Herjolf supplied the banquet from his final stocks of dried fish and seal blubber, slaughtered the last of his livestock and brought out his stores of cheese and bread. Naturally the entire community was invited to attend the feast, not just for food to fill their aching bellies but to hear what the Sibyl would say. Herjolf's wife arranged a long table running the full length of their hall. Crosswise at the head of the table and raised slightly above it where it could be seen by everyone, a seat of honour for the Little Sibyl was placed – a carved wooden chair with a cushion stuffed with hens' feathers.

While the guests were assembling, a man was sent to escort Thorbjorg from her home. When she arrived, it was immediately clear that the Little Sibyl had acknowledged the gravity of the emergency. Normally when called upon to practise seidr she arrived dressed in her everyday homespun clothes, and carrying only her seidr staff, a wooden stick about three feet long carved with runes and hung with withered strips of cloth. But when Thorbjorg was led into the great hall that evening she was dressed in clothes no one had ever seen her wear before: a long overmantle of midnight blue reaching almost to the ground and fastened across the chest with cloth straps worked with intricate designs in red and silver thread. The entire surface of the cloak was encrusted with patterns of small stones, not precious stones but pebbles, mottled and marbled and all smooth from lying underwater. They shimmered as if still wet. They were magic 'waterstones' said to contain the spirits of the river. Around her throat the volva wore a necklace of coloured glass beads, mostly red and blue. Her belt was plaited from the dried stalks of mushrooms and fungi, and from it hung a large cloth pouch, in which she kept her collection of dried herbs, charms and the other ingredients for her sorcery. Her feet were encased in heavy shoes made of calfskin, the hair still on them, and laced with heavy thongs with tin buttons on the ends. Her head was hidden within a dark hood of black lambskin lined with the fur from a white cat. On her hands were mittens also of catskin, but with the fur turned to the inside.

Had it not been for her familiar seidr staff the guests would have found it difficult to recognise Thorbjorg. The staff was of pale honey-coloured wood, much worn and slick with handling, and the knob at the end was bound in brass and studded with more of the 'waterstones'. There were, it seemed, more ribbons than usual.

As she arrived, Herjolf, who had been waiting to greet her at the door of the long hall, was surprised to find himself looking at the back of her black hood. Thorbjorg was walking backwards. The entire assembly fell silent as her host escorted Thorbjorg down the length of the hall, still facing the main entrance door. Herjolf named each person who was present as they drew level. The Sibyl responded by peering out from under her black hood and into their faces but saying little, only giving the occasional sniff as if smelling their presence.

When the volva was safely settled on her high seat, the meal was served and everyone ate with gusto, though many kept glancing up at Thorbjorg to see how she was behaving. She did not eat with the everyday utensils, but pulled from her pouch a brass spoon and an ancient knife with a handle of walrus ivory bound with two copper rings. The blade of the knife was very worn and pitted, as if it had been buried in the earth a long time, and the onlookers noted the point was broken. Nor did she eat the same food as everyone else. She asked for, and was given, a bowl of gruel prepared with goat's milk and a dish made of the hearts of all the animals slaughtered for the feast.

When the meal was over and the tables cleared, Herjolf stood up. 'Sibyl, I hope that everything that has been arranged this evening has been to your satisfaction,' he announced in a voice that carried the length of the hall. 'We have all assembled here in the hopes that in your wisdom you will be able to tell us how long the famine will last, and whether there is anything we can do to end our difficulties.'

'I need to spend longer in this house,' she answered. Her voice was thin and wheezing as if she had difficulty in breathing. 'I have yet to absorb its spirit, to learn the portents, to feel its soul. It is too early to give any judgement. I will stay here on this seat, all this night, and tomorrow afternoon I believe I will be able to reply to your question.'

There was a general sigh of despondency. Those who lived close enough to be able to walk to their homes through the dark left the building. The others bedded down for the night in Herjolf's hall and waited anxiously for the long, slow spread of dawn, which comes so late at that season that the light begins to fade almost as soon it reaches the earth.

The next afternoon, when the audience had reassembled, a hitch arose. The Sibyl unexpectedly declared that she needed the help of an assistant. She required someone to sing the proper seidr chants as her spirit began to leave her body. The chants would help free her spirit to start on its journey to the otherworld. There was consternation. The Sibyl had never requested an assistant before. Herjolf turned to face the crowd and appealed to everyone in the hall – if anyone could help, please would they step forward. His appeal was met with silence. The Sibyl sat on her high seat, blinking and peering down impatiently. Herjolf repeated his appeal, and to everyone's surprise Gudrid stepped forward quietly. 'Do you know any seidr?' Herjolf asked in astonishment. Gudrid's own father, Thorbjorn, must have been equally startled. He was gaping with surprise. 'Yes,' replied Gudrid quietly. 'When I was a foster child in Iceland to my father's friends Orm and Halldis, it was Halldis who taught me the warlock songs. If Halldis were here today, she would do it better, but I think I can remember all the words.' The Little Sibyl gave a sceptical grunt, and beckoned Gudrid close to her. She leaned over and must have asked the young woman to say a sacred verse to test her because Gudrid sang some refrain in a voice so low that no one could make out more than a few words, most of which seemed to be in some strange sort of language. The Sibyl nodded curtly, then settled back on her cushion.

At that point Gudrid's father, Thorbjorn, normally very easy-going, broke in. 'I'm not having my daughter involved in any witchcraft,' he announced loudly. 'That's a dangerous game. Once started, no one knows where it will end.'

'I'm neither a witch, nor a seeress, but if it will help our situation I am prepared to take part,' Gudrid told him firmly.

Thorbjorn took this rebuff badly, turned on his heel and pushed his way out of the crowd and left the building, muttering that at least he would not have to witness his daughter's disgrace.

'The spirits are still wary and obscure to me,' the Sibyl said after a short silence when the audience had settled down. 'They must be calmed and called to attend us.' She gestured to Gudrid, who exchanged glances with several of the farmers' wives. As their husbands looked either curious or uncomfortable, these women pushed through the crowd, and under Gudrid's instructions formed a small circle. There were perhaps half a dozen women facing inwards, Gudrid standing in the centre. As the crowd hushed, she began to sing the words of the warlock song. She had a high clear voice and sang without any trace of embarrassment. The women around her began to sway quietly to the rhythm of the voice, then their hands reached out and joined, and their circle began slowly to shuffle sideways, the direction of their rotation against the sun. Husbands and sons looked on, half-fearful and half-amazed. This was woman's work, something that few of the menfolk had ever guessed. Gudrid sang on, verse after verse, and the older women, softly at first, then more loudly, began to echo the refrain. To some of the audience the songs seemed at times like a lullaby that they had heard as children, though only Gudrid appeared to know all the verses and when to change the rhythms. She sang without a tremor until finally her voice died away, the women slipped back into the crowd and the volva looked down at Gudrid. 'I congratulate you,' she announced. 'Whoever taught you, taught you well, and the spirits have responded. I can feel them now, assembling around us and ready to carry my spirit to the Gods.'

She beckoned Gudrid to stand closer and began to croon softly. Gudrid must have recognised the chant, for she began to respond, catching the refrain, repeating the stanzas, changing a line, adding a line. Back and forth went the chant between the two women, their voices weaving together, and the volva began to rock back and forth in her chair. Then the words made a circle on themselves. There were repetitions and long pauses. People in the crowd began to shuffle their feet, glance at one another, then turn their gaze back to the blue-cloaked figure on its high seat. Not a person left the hall. Finally, after a little more than half an hour, the Sibyl's voice slowed. Gudrid, still standing beside her, seemed to sense that her role was at an end. The volva's head sank forward on her chest, and she appeared to be both awake and asleep. For a long moment nothing happened, and then very slowly the volva raised her head and looked straight down the crowded room. She nodded to Gudrid, and Gudrid quietly walked back to the edge of the crowd of onlookers, turned and faced the Little Sibyl.

Herjolf cleared his throat with a nervous cough. 'Can you tell us the answer to the question we all ask?' he said. The volva's reply was matter of fact. 'Yes, my dream was clear and cloudless. My spirit circled up through the air and I saw ice breaking in the fjord. I saw the first signs of new grass even though the migrating birds had not yet come to feed and prepare their nesting sites. The air was warm around me though the day was still short. Spring will come very early this year and your trials will finish within a few days. The hunger you are suffering will be at an end and no one else will die. You have put your trust in the Gods, and you will be rewarded.'

Unexpectedly the volva turned towards Gudrid and spoke directly to her. 'And for you,' she said, 'I also have a prophecy. My spirit messengers were so charmed by your seidr knowledge and the songs you sang that they have brought me news of your destiny. I can now reward you for the help you have given me. You are fated to make a distinguished marriage here in Greenland, but it will not last for long. Rather, I see how all your links lead you towards Iceland and its peoples. In that land you will give rise to an illustrious family line and, through its people, you will attain an enduring renown.'

Tyrkir came to the end of his story.

'So you see, Thorgils,' he said, 'that's why Thorvall thought, when you imitated the hopping One Foot in your game, that you might have inherited seidr skill, the power of spirit flight, through your foster mother. Gudrid herself could be a skilful volva, if only she did not consort so much with White Christ fanatics.'

I knew what Tyrkir meant. Ever since Gudrid had come back from Lyusfjord, she had been spending time with Leif's wife Gyda, a zealous Christian. The two women were often seen visiting the White Rabbit Hutch together. Tyrkir and Thorvall found it worrying that someone so gifted with the skills and knowledge of the Old Ways was drifting towards the newfangled Christian beliefs. Gudrid's interest in Christianity shook their own faith in the Old Gods, and they felt uneasy. They did not realise, as I do now, that the underlying truth is that good pagans make good Christians and vice versa. The choice of religion is less important than the talents of the person who is involved. The same is true of generals and politicians, as I have noticed during my travels. I have seen that it makes no difference whether an outstanding military commander is clad only in skins and painted woad, or in a gilded helmet and a beautifully tailored uniform of Persian silk as worn by the horse-warriors of the kingdom between the two great rivers. The martial genius is identical, and the brilliant, decisive reaction to the moment is the same whatever the dress. Similarly with politicians. I have listened to speeches delivered at a flea-infested tribal council meeting held around a guttering campfire in a bare forest glade which, if prettified with a few well-polished phrases, could have been the same as I heard from a conclave of the highly trained and perfumed advisers to the Basileus. I am talking about Christ's supposed representative on earth when he sits on his gilded throne in a chamber banded with porphyry and pretends that he is the incarnation of a thousand years of learning and refined civilisation.

The saddest aspect of Gudrid's drift towards the White Christ ways, now that I look back on it, is what a waste it proved to be. My foster mother would have made a truly remarkable priestess of the Old Ways if she had preferred to study under the Little Sibyl. For it is a striking feature of the old beliefs – and it would appal the monks around me if they knew – that the majority of its chief experts were women. There are fifteen different words in the Norse language to describe the various female specialisms in seidr, but fewer than half that number of words for male practitioners. Even Odinn the shape-changer has a strong element of the female about him, and you wonder about his enthusiasm for disguising himself as a woman. By contrast the White Christ expects his leading proponents to be male and women are excluded from their inner priesthood. Thus Gudrid diminished her horizons on the day she formally professed the faith of the White Christ. If she had followed the Old Ways she could have been respected and influential and helped those among whom she lived. But as a devout and saintly Christian she was finally obliged to become an anchoress and live on her own. However, that brings me far ahead of my story . . .

Thorvall and Tyrkir tried their best to make me understand that unless the Old Ways continued to be practised, they would soon be submerged by the advancing tide of White Christ beliefs. The speed with which the White Christ faith had taken hold in Iceland alarmed my tutors, and they feared that the same would happen in Greenland. 'I don't know how the White Christ people can claim to be peaceful and gentle,' said Thorvall sourly. 'The first missionary they sent to Iceland was a ruffian named Thang-brand. He swaggered about the countryside browbeating the farm-ers into taking his faith, and when he was teased about his crazy ideas, he lost his temper and killed two Icelanders in fights. To try to control him, a meeting was arranged between him and a learned volva at which the two of them would debate the merits of their beliefs. The volva made Thangbrand look an utter fool. He felt so humiliated that he took ship for Norway, and the volva proved her worth by asking Thor to send a storm, which nearly sank his ship on his journey home.

'The Icelanders were far too easy-going,' Tyrkir added. 'When the missionaries came back to Iceland some years later and began their preaching all over again, the farmers had no more stomach for the endless debates and quarrels between those who decided to take the new faith and those who wanted to stay with the old ways. They got so fed up that their delegates met at the Althing with instructions to ask the Lawspeaker to come up with a solution. He went off, sat down and pulled his cloak over his head, and thought about it for nearly a day. Then he climbed up on the Law Rock and announced that it would be less bother if everyone accepted the new religion as a formality, but that anyone who wanted to keep with the Old Ways could do so.

'We completely failed to see that the White Christ people would never give up until they had grabbed everyone. We were quite happy to live side by side with other beliefs; we never presumed to think that our ideas were the only correct ones. We made the mistake of thinking that the White Christ was just another God who would be welcomed in among all the other Gods and would coexist with them peaceably. How wrong we were.'

Inevitably, my education in paganism was patchy. Thorvall and Tyrkir often confused folklore with religion, but in the end it did not matter much. I soaked up the welter of information they gave me. Tyrkir, for example, showed me my first runes, cutting the rune staves on small flat laths of wood and making me learn his futhark, the rune alphabet, by heart. He taught me also to read the staves with my eyes shut, running my fingers over the scratches and translating them in my mind. 'It's a skill that can come in handy,' he said, 'when you want to exchange information secretly, or simply when the message is so old and worn that you cannot see it with the naked eye.' I tried hard to repay my tutors by having significant dreams which they could interpret. But I found that such dreams do not come on demand. First you have to study the complex paths of the Old Ways, and then you must know how to enter them, sometimes with the help of drugs or self-mortification. I was still too young for that, and I was reluctant to approach my foster mother to ask about her seidr knowledge because she was growing more Christian by the day, and I was uncertain if she would approve of my growing interest in the Elder Faith.

Besides, that next winter Gudrid was distracted by much more down-to-earth events. Her father, old Thorbjorn, had died not long after our return from Lyusfjord, and Gudrid, as his only surviving child, had inherited everything. Next, Thorstein the Black announced that he would not return to the farm in Lyusfjord. He felt it was an unlucky spot for him and he did not feel like starting there all over again as it would mean finding a new partner to help run the farm. So by January he had found a buyer to purchase the farm as it stood, paying him in instalments, and this meant he could reimburse Gudrid for her deceased husband's share. The result was that Gudrid, who was still without a child of her own, still beautiful, still young, was now a wealthy woman. No one was much surprised when, within a year of being made a widow, my glamorous foster mother was approached by an eligible new suitor and that she agreed to his proposal of marriage. What did surprise everyone was that her husband announced soon afterwards that he was fitting out a ship to travel to Vinland and establish a new and permanent settlement at the same spot where the two Eriksson brothers, Leif and Thorvald, had previously set their hopes.

SEVEN

WHY DID GUDRID'S new husband, Thorfinn Karlsefni, decide to try his luck in far-off Vinland? Partly, I think, because he felt he owed a debt of honour to my father, Leif. By Norse custom, when a man wishes to marry, he first seeks formal permission from the bride's senior male relation. In Gudrid's case this was Leif and he readily agreed to the match. When Leif suggested the Vinland project to Thorfinn soon afterwards, I believe that Thorfinn, who had an old-fashioned sense of family loyalty, felt that he should take up the project. Leif still believed that Vinland could be a new and prosperous colony for the Greenlanders and, though he was too busy as head of the family at Brattahlid to go there himself, he did everything he could to support the new venture. He offered Thorfinn the loan of the houses he had built there, which were technically still his property, as well as the help of several key members from his own household. Among them were my two secret tutors – Thorvall the Hunter and Tyrkir the Smith – and two slaves Leif had acquired on the same fateful voyage which brought him to my mother's bed in Orkney.

I had always been curious about Haki and Hekja because I saw them as a link to my own enigmatic past. They were husband and wife, or that is what everyone took for granted. On the other hand, they may have had no choice but to live together as a couple since fate had thrown them together. They had been captured in a viking raid somewhere on the Scottish coast and shipped to Norway, where, like Tyrkir, they were put up for sale in the slave market at Kaupang. One of King Olaf Tryggvason's liegemen bought them as a pair. He presumed the two captives were Christians and thought that he could get into the good graces of his king if he made a gift of them to his monarch. King Tryggvason could then gain public credit and reputation by giving the two slaves their freedom. To their owner's dismay, it turned out that Haki and Hekja were not Christians at all, but adherents of some pagan belief so obscure that no one had any idea what their mutterings and incantations meant. Olaf kept them at his court for only a few months, but the two Scots showed no aptitude for household work. They were only happy when they were out on some high moor or open fell that reminded them of their homeland. So when my father Leif visited the court, the Norwegian king got the two seemingly useless slaves off his hands by presenting them to Leif with the remark that he hoped that one day he would find some use for these two 'wild Scots', as he put it, whose only skill seemed to be how swiftly they could run across open country. Leif found the perfect work for Haki and Hekja as soon as he got back to Greenland. The couple made excellent sheep and cattle herders. They would spend each summer on the farthest heath lands, where they made themselves temporary shelters by thatching over natural hollows with branches and dried grass. Here they lived snugly like summer hares in a form, a resemblance enhanced by their extraordinary speed on foot. They could run down a stray sheep with ease, and they were particularly valuable when it came to chasing wayward animals during the autumn drive, when the livestock had to be brought down from the hinterland and put into the winter barns. For the rest of the year they busied themselves with odd jobs round the farm, where I used to watch them surreptitiously, wondering if my mother with her Irish blood had possessed the same mixture of fair skin and dark hair, and I tried without much success to understand the words that passed between the two Scots in their guttural, rippling language.

Karlsefni's expedition was the largest and best-equipped venture for Vinland up to that time. It numbered nearly forty people, including five women. Gudrid insisted on accompanying her new husband and she took along two female servants. There were also two farmers' wives, whose husbands had volunteered to help clear the land during the early days of the settlement in return for a land grant later. These two couples were too young to have had children of their own and Thorbjorn, Karlsefni's five-year-old son by an earlier marriage, was left behind in Brattahlid with foster parents. So the only child on board the knorr was myself, aged nearly eight. I had lobbied my father Leif to let me join the expedition and he readily agreed, to the open satisfaction of his harridan wife, Gyda, who still could not stand the sight of me.

The knorr which was to carry us westward belonged to Thorfinn. She was a well-found ship and had served him for several years in trade. Now he purchased a second smaller boat to serve as a scouting vessel. With characteristic competence Karlsefni also set about compiling a list of what was needed to establish the pioneer farm. After talking with Leif and the other men who had already been to Vinland, he loaded a good stock of farm implements – hoes, axes, saws and spades and the like – blacksmith's tools, a supply of rope and several bags of ship's nails in case we had to make repairs, as well as three dozen rolls of wadmal. This wadmal was an essential. It is cloth made from wool hand-plucked from our sheep and steeped in tubs of urine to remove the worst of the sticky wool grease. The women spin this fibre into yarn, then weave long bolts of the cloth on a simple loom suspended from the ceiling of the main room. The better-quality wadmal is set aside to make the sails of our ships while the coarser grade is turned into garments, blankets, sacks, anything that requires a fabric. Most wadmal is the same dingy brown as when the sheep had worn the wool, but sometimes the cloth is dyed with plant juice or coloured earth to produce more cheerful reds, greens and yellows. A special wadmal soaked in a mixture of sheep's grease and seal oil is nearly waterproof. This was the cloth we used to make our sea-going cloaks for the voyage – the same garment that my father gave my mother as his going-away present.

Downwind, anyone would have thought we were a mobile farm when we set sail. A small bull and three milch cows took up most of the central hold, and the smell of the cattle and wisps of dried hay from their stack of feed drifted out across the water in our lee. For the first few hours there were farmyard sounds as well because the cows kept up a low, distressed mooing before they settled to their strange new routine.

With youthful zeal I had expected instant adventure and excitement the moment we cleared the land, but like the cattle I soon found that life aboard followed the same routine as at home. I had chores to do – give the animals fresh water to drink, keep their hay topped up, clear the cattle dung. Our knorr proceeded at a stately pace, towing the scouting boat behind on a thick cable. The sea was calm, and there was nothing to see except for the escort of seabirds hovering over us and an occasional flock of black and white waterfowl with massive thick beaks, which swam along the surface of the sea beside us, occasionally ducking down and speeding ahead underwater. When I asked Thorvall why these birds did not take to the air and fly, he laughed. 'They do not know how to fly,' he said. 'The Gods gave them wings more like fish flippers. They swim when they want to travel, even from one country to another, from Iceland to Greenland, from Greenland to Vinland. That's how our sailors first guessed that there must be land to the west. When they saw the swimming birds heading out in that direction.'

This was the third of the many, many voyages of my lifetime, and I believe that Odinn had a hand in sending me upon the journey as he deliberately provoked in me the wanderlust which would bind me to him as the Far-Farer. I had been a babe in arms when my mother sailed with me from Birsay to Iceland, and still too young to remember much when I went with Gudrid from

Iceland to Greenland and suffered shipwreck. But now the crossing from Brattahlid to Vinland made a deep and lasting impression on me. There was a sense of travelling towards the new and unknown, and it was a drug. Once tasted, I could never forget it, and I wanted more. It would make me a wanderer all my life, and that is what the All-Father intended.

My first sensation on the westward journey was the slow, rhythmic motion of the fully laden knorr. She swayed up and down over the long, low swells in a seemingly endless repetition of the same movement, rising and falling, and giving a slight lurch as each swell passed beneath her keel. Looking up at the mast top, I saw the pattern repeated constantly in the steady elliptical circles that the weathervane made against the sky. And just behind each movement came the same sequence of sounds – the regular creak of the mast stays taking up the strain each time the vessel rose, the slight thump as the mast moved in its socket, the wash of the bow wave as the prow of the knorr dug into the sea and, when the vessel checked, the soft thud of a loose item rolling across the bilge and striking the hull. I found something hypnotic and comforting about the way that life on board took on its own rhythm, set by the timing and order of our meals. The sequence began at dawn with rismal when the night watch ate a cold breakfast of dried bread and gruel; in mid-morning came dagmal when the entire crew, except for the helmsman and lookout, gathered round the little charcoal fire lit on a stone slab balanced on the keelson and out of the wind and consumed the only hot meal of the day, usually a broth, though sometimes there was fresh fish or boiled seagull if we had been able to catch anything. Finally, as the sun went down, we ate the nattmal, again a cold meal of skyr, sour milk, and gruel.

On the very first night, as soon as it was dusk, Thorvall brought me to a quiet corner of the deck and made me gaze upwards past the dark outline of our sail. It was still early in the season so the night was dark enough for the stars to be visible. 'The vault of the sky,' he said, 'is the inside of Ymir's skull, the ancient frost giant. Four dwarves, Austri, Vestri, Nordri and Sudri, sit in the four corners and they took molten particles and sparks and placed them as stars, both wandering and fixed, to illuminate the earth. That way the Gods made it possible for us to guide our way at night.' He pointed out to me the leidarstjarna, the Pole Star, and how it was always at the same height in the sky on our right hand as we moved through the night. Thorvall was in his element when he was on the sea, and every day at noon he would produce a little wooden disc with small notches on the rim and lines scratched on its surface. He held it up in the sunlight so the shadow from a small pin in the centre of the disc fell across the engraved face, then he grunted directions to the helmsman.

'Trust the Gods,' he told me. 'As long as the wolves chase Sol, she will move across the sky and we can follow beneath her.'

'What if it is too cloudy and we cannot see the sun?' I ventured.

'Be patient,' he growled.

It was not cloud but a dense fog which shrouded the sun two days later. The fog was so thick that we seemed to be gliding through a bowl of thin milk. Drops of water condensed on the walrus-hide ropes of the rigging, the deck planks were dark with moisture, and we could not see farther than fifty paces. We could have been sailing in circles for all we knew, and the helmsman was edgy and nervous until Thorvall produced a flat stone from a pocket in his sea cloak. The stone was thin and opaque. Thorvall held it up to the light and peered through it, turning the stone this way and that, his arm held out straight. Finally he pointed ahead, slightly to the steering-board side of the ship. 'That course,' he ordered and without question the helmsman obeyed him.

Apart from two days spent groping our way through the fog and relying on what Thorvall called his sunstone, we had remarkably good weather and a smooth passage. Thorvall had absolute faith in Thor's power over the weather and the sea conditions, and whenever he caught a fish on the hook and line he always trailed behind the boat, he made a point of throwing a small part of the catch back into the sea as a sacrifice. No one dared to scoff at him openly for doing this, though I did notice some of the crew members, the baptised ones, exchange amused glances and snigger.

Certainly Thorvall's gifts to Thor seemed to be remarkably effective. No one was seasick except for Gudrid, whose servants looked after her as she vomited, and it was on the morning of the ninth day after leaving Brattahlid that Thorvall gave a deep sniff and said firmly, 'Land.' By evening we could smell it too, the unmistakable scent of trees wafting to us from the west. On the morning of the tenth day we saw on the horizon the thin flat smudge that was the edge of Vinland, and twenty-four hours later we were close enough for Tyrkir and Thorvall and the other veterans to establish our exact position. With the help of Thorvall's wooden disc our knorr had made a near-perfect landfall. By general opinion we were only a day's sail from the place where we would find Leif's cabins.

The land was vast. The coastline extended across our ship's bow, as though the country would go on for ever in each direction. Behind the coast, in the interior, I could see the dark green swell of an immense forest, where the land rose in a succession of low hills as far as the eye could see. The shore itself was one low, grey headland after the another, divided by deep bays and inlets. Occasionally there were beaches of sand, but for the most part the foreshore was a jumble of sea-worn rocks, where the waves rumbled and surged. The colours of the stones were drab except where a crust of seaweed and lichens added touches of green and brown. To anyone from more southerly climates, the shore of Vinland would have looked like a bleak and forbidding place. But we had come from barren Greenland and, before that, from Iceland with its equally harsh landscape. Vinland showed great potential to the farmers among us. They noted the early growth of wild meadow-grass speckling the land behind the beach and the first flush of shoots on the low bushes of willow and alder. The bull and three cows on board also sensed the pasture and became restless to get ashore. We kept a sharp lookout for signs of

Skraelings and Tyrkir probably kept an eye open for his mysterious unipeds. But nothing moved. The land seemed empty.

Neverthless Karlsefni was cautious. He remembered Thorstein's death at the hands of the Skraelings and summoned our two 'wild Scots', Haki and Hekja. He told them that he was going to put them ashore so they could make a wide sweep inland. If they encountered Skraelings, they were to avoid contact, stay hidden, and try to assess the numbers of these strange people. After three days the two scouts were to report back to the beach, where our vessel would be anchored close by. Haki and Hekja each filled a satchel with dried food, but took nothing else. They were both wearing their usual dress, nothing more than a coarse blanket with a slit through which to put the head. There was a hood for when it rained, but otherwise the garment was so basic that it was open at the sides except for a single loop to fasten the cloth between the legs. Underneath they were naked. Both scouts clambered down into our small tender, and Thorvall and a small crew rowed them to the beach. There the Scots slipped into the water and waded to land before walking up the beach and disappearing into the scrub. Apart from a knife, they carried no weapon or tool, not even a steel and flint for making fire. 'If the Skraelings catch them, they'll think we've come from a tribe more wretched than themselves,' someone said as we backed our oars and manoeuvred the knorr to a safe distance, well out of arrow range.

Those three days seemed like an eternity for an eight-year-old boy. Karlsefni flatly refused to let anyone go ashore. We had to sit on the knorr, impatiently watching the run of the tide, trying to catch fish but without much success, and looking for signs of movement on land and seeing nothing until, suddenly, the slim figures of the two runners reappeared. Thorvall and a couple of the men went in the scouting boat to pick them up, and the two Scots returned with encouraging news. They had seen no Skraelings, they said, nor any sign of them.

We arrived at Leif's cabins at noon on the second day of coasting, but did not go ashore until Thorvall and four of the men had gone ahead, armed and alert, to check the abandoned huts, looking for strangers. But they found no sign that anyone had been there since the unlucky expedition two years earlier. Our scouts waved to us to bring the knorr into the anchorage, and by nightfall the entire expedition was safely ashore and setting up the wadmal tents which would be our homes until we had refurbished the semi-derelict cabins.

Three winters of rain and wind and snow had beaten on the turf and stone walls of Leif's cabins until they were slumped and crumbled. The rafters had fallen in. Weeds and wild grass grew on the floors. The original cabins had been constructed only for short-term occupation, so they had been roofed over with wadmal to keep out the weather. Now that we were here to stay, we needed something much more sturdy and permanent. So we began to mend and enlarge the cabins, build a big new longhouse, clear the land for our cattle, dig latrines. Our knorr, which had appeared to be so amply laden when we started out, now seemed to be a meagre source of supplies. The cattle had taken up most of the available cargo capacity, and Karlsefni had brought tools for the future, not food for the present. So we nearly starved during that first month. Of course there was no question that we would kill and eat the cattle. They were the beginning of our herd, or so we hoped. We had no time to investigate the fishing or check the forest to see if there was any wild game. Instead we laboured from dawn to dusk to cut and carry and stack hundreds of turf blocks for the main walls of our new longhouse. Soon people began to complain of hunger and how they needed proper food, not thin watery porridge, if they were to work so hard. The Christians among us began to pray to their God, seeking his help to alleviate their distress. They set up their cross-shaped symbol at one edge of the settlement, and when Thorvall – rather provocatively, I thought – built a little canopied shelter on the opposite edge of the settlement and made a pile of stones under it as his altar to Thor, there was very nearly a fight. The Christians accused him of being an arch-pagan. Thorvall warned them that he would knock down any man who interfered with his Thor altar.

Karlsefni had assigned Thorvall to help the house-builders rather than hunt. His great strength was very useful when it came to lifting up the turf sods as the walls grew higher and higher. But everyone could see that Thorvall was itching to explore. Finally, when hunger was really pinching, Karlsefni gave Thorvall permission to go hunting, though most of us wondered how just one man could find and kill enough wild game to feed forty hungry mouths. Thorvall said nothing, but gave one of his unsociable grunts, gathered up his spear and made ready to leave. As he left the camp, he went first to his little altar, took off one of the polar-bear teeth from his necklace and laid it as an offering on the top stone. Then he walked off into the thick brushwood. Within moments he had vanished.

Thorvall was away for three days, and when he did not reappear Karlsefni and the other senior men began to worry. Once again there was talk of the Skraelings and speculation that they had captured or killed our hunter. Finally Karlsefni called for volunteers to join a small search party to look for Thorvall. Karlsefni announced that he himself would lead the searchers. They were to take weapons and be on the lookout for Skraelings as well as Thorvall. There was a certain amount of reluctance to join the search party because Thorvall was not a popular figure, particularly among the Christians. Some said that if the Skraelings had got the surly curmudgeon, then it was good riddance. Naturally Tyrkir was willing to look for his friend, so too were the two Scots, and I managed to attach myself to the little group because I could be spared from the house-building.

After all this, finding Thorvall was very easy. Haki and Hekja ranged ahead, quartering back and forth through the undergrowth like a pair of hounds, and to all our surprise returned on the third day to say that they had found Thorvall on a nearby headland, but he had refused to come back with them. Thinking that Thorvall might be injured, we fought our way through the underbrush and arrived, exhausted and scratched, to find Thorvall lying stretched out on the ground on the flat crest of a small headland overlooking the sea. To the fury of the Christians, and the relief of his friends, Thorvall was in good health. Indeed, he looked remarkably relaxed as he lay on his back, gazing up at the sky and apparently talking to himself, occasionally itching himself rudely. For a moment I thought our hunter had leave of his senses or had got hold of some alcohol and was drunk. One of our group, a Christian named Bjarni, began shouting angrily at Thorvall, demanding what on earth he was playing at. Thorvall rose to his feet, and scowled at his interrogators.

'There's nothing to hunt here,' he told them, 'at least, not enough to feed forty people in a hurry. Just some small animals and birds. Maybe later, when I've more time to explore the land, I'll find the places where I can set traps for the larger animals. So I composed a poem to Thor's honour, and was reciting it for him, and asking him to provide for us.'

'Thor! You heathen!' yelled Bjarni. 'How do you imagine that your blundering oaf of a God can help us. You might as well pray to the sea to give us some food.'

'Maybe he will,' Thorvall replied gruffly.

We all walked back to the camp and Thorvall received black looks from many of the settlers. Several of them turned their backs on him. I heard a number of comments that he was a cantankerous fool, riddled with superstition, too lazy to go hunting properly, and had been idling away his time, while others had been doing all the hard work on the house-building.

Next morning one of the men went out along the strand to gather driftwood for our cooking fires and came stumbling excitedly back into camp.

'Everyone, bring your knives and axes. There's a dead whale lying on the beach,' he shouted. 'It must have been washed up in the night. There's enough meat there to feed us for a couple of weeks!'

Thorvall, who had been sitting near the campfire, raised his shaggy head and let out a great roar of triumph. 'There, you White Christ fanatics, Old Red Beard liked his praise poem and he's sent us food from the sea. Now go and fill your envious bellies.'

We all hurried along the beach and were soon hacking up the whale. It was perhaps twenty-five feet in length, and of a type that none of us had ever seen before, not even Karlsefni, who had seen many different types of whale during his travels as a merchant. But the carcass cut like any other whale's, with a good three-inch-thick layer of blubber which we peeled away in strips to get at the rich, dark red meat. It was a magnificent find. The blubber we would use as fat for cooking or eat salted, while the dark red meat we grilled and ate straight away – it tasted like well-hung beef. Thorvall took his chance to gloat over the Christians, teasing them about how Thor had turned out to be more generous than their Christ. Eventually they became so exasperated that they said that the meat was cursed and that it gave them stomach cramps and we should throw away the profane flesh. But I noticed that they ate a full meal before they made a gesture of throwing some of the offal into the tide.

The stranded whale ended our famine because over the next few weeks the land began to reward us with her bounty. Leif had sited his cabins on the lip of an estuary, where two small rivers merged before emptying into a shallow tidal estuary. Both rivers teemed with fish. One of my earliest tasks was to dig a series of trenches in the sand shallows at low tide. Shoals of halibut and other flat fish regularly came swimming into the lake on the high tide to feed and as the water receded were left stranded in my trenches. For variety I also picked up clams and mussels on the wide curve of the beach, or helped the adults set nets for the magnificent salmon and sea trout which swam up the rivers. By our Greenlandic standards nature was extraordinarily bountiful. The meadows by the river mouths were covered in tall wild grasses and gave good pasture for our cattle, which usurped the deer whose tracks we could clearly see on the river banks. The most travelled of our colonists had never laid eyes on such stands of trees, mostly softwoods, but with some trees completely unknown. One yellow tree, very like our birch, provides timber as tough as our native oak, and another tree with a three-pointed leaf gives a beautiful ingrained wood that Tyrkir gloated over, turning and polishing it so that it glowed with a deep honey colour. As a timber-starved people, we scarcely knew what to do first: whether to cut down small trees to make our houses or to fell the larger ones and set them aside to season so that we could take a precious cargo across to Greenland.

By late summer there was an almost continuous natural harvest along the fringes of the forest. The wild cherries were the first to bear fruit, followed by an abundance of hazelnuts and then an array of wild berries swelling and ripening on the bushes and shrubs, speckling them with red and purple, dark blue, crimson and gold. Many plants we recognised – blueberries, cloudberries, raspberries, loganberries and cranberries. But there were several which were new to us, and sometimes so highly coloured that at first we were suspicious they were poisonous. I was given the job of hiding in the undergrowth and watching to see whether the wild birds fed on them. If they did, then we gathered this fruit as well, drying what we could not eat immediately for our winter provisions.

Only the soil was a little disappointing: it was light and thin and not as rich as we had hoped, lying in a shallow skin over the estuary sand and gravel. But it was no worse than much of the soil in Greenland and Iceland, and our farmers did not complain because they were compensated by the excellence of the hunting. In the long days of summer we trapped deer on the edges of the meadows and snared wild duck, which gathered in vast numbers on the meres and bogs. Scarcely a month after we landed there was a whale drive. A small school of pilot whales ventured into the bay at high water, and we managed to get behind them in the rowing boats and drive them up into the shallows just at the critical moment when the tide turned, so that the animals were unable to retreat and lay awkwardly in the shallows. It was a slaughter. The water was striped with wavering red bands of blood as every able-bodied person waded into the water, knife or axe in hand. We must have dispatched at least twenty of the animals in a gory frenzy, with the beasts thrashing in their last agonies and the foam pink with their blood. After we had tugged the corpses ashore, skinned and cut them into pieces, we had enough meat to last three months.

Tyrkir set up his workshop and a smithy down by the river. Digging in the swamp behind the settlement, he turned up loaf-shaped lumps of a hard encrusted stone which he said he could smelt into soft iron for replacement tools when they were needed. He announced that he required an assistant to help him with the work and made sure that I became his apprentice. In his little smithy he showed me how to build the small kiln of clay and stack it with alternate layers of charcoal and the bog iron, then ignite the mixture and wait until the fierce heat had done its work, before breaking open the kiln and scraping out the lump of raw iron from the embers. As I supplied more charcoal and operated the bellows, and he refined and forged and shaped the metal, he talked earnestly to me about the Old Gods and their ways. Watching Tyrkir heat and hammer the metal, then quench it in water, I was fascinated by the almost magical process whereby our metal tools were produced, and I readily accepted Tyrkir's central theme that there is an indissoluble bond between knowledge of metalwork and magic. Tyrkir would mutter simple charms through the smoke and steam, and grunt invocations to the Gods as he scrupulously observed his craft's taboos. He never allowed two blades to lie one across the other. He sprinkled a pinch of salt on the fire when we began work in the morning, and at the end of the day he always placed his working hammer on the small altar he had built for Thor. And when he finished an item, whether a billhook or a spearhead, he would mutter a small prayer and gather a few leaves, then pound them into a green paste and smear them on the hot metal as an offering. 'The juice gives strength to the metal,' he told me as I held the cooler end of some spearhead or sickle with a cloth around my hand and plunged it into the quenching tub with its hiss of steam.

In the smoke-grimed little smithy Tyrkir took breaks from pounding at the glowing metal to tell what he knew of the galdra, the charms and spells that make up the bulk of seidr lore. 'There are hundreds,' he told me. 'Each produces a different result suitable for a different occasion. How effective they are depends on the user's experience and skill. I know only a few, perhaps a couple of dozen, and they are mostly related to my work with metal. I never complete a sword for war, a sea knife for a sailor, or a spearhead for a hunter without reciting the correct galdra for the purpose it will serve. But these are craftsmen's galdra. There are more powerful ones, above all at times of combat. There is one to calm the rage in a warrior's heart, another to sing behind a shield as the charge is launched, which will guarantee that all your comrades-in-arms emerge from the fray unscathed, while a third gives the enchanter the quickness to catch an arrow flying through the air. A fourth, if spoken over a goblet of water which is then thrown over a warrior, ensures that he survives the forthcoming battle, perhaps wounded, but alive.'

Tyrkir failed to notice that I was not attracted by martial prowess and muscular feats and stories of bloodshed. To tell the truth I was always a little frightened of my dwarfish mentor and the hard-edged bitterness he sometimes showed when he told the more gory tales. He relished telling me how Volund, the master smith and 'prince of elves', had lured the young sons of King Nidud into his forge and, as they peered into his chest of treasure, lopped off their heads. 'You know why he did that, Thorgils?' Tyrkir asked as he fused a strip of harder steel into the soft iron blade of a sickle to give it a sharper edge. 'Volund did that to revenge himself on Nidud. Volund was so skilled at metalwork that the evil Nidud kidnapped him, then lamed him so he could not escape and forced him to work as a royal goldsmith. Volund bided his time until he could lure Nidud's greedy and stupid sons into his workshop. There he killed them and made splendid jewels from their eyeballs, brooches from their teeth and silver-plated bowls from their skulls. To their mother he presented the jewels, to their sister the brooches and to their father the bowls.' Tyrkir gave a grim smile of satisfaction. 'And in the end he seduced the Princess Bodvild and left her with child, before he cunningly fashioned wings of metal and flew away from his captivity.'

Gudrid was pregnant. People now understood why she had been seasick on the outward voyage and why she had insisted on bringing two serving women with her from Brattahlid. Most of the settlers took her pregnancy as a good omen. It meant that our little colony would flourish and grow. I wanted to be happy for Gudrid, like everyone else, but I was confused and unsure. For most of my young life I had seen myself as Gudrid's true son, and now it seemed that I was to have a rival for her affections.

In the late autumn of that first year in Vinland Gudrid gave birth to a healthy, squalling male child. He was given the name Snorri, which means 'unruly' or 'argumentative', and he was the first of our race to be born in that distant Norse outpost. Perhaps he is the only one ever to be born there. I do not know because for many years I have not had any direct news from Vinland. Nor, I suppose, has anyone else. Instead I have only the memory of the great rejoicing and excitement on the day when Snorri arrived in this world and how Thorfinn, the proud father, gave a birthday feast in our fine new longhouse. Perhaps it was the first stirring of jealousy within me, or perhaps it was my sixth sense that produced a sense of foreboding within me. But that evening, as we all gathered in the longhouse and sat along the side benches and listened to Thorfinn call toasts to celebrate the arrival of our first child, I felt a nagging certainty that those golden early days of our colony were numbered.

EIGHT

THE HERALDS OF our failure came just three days later. It was almost noon on a mild sunny day and the colonists were spread out doing their usual daily tasks, some fishing, a few absent in the forest hunting and tree-felling, the majority working in and around the houses or clearing gardens. The women, I remember, were preparing food, for I recall the smell of venison roasting on a spit over an open fire. One of the builders was up on the roof of a house, checking that the turves were binding together properly to make a watertight seal, when he straightened to ease his back and happened to glance out to sea. He stopped in surprise and shouted, pointing out along the coast. His cry alerted all of us in the settlement and we turned to look. Around the end of the farthest low spit of land a cluster of small boats was approaching. At that distance they looked no more than black needles, but it was quite obvious what they were: Skraelings. Everyone stopped whatever they were doing, and a shiver of apprehension passed through the crowd. It must be remembered that we were farmers and fishermen, not seasoned warriors, and the arrival of these strangers in this isolated land sent a chill of fear down our spines. 'Be as friendly as possible. Act normally,' warned Thorfinn. 'Don't make any sudden movements, but don't let them come too close either. We'll just wait to see what they want.'

The little Skraeling flotilla – there were nine of their skin boats – slowly paddled closer. The boatmen seemed to be as surprised and cautious as we were. They slackened their pace and drifted their boats gently through the shallows, keeping about fifty paces offshore as they watched us, staring curiously. Neither side said a word. There was a tense silence. Then one of the Skraelings stood up in his boat – it was a narrow, trough-shaped vessel, not very well made – and began to wave his arm in circles above his head. In his hand was some sort of blade, which made a low humming sound, halfway between a gentle roar and a mutter.

'What do you think that means?' Thorfinn asked his second-in-command, a man called Thorbrand Snorrisson.

'It could be a sign of peace,' he replied, 'They don't seem very hostile.'

'Then we had better respond in the same way,' answered Thorfinn. 'Take a white shield and go into the water up to your knees. Hold up the shield so they can see it clearly.'

A white shield is our standard signal of peace, recognised and used even among the wild Irish and distant German tribes. A red shield displayed means war. Anyhow, the Skraelings seemed to understand the gesture; they gently turned their boats towards us and paddled inshore. We all stood motionless as they touched land, and the men climbed out of their boats and advanced hesitantly up the beach.

We could see that they were exactly like the people that my uncle Thorvald's crew had attacked and killed. The men – there were no women in the party – were dark-skinned and a little smaller than us in stature. They had the same almond-shaped eyes and lank, very black hair worn long and loose, right down to their shoulders. Their cheekbones were high and prominent, and this gave their faces a menacing look. I noticed that their eyes were uniformly dark brown, almost black. They must have been a hunting party because there was very little in the boats except for some hunting spears and nondescript bundles wrapped in rawhide. Thorfinn suspected that they were as startled as we were by the encounter. At any rate, there was a very long silence, while both parties looked one another over, and then the leader of the Skraelings called out something in an unintelligible language and the entire group deliberately got back into their boats, shoved off and paddled away, from time to time looking back over their shoulders.

As the Skraeling boats disappeared on their original route up the coast, we returned to our chores. You can imagine the chatter and speculation about when the Skraelings would reappear and what they intended. No one doubted that this was only the preliminary encounter.

The Skraelings took us even more unawares on their next visit by appearing from the landward side of the settlement. It must have been about six months later, and how they got so close to the settlement without being detected was alarming. At one moment we were going about our usual routine, and the next instant a couple of dozen Skraelings were walking down from the edge of the woods towards us. They seemed to have sprung from the ground. It was lucky that they came peacefully for we were taken totally off guard. Indeed, we were all dithering, not knowing whether to run for our weapons, cluster together or go forward to meet the Skraelings with another peaceful gesture, when, as luck would have it, our bull began to bellow. He was with the cows in the nearby meadow, and possibly the scent of the Skraelings – for they did smell rather powerfully – disturbed him. He let out a series of thunderous bellows and this terrified our visitors. Glancing back over their shoulders, they scampered for the safety of our houses as though pursued by a monster. Several of our more timid men had already taken up position inside the houses, the better to defend themselves, and had already shut the doors. The next thing they knew, the terrified Skraelings were beating on the door planks, crying out in their strange language, pleading to be let in. The Norsemen, thinking that an attack was in progress, pushed desperately against the doors from the inside, trying to keep them shut. For us who were outside the situation, once so fraught, was now totally comic. It was clear that the Skraelings meant no harm, and the fainthearts inside the houses were in a panic at the unseen onslaught. Those of us who could see what was happening burst into roars of laughter. Our guffaws reassured the Skraelings, who calmed down and began to look sheepish, and after a few moments the frightened house defenders began to peek out to see what had happened, only to make us scoff even more loudly. This ludicrous situation proved to be the ideal introduction – there's nothing like two sides making public fools of themselves and accepting the fact for a sense of mutual understanding to develop. With sign language and smiles the Skraelings began to open the packs they had been carrying. They contained furs, splendid furs, the pelts of fox and marten and wolf and otter. There were even a couple of glossy black-bear pelts. The quality was like nothing we had seen before, and we knew they would fetch a premium price in any market in Norway or Denmark. There was not one of us who did not begin to wonder what we might trade with the Skraelings in exchange.

The obvious item was metal – for we had noted that the Skraelings possessed only stone-tipped weapons. But Thorfinn was quick off the mark. He ordered sharply that no one was to trade weapons or metal tools to the Skraelings. Better weaponry was the only advantage we possessed against their superior numbers. Everyone was standing around racking their brains about what to do next and the Skraelings were gazing around curiously, when one of the women in a gesture of hospitality fetched a pail of milk and a wooden dipper. She offered a dipper of the milk to the leader of the Skraelings. He stared at the liquid in puzzlement, sniffed it suspiciously and then cautiously tried a sip, while the woman indicated that he should drink it. The Skraeling was delighted with the taste of milk. He must have also believed that it was a rich and rare substance, for he delved in his pack and offered the woman a marten skin. She had the wit to accept it. Another Skraeling stepped forward and gestured he wanted to try drinking milk, and before long the entire group were clustering around, reaching for the ladle and handing over valuable furs and pelts in exchange.

Even as an eight-year-old lad, I had seen the drunks at Brattahlid so desperate as to give their last coins for a draught of wine or strong mead, but this was the only time in my long and varied life that I have ever seen anyone pay so handsomely for mere cow juice. What is more, the Skraelings were totally happy with the bargain. After they had parted with their entire stock of furs, even leaving behind their empty packs, they were content to walk back into the forest, carrying their barter profit in their bellies, while we gleefully stowed away a small fortune in Vinland furs.

But however peacefully the Skraeling visit had turned out, their arrival had a more sinister implication. The following day Thorfinn told us to stop all our other work and start building a palisade around the settlement. We did not need urging. All of us had an uncomfortable feeling that our peaceful and profitable relationship with the Skraelings might not last. Everyone remembered how the Skraelings had killed Thorvald Eriksson with their darts on his earlier expedition to this land, and that a massacre by our men of eight Skraelings from their hunting party had preceded his lone death. If the Skraelings behaved like us, then they might still be looking for more blood vengeance to balance the account. Like one of those sea anemones who retract their tentacles when they sense danger, we shrank back inside a safer perimeter. The outlying houses were abandoned and the entire community shifted to live within the shelter of the palisade, just in case the Skraelings returned with less peaceable intentions. The only structure to remain outside the stockade was Tyrkir's little smithy down by the river, where he needed access to the bog iron and running water.

THE SKRAELINGS DID not return until the beginning of the following winter, when baby Snorri was nearly a year old. By then we felt we were getting the measure of this new land. We had cleared back the surrounding brushwood for additional pasture, fenced two small paddocks for our cattle, which now included three healthy calves, improved and strengthened the walls and roofs of our original hastily built dwellings, and our people were beginning to talk about the prospect of sending our knorr back to Greenland with a cargo of timber and furs, and attracting more settlers to join us. We had lived through the full cycle of the seasons, and though the winter had been cold and dreary, it had been no worse than what we had known in Greenland. Our settlement had begun to put down roots, but – as we soon learned – those roots were shallow.

This time the Skraelings came in much greater strength, and by land as well as by water. One group of about a score of hunters emerged from the forest, while their comrades paddled directly into the bay in glistening, grease-treated skin boats. Their visit seemed to have been planned well ahead of time because both groups were seen to be carrying no weapons, only their packs of furs. This time one of our fishermen had spotted the Skraelings at a distance and come ashore to warn us. Thorfinn, worried by their greater numbers, had already ordered the entire community to enter the stockade and shut the gate. So when the Skraelings approached they found no one to greet them. The fields and the beach were deserted. They came up to the palisade and hesitated. Thorfinn called out, asking what they wanted, but of course they did not understand a word of our language and we had no way of understanding their reply. Then one of the Skraelings, a tall, good-looking man who must have been their chieftain, lobbed his pack over the top of the palisade. It landed on the earth with a soft thump and we found it contained five grey wolf pelts. Clearly this was the result of their summer trapping and the Skraelings had come again to trade. 'Let's see if we can sell them only milk again,' Thorfinn warned us. 'Remember: on no account let them get their hands on our weapons.' The stockade gate was cautiously open and we began to trade.

It was not quite as easy as before. The strange dark-skinned men were still eager to barter furs for milk, but when the milk was all drunk they still had more pelts for sale, and pointed to the red wadmal, which one of the colonists was wearing as garters. In the beginning we offered a hand's span of red cloth cut from the bolt for every pelt. This they accepted and immediately tied the pieces of cloth around their heads, preening in the gaudy decoration. But then the supply of red cloth ran low and it was only possible to offer them a single ribbon of red cloth, barely a finger wide, for each pelt. To our astonishment, the Skraelings were just as happy as before to make the bargain, and kept on dealing until their stock of fur was used up.

When the trading for milk and red cloth had ended, the Skraelings lingered. They strolled among our men, gingerly picking up various implements and testing their weight and wondering at their purpose. Clearly these were people who had never handled a spade or sickle, though I suspect that, hidden in the edge of the forest, they had often watched us farming. They did not mean any harm, I'm sure, and were merely inquisitive. But quick as a flash one of them leaned forward and tugged a scramsaxe from the belt of a man called Hafgrim. Startled, Hafgrim gave a shout of surprise and tried to seize the culprit Skraeling in order to retrieve his long knife. But the Skraeling was too quick for him and twisted away. The entire group of Skraelings scattered like a shoal of frightened minnows and began to run back towards the woods, several of them still with our farm tools in their hands. One Skraeling was so terrified that he ran in the wrong direction, past the smithy, and Tyrkir, who had gone back to work, emerged from the doorway just at the right moment to stick out his foot and trip him up. As casually as if he were in a salmon stream, Tyrkir then reached inside the smithy, produced a heavy fish spear he had been mending and killed him. I shall never forget the sight of my first battle corpse, the half-naked Skraeling, suddenly a pathetic, scrawny, broken figure, sprawled half in and half out of the peat stream, his bright red headband smeared with mud.

Thorfinn immediately called an assembly to discuss what we should do next. Everybody crowded into the open space in front of the longhouse and in the nervous aftermath of that tragic brawl it was not long before people were shouting irritably at one another, arguing about the best tactics to defeat the Skraelings. No one doubted that the Skraelings would return and seek revenge.

I do not know whether the next, and final, visit of the Skraelings was an accident or intentional and if they came to exact retribution for the man killed outside Tyrkir's smithy. For more than a year we mounted guard over the colony. Day and night there was a watcher stationed on the headland to keep a lookout for Skraeling boats, and another lookout scanned the edge of the forest, where it lapped down towards our stockade. Then came the fateful day when the coast watcher came panting up from the beach to announce that a large Skraeling fleet was rounding the headland. He had counted at least thirty of the needle-shaped boats and half a dozen larger canoes, each paddled by a dozen men. No one seemed to have noticed that the new Skraeling threat came from the south, and that the men we had driven off had run away in the opposite direction, to the north.

Thorfinn had planned it all out. As the Skraeling fleet aproached the beach, a handful of our men, led by the same Thorbrand Snorrisson who had stood alongside Thorfinn at the first encounter with the Skraelings, took up position on the foreshore, displayed their red shields and called out a fighting challenge. For a short while the Skraeling fleet hung back, the paddlers either suspicious or puzzled by the belligerent behaviour of the white men. Then, as our champions continued to shout defiance and wave their weapons, the Skraelings decided to accept the challenge. The Skraeling men rose to their feet in the skin boats and began to wave the same thin-bladed implements over their heads that they had employed on their very first visit, the flail-like implements that might have been mistaken for the flat wooden lath known as a weaver's sword. Only this time the sound they produced was entirely different. Instead of a low muttering hum, the noise was a loud and angry buzz, almost the sound of an enraged swarm of bees. Then, as more and more of the whirling flails joined in, the sound swelled in volume until it became a cataract of noise, filling the air until it seemed that the blood was roaring in our ears. Finally, the noise altered again as the sound-makers began to coordinate the movements of their flails, and the sound began to come rushing towards us in wave after wave, rising and falling in volume as it beat upon our senses.

Presumably, this extraordinary resonance was intended to frighten or dismay our small group of men down on the beach and it worked. Numbed by the vibrating din, they stood rooted to the ground. This was their error. While the Skraeling boats were still some distance away from the shoreline, a shower of darts suddenly came skimming through the air from the flotilla and began to patter down around our men in a deadly hail. The Skraelings were using some sort of dart launcher, a flat board a cubit long that made an extension to their throwing arm and gave an astonishing range to their missiles. Three of our men were struck by the darts, two were killed outright, and scarcely a member of our advance party was not injured in some way. As the Skraelings came into close range, they began to fling another strange weapon at us – spears which pulled behind them some sort of round float attached by a short length of line. The weird and startling appearance of these floats hurtling through the air frightened our men as much as the war sound of the flails. As they went skimming through the air over their heads and bounced on the ground, our men feared that the Skraelings were unleashing some sort of magic weapon.

Now the Skraelings were climbing out of their boats and running up the beach, waving lances and stone-edged knives, trying to come to grips with our advance guard. The Norsemen turned and fled, as was Thorfinn's plan, for they were really decoys. When the Skraelings came level with the dead bodies of our two slain, their leader was seen to reach down and pick up the axe from the corpse of Thorbrand Snorrisson. The Skraeling leader must never have seen a metal axe before, because he hefted it and then hacked experimentally at a nearby rock. The axe head broke, and thinking it was useless because it did not cut the rock, the Skraeling leader threw it into the sea with a gesture of disgust. A few moments later he learned what a metal blade can do on human flesh because by then the decoy party of colonists, with the Skraelings in pursuit, had fallen back as far as the edge of the forest, where Thorfinn had hidden the main body of the settlers in his ambush. The bulk of our men came charging out of the brushwood at full tilt, waving their weapons and roaring their war shouts. The Skraelings did not have a chance. They were lightly clad, held no shields, and even their lances could be sheered through with a swingle sweep of a metal sword. The rush of Norsemen bowled over the Skraelings, and before they could flee four Skraelings were killed, two of them victims to the heavy axes of the Norse farmers. The whole encounter was over in an instant. The Skraelings took to their heels in panic and either ran for the edge of the woods or back to their boats, which they pushed off and fled in as fast as they could paddle.

When I helped bury the corpse of Thorbrand Snorrisson I found that the small dart which had killed him looked more like a hunting weapon than a man-killing implement. As for the mysterious spears and their attached floats, they proved to be sealing harpoons with an inflated bladder attached to mark the spot where the seal has dived when it is wounded. I did not voice my opinion to the jubilant settlers – they would have thought me utterly impertinent – but I came to the conclusion that the Skraelings had not come prepared for war and we did not deserve our victory. The Skraelings were a large hunting party and would have passed by us peaceably if we had not challenged them with our red war shields and shouted defiance.

Yet, in the greater scheme of our Norse involvement in Vinland, I don't think it would have made any difference in the end. Even if we had realised that the Skraelings meant us no harm on that occasion, they would probably have come back on a later visit to drive us away from the lands where they lived. And, of course, we took the Skraelings to have the same responses as ourselves – when the Norse feel threatened, their natural reaction is to turn and fight, to protect their territory. They seldom consider the long-term consequences of such action, and they rarely back down. That day on the beach at Vinland our men were too frightened and too desperate to act in any other way than with violence.

It was that feeling of being under threat that lost us Vinland. We stayed for the winter – the season was too advanced to think of moving anywhere – but all through the winter months we worried and fretted that the Skraelings would return. 'This is a rich and fertile land,' was how Thorfinn put it to us on the day we assembled to make a final decision about leaving. 'Of course, we can visit from time to time and cut shiploads of fine timber for ourselves. But we would be foolish to think that we can establish ourselves here in the face of superior numbers of hostile Skraeling. In the end they would overwhelm us.' There was no dissenting voice. We knew we were too isolated and exposed. In the spring we reloaded our knorr with the products of our labour – seasoned timber, dried fruit, a rich store of furs, carved souvenirs of that splendid honey-coloured wood, the dried skins of some of the more colourful birds complete with their feathers – and we set sail for Greenland.

As our travel-worn knorr felt the wind and began to gather speed, I looked back at the gently sloping beach in front of Leif's cabins. On the very last morning of our stay I had stood barefoot in the sand and dug a final channel in the hopes of trapping a flounder, just as I had done when we first came there. Already the incoming tide which had floated the knorr off the landing beach, had washed away every trace of my labour. The only mark of my efforts to harvest the sea were a few piles of empty mussel shells just above the line of seawrack. A hundred paces farther up the beach, over the first swell of the dunes, I could just see the roofs of the turf houses we had abandoned. Already their humped shapes were merging into the distance, and soon they would be lost to view against the forest background. Everyone of us aboard the knorr was looking back, even the helmsman was glancing over his shoulder. We felt regretful but we did not feel defeated, and the one unspoken thought in our minds was that perhaps there were

Norsemen still left alive in that vast land and we were abandoning them to their fate.

I was thinking of one person in particular – my hero and tutor, Thorvall the Hunter. He had disappeared midway through our time at Leif's cabins when the bickering between ardent Christians and Old Believers reached such a pitch that Thorvall announced that he did not intend to stay any longer with the group. He would explore along the coast and find a more congenial spot. Anyone who wanted to accompany him was free to do so. Four of our men chose to go with him and Thorfinn gave them our small scouting boat, possibly because Gudrid encouraged him to do so. More than once she said that she did not want Snorri growing up in the company of men like Thorvall with their heathen ways. I was downcast for several days after Thorvall and his few companions rowed off, heading north along the coast. When we heard nothing more from them, I presumed with everyone else that Thorvall and his companions had been captured and killed by the Skraelings. It was what we Norse would have done to a small group of interlopers.

NINE

BACK IN BRATTAHLID, we received a muted greeting from the Greenlanders. The general opinion was that our expedition had been a wasted effort and it would have been better if we had stayed at home. Faced with this dispiriting reception, Thorfinn announced that he would spend only a few weeks in Greenland, then head onwards with his ship to Iceland. There he proposed to return to his family in Skagafjord, and set up house with Gudrid and their two-year-old son. This time I was not invited to accompany them.

Abandoned – or so I felt – by Gudrid and with only wizened Tyrkir as my mentor, I became morose and difficult. After nearly three years' absence in Vinland, my moodiness deepened when I found I had drifted apart from my circle of boyhood friends in Brattahlid. Eyvind, Hrafn and the others had continued to grow up as a group while I was away. They showed an initial curiosity about my descriptions of life in Vinland, but soon lost interest in what I had seen or done there. The boys had always regarded me as being a little odd, and now they judged that my lonely life in Vinland as the only child of my age, had made me even more solitary. We no longer had much in common.

The result was that I began to nurse a secret nostalgia for Vinland. My experiences in that strange land helped define who I was. So I yearned to return there.

The opportunity to go back to Vinland was a complete surprise when it came, because it was arranged by the last person in the world whom I would have expected: my aunt Freydis. While I had been away in Vinland, she had matured from a scheming nineteen-year-old into a domineering woman, both physically and mentally. She had put on weight and bulk, so now she was big and buxom, full-bosomed and with heavy arms and a meaty face that would have been better suited to a man. She even had a light blonde moustache. Despite her off-putting appearance she had managed to find a husband, a weak-willed blusterer by the name of Thorvard, who ran a small farm at a place called Gardar. Like the majority of the people of the area, he lived in fear of Freydis's temper, with its violent mood swings and bouts of black anger.

Freydis, who never lost the chance to remind people that she was the daughter of the first settler of Greenland, took it into her head that Thorfinn and Gudrid had been incompetent as pioneers in Vinland and that she, Freydis, could do better. She was so vehement on the topic that people listened to her. Leif's cabins, Freydis pointed out, were still the property of her half-brother, and she announced that the Eriksson clan should return to their property and make it flourish, and she was the person to do it. She began by asking my father for permission to reoccupy the huts. Leif prevaricated. He had decided that he would not waste any men or resources in Vinland after his failed investment with Thorfinn. So he put off Freydis with the promise that he would lend her the buildings and even loan her the family knorr, but only if she managed to raise a crew. However, when Freydis put her energies into a project there was nothing and no one who could stand in her way.

To everyone's astonishment Freydis produced not one crew, but three, and a second vessel as well. The way it happened was this: the spring after my return from Vinland with Gudrid and Thorfinn, a foreign ship jointly owned by two brothers from Iceland, Helgi and Finnbogi, put in to Brattahlid. She was the largest knorr that anyone had ever seen, so big that she carried sixty people on board. Helgi and Finnbogi had decided to emigrate to Greenland and had brought along their families, goods, cattle, and all the necessary paraphernalia. Naturally the two brothers went to see Leif to seek his advice on where they should settle. But on meeting the new arrivals, Leif was not at all keen to welcome them, for it was abundantly clear that the Icelanders were a very rough lot. Like Erik the Red before them, they had left Iceland to escape a violent blood feud which had involved several deaths. Three of the men had murder charges hanging over them. Leif could easily imagine the quarrels and violence if the newcomers tried unsuccessfully to settle the marginal lands, and then started to edge towards the better lands closer to the water. So while my father greeted the two brothers with a show of hospitality, he was very anxious that they should not stay too long. He advised them to proceed farther along the coast and find new land to the north – the farther away from Brattahlid the better was his unspoken opinion.

At that crucial stage, just when Leif was hoping to be rid of the newcomers and the Icelanders were getting restless, Freydis, the born schemer, saw her chance. She travelled from her home in Gardar to call on Helgi and Finnbogi.

'I'm putting together an expedition to sail to Vinland and reoccupy Leif's cabins,' she said to them. 'Why don't you join forces with me? There is plenty of good land there, which I can allocate to you as soon as we are established.'

'What about the Skraeling menace?' Finnbogi asked. 'We heard that Thorfinn Karlsefni reckoned that no Norseman could ever hold Vinland in the face of Skraeling hostility.'

Freydis brushed the question aside. 'Karlsefni was a coward,' she said. 'All his talk of the danger from the Skraelings and how numerous they were was just an excuse to cover up the fact that he and his settlers had been incompetent. If you join with me, our group will be too numerous for the Skraelings to attack.'

She proposed that Helgi and Finnbogi supply thirty settlers. She would match this number and their combined force would discourage the Skraelings. She already had her own list of volunteers from Brattahlid and Gardar. They were mostly her cronies, one or two malcontents and several failed farmers who had nothing to lose by throwing in their lot with Freydis. Personally I disliked Freydis as much as ever and trusted her even less, but my name was also on her list. Against my better judgement and, in a fit of discontent and longing for Vinland, I had volunteered to join my aunt's crew. Like my father Leif, I had never thought Freydis would succeed in mustering a full expedition, and when she succeeded, I feared I would seem cowardly if I had backed out at the last moment. My immaturity also had something to do with the decision to go with Freydis. At the age of twelve I was being both fickle and obstinate. Joining her expedition seemed to me the only way of escaping from my troubles now that Gudrid and Thorfinn had left for Iceland and I felt depressed at the prospect of living out my life in the confines of Brattahlid. Once again the wanderlust that Odinn had implanted in me was stirring.

So for the third time Leif's venerable knorr sailed for Vinland, the very same vessel which ten years earlier had rescued me as an infant from the reef. My destiny seemed intimately connected with that vessel, though by now she was distinctly shabby and worn. Her mast had snapped in a heavy gale and been fished with heavy splints. Her hull was out of true, with a distinct droop where she had been overloaded so often that she sagged amidships. Many of her planks were rotten or had been damaged, and due to the shortage of good timber locally, they had been replaced with short lengths which made a clumsy patchwork. Even when recaulked and rerigged, she was barely fit for sea, and as we sailed west, I found myself not just cleaning cattle dung, but joining every able-bodied man in the crew to bail out the bilges every four hours to keep our vessel afloat. Our consort, the big new Icelandic ship, did nothing to help us. From the start there was no cohesion in our expedition whatsoever. The larger knorr would draw close as we lay there wallowing on the swell, tipping water over the side from buckets, and her ruffianly crew would jeer at us.

Tyrkir did not come with us. He had finally been given his formal freedom from slavery. A stickler for tradition, Tyrkir held a little ceremony to mark his manumission. He obtained a supply of grain and some malt and brewed a great cauldron of beer, then he invited every one of the Erikssons and their children to Thorvall the Hunter's old empty cabin, where Tyrkir had now installed himself. When everyone was gathered, he formally presented my father Leif with the first drinking horn of the new beer and a small loaf of bread and salt, which he had obtained by burning seaweed. Then he handed beer, bread and salt to all the other senior members of the family, one by one, and they pronounced him to be a free man and his own master and offered their congratulations. Considering that Tyrkir was still far from his German birthplace, from where he had been kidnapped as a youth, it was remarkable how emotional and happy he was. When the ceremony was over, he hung up the drinking horn by a leather thong on a peg just beside the entrance to his cabin, a proud reminder that he was now a free man.

No such camaraderie marked the arrival of our two knorrs at Leif's cabins. The Icelanders and the Greenlanders might as well have belonged to two different expeditions. Ashore the two groups bickered constantly. It all began with an argument about who was to occupy the longhouse which Karlsefni had built. Helgi and Finnbogi wanted to claim it, but Freydis retorted that all the buildings, including the cowsheds, belonged to her family and she would exercise her right to occupy all of them. She pointed out that she had never offered the Icelanders free accommodation, only a chance to settle the land. If they wanted shelter, they should build it for themselves. Helgi and Finnbogi's people were so enraged that they almost started a fight on the spot. But they paused after they counted up the men that Freydis had mustered. It seemed that Freydis had cheated. Instead of manning her ship with thirty men as agreed, she had smuggled aboard five extra settlers to Vinland, some of the most turbulent characters from Brattahlid, and her faction had the advantage of numbers. So the

Icelanders had to build two longhouses to accommodate themselves and their wives and children, and of course the Greenlanders did not help them. One group laboured at the building, while the other went fishing and hunting and tended their cattle. This time it was the Greenlanders who did the jeering at the sweating Icelanders.

What had begun with mere selfishness degenerated into unconcealed malice. Freydis's people not only refused to assist the Icelanders with their house-building but would not lend them tools for the work. They even demanded to be paid for any share of the fish and game they caught, insisting that the Icelanders pledge future profits from the colony. Very soon the two groups were not on speaking terms, and the Greenlanders were deliberately angering the Icelanders by ogling their women and passing lewd remarks. Freydis's husband Thorvard was too weak and hesitant to stop this reckless behaviour, and Freydis herself seemed positively to approve of it.

I stayed well out of this quarrel. I wanted no part of the growing animosity and I began to appreciate how Thorvall felt when there was bad blood between the Christians and the Old Believers. Obdurate bloody-mindedness is characteristic of the Norse. If someone receives a slight, or even imagines that he or she has done so, then they never forget. If they do not obtain immediate satisfaction, they nurse the grudge until it overshadows their daily lives. They plan revenge, seek allies for their cause and eventually take their retribution.

To avoid the poisonous atmosphere of the settlement, I began making long excursions deep into the forest. I claimed that I was going hunting, but I seldom brought back anything more than the wild fruit and roots that I had collected. Nevertheless, I would stay away from the settlement for two or three days at a time and my absence was barely noticed. Everyone was too engrossed in their own selfish concerns. On one of these trips, heading in a direction that I had never tested before, I heard a sound which puzzled me. It was a gentle, steady, rhythmic beat. I was following a deer path through dense underbrush and walked in the direction of the noise, feeling curious rather than fearful. Soon I smelled woodsmoke and, coming into a small clearing, saw that smoke was rising from what appeared to be a large pile of branches heaped up against a tall tree on the far side of the clearing. Looking closer, I realised that the pile of branches was in fact a simple lean-to shelter and the sound was coming from inside it. I had stumbled upon Skraelings.

Looking back on that moment, I imagine that most people would have stepped quietly back into the cover of the underbrush and quickly put as much distance as possible between themselves and the Skraeling hut. This would have been logical and sensible. Yet this thought never occurred to me. On the contrary, I knew with absolute certainty that I had to go forward. I knew, also, that no harm would come to me if I did. Later I was to come to understand that this sense of invulnerability mingled with curiosity and trust is a gift that I have naturally. I felt no fear or alarm. Instead a strange numbness ran right down through my legs, almost as if I could not feel my feet, and I felt I had no control over what my limbs were doing. I simply walked forward into the clearing, went across it to the entrance of the shelter, stooped down and pushed my way in.

As I straightened up inside the smoke-filled interior of the little lean-to, I found myself face to face with a small, thin man, who was flicking some sort of rattle steadily from side to side. It was this rattle which had made the rhythmic chinking sound I heard. The man must have been about sixty years old, though it was difficult to tell because he looked so different from any other human I had yet seen. He was no taller than me, and his narrow face was very brown and deeply lined, and framed with long, lank, black hair which hung down to his shoulders. He was dressed entirely in deerskin, from the jacket to the slippers on his feet. Above all he was very, very thin. His hands, his wrists where they emerged from the sleeves of his rough jacket, and his ankles were like sticks. He glanced up as I entered and the expression in his narrow brown eyes did not change as he looked straight into my face. It was almost as if he was expecting me, or he knew who I was. He gave me a single, long glance, then looked down again. He was staring down at the figure of another Skraeling, who was lying on a bed of branches and was obviously very ill. He too was dressed in animal skins and covered with a deerskin wrap. The man seemed barely conscious and was breathing erratically.

How long I stood there I have no recollection. All notion of time was absorbed into the hypnotic beat of the Skraeling rattle and I was completely relaxed. I too looked down at the invalid, and as I gazed at his recumbent body, something strange happened to my senses. It was as if I was looking through a series of thin veils arranged within the man's body and, if I concentrated hard enough, I could shift aside a veil and pass forward and see deeper and deeper inside, past his external form and into the man's interior. As each veil was passed, my vision became more strained until I could progress no further. By then I knew that I was seeing so far inside the sick Skraeling that I could distinguish the interior shape of his spirit. And that shape, his inner soul, was emitting a series of thin flickers, too light and frail to be sustained. At that moment I knew he was mortally ill. He was too sick to be saved and no one could help him. Nothing like this insight had ever happened to me before, and the impact of the premonition broke through my own inner calm. Like someone struggling to come awake from a deep sleep, I glanced around to try to grasp where I was, and I found myself looking into the eyes of the Skraeling with the rattle. Of course I did not know a single word of his language, but I knew why he was there. He was a doctor for his sick comrade, and he too had been peering into the invalid's soul. He had seen what I had seen. I shook my head. The Skraeling looked back at me quietly and I am sure he understood. Without any hurry I pushed my way out of the lean-to, then walked back across the clearing and away into the underbrush. I was confident that no one would follow me, that the Skraeling would not even mention my presence to his fellows, and that he and I shared something as close as any ties of tribe or race.

Nor did I tell Freydis, her husband, Thorvard, or anyone else in the camp about my encounter with the two Skraelings. There was no point in trying to explain it. They would have thought that I was hallucinating or, in view of what happened a month later, they would have seen me as a traitor who had failed to warn them that the Skraelings were closing in.

They came when the leaves on the trees had turned to the vivid reds and russets and yellows which herald the arrival of winter in those lands. Later we guessed that the Skraelings had needed to assemble their menfolk, who had dispersed to hunt and gather food for the winter, before they made their united effort to drive us away. Certainly the fleet of canoes which came paddling towards us that late autumn morning was twice the number of anything we had expected, though many of our more belligerent settlers had been waiting eagerly for the encounter. For weeks they had endlessly discussed their tactics and boasted how they would crush the Skraelings. So when the Skraeling canoes eventually approached the land, our main force rushed down to the beach and showed their red shields in defiance. For their part, the Skraelings stood up in their canoes and – as they had done the first time I ever saw them – they began to whirl their strange humming sticks through the air. Only now I noticed that they did not swing them with the sun as before, but in the opposite direction, and as they they whirled them faster and faster the air was again filled with a dreadful droning sound that seemed to work right inside our heads.

Our men were still on the edge of the surf, shouting insults and defiance, when the first Skraeling missiles struck. Once again the range of their dart throwers took our men unawares. Two grunted in surprise and slumped down so suddenly that their comrades turned round in puzzlement.

Unnerved, our men began to fall back. They retreated up the beach in disorder, leaving the corpses at the water's edge. We watched the Skraeling flotilla paddle right up to the beach unopposed and their warriors step ashore.

The mass of the Skraelings advanced up the beach towards us.

There must have been nearly eighty of them and they kept no particular order or discipline, but neither did our men, who were scampering back towards the settlement. What followed was a chaotic and deadly brawl, which I watched from the shelter of a dense willow thicket, where I had been sent by Freydis's husband Thorvard when the Skraeling boats first appeared. Earlier I had told Thorvard how the Skraelings had been terrified by the bellowing of our bull on my first visit to Vinland. Now Thorvard told me to run and catch one of the bulls we had brought with us and produce the animal as our secret weapon. But by the time I had brought the animal to the willow thicket, ready to drive it into the open, our forces were about to gain an even more spectacular advantage.

Our men were fleeing back along the bank of one of the small rivers leading up from the strand. Later they claimed that a second band of Skraelings had emerged from the forest and was blocking their line of retreat towards the settlement, though this was a fabrication. The real problem was that our men had no leadership or cohesion. Once again the Icelanders and Greenlanders were behaving as though they were complete strangers to one another, and neither group showed any sign of helping the other. In their panic-stricken haste men were tripping over and picking themselves up, then running onward and bumping into one another as they glanced over their shoulders to see if any more of the Skraeling darts were on their way, or if the Skraelings were pressing home the attack. At this point, when it seemed that our forces were beaten, we were saved by a berserk.

The term berserk has now such common currency that it is known to nations far beyond the Norse world. All agree that the word describes someone so brimming with fighting rage that he performs extraordinary deeds on the battlefield with no regard for his own safety. Some say that in his fury the berserker howls like a wolf before he attacks, others that he foams at the mouth and bites the rim of his shield, glares at his foe, snarls and shakes before he strikes. A true berserk scorns any notion of armour or self-protection and wears only a bearskin shirt as a mark of his role. Sometimes he wears no shirt at all and goes half-naked into battle. This I have heard, and much more besides, but I have never heard tell of what appeared that day as our men fought the Skraelings – a female berserk.

Our situation was desperate. Our ill-disciplined men were degenerating into a worse rabble. A few of them had turned to skirmish with individual Skraelings, while others were scrambling along the river bank, fleeing ignominiously. One or two were shouting for help, or standing open-mouthed and apparently shocked by the reality of hand-to-hand fighting. It was shameful.

Just at that moment the gate of the settlement palisade banged open, and out rushed a frightful figure. It was Freydis. She had been watching the rout and was appalled by the cowardice of our men. She was in a fury. She came running full tilt down the slope towards the battle, roaring with anger and cursing our men as cowards and poltroons. She made an awesome sight, with her massive bulk, thick legs like tree trunks pounding the ground, red-faced, sweaty and her hair streaming behind her. She was wearing a woman's underdress, a long loose shift, but had discarded her overmantle so as to be able to run more swiftly, and now the undershift flapped around her. She thundered down the slope like an avenging heavyweight Valkyrie and, coming on one of the Norsemen who was standing futilely, she gave him a hefty blow with her meaty arm, which sent him flying, and at the same time snatched the short sword from his hand. She was in a blinding rage, more with her own men than with the Skraelings, many of whom had stopped and turned to look in shocked amazement at this huge, blonde woman raging with obscenities. Freydis was incandescent with anger, her eyes rolling. 'Fight like men, you bastards!' she bellowed at our shamefaced settlers. 'Get a grip on yourselves, and go for them!' To emphasise her rage, to shame our men and work herself into an even greater frenzy, Freydis slipped aside her shift, pulled out one of her massive breasts and gave it a great stinging slap with the flat of her sword. 'Come on!' she screamed to her followers. 'A woman could do better.' And she flung herself at the nearest Skraeling and slashed at him with the weapon. The wretched man, half her size and strength, put up his spear shaft to ward off the blow, but Freydis's sword chopped through the timber cleanly and dealt him such a terrific blow on his neck that he crumpled up instantly. Freydis then swung round and began lumbering at full speed at the next Skraeling. Within seconds the invaders broke and ran back towards their canoes. They had never seen anything like this, and neither had our men. Puffing and panting, Freydis churned along the beach, taking wild swipes at the backs of the departing Skraeling, who did not even attempt to turn and throw darts at her. Our attackers were utterly nonplussed, and they left a panting Freydis standing in the shallows, her loose shift soaked at the hem, great patches of sweat staining her armpits, and splashes of Skraeling blood across her chest.

It was the last time we saw the Skraelings. They left seven of their number dead on the beach, and when we examined them I found that they were not like the healer I had met in the branch shelter in the woods. These Skraelings who had attacked us were shorter in stature, broader, and their faces were generally flatter and more round than the man I had met. They also smelled of fish and wore clothes more suited to the sea than the forest – long sealskin jerkins and heavy leggings. We stripped their bodies of any useful items – including some finely worked spearheads of bone, then carried their bodies to the top of a nearby cliff and threw them into the tide. Our own dead – there were three of them – were buried with little ceremony in shallow graves scraped out of the thin soil.

Our victory, if such an inglorious encounter deserves the name, made the resentment within our camp even worse. Icelanders and Greenlanders heaped blame on one another for being cowards, for failing to come to help, for turning and running instead of making a stand and fighting. No one dared look Freydis in the face, and people slunk about the settlement looking thoroughly ashamed. To make matters worse, winter came on us within a few days and so swiftly that we were caught unprepared. One morning the weather was crisp and bright, but by afternoon it began to rain, and the rain soon turned to sleet, and the following morning we woke up to find a heavy covering of snow on the ground. We managed to get the cattle rounded up and put into the sheds, but we knew that if the winter proved to be long and hard we had not gathered sufficient hay to feed the cattle through to springtime. And the cattle would not be the only ones to suffer. The Icelanders had spent so much time on the construction of their new longhouses during the summer months that they had not been able to catch and dry enough fish for a winter reserve or save a surplus of sour milk and cheese. Their winter rations were very meagre, and when they suggested to Thorvard and the Greenlanders that they should share their food supplies, they were brusquely told that there was not enough to go round. They would have to fend for themselves.

That winter did prove to be exceptionally long and bitter, and in the depths of it we were hardly able to stir from our longhouses for the deep snow, ice and bitter cold outside. It was the most miserable episode of our entire Vinland experience. In the longhouse of the Greenlanders, where I lived, life was hard. Our daily intake of food was quickly reduced to tiny portions of gruel with a handful of dried nuts which we had gathered in the autumn, and perhaps a few flakes of dried fish as we huddled around the central fire pit, nursing the embers of our small stock of firewood. All our cattle were dead by midwinter. We were feeding them such short rations that they never gave any milk anyhow, and we killed them when the fodder ran out entirely, though by then they were so scrawny that there was hardly any flesh on their bones. I missed my two mentors, Tyrkir and Thorvall. Before, in Vinland, they had been on hand to help pass the long dark hours with their tales of the Old Gods or instructing me in the Elder Lore. Now, with both men gone, I was reduced to empty daydreaming, turning over in my mind the tales they had told and trying to apply them to my own circumstances. It was at this time, in the depths of uncommonly harsh Vinland winter, that I first began to pray to Odinn, making silent prayers partly for my own solace, and partly in the hopes that he would come to help, to make the winter pass away, to reduce the pangs of hunger. I made sacrifices too. From my tiny ration of food, I would set aside a few dried nuts, a shred of meat, and when no one was looking I would hide them in a crevice in the longhouse wall. They were my offerings to Odinn, and if the mice and rats came and ate them, then – as I told myself – they were either Odinn in disguise or at least his ravens, Hugin and Munin, who would report back that I had made my proper obedience.

If our lives were pinched in the longhouse of the Greenlanders, the conditions in the two houses occupied by the Icelanders were far, far worse. Two of their men had received crippling wounds in the Skraeling attack, and while in summertime they might have been able to recover from their injuries with adequate food and warm sunshine, they failed to survive the fetid gloom of their longhouses. They lay wrapped in their lice-ridden clothes and with almost nothing to eat until they died a lingering and famished death. Theirs were not the only Icelandic deaths that winter. One of the longhouses was infected with some sort of coughing sickness which killed three of the settlers, and then a child, driven to desperation by hunger, wandered out into the black winter night and was found a few paces from the entrance next morning, frozen to death. A malignant silence settled over the three longhouses, which became no more than three long humps in the snow. For days on end nothing stirred.

Our longhouse was the most westerly of the three, and only occasionally did someone venture outside and walk through the thick snow to visit our immediate neighbours. For two months no one at all from our longhouse went as far as the second of the Icelandic houses, and when someone did – it was Thorvard, Freydis's husband – he found the door was banked up with snow as if no one had emerged for days. When he levered open the door and went inside, he found the place was a mortuary. A third of the people were dead of cold and hunger, and the survivors looked no more than bundles of rags, scarcely able to raise themselves from where they lay on the side benches.

There was more bad news when one of our own men came back from the beach, where we had stored the two knorrs for the winter. At the time of the first, unexpected snow we had dragged the two vessels on rollers up above the high-tide line, propped them up on wooden baulks, and heaped banks of shingle around them as a protection from the blizzards. Then we covered them with tents of wadmal. But a winter gale had stripped away the covers from the elderly vessel that Leif had loaned us, and snow had filled her. A false spring day with its sudden thaw had melted the snow to water, which filled the bilge. That same evening a sudden drop in temperature turned the water into ice, which expanded and split the garboard plank, the key plank which ran the length of her keel. When our carpenter tried to mend the long and dangerous crack he found that the bottom of our ship was entirely rotten. Every time he tried to replace a section of plank, the adjacent area of hull crumbled away. The carpenter was a grouchy and bad-tempered man at the best of times, and now he reported to Thorvard that he refused to waste his time trying to make the decayed old vessel seaworthy.

By that stage, I think, Freydis had already made up her mind that the colony was a failure and that we would have to evacuate Leif's cabins yet again. But she kept the idea to herself and, with typical guile, prepared for the evacuation without alerting anyone else. Her immediate problem was the damage to our knorr. We needed a vessel to carry us away from Vinland and our ancient and rickety knorr was no longer seaworthy. One possible solution was for all the settlers, both Icelanders and Greenlanders, to evacuate the colony by cramming aboard the Icelanders' large, newer vessel. But given the history of bad blood between the two groups it was very unlikely that the Icelanders would agree to this arrangement. Alternatively the Icelanders might lend us their vessel for the evacuation if we promised to send the ship back to them once we had safely arrived in Greenland. Though why the Icelanders should trust us to do this was an open question. And even if the Icelanders were so generous, Freydis knew that there was a more acute problem to confront: if the Icelanders stayed behind in Vinland and somehow managed to make a success of the venture, then by customary law the possession and ownership of the entire settlement would pass away from the Erikssons and transfer to Helgi and Finnbogi and their heirs. They would no longer be Leif's cabins, but Helgi and Finnbogi's cabins, and this was a humiliation which Freydis, the daughter of Erik the Red, could not bear.

Her solution to the dilemma was as artful as it was demonic. It depended on that fatal Norse belief in personal honour.

Very soon after the spring thaw, a real one this time, she walked over to visit the nearest Icelandic longhouse. It was early in the morning, at first light, and I saw her go because I had slipped out of the longhouse to get some badly needed fresh air after a fetid night spent among the snoring Greenlanders. I was loitering near one of the empty store sheds. I always tried to stay well clear of Freydis, so when I saw her I stepped behind the shed until she walked past. I watched her push open the door of the Icelanders' longhouse and go inside. When she reappeared she was accompanied by Finnbogi, who was wearing a heavy coat to keep out the cold. The two were intending to walk in my direction, and once again I shrank back from view. They halted, less than ten paces away, and I heard Freydis say, 'I've had enough of Vinland. I've made up my mind that my people should leave the colony and return home. For that I need to buy your knorr because our vessel is no longer fit for the journey to Greenland. We'll sail away from here, and if you, Helgi and your people want to stay on, then the settlement is yours.'

Finnbogi must have been taken by surprise, for there was a long pause and then he answered that he had no objection to her proposal but would first have to check it with his brother. I heard the soft crunch of his footsteps receding on the slushy snow as he returned to the Icelanders' house. I waited to give Freydis time to get back to our own longhouse, and then scuttled there as fast as I could, knowing instinctively that something was very wrong. It was not my second sight which warned me. It was my long experience of Freydis. Speaking to Finnbogi, her voice had carried that hint of treachery and manipulation that had preceded the unpleasant tricks she had inflicted on me back in Brattahlid in my father's house. That tone of deceit convinced me that Freydis was planning something unpleasant. Quite how foul her plan was soon became apparent.

I got into the longhouse just in time to hear Freydis deliberately provoke her weak-willed husband Thorvard into losing his temper. That was another of Freydis's techniques I recognised. Thorvard must still have been in bed when Freydis returned to the longhouse and climbed in beside him, for he kept repeating his question. 'Where have you been? Where have you been? You have got cold, wet feet, and the hem of your shift is damp, so you must have been outside.' At first Freydis refused to answer. Then finally, when Thorvard was truly irritated with her grudging silence, she said that she had been to see Finnbogi and his brother to ask them for the sale or loan of their knorr.

'They refused my request outright,' she said. 'They laughed in my face, and then insulted me. They said I was becoming more like a man every day, and that you, not I, should have come to discuss the matter with them. Finnbogi even went so far as to hit me, knocking me to the ground.'

Thorvard began to bluster. He had a good mind to go out and give the brothers a good thrashing, he said. Freydis pounced on his bravado. 'If you were more than half a man,' she retorted scathingly, 'you would do more than just lie in bed threatening the two ruffians who have humiliated me. A real man would go off and avenge my honour. But you, you little worm, you are such a coward that you will do nothing. I know you and your faint-hearted ways, and so too do half the people in Brattahlid. When we get home, I'm going to divorce you on the grounds of cowardice, and there's no one who would not sympathise with me.'

As usual, my aunt knew how to twist the knife. Cowardice is

almost the worst and most shameful ground for summary divorce in Norse society, exceeded only by homosexual acts. Her goading was more than Thorvard could bear. He leapt out of bed, threw on his clothes and grabbed an axe and a sword. Moments later, with Freydis at his heels and calling on the other Greenlanders to follow their leader, Thorvard was slipping and slithering along the muddy path to the Icelanders' longhouse. He slammed his way into the building, ran across to where Helgi was sitting on his bed, sleepily thinking over Freydis's proposal to buy the knorr, and with a great swipe he sank his axe into Helgi's chest, killing him. Within moments a massacre was in progress. More and more of the Greenlanders appeared, brandishing their weapons and hacking and stabbing at the unfortunate Icelanders, who were taken by surprise. There were curses and shouts as the Icelanders rolled off their sleeping benches and scrabbled to find their weapons and defend themselves. But they were at too much of a disadvantage. Most of them were killed while they were sleepy or unarmed.

Too young to have been called upon to join the attack on the Icelanders, I heard the shrieks and clamour of the massacre and ran to the side entrance of the Icelanders' longhouse, arriving on the scene just in time to see Freydis pick up Helgi's sword from under his bed and make sure that his brother Finnbogi did not have a chance to reveal the truth by running him through so powerfully that the blade emerged a hand's breadth out of his back. She then wrenched the blade clear and joined in the general bloodbath.

Again Norse custom had its malign influence. Once the massacre had started, there was no going back. Every man knew the pitiless truth. The moment that the first mortal blow had been struck, it was better to kill every last Icelander. Any survivor was a potential witness, and his or her evidence about the murders would lead to a cycle of revenge if a report of the atrocity reached their families back in Iceland. Contributing to this stark policy was the killing frenzy which now gripped the Greenlanders. They killed and killed and killed until they were tired. Only when every adult Icelander, male or female, was dead did they stop the slaughter. By then only five Icelanders were left alive, three boys and two girls, and they were huddled in a corner, wide-eyed and speechless with shock as they watched their parents cut down. Murdering the children was beyond the capacity of even the most blood-crazed Greenlander, but not Freydis. She ordered the men to complete the job. They looked back at her, panting with exhaustion, their swords and axes streaked with gore, their clothes spattered with blood, and the red madness slowly fading from their eyes. They looked drained and tired, and did not move. Freydis raised her borrowed sword, and screamed at them. 'Kill the brats! Kill them! Do as I say!'

I was well inside the longhouse. Appalled by the sight of what seemed like so many limp and blood-soaked bundles of clothing lying on the floor, I crept along the side wall and sank down into a corner, wishing that I was somewhere else. I sat with my back to the wall, trying to make myself invisible, with my arms around my knees and my head down. Hearing Freydis's harridan shriek I raised my head and saw her become grim and calm. Her sway over the men became almost diabolic. She seemed to dominate them like some awful creature from the Hel of the Gods, as she ordered the men to bring the children one by one before her. Such was her authority that the men obeyed, and they led the children to stand in front of her. Then, teeth clenched, she beheaded each child.

I vomited pale, acid bile.

FREYDIS NOW ORDERED that everything that would burn was to be collected and heaped around the bases of the heavy timber posts supporting the turf roofs of the longhouses. Wooden benches, scraps of timber, old rags, anything combustible was piled up. Then Freydis herself went down the line of pillars, setting fire to the materials. She was the last person to leave each building and heave the big door shut. By midday we could see that smoke, which had been issuing from the smoke hole, was also seeping out from the sides of the building, where the turf wall joined the roof.

The whole structure of the longhouse began to look like a smouldering charcoal burners' mound as the turf and wattle interior walls eventually caught fire. The heat steadily built up until we could feel it from forty paces away. Around the fire the last of the snow melted and turned to slush, and in the end the long curved roofs simply fell in with a soft thump, a few sparks curled up into the sky, and the remains of the longhouses which the Icelanders had spent three months building became their funeral pyres. Looking at the ruins, it was obvious to us that in a few winters there would be scarcely any trace that they had ever existed.

Freydis summoned us to a meeting in our own longhouse late that evening. We gathered in a glum silence. Many of us were ridden with guilt, a few were trying to boost their spirits by bragging that it was exactly what the Icelanders had deserved. But Freydis was clear-headed and unmoved. 'The only trace of the Icelanders' existence now lies in our heads,' she told us fiercely. 'No one else will know what has happened, if we keep our mouths shut about the events of this day. We, who are responsible, are the only witnesses. Here on the edge of the world there is no one else to observe and report. We control the only knowledge of what has happened.' Freydis promised us that we had been justified in destroying the Icelanders. Again she produced the lie that she had asked Finnbogi for the loan of the knorr and been refused. 'The Icelanders denied us their knorr,' she said. 'If we had not seized the initiative, they would have sailed away, leaving us behind to our deaths. We acted in self-defence by striking first. What we have done was to save our own lives.'

I do not know how many of us believed her, perhaps a few. Those who did not were either too ashamed or too shocked or frightened of what might happen if they disagreed to speak out. So we kept quiet and followed Freydis's orders when she told us to load the knorr with our possessions and a cargo of valuable Vinland timber to take back to Greenland, for even at that late stage Freydis was determined to make a profit from her venture.

We were so keen to get away from that sinister place that we had the boat loaded and ready to sail within a week. Then Freydis ordered that our longhouse, too, should be set on fire. She told us that when we returned to Greenland we were to say that we had decided to abandon the colony, but the Icelanders had elected to stay, that Freydis and Thorvard had purchased the knorr, and when last seen the Icelanders had been thriving and prosperous and alive. Should anyone in later years visit the site, all they would find would be the burnt-out ruins of the longhouses, and of course they would presume that the Skraelings had overwhelmed the settlement and destroyed every last colonist.

TEN

SUCH A MONSTROUS event could never be kept a secret. When we reached Brattahlid, our people were delighted to see us safely back, though disappointed to hear that once again our plans for a permanent settlement in Vinland had been abandoned. Freydis went immediately to her farm at Gardar, taking her followers with her. Some she bribed to keep quiet about the massacre of the Icelanders, others she threatened with death if they should reveal the details. Given her reputation for violence, these threats were very effective. But rumours soon began to leak out, like the smoke which rose from the smouldering longhouse. Some former Vinlanders blurted out the grisly details when they were drunk. A few shouted aloud during their nightmares. Most were clumsy liars, and inconsistencies in their stories were noticed. Finally, the swirl of rumour and doubt became so powerful that Leif himself decided he must get at the truth of what was happening with his property in Vinland. He asked his half-sister to visit him at Brattahlid, and when she refused, he had three of her thralls arrested and tortured to reveal what had really gone on at Leif's cabins. They quickly revealed the horrors of Vinland, and Leif was appalled. He could not bring himself to punish his half-sister directly, for that would violate his ties of kinship. But he pronounced a curse on her and her progeny and shunned her for the rest of his life.

He also refused to have under his roof anyone who had been involved in these despicable events. The result was that I, who had been an innocent bystander to the massacre, was banished from his household.

For me, it was out of the question to live in Gardar with Freydis. We had a mutual dislike and my presence would have reminded her of the blood-stained episode which was to blight the rest of her life. For a few weeks I lived with Tyrkir, now an old man with failing eyesight, in his cabin on the outskirts of Brattahlid, until my father Leif could make plans for me, his bastard child, to be shipped away. He arranged a passage for me aboard the next trading vessel that arrived and made it clear to me that it did not much matter where I went. I said goodbye to Tyrkir, who was probably the only person genuinely sorry to see me leave, and at the age of thirteen began yet another sea journey, this time heading eastward.

Deep down, I suppose I was hoping that I might be able to find Gudrid again and be accepted back into her affections. I had heard nothing from her since she and Thorfinn and young Snorri had left Greenland to return to Thorfinn's people in Iceland. But for me Gudrid was still the person who had shown me the greatest kindness in my childhood, and I had no plan save for a vague notion of presenting myself at her new household to see if she would take me in. So when the ship called in at Iceland I told the captain that I would be going no farther with him. It may have seemed a rash decision to set foot in a country, several of whose people had been victims in Vinland, but news of the massacre had not yet spread and I discovered within days that the extermination of the Vinlanders was not the unique atrocity that I had imagined. Every farmer in Iceland was talking about the climax to a more local feud which, in its gruesome details, provided a freakish echo of the Vinland atrocity.

The feud had been going on for years, driven by the hatred of Hallgerd, the malevolent wife of a farmer named Gunnar Hamundarson, for her neighbour Bergthora, wife of Njal Thorgeirsson.

The feud had started with a quarrel over a dowry and had spread to include dozens of kinsmen and outsiders, leading to a series of killings and revenge murders. The autumn before I arrived a gang of Hallgerd's faction had surrounded the farmhouse in which Njal and his wife lived, blocked up the doors and set it on fire, burning to death nearly everyone inside, including Njal's three sons.

For me the story was a grisly reminder of Vinland, but for the sweating farmer from whom I heard the tale after I came ashore it was the juiciest gossip of the day. I was helping him stack hay in his barn to pay for my night's lodging. 'It'll be the high point of the next Althing, of that you can be sure,' he said as he wiped the back of his hand across his shiny forehead. 'It'll be a confrontation the like of which has not been seen for ages. Njal's people are bringing a lawsuit against the Burners, seeking compensation for his death, and the Burners are sure to bring along as many of their own supporters as they can muster to defend their action. And if that maniac Kari Solmundarson also shows up, the Gods only know what is likely to happen. I wouldn't miss it for all the looted silver in the world.'

Kari Solmundarson was the name which kept cropping up whenever people discussed the possible repercussions of the Burning, as people had taken to calling it. He was Njal's son-in-law and had escaped from the blazing building after the roof fell in by running up a fallen rafter, where it lay aslant against the gable wall, then leaping out through the smoke and flames as his makeshift ladder collapsed behind him. The Burners had surrounded the building and were waiting to kill any fugitives. But they failed to spot Kari in the gathering darkness, and he slipped through the cordon, though his clothes and hair were so charred by the heat that he had to plunge into a small lake to extinguish the embers. Now he had sworn to exact revenge and was criss-crossing Iceland, rallying Njal's friends to the cause and swearing bloody vengeance. Kari was a foe the Burners would have to take seriously according to everything I heard. He was a skilful warrior, a vikingr who had seen plenty of action overseas. Before he came to Iceland and married Njal's daughter, he had lived in Orkney as a member of the household of Earl Sigurd, lord of that country, and had distinguished himself in several sharp battles, including a famous encounter with a gang of pirates when he had rescued two of Njal's sons.

The moment I heard Kari's story, my half-formed idea of trying to track down Gudrid was replaced by a new and more attractive scheme. I added up the years and calculated that when Kari Solmundarson had served the Earl of Orkney, he might well have met my mother, Thorgunna. He was in Orkney at about the time she seduced Leif the Lucky, to the amazement of all at Earl Sigurd's court, and conceived a son. If I could locate Kari and ask him about those days in Birsay, maybe I would have the chance to learn more about my mother and who I was.

The place to find Kari, if the farmer was correct, was at the next Althing.

As this memorial is intended, if only in my fantasy, to redress some of the lapses which the good Adam of Bremen is likely to make in his history and geography of the known world, perhaps I should say something about the Althing, because I doubt if the cleric of Bremen has ever heard of it, and it is a remarkable institution. Certainly I never came across the like of it elsewhere in my travels. The Althing is how the Icelanders rule themselves. Every year the leading farmers in each quarter of the island hold local meetings, where they discuss matters of common interest and settle disputes among themselves. Important topics and any unresolved lawsuits are then brought to the Althing, a general conclave, which always assembles in July after ten weeks of summer have passed. Only the wealthier farmers and the godars or chieftains have any real role in the actual law-making and courts of justice. The common folk merely look on and support their patrons when called upon to do so. But the gathering is such a combination of fairground, congress and gossip shop that every Icelander who can make the journey to Thingvellir does so. Listening to the lawsuits is a spectator sport. Plaintiffs and defendants, or their representatives, appear before sworn juries of their equals and make their appeals to the customs of the country. This is where the Lawspeaker has an important role. He acts as umpire and decides whether the customs are fairly quoted and applied. In consequence the arguments often take on the flavour of a verbal duel, and the Icelanders, who enjoy courtroom revelations as much as anyone else, cluster round to listen to the rhetoric, while analysing who is being most skilled in twisting the law to their own ends or outsmarting the opposition. If they are looking for such lawyers' tricks, they are rarely disappointed.

Some might say that the Althing is an ill-advised way to run a country's affairs, and feel that these are best conducted by a single wise ruler, whether king or queen, emperor, lord or regent. If a single ruler cannot be found, then a small council of five or six is more than enough. The notion that Iceland's affairs should be conducted by the mass of its citizens assembling once a year on a grassy pitch does seem very odd. But this is how the Icelanders have arranged matters ever since the country was first settled nearly two hundred years ago, and in truth its way of government does not differ so very much from the councils of kingdoms where the barons and nobles form their rival factions and compete with one another for the final verdict or advantage. The only difference is that Iceland lacks a single overlord, and this leaves the factions to settle the scores directly among themselves when legal arguments are exhausted. This is when the weapons take over from words.

Thingvellir, the site of the annual Althing, is an impressive location. In the south-west of the country and about five days' ride inland from Frodriver, where my mother spent her last days, it is a grassy area at the base of a long broken cliff, which provides sheltered spots for pitching tents and erecting temporary cabins among scattered outcrops of rock. One particular rock, known as the Lawgiver's Rock, makes a natural podium. Standing on top of this, the Lawspeaker opens the proceedings by reciting from memory the traditional laws and customs of the land to the assembled crowd. There is so much law for him to remember that the process can take two or three days, and when I was there the White Christ priests were already suggesting that it would save time just to write down the laws and consult them as necessary. Of course, the priests knew very well this meant that they, the book-learned priests, would eventually control as well as interpret the legal system. But as yet the change from memory to the written page had not been made, and to the irritation of the White Christ faction the Lawspeaker still went to the nearby Oxar River on the first day of the Althing and hurled a metal axe into the water as an offering to the Old Gods.

THE FACTION SUPPORTING the Burners arrived in style. They came as a group, about forty of them, riding those small and sturdy Icelandic horses. They were armed to the teeth because they feared an ambush organised by Kari. Their leader was a local chieftain, Flosi Thordarson. He had planned and organised the incendiary attack, though he did not boast about it as much as several of the other Burners, who arrived at Thingvellir gloating over the death of Njal and bragging that they would finish the job by putting paid to Kari as well, if he dared show his face. By contrast Flosi preferred to work with his head rather than by brawn. He knew that the Burners had a very weak case when it came to defending their actions before the courts set up at the Althing. So he used a classic strategy: he resolved to bribe the best lawyer in Iceland and rely on his legal hair-splitting to get the Burners acquitted.

The lawyer he picked was Eyjolf Bolverksson, generally considered to possess the most wily legal mind in the country. Eyjolf had already set up his booth at Thingvellir when Flosi went looking for him. Flosi, however, had to be careful about being seen negotiating in public with Eyjolf because Icelandic custom dictates that a lawsuit can only be conducted by the party directly concerned or by a deputy with a recognised relationship such as kinship or a debt of honour. Legal advice is not meant to be for profit or hire. Eyjolf had no prior connection with the Burners, and it is very unlikely that he believed in their innocence. But Eyjolf had a reputation for avarice and, like many lawyers, he was perfectly willing to sell his skills if the payment was high enough. So initially he rebuffed Flosi, telling him that he would not act on his behalf. At most he was allowed to act as a friend of the court and give impartial advice. But when Flosi quietly took him off to one side and offered him an arm bracelet of solid gold, Eyjolf accepted the bribe and agreed to act for him, assuring Flosi that no one else knew so intimately the twists and turns of the back alleys of Icelandic custom and that he would find a way which would allow the Burners to escape punishment.

I know all this because, by then, I had been set to spy on Flosi.

Four days before the Burners arrived at the Althing, Kari Solmundarson slipped quietly into Thingvellir. I would not have guessed from his appearance that Kari was the formidable warrior of his reputation. He was only of average height and rather slim, and he scarcely looked as if he could heft a battleaxe to good effect. He had a narrow face with a long nose above a small mouth, and his brown eyes were rather close set. Unusually for a fighting man, he kept his beard very neat and trim and tied back his hair with a browband of dark grey. Only when he was ready to do battle did he remove the browband and his magnificent head of hair become a warrior's mane. But if you looked past the sober style of Kari's dress, his movements gave him away. He was as supple as an athlete, always quick and fluid, and constantly alert like some sort of hunting animal. A bystander pointed Kari out for me just as Kari was about to enter the booth of one of his potential allies. I walked up behind him, out of his line of vision. Yet he sensed my presence, suddenly whirled about to face me, and dropped his hand to the hilt of the short sword in his belt. When he saw only an unarmed boy, he relaxed.

'Are you Kari Solmundarson?' I asked.

'I am,' he replied. 'Who are you, lad? I don't think I have seen you before.'

'I'm Thorgils Leifsson, though perhaps it might be more accurate if my name was Thorgils Thorgunnasson.'

He looked more than a little startled. 'Thorgunna the w—' He stopped himself. 'Thorgunna, who came from Ireland to Earl Sigurd's court?' he asked.

'Yes, I grew up in Greenland and the west, and only arrived here recently. I was hoping you could tell me something about my mother.'

'Well, well, you're Thorgunna's son. I did know your mother, at least by sight, though we exchanged only a few words,' Kari replied, 'but right at this moment I don't have time to spend chatting about those days. I've got much to do here at the Althing, but if you want to tag along with me, perhaps there will be a moment when I will be able to tell you a little of what you want to know.'

For the rest of that day, and the next, I followed Kari as he went from booth to booth, talking to the godars who had known his murdered father-in-law. Sometimes he was successful in enlisting their support for the case against the Burners, but just as often he was told that he would have to look after his own interests as the Burners were too powerful and anyone helping Kari would be victimised. In one booth we found a tall, rather gaunt man, lying on a bed with his right foot wrapped in bandages. The invalid was Thorhall Asgrimmsson, Njal's foster son.

'Thank the Gods that you managed to get here,' said Kari, obviously pleased.

'The travelling was painful, but I managed it by taking it in slow stages,' Thornhall replied. 'The infection is so sore that I can hardly walk.'

He pulled aside the bandages and showed his right ankle. It was swollen to three times its normal size. In the centre of the swelling a great pus-filled boil seemed to pulsate with heat. In the centre of the boil, I could see the focus of the infection: a black spot like an evil fungus ringed with a fringe of angry red.

'The court case against the Burners will probably be called the day after tomorrow. Do you think you will be able to attend?' asked Kari.

'I doubt it, unless the boil bursts by then,' Thorhall replied. 'But even if I can't attend in person, I can follow the case from my bed here and offer advice if you keep me informed of the details of each day's proceedings.'

'I'm really grateful, and can't thank you enough for coming to the Althing,' Kari said.

'It's the least I can do,' Thorhall said. 'It was your father-in-law Njal who taught me nearly everything I know about the law and I want to see justice done to his murderers.' He paused and thought for a moment. 'In fact, my disability could be useful. Very few people know that I am here, cooped up on this bed, and I think that it should stay that way. We might work a surprise on them.' He glanced at me. 'Who's this youngster?'

'He's just come from Greenland, grew up there and in a place called Vinland.'

Thorhall grunted. 'What do you know about the arrangements Flosi and the Burners are making for their defence at the trial?'

'It's said that they are going to try to get Eyjolf Bolverksson to lead their defence.'

'Officially he shouldn't be taking the case,' said Thorhall, 'but knowing how greedy he is for money, I expect he will be bought. If he is lining up against us, then it would be helpful to know.' His glance fell on me. 'Perhaps this lad could make himself useful. I doubt if anyone around here knows who he is, and he wouldn't stand out in a crowd.'

Then, speaking directly to me, he asked, 'Could you do something for us? If you had Flosi and the chief Burners pointed out to you, do you think you could stick close to them and report back to us how they are getting on in their campaign to recruit allies for their court hearing?'

It was the first time that anyone had ever showed such confidence in me and I was flattered. Equally important, Thorhall's suggestion appealed to my sense of identity. Odinn, as I mentioned earlier, is the God of disguises, the listener at the door, the stealer of secrets, and the God whose character and behaviour appeals to me most. Here was I, alone in a new country, being asked to spy in a matter of real importance. To accept the invitation would be a homage to Odinn and, at the same time, it would be a way of earning the confidence of the man who could tell me about my mother.

So it was that, three days later, I was crouching in a cleft of rock, barely daring to breathe. Not ten paces away was Flosi Thordarson, leader of the Burners, together with two of his leading supporters, who I would later learn were Bjarni Brodd-Helgason and Hallbjorn the Strong. With them was the eminent legal expert Eyjolf. He was easy to recognise because he was a dandy who liked to strut around the Althing wearing a flashy scarlet cloak and a gold headband, and carrying a silver-mounted axe. We were all a short distance behind the lip of the Almmana Gorge, out of sight of the meeting place below. Clearly the four men had come to this isolated spot for a private conference, thinking it an ideal place to talk freely, after they had left their retainers to keep a lookout. I had seen the group leave the cluster of booths at the Althing and begin to walk along the path leading to the clifftop, and I had guessed where they were going. Scrambling up ahead of them, I flung myself down on the grass so I was not visible against the skyline. After catching my breath and waiting for the pounding of blood in my ears to cease, I raised my head cautiously and looked to my right. A moment later I was wriggling backwards anxiously and trying to burrow into cover. The four men had chosen to sit down alarmingly close to me and begin their discussion. Fortunately the Thingvellir cliff is made of the rock the Icelanders call hraun. It oozes from the ground as a fiery torrent when the Gods are angry and, when it cools and hardens, develops cracks and slits. Into one of these clefts I slid. I was too far away to hear anything more than the occasional scrap of conversation when one or another raised his voice, but it was clear that some negotiations were going on. The outcome must have been satisfactory because the next thing I saw as I peeked cautiously from my hiding place, was Flosi pull off his own arm a heavy gold bracelet, take Eyjolf's arm and slip the bracelet onto it. I could tell that the bracelet was valuable from the way it gleamed briefly in the watery sun, and Eyjolf lovingly ran his finger over it. Then Eyjolf carefully slid the bracelet farther up his arm, under the sleeve of his coat where it would not be seen.

At this point I had no idea of the significance of the transaction. When the four men got to their feet and walked back along the path to rejoin their waiting retainers, I waited silently, still pressed to the ground, until I guessed that the others must be gone. Then I slipped quietly back to the booth, where Kari was conferring with Thorhall, and reported what I had witnessed. Kari scowled and muttered something about making sure that Eyjolf did not live to enjoy his bribe. Thorhall, lying on his cot, was more phlegmatic. 'Eyjolf's a tricky customer,' he said, 'but he may not be quite the invincible lawyer that he thinks he is.'

The eagerly awaited lawsuit began next morning before a large and expectant audience. One after another, various members of Kari's faction stood at the foot of the Law Rock and took it in turns to pronounce the accusations. The most eloquent speakers had been chosen, and the legal formulae rolled out sonorously. They accused Flosi Thordarson and his allies of causing the death of the Njalssons 'by internal wound, brain wound, or marrow wound' and demanded that the culprits be neither 'fed nor forwarded nor helped nor harboured' but condemned as outlaws. Further, they demanded that all the goods and properties of the accused be confiscated and paid as compensation to the relatives of the dead family and the people living in their area. It was then that I noticed how the crowd assembled round the law court were standing in separate groups. If I had not been a newcomer, I would have identified much sooner how those who supported the Burners were standing well apart from the band of men allied with Kari and the Njalsson faction. Between them, acting as a buffer, stood a large crowd of apparently neutral bystanders, and it was just as well they did so because both Kari's men and the Burners had come fully armed to the Law Rock and were wearing tokens – ribbons and emblems attached to their clothes – which signalled their loyalty and that they were ready for a fight.

For the moment, however, both sides were prepared to let the lawsuit take its course. The first day of the court case was occupied entirely with Kari's people laying accusations of murder or conspiracy to murder against the Burners. The second and third days saw legal arguments over which court had the power to try the cases, and who should be on the juries. Eyjolf proved to be every bit as slippery as his reputation suggested. He tried every wily trick in law to delay or deflect the accusations, and even came up with several variations which were entirely new. He fastened on tiny procedural irregularities which he claimed rendered the prosecution irrelevant. He discredited witnesses on minor technical points and had so many jurors disqualified for the most arcane reasons that Kari's side were driven to summoning up and enrolling nearly a dozen substitute jurors. Eyjolf bent and twisted the law this way and that, and the Lawspeaker, a man named Skapti, was constantly being called on to adjudicate. Invariably he found in favour of the clever Eyjolf.

At the end of each day the crowd, who greeted each new legal subtlety with a murmur of appreciation, judged that the Burners had the upper hand. But then next morning the spectators had to reverse that opinion because they had not reckoned with Kari's hidden adviser, Thorhall, lying in his booth nursing his grotesque boil. I was kept employed constantly running back and forth to Thorhall to report every latest twist in the legal wrangling. Thorhall, grimacing with discomfort, red-faced and tears of pain running down his cheeks, would listen to what I had to say, though the legal wording was so ornate that half the time I did not know what it was that I was reporting. Then he would wave me away to return to the law court and wait my next errand while he mulled over the fresh scrap of news. That evening he and Kari would have a consultation, and Kari or his representative would appear before the Lawspeaker the following morning and produce Thorhall's counter-argument, which would save the day and allow the prosecution to proceed. The Lawspeaker several times remarked that he did not know there was anyone who knew the laws so thoroughly. One little wrangle, I remember, turned upon whether the ownership of a milch cow entitled an individual to sit on the jury as a person of property. Apparently it did.

After four labyrinthine days, the case finally ended with a verdict. Despite all his twisting and turning Eyjolf had failed to get the case thrown out and the Burners were found guilty by the forty-two members of the jury. At that moment Eyjolf produced his master stroke: the verdict was invalid, he pointed out, because the jury was too large. It should have had thirty-six members, not forty-two. Kari and his faction had fallen into the trap that Eyjolf had set right at the beginning. His strategy had been to challenge repeatedly the composition of the jury, until he had lured Kari's faction into agreeing to an excess of jurors. On this technicality, the case against the Burners collapsed. Promptly Eyjolf turned the case on its head. He announced that Kari's prosecution had been malicious and that he was indicting Kari and his followers for false accusation and demanded that they, not the Burners, should be pronounced outlaws.

Kari came with me this time as we hurried back to Thorhall's booth to report the disaster. It was just past noon, and we left a crowd of onlookers clustering round Eyjolf and the Burners and excitedly offering their congratulations. Kari pushed past the door flap and summarised the situation in a few words. Thorhall, who had been lying back on his cot, swore loudly, sat up and swung his tender foot onto the ground. I had never seen a man look so angry. Thorhall groped under the cot and pulled out a short stabbing spear. It was, I remember, a particularly fine weapon, razor sharp, its blade inlaid with some fine silver work. Lifting up the spear with both hands, Thorhall brought it plunging down on the enormous boil on his ankle. There was a sickly squelching sound and I could almost hear the pus and blood as it burst out. A fat gob of pus slopped on the earth and there was a splatter of black blood across the earth floor as the putrefaction exploded. Thorhall let out a brief moan of pain as the boil was lanced, but a moment later he was on his feet, spear in hand and with bits of his own flesh still on the blade, striding out of the door, not even with a limp. Indeed, he was walking so fast that I found it difficult to keep up with him. I noticed that Kari, who was matching Thorhall stride for stride, had pulled off his browband, shaken out his hair, and had clapped a helmet on his head.

Thorhall came barging into the back of the crowd loyal to the Burners. The first person he encountered was one of Flosi's kinsmen, a man called Grim the Red. One look at Thorhall's furious expression and the spear in his hand, and Grim raised his shield to protect himself. Barely pausing, Thorhall rammed the spear into the shield with such force that the shield, an old and badly maintained wooden one, split in two. The spear blade carried right through Grim's body so that the point came out of his back between his shoulders. As Grim dropped to the ground, someone from the far side, from Kari's faction, shouted out, 'There's Thorhall! We can't let him be the only one to take revenge on the Burners!' and a furious melee broke out. Both sides drew their weapons and flung themselves at their opponents. So I saw what, in the end, is the deciding factor of Icelandic justice.

I also understood how Kari had got his reputation as a fighter. He came face to face with two of the Burners – Hallbjorn the Strong and Arni Kolsson. Hallbjorn was a big brute of a fellow, heavy-boned and broad-set. He was armed with a sword, which he swung at Kari, a low scything sweep at his legs, hoping to cripple or maim him. But the big man was too ponderous. Kari saw the blow coming. He leaped high in the air, drawing his knees up to his chest, and the sword swept harmlessly under him. Even as Kari landed, he struck with his double-bladed battleaxe at Arni Kolsson, a hit so shrewdly directed that it caught the victim in the vulnerable spot between shoulder and neck, chopping through the collarbone and splitting open his chest. Mortally wounded, Arni fell. Turning towards Hallbjorn, who was getting ready to take a second swing at him, Kari sidestepped and used his axe backhanded. The blade glanced off the lower edge of Hallbjorn's shield and carried downward, severing the big toe from Hallbjorn's left foot. Hallbjorn gave a howl of pain and hopped back a step. One of Kari's friends now rushed in and gave Hallbjorn such a shove with his spear that the big man toppled backwards in a heap. Scrambling back to his feet, Hallbjorn limped back in the crush of people as fast as he could set his injured foot on the ground. With each step he left a small splash of blood.

Next I witnessed something I have seen only four or five times in my life, even though I was to take part in quite a number of battles. Standing a little behind Kari, I saw a spear came hurtling at him, thrown by one of the Burners. Kari, who was not carrying a shield, sidestepped and caught the weapon left-handed in mid-air. At that instant I realised that Kari was ambidextrous. He caught the spear, as I say, left-handed, turned it and flung it back straight into the crowd of Burners and their supporters. He did not take aim, but threw as a reflex. The spear plunged into the crowd, killing a man.

By this stage men from both factions were trading blows with swords and axes and daggers, slamming shields in one another's faces, headbutting, wrestling hand to hand. This was not a military encounter between trained soldiers, disciplined and skilled in the use of arms. It was an ugly brawl between enraged farmers, and no less dangerous for being so.

The Burners and their friends began to fall back in disorder, and as the retreat began, Kari, the experienced fighter, picked his targets. He looked around for the men whom I had identified to him, those who bribed Eyjolf at the meeting at the gorge. One – Hallbjorn the Strong – was already in retreat with his injured foot, the other was Bjarni Brodd-Helgason. Seeing Bjarni in the scrimmage, Kari began to press towards him. There was no room for Kari to use his axe in the thick of the turmoil. Instead, again with his left hand, he snatched up a spear which someone had thrown and which was sticking up from the ground, and slithered the weapon through a gap between two men. His intended victim swung his shield round just in time to deflect the stab, which otherwise would have spitted him. With Kari extended fully forward, Bjarni saw his chance. As a space opened up, he darted his sword at Kari's leg. Once again Kari's remarkable agility saved him. He jerked back his leg, pivoted like a dancer, and in a moment was poised again and making a second spear thrust. As he lunged forward, Bjarni's life was saved by one of his retainers running forward with a shield. Kari's spear penetrated the shield and gashed the man in the thigh, a deep wound which was to make him a cripple for the rest of his life. Kari swayed back, preparing to strike a third time. He had dropped his axe and, holding the spear with both hands, thrust straight at Bjarni. The Burner threw himself sideways, rolling on the ground so the spear passed over him, then got back on his feet and ran for his life.

The fighting was now getting hazardous for the onlookers. The retreating Burners had to pass between the booths of several godars who had been friends with their victim, Njal. These godars and their retainers deliberately blocked the way, jostling and taunting the unfortunate Burners. Their taunts soon turned to blows and it seemed that the entire Althing was about to disintegrate into a general battle. A man named Solvi, who belonged to neither faction, was standing beside his booth as the Burners streamed by. Solvi was cooking a meal and had a great cauldron of water boiling over the cook fire. Unwisely he made a remark about the cowardice of the Burners, just as Hallbjorn the Strong was passing by. Hallbjorn heard the insult, picked up the man bodily and plunged him head first into the cauldron.

Kari and his allies chivvied the Burners through the booths and back towards the bank of the Oxar River. Both sides began to suffer losses. Flosi hurled a spear which killed one of Kari's men; someone else wrenched the same spear from the corpse and threw it back at Flosi, injuring him in the leg, though not badly. Once again it was Kari, the professional fighter, who did the most damage. Of the men who had almost humiliated him at the court, the key figure was Eyjolf the lawyer. Now Kari was out for revenge. As the Burners began to cross the river to safety, splashing their way through the milky-white shallows, Thorgeir Skora-Geir, who had been fighting alongside Kari all the time, saw the lawyer's scarlet cloak.

'There he is, reward him for that bracelet!' Thorgeir shouted, pointing to Eyjolf.

Kari seized a spear from a man standing beside him and threw it. The trajectory was flat and low, and the spear took Eyjolf in the waist and killed him.

With Eyjolf's death, the fighting began to subside. Both sides were exhausted, and Kari's faction were unwilling to cross the river and advance uphill against the Burners. One last spear was thrown – no one saw who flung it – and it struck down one more Burner. Then several of the leading godars arrived, among them Skapti the Lawspeaker, with a large band of their followers. They placed themselves between the two groups of combatants and called a halt to the fighting. Enough blood had been spilled, they said. It was time to make a temporary truce, and try to settle the dispute by negotiation.

To my astonishment, I now learned that conflict and killing in Iceland can be priced. Half a dozen godars assembled before the Law Rock and formed a rough-and-ready jury to calculate who had killed whom, how much the dead man was worth, and who should pay the compensation. It was like watching merchants haggle over the price of meat.

The weary fighters, who had been hacking at one another a moment before, were now content to lean on their shields or sit down on the turf to rest while they listened to the godars make their tally. The killing of this man was balanced by the killing of someone on the other side, the value of that wound was set at so many marks of silver, but that sum was then set against an injury on the opposite side, and so forth. In the end the godars decided that the losses that the Burners had sustained at the Althing brawl made up for the deaths they had inflicted on Kari's faction on previous occasions, and that both sides should make a truce and waive their claims for compensation. The original outstanding matter – the Burning of Njal and his family – was also settled. Compensation was to be paid for Njal's death, also for the death of his wife, and the Burners were to suffer outlawry. Flosi was banished for three years, while four of the more belligerent Burners – Gunnar Lambason, Grani Gunnarsson, Glum Hildisson and Kol Thorsteinsson – were banished for their lifetimes. However, in a spirit of compromise, the sentence of outlawry was not to take effect until the following spring, so that the chief malefactors could spend the winter arranging their affairs before beginning their period of banishment from Iceland.

The one man for whom no compensation was either sought or paid was Eyjolf. His underhand ways, it was commonly agreed, had brought the law into disrepute. One by one, the various farmers shook hands on the agreement, and thus ended what was, by all accounts, the most violent battle ever to take place before Logberg, the Law Rock.

ELEVEN

'OUTLAWRY FOR THREE years – that I can accept, but it's not for a youngster,' Kari explained later that evening. He had remembered me, even after all the violence of the day, and summoned me to the booth where he was staying. There he told me as much as he could remember about my mother Thorgunna in Orkney – including the details which I have given earlier – and now he was trying to make me understand why I had to fend for myself. When the godars announced their decisions at the Law Rock, Kari had been the only person to reject their judgement. He refused to acknowledge that the killings and maimings of the recent skirmish could be equated with the murders committed by the Burners on Njal and his family. 'In front of the most influential godars in the land, I declared that I refused to give up my pursuit of the Burners,' he went on, 'That means that sooner or later they will condemn me to outlawry and force me to leave Iceland. If it is lesser outlawry, then I must stay away for three years. If I come back before the time is complete, then my sentence is increased to full outlawry and I will be banished for life. Anyone declared an outlaw and still found in Iceland can be treated as a criminal. Every man's hand is against him unless he has friends willing to take the risk of protecting him. He can be killed on sight, and the executioner can take his property. It is no life for you.'

I still asked Kari if I could continue to serve him. But he refused. He would have no retinue or following. He would act alone in pursuing his vengeance, and a thirteen-year-old lad would be a hindrance. But he did have a suggestion: I should travel to Orkney, to the earl's household, and find out more details about my mother for myself. 'The person there who might have some more information for you is the earl's mother, if she is still alive. Eithne is her name, and she and Thorgunna got on particularly well. Both came from Ireland and they used to sit for hours at a time, quietly talking in Irish to one another.'

And he promised that if he himself was ever going to Orkney, then he would take me with him. It was my reward for spying on the Burners during the Althing.

Kari's revelation that on Orkney, in the person of the earl's mother, I might find a source of direct information about my mother completely eclipsed my earlier, ill-formed scheme of trying to rejoin Gudrid and Thorfinn. There were another six days before the Althing would be closed and the people dispersed to their homes, and I spent those six days going from booth to booth of the more important landowners, looking for work. I offered myself as a labourer, willing to spend the autumn and winter on a farm doing the same humdrum jobs I had performed in Greenland. In return I would receive my board and lodging and a modest payment when spring came. I realised that the payment would probably be in goods rather than cash, but it should be enough to buy my passage to Orkney. As I was rather weakly looking, I encountered little enthusiasm from the farmers. Winter was not the season when they needed extra hands, and an additional employee in the house had to be fed from the winter stocks of food. My other failing was that no one knew who I was. In Iceland's close-knit society that is a great disadvantage. Most people are aware of a person's origins, where he or she comes from, and what is their reputation. The people I spoke to knew only that I had been raised in Greenland and had spent some time in Vinland, a place few of them had even heard of. They were puzzled that I did not speak with the vocabulary of an ordinary labourer – I had Gudrid to thank for that – and I was certainly not slave-born, though once or twice people commented that my green-brown eyes made me look foreign. I supposed that I had inherited their colour from Thorgunna, but I could not tell them that I was Thorgunna's son. That would have been disastrous. I had made a few discreet enquiries about my mother, without saying why I wanted to know. The reactions had been very negative. My informant usually made some comment about 'foreign witches' and referred to something called 'the hauntings'. Not wanting to seem too curious, I did not pursue my enquiries. So, with the exception of Kari, I told no one about my parentage.

Thus my anonymity, which had been a help when Kari set me to spy on the Burners, was now a handicap, and I became anxious that I would not find a place to spend the autumn and winter. Yet, someone had made a very accurate guess as to who I was, and was keeping an eye on me.

He was Snorri Godi, the same powerful chieftain whose half-sister Thurid Barkadottir had stolen my mother's bed hangings at Frodriver.

Thus when I arrived from Greenland, bearing the name Thorgils, and of the right age to be Thorgunna's son, Snorri Godi guessed my true identity at once. Typically, he kept the knowledge to himself. He was a man who always considered carefully before any action, weighed up the pros and cons, then picked the right moment to act. He waited until I approached him at his booth on the penultimate day of the Althing, looking for work. He gave no indication that he knew who I was, but told me to report to his farm at a place called Tung five or six days' distance to the north-west at the head of a valley called Saelingsdale.

Snorri's bland appearance belied his reputation as a man of power and influence, and it would have been difficult to give him a nickname based on his physical looks. Now in late middle age, he was good-looking in a neutral way, with regular features and a pale complexion. His hair, once yellow, had turned grey by the time I met him, and so had his beard, which once had a reddish tinge. In fact, everything about Snorri was rather grey, including his eyes. But when you looked into them you realised that the greyness was not a matter of indifference, but of camouflage. When Snorri watched you with those quiet, grey eyes and with his expression motionless, it was impossible to know what he was thinking. People said that, whatever he was thinking, it was best to be on his side. His advice was sound and his enemies feared him.

Snorri turned that quiet look on me when I reported to him on the day I arrived at his farmhouse. I found him seated on a bench in the farthest shadowy corner of the main hall. 'You must be Thorgunna's son,' he said quietly, and I felt my guts coil and tighten. I nodded. 'Do you possess any of her powers?' he went on. 'Have you come because she sent you?'

I did not know what he was talking about, so I stood silently.

'Let me tell you,' continued Snorri, 'your mother left us very reluctantly. For months after her death, there were hauntings at Frodriver. Everyone knows about your mother's reappearance stark naked when they were taking her corpse for burial. But there was more. Many deaths followed at Frodriver. A shepherd died there under mysterious circumstances soon afterwards, and his draugar, his undead self, kept coming back to the farm and terrifying everyone living in the house. The draugar even beat up one of the farm workers. He met the worker in the darkness of the stable yard and knocked him about so badly that he took to his bed to convalesce and never recovered. He died a few days later, some said from pure fright. His draugar then joined the shepherd's draugar in tormenting the people. Soon half a dozen of the farm workers, mostly women, got sick and they too died in their beds. Next, Thorodd, the man who had given your mother a roof over her head when she came from Orkney, was drowned with his entire boat crew when they went to collect some supplies. Thorodd's ghost and the ghosts of his six men also kept reappearing at the house. They would walk in and sit down by the fire in their drenched clothes and stay until morning, then vanish. And for a long time afterwards there were mysterious rustlings and scratching at night.'

I remained silent, wondering where Snorri's talking was leading. He paused, eyeing me as if to judge me.

'Have you met my nephew, Kjartan?' he asked.

'I don't think so,' I replied.

'He was the only person who seemed to be able to quell the hauntings,' Snorri went on. 'That is why I'm sure your mother's spirit was responsible because in her life she really desired that young man. I think that even as a ghost she still lusted for him until finally she understood that he had no wish for her. She came back one last time, in the form of a seal, and poked her head up through the floor of the farmhouse at Frodriver. She was looking at him with imploring eyes, and Kjartan had to take a sledgehammer and flatten her head back down into the earth with several strong blows before she finally left him alone.'

I still did not know what to say. Had my mother really been so enamoured of a young teenager, scarcely three years older than I was now? It was unsettling for me to think about it, but I was too naive as yet to know how a woman can become just as hopelessly attracted by a man, as the other way around.

Snorri looked at me shrewdly. 'Are you a follower of the White Christ?' he asked.

'I don't know,' I stammered. 'My grandmother built a church for him in Brattahlid, but it wasn't used very much, at least not until Gudrid, who was looking after me, took an interest in going there. We didn't have a church in Vinland, but then we didn't have a temple to the Old Gods either, we only had the small altar that Thorvall made.'

'Tell me about Thorvall,' Snorri asked, and I found myself describing the cantankerous old hunter – how he had placed his trust in Thor, and vanished mysteriously, and was believed killed by the Skraelings. Snorri made no comment, except to ask an occasional question that encouraged me to talk further. When I told Snorri about Tyrkir and how I had worked alongside him in the smithy and learned something of the Old Ways, Snorri cross-examined me about Tyrkir's background, what the wizened German had told me of the various Gods and of their different legends, and how the world was formed. Occasionally he asked me to repeat myself. It was difficult to guess what Snorri was thinking, but eventually he stood up and told me to follow him. Without another word, he led me out of the house and across to one of the cattle byres. It was little more than a shed and from the outside looked like a typical cattle stable, except that it was round not oblong, and the roof was higher and rather more steeply pitched than usual. Snorri pushed open the wooden door and closed it behind us when we went in, shutting out the light.

When my eyes had adjusted to the dim interior, I saw that there were no cattle stalls. Instead the building was empty. There was only a bare earth floor and rising from it a circle of wooden poles supporting the steep cone of the roof, with a hole at the apex to let in the light. Then I realised that the poles were not necessary to the structure of the building.

'I built this four years ago when I moved here from my father's home,' Snorri was saying. 'It's a bit smaller than the original, but that does not matter. This does.' He had walked to the centre of the circular earth floor, and I now saw there was a low, round stone, very ancient and almost black, directly under the sky hole. The rock seemed to be natural, and was not carved or shaped in any way. There were irregular bumps and protuberances so that it was slightly misshapen. There was a shallow depression on its upper surface, like a basin.

Snorri walked over casually and picked up something which had been left lying in the basin. It was an arm ring, apparently made of iron and without any markings. Snorri handled its smooth surface, for it was much worn, then slipped it on his right arm, pushing it up just above his elbow. He turned to me. 'This is the priest's ring, the ring of Thor. It was my father's, and it is as precious to me as the cross of the White Christ. I continue to use it because

I know that there are times when Thor and the other Gods can help us here in Tung as they did my father and my grandfather before him.'

He was standing in the shaft of light that came in through the smoke hole so I could see his expression. His voice was utterly matter of fact, not in the least mystical or reverential. 'When Kjartan and the others came to ask my advice about the hauntings I went to the temple and put on the arm ring. Thinking about the hauntings and deaths, it came into my mind that the deaths might have something to do with the bed hangings that your mother left. She had said they were to be burned, but Thorodd, egged on by his wife Thurid, failed to do so. They kept some of the bedlinen, and somehow that brought the deaths and sickness. So I ordered that every last scrap of linen, sheets, hangings, drapery, everything, should be taken down and committed to the flames, and when that happened the sickness and death stopped. That is how Thor helped me to understand.'

'And did that stop the hauntings also? Was my mother ever seen again?' I enquired.

'Your mother's fetch was never seen again. The other hauntings ended when the White Christ priests went to the house and held a service to drive out the draugars and ghosts they like to call godless demons,' Snorri told me. 'They knew their job well enough to perform the matter correctly in the old way. The ghosts were summoned to appear and stand trial, just like in a law court, and told to leave the house. One by one the ghosts came, and each promised to return to the land of the dead. If the Christians believe that the White Christ himself appeared as a draugar after his death, then it is not so difficult to believe in ghosts that rise up through the floor as seals.'

Snorri slid the ring of Thor off his arm and replaced it on top of the altar.

'What made Thorvall and Tyrkir take so much trouble to teach you about the Old Ways?' he asked.

'They began after I became a uniped,' I said, and explained how my childish game had led them to believe that I could spirit-fly.

'So it seems that, like your mother, you do have seidr powers. That's how it usually is. The gift passes down through the family,' Snorri commented.

'Yes, but Tyrkir said that my spirit, my inner self, should also be able to leave my body and travel through space to see what is happening in other places. But that has never happened. It is just that at times I see people or places in a way that others do not.'

'When was the last time?' Snorri asked quietly.

I hesitated because it had been very recently. On the way to Tung I had stayed overnight at a large farm called Karstad. The farmer had been away when I called at the door and his wife had answered. I had explained that I was walking to Tung and asked if I could sleep the night in a corner of the main hall. The farmer's wife was old-fashioned; for her a stranger on the road was always to be given shelter, and she had put me with the household servants, who had provided me with a wooden bowl of sour whey and a lump of bread. Shortly before dusk the farmer had come in, and I was puzzled to see when he took off his cloak that the left side of his shirt was heavily soaked with fresh blood. But instead of enquiring what was the matter, his wife ignored the bright red stain and proceeded as if everything was normal. She produced the evening meal and her husband sat at the table, eating and drinking as if nothing was the matter. After the meal he walked over to be nearer the fire, pulled up a bench and began mending some horse harness. As he walked across the room, he came right past me where I was seated, and I could not keep my eyes off his blood-stained shirt. The gore still glistened. 'You see it too?' asked a thin, cracked voice. The questioner was so close that I jumped with fright. Turning, I found that an old woman had seated herself beside me and was looking at me with rheumy eyes. She had the mottled skin of the very elderly. 'I'm his mother,' the old woman said, nodding towards the farmer, 'but he won't listen to me.'

'I'm sorry, I'm a stranger,' I replied. 'What won't he listen to?'

I expected to hear the usual ramblings of an aged mother about her grown-up son, and I was preparing to invent some sort of an excuse – that I needed to visit the latrine – so that I could avoid this crazy old crone, when she went on, 'I've warned him that he will be hurt and hurt badly.'

Suddenly I felt giddy. Did she mean that she also saw how the man was bleeding heavily? And why had she spoken in the future tense? The blood seemed real enough to me.

I glanced across at the farmer. He was still unconcerned, pushing the awl through a broken horse harness. His shirt was sticking to his side it was so wet with blood. 'Why doesn't he take off the shirt so someone can attend the wound and staunch the bleeding?' I said in a low voice.

She laid a withered hand on my wrist and held tight. 'I knew you could see,' she said fiercely. 'I've been watching your face just as I've been watching that stain on his shirt for nearly three years past and still he won't listen to my warning. I told him to kill the creature, but he hasn't done so.'

This did not make sense, and I began to revert to my idea that the old woman was addled. 'Haven't you heard it?' she enquired, still holding me with her claw of a hand, thrusting her head forward until it was only a few inches from my face.

At this point her mutterings had lost me completely, and I was feeling uncomfortable, shifting in my seat. The farmer, sitting by the fire, must have noticed because he called out, 'Mother! Are you still going on about Glaesir. Leave the youngster alone, will you. I told you I don't believe there's any harm in the animal, and if there is I can deal with it.'

The old woman made a sniff of disgust, got slowly to her feet, and moved off down the hall. I was left to myself.

'Ignore her, young fellow,' called the farmer. 'And I wish you a safe journey wherever it is that you are going.'

'Was the farmer's name Thorodd?' asked Snorri, who had been standing silently, listening to my account.

'Yes, I think so,' I answered.

'He farms over at Karstad all right and there's a young bull in his herd called Glaesir. It's an animal you couldn't miss, spotted, very handsome. Frisky too. Some people think the animal is inhabited by the spirit of another Thorodd, a man called Thorodd Twist-foot. I had several quarrels with him. The worst was about the right to cut timber in a small woodland he owned. He got in such a rage that he went home and had a fit. Next morning they found him dead, sitting in his chair. They buried him twice. After the first time, when his ghost began plaguing his old farm, they dug up the corpse and shifted him to a hilltop, where they buried him under a big cairn. Then, when that didn't work and his ghost kept reappearing, they dug him up again. The grave diggers found that the body had not rotted away but just turned black and stank, so they burned the corpse to ashes on a pyre. Some say that the ash blew onto a nearby beach and was licked up by a cow feeding near the shoreline. The cow later gave birth to two calves, a heifer and a young bull calf. That's the one they call Glaesir. The Thorodd you met has a mother with second sight, or so it's said, and ever since that bull calf got on the farm, she's been wanting someone to kill it, saying that it will do terrible damage. Did you see the calf? He's a young prize bull now. Quite remarkable colouring.'

'No, I left the farm at first light next morning,' I replied. 'I wanted to get on my way early, and I didn't see Thorodd's mother again. I expect she was still asleep when I left. And there was nobody about, except for a few farm servants. I don't know anything about Glaesir. I just know that the farmer looked as if he had a serious injury to his side.'

Snorri was trying to assess what I had just told him. 'Maybe you do have second sight,' he said, 'but it's not quite in the usual way. I don't know. You seem to have it only when you are with others who also possess the gift. Like a mirror or something. You are young, so perhaps that will change. Either the sight will grow stronger or you will lose it altogether.'

He shrugged. 'I don't have the sight, though some people think

I do,' he said. 'My common sense tells me what is likely to happen, and the result is that many believe that I can see into the future or into men's minds.'

Whether Snorri believed I had the sight or not, from that moment onward he treated me as something more than a itinerant farm labourer. At the end of the day's work I was seated not among the farmhands down the far end of the hall, but alongside Snorri's large and rather boisterous family, and when he had free time – which was not often because he was such a busy man – he would continue with my education in the lore of the Old Gods. He was more knowledgeable in these matters than either Tyrkir or Thorvall the Hunter had been, and he had a more elegant way of explaining the intricacies of the Old Ways. Also, whenever Snorri went into the Thor temple, he expected me to go with him.

Such visits were surprisingly frequent. Local farmers came to pay their respects to Snorri as the local chieftain and ask his advice, and they spent hour after hour in the evenings, talking politics, negotiating land rights, discussing the weather and fishing prospects, and mulling over whatever news reached us via travellers or traders. But when the talking was over, and especially if the farmers had brought their families, Snorri would beckon to me and we would all walk across the farmyard to the temple shed, and there Snorri would hold a small ceremony to Thor. He would put on the iron arm ring, say prayers over the altar stone and present to Thor the small offerings brought by the farmers. Cheese, chickens, haunches of dried lamb were placed on the altar, or hung from nails driven into the ring of surrounding wooden pillars. These pillars were tied with ribbons brought by the farmers' wives, together with scraps of children's clothing, milk teeth wrapped in packets, embroidered belts and other personal articles. Frequently the women would ask Snorri to look into the future for them, to prophesy what would happen, what marriages their children would make, and so forth. At such moments Snorri would catch my eye and look slightly embarrassed. As he had warned me, his prophesies were largely based on common sense. For example, when a mother asked whom her young son would marry I noticed that Snorri often identified – though not exactly by name – the daughter of a neighbour who, like as not, had visited the temple the previous week and asked exactly the same question about her young daughter. I never found out whether any, or all, of Snorri's matrimonial prophecies came true, but the fact that the parents thenceforward nurtured the probability of a particular match for their offspring must have helped to bring it about.

However, on one particular occasion which I will always remember, Snorri behaved differently. A small group of farmers – there were about eight of them – had come to see him because they were worried about the weather for the hay harvest. That year there had been little sunshine and the hay growth was exceptionally slow. But eventually the long grass in the meadows was ready to be cut and dried, and everyone was waiting for a spell of good dry weather to do the work. But the days continued cloudy and damp, and the farmers were increasingly worried. If they did not get in their hay crop, they would be obliged to slaughter many of their cattle for lack of winter feed. A bad hay crop, or worse, no hay crop at all, would be a major misfortune. So they came to Snorri to ask him to intercede on their behalf because, of course, Thor controls the weather. Snorri led the farmers into the temple building and I went with them. Once inside, Snorri made offerings, rather more lavish than usual, and called on Thor, using the fine rolling phrases and archaic Norse vocabulary which are a mark of respect to the Gods. But then Snorri did something more. He called forward the farmers to stand around the central altar stone. Next he made them form a circle and join hands. Snorri himself was a member of the circle and so was I. Then Snorri called out to the men and they began to dance. It was the simplest of the stamping dances of the Norsemen, an uncomplicated rhythm, with a double step to the left, then a pause, a step back, a pause, and then two steps more to the left, their clasped hands swinging out the rhythm. The men swayed down and then arched back at the end of each double step.

As I joined in, I had a strange feeling of familiarity. Somewhere I had heard that rhythm before. For a moment I could not recall when and where. Then I remembered the sound that I had heard while wandering in the forest of Vinland, the strange rhythmic sound that had led me to the shelter of branches with the sick Skraeling inside, and the older man chanting over his body and shaking his rattle. It was the same cadence that I now heard from the Icelandic farmers. Only the words were different. Snorri began a refrain, repeating over and over the same phrases, and this time he was not speaking archaic Norse. He was using a language that I could not recognise. Again there seemed to be something distantly familiar about it. Several of the farmers must have known the same spell language because they began to chant in time with Snorri. Eventually, after nine circuits of the altar, left-handed against the sun, we stopped our dance, straightened up and Snorri turned to face north-west across the altar. He raised his arms, repeated another phrase in the same strange language, and then the spell session was over.

The next four days, as it happened, were bright and sunny. There was a perfect drying wind and we gathered and stacked the hay. Whether or not this was because we had performed our nature-spell I have no idea, but every farmer in the Westfjords managed to save his hay for the winter, and I am sure that each man's faith in Thor increased. Later, at a discreet moment, I dared to ask Snorri whether he thought the fine weather was the result of our incantations, and he was non-committal. 'I had a feeling in my bones that we were finally due for a dry spell,' he said. 'There was a change in the air, the moon was entering a new phase and the birds began to fly higher. Maybe the dry weather was already on its way and our appeal to Thor only meant that we were not disappointed.'

'What was the language you used when we were dancing in a circle?' I asked him.

He looked at me pensively. 'Under other circumstances you would know it already,' he said. 'It is the language of many spells and incantations, though I only know a few words of it. It is the native language of your mother, the language of the Irish.'

Four days later a messenger arrived from Karstad to ask Snorri to officiate at a burial. Farmer Thorodd was dead. During the haymaking on his farm, the young bull Glaesir had been kept confined to a stall as he was troublesome, and the labourers needed to mow the home meadows without being disturbed by the aggressive young bull. As soon as the hay was put up in haycocks, they had let Glaesir out on the stubble. First they took the precaution of tying a heavy block of wood over his horns to restrain and tire him. Glad to be free, the animal had charged up and down the largest of the home meadows. Within moments he had shaken off the block of wood and, something he had never done before, he began assaulting the carefully stacked haycocks. Ramming his horns into the stacks, he shook his head and scattered the hay in all directions. The farm workers were angry to see their work destroyed, but too fearful of the young bull to interfere. Instead they had sent word to Thorodd at the main house. He arrived, took one look at the situation and seized a stout wooden pole. Then he vaulted the low wall into the paddock and advanced on Glaesir.

Previously Glaesir had shown a unique respect for Thorodd. Alone of all the people on the farm, Thorodd was able to handle the young bull. But this time Glaesir had dropped his head and charged the farmer. Thorodd stood his ground and, as the bull closed with him, brought the heavy wooden pole down with a massive thump, striking Glaesir on the crown of the head right between the horns. The blow stopped Glaesir in his tracks and the animal stood there shaking his head in a daze. The force of the blow had broken the wooden pole in half, so Thorodd – confident of his mastery over the bull – strode forward and grasped Glaesir by the head, seeking to twist the horns and bring the animal to his knees. For a few moments the tussle went on. Then Thorodd's foot slipped on the short cut grass, and he lost his purchase. Glaesir jerked backwards and gave his head a shake which partially broke

Thorodd's grip. Thorodd managed to keep one hand on the left horn and, stepping behind the bull, boldly vaulted onto Glaesir's back, putting his body right forward on the animal's neck, intending that his weight – for Thorodd was a big, heavy man – would eventually subdue the young bull. Glaesir bolted down the field, swerving and twisting from side to side in an attempt to dislodge the burden on his back. The bull was quick and agile and stronger than Thorodd had anticipated. An unlucky leap, a change of direction in mid-air, unseated Thorodd and he began to slip to one side. Glaesir must have sensed the change, for he turned his head, placed a horn under Thorodd and got enough leverage to throw the farmer up into the air. As Thorodd fell back down towards the animal, Glaesir raised his head and the farmer fell straight onto one of the horns, which pierced his gut on the left side, low down. The horn drove deep. Thorodd fell off the bull and lay in a heap, as Glaesir, suddenly quiet, trotted off and began grazing. The farmhands ran into the field and picked up their master. They placed Thorodd on a hurdle and carried him up to the farmhouse. As they reached the door, Thorodd insisted on getting off the hurdle and walking into his own house upright. He lurched into the hall, the right side of his shirt drenched in blood. That night he died.

When the messenger finished his story, Snorri dismissed him, and waved away the small crowd who had gathered to hear the gruesome tale. Then he beckoned to me to follow him and led me to the small sleeping closet at the side of the hall. It was unoccupied and the only place where he could speak to me privately.

'Thorgils,' he asked, 'how many people did you tell about your vision of Thorodd in his blood-stained shirt?'

'No one apart from yourself.' I replied. 'I am sure that Thorodd's mother saw the blood too, but we were the only people to see it.'

'Let me give you some advice,' Snorri went on. 'Don't ever tell anyone else that you saw Thorodd's blood-stained shirt before his accident happened. In fact, I advise you not to talk to people whenever your second sight foretells anything that can be interpreted in a sinister way, particularly if there is any hint of death in it. People become fearful and nervous. Sometimes they think that a seer can cause an event to happen, and that once a seer has seen a vision, he or she shapes the future to make the vision come true, and they do this to enhance their reputations as visionaries. When ordinary people start to think like this, and some tragedy does occur, things can get very ugly. Fear leads to violence. People take revenge or try to remove the source of their fear by hurting the seer.'

'But aren't seers and volva and seidrmanna respected?' I asked, 'I thought that it was forbidden to spill their blood.'

'So it is. The last time that the people of this area mistrusted a magician, it was a man named Kolmek. He was another half-Irish like yourself, just a small farmer, who could see portents and make forecasts. A gang of his neighbours grabbed him one evening, pulled a sack over his head and bound it so tight that he choked to death. That didn't spill a drop of his blood. Nor did the way they dealt with Kolmek's wife. They accused her of black witchcraft. They carried her to a bog, tied a heavy stone round her feet and dropped her in.'

Already reticent about my dreams and second sight, I made a silent promise to myself that only in the most extreme circumstances would I disclose what my second sight revealed to me and not to others. Also I began to suspect that my flashes of second sight came from Odinn himself and, like all of Odinn's gifts, they could cause both help and harm.

TWELVE

HALLBERA WAS SNORRI'S fourth daughter. She had light freckles on healthy pale skin, rounded arms with a light fuzz of golden down, blue-grey eyes, blonde hair worn long and a face that was perfectly symmetrical. In short, she was the epitome of a normal, wholesome, good-looking Norse maiden. She adored her brothers, of whom she had eight, and she got on well with her sisters, of whom she also had eight. Indeed, if any proof is needed that Snorri Godi was more pagan than Christian, it is the fact that he had one official wife, and a second wife, whom he never married but made clear was his second consort. And he treated all their children equally. Hallbera's background in such a large and well-to-do family could scarcely have been more different from mine as an impoverished newcomer living on the fringes of her father's household. There were many times when I felt overawed by the energy and self-confidence of the Snorrissons and Snorradottirs. But I was smitten. I did everything I could to stay in her father's favour so that I could be close to this honey-gold girl. For the first time in my life I was in love.

Quite why Hallbera accepted my infatuation is something I have never been able to explain fully. There was really no reason for her to take up with such a modest prospect as myself. The only explanation that I can find is that she was bored and perhaps curious as to how to manage the opposite sex, and I was conveniently on hand to experiment with. There was nothing improper about our relationship. Hallbera and I began to meet quietly, exchange kisses and indulge in some gentle cuddling. These physical contacts made my head spin and I would feel weak for half an hour afterwards, though Hallbera never seemed to experience similar surges of emotions. She was always so robust and crisp and energetic. She was capable of emerging from an embrace, suddenly announcing that she had promised to help one of her brothers in some task, and go bouncing off in her athletic stride, her blonde hair swinging, leaving me dazed with emotion and completely baffled. I am sure that Snorri guessed at the relationship between his daughter and myself, and there is no doubt that it was known to Hallbera's mother. But neither of them chose to interfere because there were so many other children and more important matters to occupy their attention.

In the throes of calf love, I would go off for hours to some quiet corner and fall into a trance, meditating on how I could spend the rest of my life close to that glorious, milk-and-honey girl. Now I realise that I wanted more than just Hallbera. I was longing to be absorbed for ever into the embrace of a large family, where everything seemed to be in a perpetual state of sunny commotion and bustle, where there were few problems which, when they did arise, were solved in moments by mutual help and support. In short, I was feeling lonely and insecure, and my view of Snorri's family was a fantasy which overlooked the fact that my darling Hallbera was no more than a thoroughly normal, conventional young woman in the blush of her maidenhood.

The conversation that autumn was all about a local bandit by the name of Ospak, and what should be done about him. Listening to the discussions, I learned that Ospak had plagued the region for many years. He had always been a bully. A brute by nature and in stature, he had started his mischief when he was still in his teens, knocking about his neighbours and generally terrorising them. As he grew to middle age, he graduated to systematic oppression of the people living within reach and a gang of similar-minded ruffians soon clustered around him. On one notorious occasion he and a gang of his toughs showed up when a dead fin whale had been stranded on a beach. By Icelandic law the division of anything washed up on a beach is strictly controlled. Each stretch of rocky foreshore belongs to the farmers who own the driftage rights there. Dead whales, lengths of driftwood, bits and pieces from boat wrecks, are all considered valuable. They are so precious, in fact, that the first pioneers developed an ingenious system of selecting where to build their homes. Sailing along the new-found coast, the captain of the vessel would throw overboard the carved wooden panels that traditionally stand on each side of the high chair in a Norse hall. Later, going ashore, the new arrivals would range the coast looking to see where the panels had washed up. There they built their home and claimed the beach rights because they knew that the sea currents would supply an endless source of bounty at that spot.

On the day the fin whale washed up, the farmers who owned the driftage rights went down to the beach early in the morning to check what the sea had cast up. The previous night there had been a great gale from the direction which normally brought the best flotsam, and sure enough the carcass of the whale, dead from natural causes, was found lying in the shallows. The farmers went home, fetched their cutting spades and axes and began to butcher the dead whale. They had peeled back the blubber and got as far as cutting up large chunks of the meat, stacking it in piles ready to be shared out, when Ospak appeared. He had no driftage rights, but knew the wind and waves as well as anyone and had rowed across the bay with fifteen of his gang, all heavily armed. They came ashore and demanded a share of the meat, only to be told by one of the farmers, a man named Thorir, that if the other workers agreed they would sell Ospak what he wanted. Ospak gruffly told Thorir that he had no intention of paying and instructed his men to begin loading their boat. When Thorir objected, Ospak struck him on the ear with the flat of an axe blade and knocked him unconscious. The rest of the farmers, outnumbered, were in no position to resist. They had to look on while Ospak and his men filled their boat with as much meat as they could carry, and rowed off, taunting their unfortunate victims.

The following year Ospak's behaviour became even more wild. He and his men took to raiding isolated farms and looting them, often tying up the farmer and his family. They carried off whatever valuables they could find, all spare stocks of food, and drove away the cattle and horses. They operated with impunity because the farmers were poorly organised, and Ospak had taken the trouble to fortify his own farmhouse so strongly that it was dangerous to counter-attack. His following increased to at least twenty men, all desperadoes attracted by the chance of easy pickings. But the more men Ospak recruited, the more he had to extend his raids to obtain them enough supplies. So the vicious cycle continued unabated. Some time before I joined Snorri's household, Ospak and his men had raided Thorir's farm, pillaged it and dragged Thorir outside and killed him. The raiders then headed on towards a farm owned by another of the men who had been at the whale kill, and against whom Ospak bore a grudge. Fortunately Alf, known as Alf the Short, was fully dressed and still awake when the raiders arrived, though it was late in the evening when most people would have been in bed and asleep. Alf managed to slip out of the rear of the house as the raiders battered down the front door, and he ran off across the moor, heading for refuge with Snorri, who was one of the few men in the district too powerful for Ospak to meddle with.

Snorri heard Alf's tale and his plea for help. But though he gave Alf shelter for as long as he wanted to stay, Snorri waited several months without taking any action against Ospak. For this Snorri was criticised by many, but it was typical of his style. Snorri never did anything in haste, and only after he had made meticulous preparations did he reveal his hand. He wanted more information about Ospak's defences, and asked if I would visit Ospak's fortified farm. Ostensibly I was calling to look for work. In reality I was, once again, a spy and – as Snorri made this request just when I was in the full fever of my passion for Hallbera and badly wanted to impress her – I accepted without hesitation.

It took me two days to walk across country to Ospak's stronghold, and as I approached his farmhouse I could see that he had built a tall palisade made of timber and closed the entrance to the stockade with massive double gates. Round the inside of the palisade ran an elevated walkway, which would allow the defenders to stand at the rampart and hurl missiles down at any attackers who came too close. Even more daunting was the garrison. I saw at least twenty heavily armed men, including one ugly specimen who affected the old-fashioned style of weaving his long beard in plaits, which he arranged in a mat down his chest. Snorri had already told me about this flamboyant villain, who went by the name of Hrafn the Vikingr. He was a simple-minded, lumbering sort of oaf who drank away his spoils and was already under sentence of full outlawry for committing a random murder.

I also laid eyes, for the first time, on a second, rather more intriguing outlaw at Ospak's farm. When I walked in through the massive wooden gates I saw a young man sitting in the farmyard on a bench, moodily carving a piece of wood with his knife. I remember he was wearing a brown tunic and blue leggings, and that he seemed to control a repressed fury. The pale shavings were curling up from his knife blade and jumping into the air like nervous insects. Only the breadth of his shoulders, his long arms and powerful hands gave a hint of how he had earned his name, Grettir the Strong. I was interested to meet him because he was only two years older than myself, yet already infamous throughout Iceland. He was not a member of Ospak's band but visiting the fortified farm with his sister, who was betrothed to Ospak's son. All sorts of stories were circulating about Grettir the Strong. Even as a young boy he had been uncontrollable. He wilfully disobeyed his parents, refused to help on the family farm and spent most of his time sprawling lazily in the house. When forced to get to his feet and carry out any chore, Grettir made sure he did it in such a way that he was never asked to do the same job again. Sent to lock up the poultry for the night, he left the chicken-shed door ajar so the birds escaped onto the moors. Told to groom the prize stallion, he deliberately scored its back with a sharp knife point so the wretched animal was invalided. He was an impossible youth, wayward and perverse. Nor was he affable with his contemporaries. He was always picking fights, quarrelling and brawling, and he made few friends. I had first heard his name mentioned that winter when I and several of Snorri's younger children were out on the frozen fjord, playing an ice game. We had divided into two teams and were using shaped sticks to hit a small ball through a mark. One of my team lost his temper and rushed at an opponent, threatening to smash him on the head with his stick. It was called 'doing a Grettir'. I found out that Grettir had famously attacked an opponent during the ice game and nearly killed him when he hit the boy so hard that his skull cracked. Three months later Grettir killed a man in a quarrel over, of all things, a leather flask of skyr, sour milk. After that brawl, Grettir was sentenced to lesser outlawry, and when I met him he was in the second grace year, preparing to leave Iceland and seek service with the King of Norway. At that time I had no inkling that one day Grettir would become perhaps my closest friend.

Ospak bluntly turned me away, saying that he had no work for me. However, in the few hours I spent inside his stockade I was able to glean enough information to report on Ospak's force and defences to Snorri when I got back to Saelingsdale.

I told Snorri what I had seen, and as usual he made little comment. He had been talking with the local chieftains about organising a unified attack on the brigands, and he was prepared to wait until all his allies were free to join him, and also for an excuse to assemble them without arousing Ospak's suspicions. The one person he did summon to Saelingsdale in advance of his attack was a former member of his household who had now set up as a farmer on his own account – Thrand Stigandi.

Thrand was the sort of person who causes people to lower their voices nervously when they catch sight of him. A head taller than any other man in the neighbourhood, he had a leathery, competent air and was known to be handy with sword and axe. He also looked formidable, with a craggy face, a great prow of a nose, and bushy eyebrows that he could pull down in a ferocious scowl. Anyone facing Thrand in a quarrel would have second thoughts about resorting to physical violence. But within moments of Thrand walking into Snorri's house I knew that there was another, hidden reason why Snorri had summoned him. When Thrand entered the main hall, I was standing slightly to the left of the entrance, and as he came into the room, he glanced to one side and caught my eye. The moment that happened he paused in his stride and waited for the space of a heartbeat. In that instant I recognised the same cool, calm look I had seen eighteen months before in Vinland, on the day I had stumbled across the two Skraelings in the forest. It was in the eyes of the Skraeling shaman when I blundered into the sick man's shelter. I guessed at once that Thrand was a seidrman, and my intuition was confirmed when Snorri and Thrand went that same evening to Thor's temple and spent many hours there. Thrand, I was sure, was communing with the God.

Thrand's arrival had the same effect on me as when I saw the blood-stained shirt in the company of Thorodd's mother, or when I saw the ghost of my dead uncle with Gudrid. The presence of someone who could also see into the spirit world aroused the spirit energy within me. On the second night after Thrand's arrival I had my first omen dream.

I dreamed of a farm that was under attack. Half awake, half asleep, I was in a dimness that was neither night nor day. The attackers had surrounded the building and were pressing home their assault with great ferocity, and I was conscious of the shouts of the combatants and the screams of women inside the building. Several times the thud of blows jolted me part awake, though they were sounds that could only have existed within my dream. The first time I woke, I told myself that my nightmare was a memory of all the horrors that I had heard about the Burning when Njal and his family had been massacred. But as I slipped back into the nightmare I realised that the farm I was watching was not being attacked with fire. There were no flames, no smoke, only the figures of men running here and there, occasionally hurling themselves at the rampart. Then I saw that it was Ospak's farm, and among the assailants was Thrand. His tall form was unmistakable, but he seemed to have an owl's head, and there was something about the conflict which reminded me of how the Skraelings had fought when they attacked us in Vinland. I woke up sweating.

In the morning I recalled Snorri's warning about keeping silent about my visions, particularly if they involved death or harm, and I told no one.

Snorri moved against Ospak's farm some three weeks later and with overwhelming force. Every able-bodied worker from the farm, including myself, joined the expedition. On our march across the moor we met a column of fifty farmers led by a neighbouring chieftain, Sturla, who had brought his people to assist in the campaign. Our joint company must have amounted to at least eighty combatants, though, as usual, there were very few trained fighters among them. Everyone carried a sword or an axe, plus his dagger, but there was a noticeable shortage of defensive armour. A few men wore leather jackets sewn with small metal plates, but most of the farmers were relying on their wooden shields and thick leather jerkins to protect them from any missiles that Ospak and his cronies would hurl at them from the rampart. In our entire war band I counted only a dozen metal helmets, and one of those was an antique. Instead of the conical modern style with its noseguard, it was round like a pudding bowl and the wearer's face was hidden behind two round eyepieces. I was not in the least surprised that the man who carried that helmet was Thrand.

Ospak's scouts must have been watching the trail because when we came in sight of the farmhouse the gates were already shut and barred, and we could see his men had taken up their positions on the elevated walkway. Snorri and Sturla held a short council and agreed that to make the best use of our own superior numbers all four sides of the farm should be attacked simultaneously. Snorri found that he was facing the forces commanded by Hrafn the Vikingr, while Sturla and his men attacked the section of the rampart where Ospak led the defence.

The siege of the farmhouse opened with a barrage of rocks and small boulders which the opposing forces hurled at one another. In this phase of the battle, the defenders on the elevated walkway held a considerable advantage, as they were able to drop boulders on any of the attackers who came too close. Their weakness was their limited supply of boulders and other missiles, so Snorri's and Sturla's forces spent the first hour or so of their attack making quick feints up to the palisade, shouting insults and throwing stones, then turning to run back as they dodged the counter-hail of missiles. When the defenders' supply of stones ran low, the attackers began to run right up to the palisade, concentrating on the fortified gateway and attempting to break through by hacking and levering at the planks. This tactic, however, had little success as the gates were too stoutly built, and the assaults were beaten back. The attackers threw few spears because they tended to bounce off the ramparts, or if one flew over the wall and landed in the compound, one of the defenders was likely to pick it up and hurl it back with more dangerous effect. Only a couple of men on either side used bows and arrows because, quite simply, they are seldom used among Icelanders in their quarrels – they much prefer hand-to-hand fighting.

The rather untidy assault had been in progress for a couple of hours when it seemed to me that the enthusiasm of the attackers was waning. It was at that moment that Thrand showed his worth. Wearing his antique helmet, he sprinted forward from our group, ran up to the palisade and, using the advantage of his great height, sprang into the air so that he leaped high enough to hook the blade of his battleaxe over the top of the palisade. He then grabbed the handle of the axe in both hands and pulled himself upwards, so that he got a leg over the rampart and was able to jump down on the walkway on the far side. There he came face to face with Hrafn the Vikingr, who rushed at him with a great roar of anger. Thrand dodged the Viking's clumsy spear thrust, knocked the plait-bearded warrior off balance, and hacked at the outstretched arm that held the spear. The axe blow was perfectly aimed. It struck Hrafn on the right shoulder and severed his arm from his body. Hrafn reeled sideways, slipped from the walkway and fell with a heavy thud into the compound below. As Ospak's men looked at the fallen body of their champion in shock, Thrand took advantage of the moment to vault back over the rampart, drop to the ground and run back to rejoin us. His intervention demoralised the defenders. Ospak's men began to fight with less bravado and, seeing this, Snorri sent me with a message for Sturla, who was attacking the opposite side of farm. I was to tell him to launch an all-out assault now that the defence was in disarray.

I ran round the side of the farm, scrambling over the low sod walls that marked out the home pasture, and reached Sturla just in time to see him step forward holding a weapon that I vaguely recognised. It was a thin, flat board, about as long as a man's arm, and I had first seen it when the Skraelings attacked us in Vinland and, most recently, it had appeared in my nightmare. It was a spear thrower. Where Sturla had obtained this device I do not know. But he knew how to use it, for he ran forward until close enough to the rampart to deliver an accurate strike. Ospak must not have known what Sturla was carrying because when he saw Sturla come so close, Ospak jumped up on the lip of the rampart, made an obscene gesture, and raised a large rock above his head with both hands, ready to toss it on Sturla's head. Ospak was wearing protective armour that few Icelanders could afford – a thigh-length shirt of chain mail, which protected almost his entire body. But the action of raising the rock lifted the skirt of the chain mail and exposed his upper thigh. Seeing his target, Sturla swung the spear thrower in its arc and delivered its projectile. The spear shot upward. The iron head of the spear was long and slender, with two small flanges to serve as wings. Behind it uncoiled a loop of line. The spear's point passed clean through Ospak's thigh and, as he staggered, Sturla gathered the line in both hands and gave a tremendous jerk. Like a fish that has been harpooned, Ospak was literally plucked off the wall and pulled down to the ground. Gesturing to his companions to stand back, Sturla ran forward, drew his dagger and stabbed Ospak through the heart.

The death of their leader ended all resistance from Ospak's gang. They lowered their weapons and began shouting out that they would leave the building if they were allowed to go unharmed. A moment later the double gates of the stockade were tugged open. Snorri, Sturla and the rest of us walked into the compound to find the bandits looking frightened and exhausted. Hrafn, Ospak and one other man were the only fatalities, but many of the defenders had minor wounds and bruises. Snorri kept his word and was remarkably lenient with their punishment. He held a brief court hearing on the spot, and in his capacity as the local godi condemned the worst culprits to exile. He did not have the power to exile them from Iceland, but he could forbid them to come ever again into Westfjords on pain of being prosecuted as full outlaws at the next Althing. The men were obliged to leave their weapons behind and quit the farm immediately, never to return. Snorri treated Ospak's widow and son magnanimously. The widow, he said, had not had any choice in her husband's behaviour, and though the son had fought in the defence of the farm, he was honour-bound to do so for his family's reputation. He had not been involved in his father's brigandage, and in consequence Snorri pronounced that the widow and son could continue in possession of the farm and its lands.

Thrand Stigandi stayed on at Snorri's farm for several weeks after Ospak's defeat at the battle of Bitra, as it came to be called, and there were many who came to congratulate him on his bravery and some, more discreetly, to thank him for interceding with Thor on behalf of the law-abiding people of the Westfjords. Snorri must have told Thrand about me and I was flattered when Thrand beckoned to me one evening as supper was being cleared from the table and led me to a quiet corner, where we could not be overheard. He sat down on a storage chest and said in his deep, husky voice, 'Snorri tells me that sometimes you see things which others cannot see.'

'Yes, occasionally,' I replied, 'but I don't understand what I am seeing, and I never know when it will happen.'

'Can you give me an example?' he asked.

I thought of Snorri's warning never to reveal dreams of death to anyone, but the events were in the past and Snorri had assured me that Thrand was seidr-skilled so I told him about my dream of the battle at Ospak's farm, the owl-headed man, and the rest.

Thrand did not interrupt, and when I had finished my account, he said, 'And how many days before the fight did you have this dream?'

'Soon after your arrival here, on the night after you and Snorri spent so much time in Thor's temple,' I answered.

'I wonder if you would have had the dream earlier, in the temple itself, if the conditions had been right,' Thrand commented, almost speaking to himself. 'Some seers are lucky. Dreams come to them so easily that they need only to withdraw to some quiet place, close their eyes and empty their minds, and the visions enter their consciousness. Others must get fuddled on strong drink, or chew strong weeds, or breathe the smoke of a sacred fire, or listen to sacred chants repeated over and over again until their spirit floats free from their body.'

He got up and went to where his sword and helmet were hanging from a peg on the wall. He brought them over and showed the flat of the sword's blade to me. 'What does that mean?' he asked.

The runes were easy to decipher and simple. 'Ulfbert made,' I replied.

'Now, what about this?' he continued, holding out his antique helmet with its quaint eye protectors. He had turned the helmet upside down so I could see inside the metal bowl. From the centre, radiating down to each side, was incised a plain, thin cross, its arms ending in arrow heads which pointed back towards the intersection.

'That's the aegishjalmr,' I said, 'the helm of awe.' 'Yes,' replied Thrand, 'but what about the marks around the edge?'

I looked more closely. Around the inner rim of the helmet I could see a number of small scratches. They were badly worn, but they had been put there deliberately. Several of them I recognised immediately as rune staves in the futhark, but others were more difficult to decipher. I ran my finger round them, to feel their shapes, as Tyrkir had taught me. Several I identified as letters which Tyrkir had said were little used nowadays. In the end, I did manage to puzzle them out.

'I don't know what it means, but if I try to read out the message it would sound something like . . . a g mod den juthu pt fur . . . but I cannot be sure.'

Thrand looked thoughtful. 'No more than half a dozen people in Iceland know how to read the archaic runes,' he said. 'That's galdrastafir – rune spell. It was put there soon after the helmet was forged, and the staves make the helmet a talisman against harm to the wearer, as well as a physical protection. I would never exchange this antique helmet for a modern one. Who taught you the archaic runes?'

'An old German, a metalsmith named Tyrkir, instructed me in how to read and cut rune staves while I was in Greenland.'

Thrand said solemnly, 'The message you carve in runes is more important than just knowing what each stave represents. Quite a few people know how to carve their name, but only the initiated know the spells and charms and curses that can be written. Odinn showed rune writing to mankind and now it is merely a matter of passing the knowledge from one person to the next.'

He seemed to make up his mind about something, turned towards me and, speaking to me as if I was an adult and not a fourteen-year-old lad, he went on:

'The greatest and most profound visions require pain and sacrifice. Odinn gave one of his eyes in order to drink from the fountain of Mimir and learn the secret wisdom which allows the Gods to survive. He also impaled himself on a spear and hung for nine days from Yggdrasil, the world tree, in order to learn the secret of the runes. Only through the sacrifice and pain could he open his mind and spirit to wisdom. That is one thing which distinguishes us from the Christians. They believe that the soul lives in the heart, but we hold that it resides in the mind, and that when the mind is set free the spirit also is liberated.'

Unwittingly I had allowed my rune literacy to impress Thrand in a way that was to have painful consequences. When he was ready to return to his own farm, he suggested to Snorri that I go with him and become his pupil in seidr skills. Snorri summoned me and, watching me with those quiet grey eyes, said, 'Thrand has offered to take you on as a pupil. I believe that this is your chance to develop a talent that you were born with and which may yet compensate for the disadvantages you have already faced in your young life. For that reason I am closing my house to you and sending you away.'

Thus I began to appreciate how the acquisition of knowledge can mean pain and sacrifice, for I was heart-broken to be parted from my adored Hallbera. Years later, long after my departure from Snorri's household, I learned that she married an eminently suitable husband, the son of a neighbouring landowner whose help Snorri needed at a session of the Althing. Her young man was ideal – respectable, well-connected, reliable. He was also decidedly dull. I am sure that Hallbera was very happy with him. The last I heard was that they had their own family of seven or eight children, lived on a well-run farm on the Westfjords, and were similarly looking for suitable matches for their numerous offspring. On the few occasions when I imagine myself as that young man Hallbera could have married, I wonder whether it was Hallbera's wish to have a more settled future that made her marry her worthy husband, or whether once again it was Odinn's intervention that led her family to judge me to be no more than a pleasant and temporary diversion for their fourth daughter.

THE SUMMER THAT I spent with Thrand at his farm in the uplands behind Laxadale was perhaps the most formative period of my life.

Thrand lived by himself on a small homestead, no more than a single cabin with a barn nearby. His dwelling was sparsely furnished with only a couple of stools, a pair of wooden cots, his iron cooking pot and griddle – he did all his own cooking – and a few large storage chests, always kept locked. The walls of his cabin were bare except for several foreign-looking wall hangings with strange patterns, which I could not decipher, and a row of pegs from which Thrand hung his weapons and various satchels and cloth bundles containing his seidr materials. The place was so orderly that it was stark, and this reflected the character of its owner. My teacher in seidr was reserved and self-controlled to the point of austerity and as a result he was very difficult to get to know. I am sure he never meant to seem unfriendly but if I plucked up enough courage to ask a question, the answer was sometimes so slow in coming that I feared he thought me stupid or that he had not heard the question. When the answer came – and it always did, though I might have to wait until the next day – it was terse, accurate and clear-cut. It was to take me a long time to grow fond of Thrand, but from the start I respected him.

He was a methodical teacher. Patiently he built on the foundation of the knowledge that Tyrkir and Thorvall had imparted. Sometimes he found it necessary to correct errors. My earlier mentors had occasionally muddled the roles of the Aesir, the family of Gods, and at other times I had misunderstood their lessons. So Thrand began by putting my chaotic knowledge in some sort of order and then went on to expand and deepen the details. I progressed from my basic knowledge of the main Gods and Goddesses of the Aesir and Vanir, and became aware of an entire pantheon, and this in addition to the Norns and light-elves and dark-elves and dwarves, and frost giants and the otherworld creatures and the roles they played in the ancient cosmology. 'Everything interlocks,' Thrand was fond of saying. 'Think of the braiding roots of the World Tree, where one root tangles with another, and then reaches out to a third, and then doubles back and binds on itself, or the spreading branches above which do the same. Yet all the roots and branches have a function. They sustain Yggdrasil and they are Yggdrasil. This is how it is with ancient lore. If you have the foundation knowledge, you can follow the path of a single root or just one strand, or you can stand back and see the whole pattern.'

Committing the lore to memory was surprisingly easy. It seemed that every deed, every deity, every detail, had been set into a language that flowed and rippled seductively, or laid out in lists that marched to a steady beat. Even now, half a century later, I can count off all forty-eight names of Odinn – from Baleygr, Harbardr and Herblindi, to Herian, Hialmberi, Thekkr, Thriggi, Thundr, Unnr, Viudurr, Yrungr, and so forth. The ones that still make my heart beat faster when I hear them in my head are: Aldafadr, All-Father; Draugadrottin, Lord of the Dead; Grimnir, the Masked One; Farmognudr, Maker of Journeys and Gangleri, the Wanderer.

Tyrkir and Thorvall had told me the simple tales that illustrate the deeds of the Gods – that the earth quakes when Loki writhes in his bonds, that the gales arise from the flapping wings of the great eagle giant Hraesvelg, and that lightning is the flash of Mjollnir when Thor hurls his hammer. Now Thrand placed these tales in their wider context. He explained the relationship between deeds past and the events that still lie in the future, and how at their intersection lies what happens today. And always he emphasised that everything interweaves, so that while those who were gifted with second sight might look into the future, there was little we could do to avert what had been ordained by the Norns. Those three supernatural women hold the ultimate power, for they have decided the fate of every living creature and even of the Gods themselves.

'The greater pattern cannot be altered,' Thraud emphasised to me. 'Even the Gods themselves know that they must inevitably face Ragnarok and the destruction of the world. With all their power they can only delay that fatal time, not avoid it. How much less can we, mere mortals, alter the web that the Norns have spun for us or the marks they have cut in the timber of our lives.'

Thrand was a firm believer in divination. If fate was set, then it could be revealed by skilled interpretation. He owned a casting set of rune blocks, carved from whalebone and yellow with age. He would spread out a white sheet and throw the blocks on the sheet like dice, then puzzle over the way the symbols fell, reading the message in their random patterns and then explaining their symbolism to me. Often the message was obscure, even more frequently it was contradictory. But that, as he explained to me, was in the nature of the runes themselves. Each owned two meanings, at the very least, and these meanings were opposites; whether they occurred in light or dark conjunctions determined which was the correct sense. I found it all very confusing, though I managed to grasp most of the basic principles.

Galdrastafir, the rune spells, were more straightforward and reminded me of the smith's galdr that Tyrkir had taught me. Thrand would take practice pieces of timber and show me how to carve correctly the sequence of runes, dividing my lessons into categories: mind runes for bringing knowledge, sea runes for safe journeys, limb runes for healing, speech runes to fend off revenge, the helping runes for childbirth. 'Don't be surprised if they are ineffective sometimes,' he warned me. 'Odinn himself only learned eighteen rune spells when he was hanging on Yggdrasil, and we are presumptuous to think that we can achieve more.' The accuracy of cutting was not all, he stressed. Every stave had its own spoken formula, which I had to recite as I made the mark, and Thrand made me repeat the formula until I was word-perfect. 'Speak the words right,' said Thrand, 'and you will not have to resort to such tricks as rubbing the marks with your own blood to make the spell more potent. Leave such devices to those who are more interested in doing harm with the rune spells, not achieving good.'

Thrand also had a warning. 'If galdrastafir is done badly, it is likely to have the reverse effect from what was intended. That arises from the double and opposing nature of the runes, the dual nature of Odinn's gift. Thus a healing rune meant to help cure an invalid will actually damage their health if incorrectly cut.'

Thrand, who was by nature an optimist, refused to teach me any curse runes. And, as a precaution, he insisted that at the end of every lesson we put all the practice rune staves into the fire and burn them to ashes, lest they fell into malevolent hands. On these occasions, as we watched the flames consume the wood, I noticed how Thrand stayed beside the dying fire, gazing into the embers. I had the impression that he was far away in his thoughts, in some foreign country, though he never talked about his past.

THIRTEEN

A HORSE FIGHT marked the end of my stay with Thrand. The match between the two stallions had been eagerly awaited in the district for several months, and Thrand and I went to see the spectacle. The fight, or hestavig, was held on neutral ground for the two stallions. To encourage them, a small herd of mares was penned in the paddock immediately next to the patch of bare ground where the two stallions would fight. Naturally a small crowd had gathered to place bets on the outcome. When we arrived, the owners of the stallions were standing facing each other, holding the halters. Both animals were already in a lather, squealing and lunging and rearing to get at one another. A visiting farmer – he had probably backed the animal to win – had boldly walked behind one of the stallions and was poking at his testicles with a short stick to enrage the animal still further, which led Thrand to comment to me, 'He wouldn't be doing that if he knew his lore. He could be making an enemy of Loki and that will bring bad fortune.' I didn't know whether Thrand was referring to the story in which the trickster God Loki changed himself into a mare to seduce a malignant giant in the shape of a huge stallion, or the comic scene in Valholl when Loki is given the task of amusing the visiting giantess Skadi. Loki strips off, then ties one end of a rope round the beard of a billy goat, and the other end round his testicles, and the pair tug one another back and forth across the hall, each squealing loudly until the normally morose giantess bursts into laughter.

There was a sudden shout from the crowd as the two stallions were given slack and immediately sprang forward to attack one another, teeth bared and snorting with aggression. Their squeals of anger rose to a frenzy as they clashed, rising up on their hind legs to lash out with their hooves, or twisting round with gaping jaws to try to inflict a crippling neck bite. When all eyes were on the contest, I felt a discreet tug on my sleeve and turned to see a soberly dressed man I did not recognise. He nodded for me to follow him, and we walked a short distance to one side of the crowd, which was cheering as the two stallions began to draw blood. "Kari sent me with a message,' said the unknown visitor. 'He plans to go to Orkney, and has arranged to board a ship leaving from Eyrar two weeks from today. He says that if you want, you can travel with him. If you do decide to make the journey, you are to find your way to Eyrar and ask for the ship of Kolbein the Black. He's an Orkney man himself and an old friend of Kari's.'

I had heard nothing from Kari since the day at the Althing when he had refused to accept the godi's proposed settlement with the Burners. But plenty of rumours had reached me. It seemed that, as soon as the Althing ended, Kari launched himself on a personal and deadly campaign of revenge. He intercepted a party of Burners and their friends as they rode home from the Althing and challenged them to fight. They took on the challenge because Kari had only a single companion, a man named Thorgeir, and the Burners were eight in number. But Kari and Thorgeir had fought so skilfully that three of the Burners were killed and the remainder fled in panic. The leader of the Burners, Flosi, again offered to settle the blood feud and pay a heavy compensation for Burned Njal's death. But Kari was not to be placated. He persuaded his colleague Thorgeir to accept the settlement, saying that Thorgeir was not directly concerned in the blood feud, but that he, Kari, was a long way from settling the debt of honour that he owed to his dead family.

Kari was now outside the law and every man's hand was against him, but he refused to give up his campaign of retribution. Driven by the Norse sense of honour I mentioned earlier, he skulked in hiding for months, either living on the moors or staying with friendly farmers. He found another comrade-in-arms in a smallholder named Bjorn the White, a most unlikely associate as Bjorn was known as a braggart who boasted much and did little. Indeed, Bjorn's reputation was so low that even his wife did not think he had the courage for a stand-up fight. But Kari was a natural leader and he inspired Bjorn to excel. The two men ranged the island, tracking down the Burners and confronting them. Each time the combination of Kari and Bjorn won the day. Bjorn guarded Kari's back while the expert dueller tackled the Burners. By now fifteen of the original gang of Burners had been killed, and the rest had decided that it was wiser to begin their own period of exile and leave Iceland rather than be hunted down by Kari. In late summer the last of the Burners had departed from Iceland, intending to sail to Norway, and nothing more had been heard from them. Now, I guessed, Kari was planning to begin his own period of exile.

I told Thrand of Kari's message as soon as we got back to Thrand's cabin. My mentor's response was unhesitating. 'Of course you have to go with Kari,' he said decisively. 'There is a bond between you. Kari has kept in mind his promise he made to you at the Althing. With this offer of a passage to Orkney, he is honouring his pledge. In turn, you should acknowledge his nobility of spirit, accept his offer and go with him.' Then he made a remark which showed how – all this time – he had been aware of what was troubling me. 'If there is to be a final lesson which I want you to take away with you, let it be this: show and maintain personal integrity towards any man or woman who displays a similar faith and trust in you and you will find that you are never truly on your own.'

KOLBEIN THE BLACK sailed south from Eyrar at the end of November. It was late in the year to be making the voyage, but we had weather luck and the trip was uneventful. En route to Orkney Kari asked if we could stop at the Fair Isle, which lies between Orkney and Shetland, as he wanted to visit another of his friends, David the White, whom he had known from the days when both men were in the service of Earl Sigurd of Orkney. It was while we were staying at Fair Isle that a fisherman brought news that the Burners were nearby on Mainland, as the chief island in Orkney is called. The Burners had sailed from Iceland two weeks before us, but where we had good weather the Burners had encountered a heavy gale. Driven off course, their vessel was wrecked on the rocks of Mainland in poor visibility and they only just managed to scramble ashore. The mishap put Flosi and his colleagues in a real predicament. One of their victims at the Burning, Helgi Njalsson, was formerly a member of Earl Sigurd's retinue. There was every chance that if they were caught by the earl's people, the earl would put them to death for murdering one of his sworn men. The worried Burners spent a very uncomfortable day on the seashore, hiding in rocky clefts, camouflaging themselves under blankets of moss and seaweed, before Flosi decided that they had no choice but to walk across the island to Earl Sigurd's great hall, present themselves before the ruler of Orkney and throw themselves on his mercy.

Earl Sigurd knew at once who they were when the Burners arrived. Most of the Norse world was talking of the Burning of Njal. The earl was renowned for his violent temper and, as the Burners had feared, his initial reaction was to fly into a rage and order the visitors to be arrested. But Flosi courageously spoke up, admitting his guilt for Helgi Njalsson's death. Then, invoking an old Norse tradition, he offered to serve in Helgi's place in the earl's retinue. After some grumbling, Earl Sigurd agreed. The Burners had then pledged obedience to the earl and now were under his protection.

'Sigurd the Stout', as he was popularly known, was a pagan Norseman of the old school and proud of it. He always attracted fighting men. It was said that his two favourite seasons of the year were spring and autumn because at the first sign of spring he would launch his warships and go raiding his neighbours. He then came home for the summer to gather the harvest, and as soon as that was done he promptly put to sea again for a second round of viking. His most celebrated possession was the battle banner that his mother, a celebrated volva, had stitched for him. Its insignia was Odinn's emblem, the black raven. It was claimed that whoever flew the banner in battle would be victorious. However, in keeping with Odinn's perverse character, the person who carried the banner in battle would die while winning the victory. Given this warning, it was hardly surprising, that only the most loyal of Earl Sigurd's retainers was prepared to be his standard-bearer.

This was the man, then, in whose long hall at Birsay my mother had conducted her affair with my father Leif the Lucky, and the woman who had stitched the raven banner was my mother's confidante, Eithne the earl mother. According to the fisherman who brought us the news about the Burners, the earl mother was well advanced in years but still very much alive.

Kari decided that the most prudent time for us to cross to Mainland and arrive at Sigurd's great hall was during the Jol festival, when there should be several days of feasting and oath-taking. Sigurd still followed the old-fashioned tradition of having a large boar – an animal sacred to the fertility God Frey – led down his great hall so that the assembled company could lay hands on the bristly animal and swear their solemn oaths for the coming year. Then that evening the oath boar would be served up roast at a great banquet, at which the earl displayed his bounty by distributing vast quantities of mead and beer for his retainers and guests. For Sigurd the festival was a proper celebration in honour of Jolnir, another of Odinn's names, but he had no objection if the Christians chose to combine the earthy celebration of Jol with one of their holy days, provided they did not interfere with the priorities of eating, drinking, story-telling and carousing. Indeed, it occurred to me that it might have been under similar circumstances, fifteen years earlier, that I was conceived.

Kolbein's boat had a favourable tide under her and carried us across the strait between Fair Isle and Mainland in less than ten hours. Kolbein knew of a quiet sandy beach for our landing place, and he, Kari and I went ashore in the boat's tender, leaving a few men aboard at anchor watch. It was less than a half-hour walk over the rolling sand dunes to reach the earl's long hall, and there was still enough daylight left for me to have my first glimpse of an earl's residence. After hearing so much about the wealth and power of an earl, for which there is no equivalent rank in Iceland, I was frankly rather disappointed. I had expected to see a grand building, something with towers and turrets and stone walls. What I saw was nothing more than an enlarged version of the longhouses that I already knew from Iceland to Vinland. The only difference was that Earl Sigurd's long hall was considerably bigger. In fact it was almost three times larger than the largest home I had yet seen, with side walls that were over four feet thick. But the rest of it, the stone and turf walls, the wooden supports and the grassy roof, were identical to the domestic structures I had known all my life. The interior of this huge building was just as gloomy, smoky and poorly illuminated as its more humble cousins, so Kari, Kolbein and I were able to slip quietly in through the main doors without being noticed in the crowd of guests. We took up our positions just a few paces inside. There we could see down the length of the great hall, yet we were far enough from the central hearth, where Sigurd, his entourage and chief guests were seated. In the half-light and surrounded by a jostle of visitors, there was little chance that Kari would be recognised.

I had forgotten about Kari's exalted sense of self-honour. We arrived in the interval between the parading of the oath boar and the time when it would be served up with an apple in its mouth. This long intermission lasts at least three hours, and the assembled company is normally entertained with a programme of juggling, tumbling and music. It is also a tradition for the host of the Jol banquet to call on each of his chief guests to contribute a tale from his own experience. Scarcely had the three of us found our places in the audience than Earl Sigurd called on one of the Burners, a tall, gangling man by the name of Gunnar Lambason, to recount the story of Njal's death and the events leading up to it. Clearly Earl Sigurd thought that a first-hand account of this famous and recent event, told by one of the chief participants, would impress his guests.

From the moment Gunnar Lambason started speaking, I knew he was a poor choice for a saga teller. The Icelanders can be somewhat long-winded when it comes to narration, but Gunnar made particularly heavy going. He had a nasal voice that grated on the ear, and he often lost the thread of his tale. He also skewed the story so that it showed the deeds of the Burners in the most favourable light. As Gunnar Lambason recounted it, the Njalssons had brought their fate on themselves and throughly deserved to die in the flames and smoke of their home. When Gunnar finished his recitation, Sigurd's most important guest, a sumptuously dressed chieftain with a splendidly lustrous beard, asked how the Njalsson family had endured their final hours. Gunnar answered dismissively. They had fought well at first but then begun to cry out, begging for quarter, he said. His reply was more than Kari could stomach. Standing next to him, I had heard his deep, angry breathing as Gunnar's dreary tale proceeded. Now Kari gave a roar of fury, broke out from the little knot of bystanders and raced half the length of the hall. Like everyone else, I stood and gaped as Kari jumped over the outstretched legs of the men seated at the side benches until he was level with Gunnar Lambason, who had just seated himself and turned to see what was the commotion was.

Everyone was so startled that there was no time to react. Kari had his famous sword Leg Biter in his hand. With a single sweep of the blade Kari cut Gunnar Lambason's head from his shoulders.

Sigurd, the veteran warrior, was the first to react. 'Seize that man!' he shouted, pointing at Kari, who stood there confronting the crowd, with a pool of Gunnar Lambason's blood seeping around his feet. There was a shocked murmuring, followed by an uncomfortable silence. No one got up from their seats. At banquets it is customary for weapons to be hung up on the walls as a precaution against drunken brawling leading to bloodshed. Kari had only managed to bring Leg Biter into the hall because we arrived so late that the gatekeepers were already drunk and had failed to search him. The only other people with any weapons were Sigurd's bodyguard, and they were men who had previously served with Kari and were wary of his prowess as a fighter. Kari looked straight at Sigurd and announced loudly, 'Some people would say that I have just rendered you a service by killing the murderer of your former servant, Helgi Njalsson.' There was a mutter of approval from the onlookers and Flosi, the leader of the Burners, rose to his feet. He too turned towards Sigurd and said, 'I can speak on behalf of the Burners. Kari has done no wrong. He never accepted any settlement or compensation we offered for the deaths of his family, and he has always made it public that he intends to seek blood revenge. He only did what is his duty.'

Sigurd quickly sensed the mood of the assembly. 'Kari!' he thundered. 'You have offended our hospitality gravely, but in a just cause. With my permission, you may leave this hall unharmed. But I declare that by your action you have brought upon yourself the same outlawry for which you were condemned in Iceland. For that reason you must leave Orkney without any delay, and not return until your sentence of exile has been fully served.'

Kari said nothing, but turned on his heel and, the blood-streaked sword still in his hand, walked back quietly down the hall to where Kolbein and I were still standing. As he passed us, we both made a movement to step forward and join him. Kari nodded to Kolbein and said quietly, 'Let's go,' but to me he said firmly, 'you are to stay. I have brought you to Orkney as I promised, but you have not had time to carry out your own mission. I hope everything goes well for you. Perhaps we will meet again some day.' With those words, he stepped out of the door and into the darkness of the night. I stood watching him walk away, with Kolbein at his shoulder, until I could no longer see them in the gloom.

The earl was quickly back to his role as a genial host. Even as Sigurd's guards hauled away Gunnar Lambason's body, the earl was calling for more drink to be brought and a moment later was shouting at the cooks, demanding to know how much longer it would be before they could serve up the oath boar. I suspect that he was secretly delighted that the spectacular events would make his Jol festival remembered for years to come. The housemaids and thralls washed down the tables, and to his great credit Flosi stood up and in a loud voice asked the earl if he might have permission to retell the story of Njal's Burning, but this time with proper regard for the heroism of Njal and his family. When Earl Sigurd waved his hand in agreement, Flosi turned to the audience and announced that he would start the tale all over again, right from the beginning. His listeners nodded approvingly and settled themselves down for a lengthy discourse. Not only do Norsemen have an insatiable appetite for such narratives, but the more often a tale is told the better they seem to like it.

Flosi had barely started when Sigurd's steward was pushing through the crowd to where I was standing. 'Are you the young man who arrived with Kari Solmundarson?' he asked. 'Come with me,' he said. 'The earl wants a word with you, and so does his guest of honour.' I followed the steward through the crush of people, and found myself standing beside the earl's high seat.

Sigurd looked me up and down and asked my name.

'Thorgils,' I replied.

'How long have you known Kari?' asked the earl.

'Not very long, sir,' I answered respectfully, 'I helped him last year before the Althing, but just for a few days. Then he invited me to join him on his voyage to Orkney.'

'Why was that?' asked Sigurd.

'Because he knew that I wanted to come here to enquire about my family.'

Before Sigurd could ask me what I meant, the man seated on his right interrupted, 'What a remarkable fellow that Kari is,' he said, 'walking straight in, and carrying on his blood feud under our noses, with no thought for his own safety. Great courage.'

'Kari has always been known for his bravery,' replied Sigurd, and his slightly deferential tone made me look more closely at his guest. He was the most expensively dressed man I had ever seen. He wore at least three heavy gold rings on each arm, and his finger rings glittered with magnificent coloured stones. Every item of his clothing was of the finest material and in bright colours. His shoes were of soft leather. He even smelled richly, being the first man I had ever met who used body perfume. His sky blue cloak was trimmed with a broad margin of gold thread worked in an ornate pattern, and the precious brooch that held the cloak to his left shoulder was astonishing. The pattern of brooch was common enough. The pin pivoted on a slotted ring, and the wearer drove the pin through the cloth, turned the ring and the cloth was held in place. My father Leif had worn one very similar at feasts. But he had never worn one anything like the brooch displayed so ostentatiously by Sigurd's guest. The brooch was enormous. Its pin was nearly the length of my forearm, and the flat ring was a hand's span across. Both the pin – spike would be a better description – and the flat ring were of heavy gold. Even more amazingly, the surface of the gold ring was worked with intricate interlacing patterns, and set into the patterns was a galaxy of precious stones carefully picked for their colours – amethyst, blue, yellow and several reds from carmine to ruby. The brooch was a masterpiece. I guessed that there was probably no other piece of jewellery quite like it in all the world. It was, I thought to myself, a work of art fit for a king.

Earl Sigurd had already turned back to his dandified guest without waiting to hear my further explanation about why I wanted to visit Orkney. He was deep in conversation with him, and I caught a scowl from Sigurd's steward, who had been hovering in the background. Realising that my presence next to the high seat was no longer required, I made my way quietly back to the steward.

'No eavesdropping on matters of state,' he growled, and for a moment I thought he might know about my role as a spy for Kari at the Althing.

'Who's the man wearing the superb brooch?' I asked him.

'That's Sigtryggr, King of Dublin, and he's come here to negotiate with Earl Sigurd. Sigtryggr's looking for allies in his campaign against the Irish High King, Brian. Knowing Sigurd the Stout, I doubt that he'll be able to resist the chance of winning loot, even without the added attraction of that meddling hussy, Kormlod.'

The steward noticed that I had not the least idea what he was talking about, and beckoned to one of the hall servants. 'Here, you. Look after this lad. Find him something to eat and a place to sleep. Then something useful to do.' With that I was dismissed.

The Jol ended with the ceremonial quenching of the Julblok, a large burning log whose flames were doused with ale to ensure the fertility of the coming year, and when most of the guests had left I found myself assigned to domestic duties. Twelve days of uninterrupted revelry had left a remarkable mess in the great hall and the surrounding area. I was employed in sweeping up the debris, collecting and burning the rushes that had been fouled on the floor, raking out the long hearth, swabbing down benches, and digging out patches of sodden earth where the guests had relieved themselves without bothering to go to the outside latrines. At times I wondered whether the cattle in the byres at Brattahlid had not been more sanitary.

King Sigtryggr was still with us and some sort of negotiation was going on because I noticed that he and Sigurd the Stout spent a good deal of time in Sigurd's council room, often accompanied by their advisers. Among these advisers was Sigurd's mother Eithne. As had been reported, the celebrated volva was surprisingly well preserved for her advanced age. She must have been over seventy years old, but instead of the bent old crone that I had expected, Eithne was a small, rather rotund old woman full of energy. She bustled about, turning up at unexpected moments and casting quick glances everywhere and missing very little that went on around here. Only her thin, scraggly grey hair gave away her age. Eithne was almost bald, and she had a nervous habit of adjusting her headscarf every few moments so that no one would see her pate.

Her ears, as well as her eyes, were collecting information. I had barely begun to question the older servants about their memories of a certain Thorgunna, who had stayed at Birsay one winter fifteen years before, when I received another summons. This time it was to Eithne's retiring room at the back of the great hall. I found the earl mother standing so that the light from a small window fell directly on my face as I entered. Most windows in Norse houses are no more than open holes in the wall, which can be closed with a shutter in bad weather or when it is cold outside, but it was a mark of Sigurd's wealth and status that the window in his mother's chamber was covered with a sheet of translucent cow horn, which allowed a little of the dreary north light of winter to fall on me.

'I'm told you've been asking about Thorgunna, who stayed here a long number of years ago,' Eithne said. 'I suppose you are her son.'

My mouth must have dropped open with shock, for she went on, 'Don't look so surprised. You have the same colour of eyes and skin as she had, and perhaps the shape of your face is the same.'

'I never knew my mother,' I said. 'She sent me away to live with my father when I was still a babe in arms, and she had died by the time I came back to where she lived.'

'And where was that?' asked Eithne.

'At Frodriver in Iceland,' I answered. 'She died there when I was only three years old.'

'Ah yes, I had heard something about that,' this strange, rotund little woman briskly interrupted.

'It was said that there were portents shortly before she died and hauntings afterwards.' I ventured. 'It was something to do with her goods, with the things she brought with her, her clothes and bed hangings. At least that was what I was told. When these things were finally burned, the troubles ceased.'

Eithne gave a little snort of impatience. 'What did they think! No wonder there was trouble if someone else got their hands on a volva's sacred possessions.'

She gave another sniff. 'Your mother may have been nothing to look at, but she was skilled in other ways and I don't mean just at needlework. Those wall hangings she owned, she brought them with her from Ireland and she had stitched them herself and chanted the spell-words over them.'

'You mean like rune writing,' I commented.

Eithne gave me a patient look.

'Yes, like rune writing, but different. Men and women can both cut runes, but women often prefer to stitch their symbols. In some ways it is more painstaking and more effective. Those cloths and hangings and garments your mother cherished were powerful seidr. In the wrong hands they caused the spirits to be uneasy.'

I was about to make some comment about the earl's mystical raven flag, but thought better of it. 'I was told that you and my mother spent time together, so I was hoping you would be kind enough to tell me something about her. I would truly appreciate any details.'

'Most of our discussions were on trivial matters – or on matters which do not concern men,' she replied crisply. 'Your mother kept herself to herself nearly all the time she was here. She was a big woman – as I expect you know – and rather fierce, so most people kept out of her way. I had more to do with her than anyone else because we spoke Irish to one another, and of course she recognised that I have the sight, just as I knew she was a volva.'

'Did she say where she came from? Who her family were?' I

persisted. 'If I knew that, perhaps I could find out if I have any living relatives.'

Eithne looked at me with a hint of pity. 'Don't expect too much. Everyone thinks that they are descended from some special line, princes or great lords. But most of our forebears were ordinary folk. All I know is that your mother spoke excellent Irish and she could be well mannered when she was not being peevish, which might mean she came from a family with good social standing. She did once mention that she belonged to a tribe who lived somewhere in the middle of the island of Ireland. I don't remember its name but it might have been Ua Ruairc or Ua Ruanaid, or something like that. But the Irish tribes love giving themselves new titles and names, even changing where they live. The Irish are a restless and wandering people. I've been living in Orkney so long that I'm out of touch with what goes on there. It's possible that King Sigtryggr might recognise your mother's clan name. But, on the other hand, he may not have any idea at all. Although he's King of Dublin and has his home there, he's a Norseman through and through. You would be better advised to find your way to Ireland yourself and make enquiries there. Though don't be in a hurry, there's already war in the west and it will soon get worse. But why am I telling you this? You know that already, or you should.'

Again I must have appeared puzzled because the old woman shot me a glance and said, 'No, perhaps not. You're still too young. Anyhow, I can arrange for you to accompany Sigtryggr when he returns home, which should be some time very soon – that doesn't require second sight to anticipate. He and his men are locusts. They'll eat up our last stocks of winter food if Sigurd doesn't make it obvious that they have outstayed their welcome. I've advised him to serve up smaller and smaller portions at mealtimes, and resurrect some of the stockfish that half rotted when the rain got into the storehouse last autumn. If the smell doesn't get rid of them, nothing will.'

The old lady was as good as her word and her dietary stratagem was effective. Sigtryggr and his followers left Birsay within forty-eight hours, and I was added to the royal entourage at the earl mother's particular request. I had failed to learn anything more about Thorgunna, but was glad to leave Orkney because I had noticed how one of the Burners had started giving me occasional puzzled glances, as if he was trying to remember where he had seen me before. I recognised him as one of the men on whom I had eavesdropped at the Althing, and was nervous that he would make the connection. If he did so, it was likely that I could finish up with my throat cut.

FOURTEEN

SIGTRYGGR'S SHIP WAS a match for his magnificent dress brooch. The Norsemen may not be able to weave gossamer silks into gorgeous robes or construct the great tiled domes and towers of the palaces that I was later to see in my travels, but when it comes to building ships they are without peer. Sigtryggr's vessel was a drakkar, sleek, sinister, speedy, a masterpiece of the shipwright's craft. She had been built on the banks of the Black River in Ireland, as her crew never tired of boasting. The Ostmen, the word the Norse in Ireland use to describe themselves, build ships every bit as well as the shipwrights in Norway and Denmark because the quality of native Irish timber equals anything found in the northern lands. Coming as I did from two countries where big trees were so rare that it was unthinkable to build a large ocean-going vessel, the moment I clambered aboard the drakkar I could not resist running my fingertips along the handpicked oak beams and the perfect fit of the flawless planking. I would have been a complete ignoramus not to appreciate the gracefully sweeping lines of the long black-painted hull and the perfect symmetry of the rows of metal fastenings, the ingenious carving of the wooden fittings for the mast and rigging, and the evident care which the crew lavished on their vessel. The drakkar – her name was *Spindrifter* – was deliberately flamboyant. At anchor her crew rigged a smart wadmal tent to cover her amidships, a tent sewn from strips of five different colours, and set it up so tautly that she looked like a floating fairground booth. And as soon as we were at sea with a fair wind, they set a mainsail of a matching pattern so that the vessel crested along like a brilliant exotic bird. As a king's ship, *Spindrifter* was prettified with fancy carvings and bright paint. There were intricately cut panels each side of the curling prow, a snarling figurehead, blue, gold and red chevrons painted on the oar blades, and the intricate decorative lashing on the helmsman's rudder grip was given a daily coat of white chalk. Even the metal weathervane was gilded. *Spindrifter* was meant to impress, and in my case she did.

Most mariners, I have noticed, share a particular moment of weakness. It comes in the first hour after a ship safely clears the land and is heading out to open sea. That is when the crew lets out a collective breath of relief, sensing that they are back in their closed world that is small, intimate and familiar. The feeling is particularly strong if the crew has previously sailed together, gone ashore for a few days and then returned to their vessel. They are eager to re-establish their sense of comradeship, and that is their moment of indiscretion. As the last rope is coiled down and the ship settles on her course, they begin to talk about their time ashore, compare their experiences, comment on sights they saw and the people they met, perhaps boast of the women they encountered and speculate about the immediate future, and they do so openly. They are a crew binding together and, as our ship sailed down the inner channel from Orkney, the crew of *Spindrifter* overlooked the fact that among them was a stranger. Too insignificant to be noticed, I heard their unguarded thoughts on the success of their visit to Birsay, the prospects for the coming war and the manoeuvrings of their lord and master, King Sigtryggr.

What I heard was puzzling. Sigtryggr's kingdom of Dublin is small, but it is the richest and most strategic of all the Norse domains scattered around the rim of Ireland, and Sigtryggr was savouring its prosperity to the full. Dublin's thriving commerce was the milch cow providing him with the money for the luxuries he enjoyed so much – his jewellery and fine clothes, his splendid ship, and the best food and wine imported from France. Indeed, his income from taxing the Dubliners was so great that Sigtryggr had taken the unique step of minting his own money. No other ruler in Ireland, even their own High King, was wealthy enough to do that, and I saw one of the drakkar sailors produce a leather pouch and double-check his wages by counting out a small stack of silver coins struck by Sigtryggr's moneyers.

The more I heard the sailors brag about the wealth of their lord, the more rash, it seemed to me, that he should be about to risk such a comfortable sinecure by joining a rebellion against a grizzled Irish veteran who styled himself 'Emperor of the Irish'. This was the same High King Brian whom Sigurd's steward had mentioned, a warlord who had been rampaging up and down the country with a sizeable army, imposing his authority and winning battle after battle.

Brian Boruma claimed to be driving out the foreign invaders from his land. Yet a large part of his army was made of foreigners, chiefly Ostmen, so what really distinguished his actions was that he was as virulent a Christian in his own way as 'St' Olaf of Norway had been. He travelled everywhere with a cluster of White Christ priests. Wild-looking creatures, they seemed as convinced of their own invincibility as any berserker. These Irish holy men, according to one of the drakkar sailors, were by no means as peaceable as their profession might suggest. The sailor had been in Dublin some fifteen years earlier when Brian Boruma had entered the city and ordered the destruction of a sacred grove of trees, a temple site for Thor. A group of Old Believers had stood in the way of the woodcutters, and the Irish holy men had rushed forward and beaten them back, wielding their heavy wooden croziers like clubs. The sailor's mention of Thor's sacred grove reminded me of Snorri and his twin role as priest and ruler, and it seemed to me that this Irish High King who mixed rule and religion was a grander version of my more familiar godi, and perhaps even more ruthless.

King Sigtryggr's informers had warned that the plan for

Boruma's next campaign was to overrun Dublin once again and bring to heel the provincial ruler, the King of Leinster. So Sigtryggr was scurrying around to build up a grand alliance to defeat the expected invasion. He was using his ample war chest to hire mercenaries and looking for assistance from overseas. In Birsay he had set a clever snare, according to the crew of *Spindrifter*. He had promised Sigurd the Stout that if the Earl of Orkney came to his help, then he would arrange for Sigurd to marry Kormlod, Brian Boruma's ex-wife. This Kormlod was an irresistible bait. She was not only the divorced wife of the High King, but also the sister of the Irish King of Leinster. Whoever married her, according to Sigtryggr, would be able to lay claim to the vacant throne of Ireland after the defeat of Brian Boruma, and his claim would be supported by the Leinster tribes. Yet I noted that when the crew of *Spindrifter* talked about this scheme, they chuckled and made sardonic comments. Listening to them, it seemed to me that the Lady Kormlod was not the meek and willing consort Sigurd would have been led to expect and neither did Sigtryggr himself set much store by the plan.

Thor sent our drakkar the wind she loved – a fine quartering breeze that brought us safely past the headlands and the tide races, and into the mouth of Dublin's river without the need to shift sail or even get out our oars until we were closing the final gap across the dirty river water ready to tie up at the wooden jetty which was the royal landing place.

I had never even seen a town before, let alone a city, and the sight of Dublin astounded me. There are no towns or large villages in Greenland or Iceland or Orkney, and suddenly here in front of me was a great, grey-brown untidy sprawl of houses, shops, laneways, roofs, all spilling down the side of the hill to the anchorage in the river. I had never imagined that so many people could exist, let alone live together cheek by jowl in this way. The houses were modest enough, little more than oversized huts with walls of wattle and daub and roofed with straw or wooden tiles. But there were so many of them and they huddled so close together that it seemed there were more people living in one spot overlooking the south bank of Dublin's river than in the whole of Iceland. It was not just the sight of the houses which amazed me. There was also the smell. The river bank was thick mud littered with rotting, stinking matter, and it was clear that many of the citizens used the place as their latrine. On top of the stench of putrefaction was laid an all-pervading odour of soot and smoke. It was an early January evening when we moored and the householders of Dublin were lighting fires to keep warm. The smoke from their hearths rose through holes in the roofs, but just as often it simply oozed through the straw covering so it seemed as if the whole city was smouldering. A light drizzle had begun to fall, and it pressed down the smoke and fumes of the fires so that the smell of wood smoke filled our nostrils.

Sigtryggr's steward was waiting at the quayside to greet his master and led us up the hill towards the royal dwelling. The roadway was surfaced with wooden planks and woven wicker hurdles laid on top of the mud, but even so we occasionally slipped on the slick, damp surface. Through open doorways I caught glimpses of the interiors of the houses, the flicker of flames from an open hearth, dim shapes of people seated on the side benches or a woman standing at a cooking pot, the grimy faces of children peering round the doorpost to see us go by until unseen hands reached out and dragged them back out of sight. Sigtryggr and his cortege were not popular. The reception for the King of Dublin was very muted.

We passed through the gateway of a city wall which I had not noticed before because the cluster of houses had outgrown Dublin's defensive rampart. Then we had reached the centre of Dublin, where the houses were more spread out, and here stood Sigtryggr's residence, similar in size and shape to Earl Sigurd's hall though it was built of timber rather than turf. The only unusual feature was a steep, grassy mound slightly to the rear and right of Sigtryggr's hall. 'Thor's Mound,' muttered Einar, the sailor, who had spoken about the warlike Irish priests earlier, and who now saw me looking in that direction. 'Those mad fanatics chopped down the sacred trees, but it will take more than few axe blows to get rid of every last trace of his presence. Silkbeard still makes an occasional sacrifice there, just for good luck, though his real worship should be for Freyja. There's nothing he would like better than to be able to weep tears of gold.' Tyrkir had taught me long ago in Vinland that the Goddess of wealth shed golden tears at the loss of her husband, but I didn't know who Silkbeard was, though I made a shrewd guess. When I asked the sailor, he guffawed. 'You really are from the outer fringes, aren't you? Silkbeard is that dandy, our leader. He loves his clothes and perfume and his fine leather shoes and his rings, and haven't you noticed how much time he spends combing and stroking and fondling his chin whiskers.'

But I hardly heard his reply. I had come to a dead stop and was staring at a woman standing at the entrance to Sigtryggr's hall among the group of women and servants waiting to greet the king formally. I guessed her age at about fifty. She was very richly dressed in a long blue gown with expensive shoulder clasps, and her grey hair was held back in a matching silk scarf. She must have been important because she was standing in the front rank, next to a younger woman, who I guessed was Sigtryggr's wife. But it was not the older woman's dress which had caught my eye; it was the way that she stood, and the way that she was looking at Sigtryggr, who was now walking towards her. There was a sense of exasperation and determination on her face. I had seen precisely that look before and that same posture. I felt that I was seeing not the grey-haired matron in front of me, but another person. It was a memory that made me feel queasy. I had seen exactly that expression on the face of Freydis Eriksdottir.

'Get along and stop gawping,' Einar said from behind me.

'Who's the grey-haired woman standing in the front row?' I asked him.

'That's Sigtryggr's mother Kormlod, the Irish call her Gormlaith.'

I was utterly confused. 'But I thought that she was the person

Earl Sigurd was supposed to marry as a reward if he came to help Sigtryggr. The person who would help him become High King.'

'Precisely. Until last year she was the wife of the High King Brian, but he divorced her after some sort of a row. Now she says that Brian doesn't deserve to remain on his throne. She hates him so much that she would support whoever marries her in a bid to replace him. She's got a lot of influence because she also happens to be the sister of King Mael Morda of Leinster, and at one time she was even married to Malachi, another of the important Irish chieftains who's spent years intriguing and fighting against Brian to become the High King himself. Whatever happens in high politics in this part of the world, you can be sure that Kormlod is involved. Now you'd better report to Sigtryggr's steward and see if he can find a place for you.'

Ketil the steward gave me an exasperated glance when I finally managed to get his attention. He was bustling here and there in a self-important manner, organising the storage of various boxes and bundles that his master's embassy had brought back from Orkney, calling for food to be brought from the kitchen and served, and generally trying to give the impression that he was essential to the smooth running of the royal establishment, though in fact he seemed to be more of a hindrance. 'You can be a temporary dog boy,' he snapped at me. 'One of those Irish chiefs the king is negotiating with has sent a couple of hairy wolfhounds as a present. Apparently it's a compliment, though I call it more of an aggravation. I'm told the brutes can only be exchanged between kings and chieftains, so you'd better be sure they are kept healthy in case the donor comes on a visit. Feed them before you feed yourself.' He waved me away and a moment later was berating one of the household servants for setting out the wrong goblets for the king's meal.

My charges were hard to miss. They were skulking around the back of the hall – tall, hairy creatures, occasionally loping in embarrassed confusion from one corner to the next. I had no experience whatsoever of looking after dogs. But even I could see from the way their tails were curled tightly down between their legs and their large flappy ears were pressed close to their skulls that they were unhappy in their new surroundings. I had come across a few of the same breed of dog in Iceland, where they had been imported in much the same way as Irish slaves, so I was aware that they were not as lethal as they looked. I succeeded in coaxing them outside the king's hall and giving them some scraps which I wheedled from the kitchen staff. The dogs looked at me mournfully, their great dark, oval eyes blinking through their drooping fur, obviously recognising an incompetent, though well-meaning, dog keeper. I was grateful to the lanky beasts because they gave me an excuse to stay in the background and pretend to be busy. Whenever anyone looked in my direction, I made a show of brushing their rough, harsh coats, and the hounds were decent enough to let me do so, though I did wonder if there might not come a moment when, fed up with my incompetence, they would sink their teeth into me.

Fortunately my role as royal dog boy was never put seriously to the test. King Sigtryggr lacked any real affection for the animals, regarding them as decorative accessories akin to his fine footwear or personal jewellery. My only real duty was to see that the two hounds were prettily presented, sitting or lying near his seat whenever he held court or had meals.

Queen Mother Gormlaith scared me, and not simply because she reminded me so often of Freydis, the organiser of the Vinland massacre. There was a calculating coldness about Gormlaith which occasionally slipped out from under her elegance as the gracious queen mother. She was still a very handsome woman, slim and elegant, and she had retained her youthful grace so that with her green eyes and haughty stare she reminded me of a supercilious cat. She had exquisite manners – even condescending to make the occasional remark to the lowly dog boy – but there was a flinty hardness to her questions and if she did not get the answer she sought, she had a habit of ignoring the response and then putting on the pressure until she got the reply she wanted. I could see that she was manipulative, calculating, and that she could twist her son, the showy Sigtryggr, into doing precisely what she wanted.

And what she wanted was mastery. Eavesdropping on the high table conversations, and casually questioning the other servants, I learned that Gormlaith was not so much a woman scorned as a woman thwarted in her ambitions, which were vaunting. 'She married Boruma hoping to control the High King of Ireland,' one of the other servants told me, 'but that didn't work. Brian had his own ideas on how to run the country and soon got so fed up with her meddling that he had her locked up for three months. Brian's an old man now, but that doesn't mean he would allow himself to be manipulated by a scheming woman.'

'Is the Queen Mother really that ambitious?' I asked.

'You wait and see,' the servant replied with a smirk. 'She sent her son off to Orkney to recruit Fat Sigurd, offering herself as the meat on the hook, and she'll do anything to get even with the High King.'

Not until the middle of March, nearly seven weeks later, did I understand what the servant meant. I spent the interval as a member of Sigtryggr's household, carrying out domestic duties, learning to speak Irish with the slaves and lower servants, as well as feeding and exercising his two dogs as their guardian. If I have given the impression that the Norse people are uncouth and unwashed savages with their raucous drinking bouts and rough manners, then my descriptions have been misleading. The Norse are as meticulous in their personal cleanliness as circumstances will allow and, though it may seem unlikely, their menfolk are great dandies. And of course King Sigtryggr fancied himself as an arbiter of good taste and style. The result was that I spent a good deal of my time pressing his courtiers' garments, using a heavy, smooth stone to flatten the seams of the surcoats and cloaks from their extensive wardrobes which they changed frequently, and combing not just the rough hair of the two dogs, but also the heads of the royal advisers. They were very attentive to their hairstyles, and would even specify the length and fineness of the teeth on the combs I used. There was a special shop in Dublin, where I was sent to purchase replacement combs, specifying that they should be made of red-deer antler and not common cattle horn.

It was at a noon meal, one day in early spring, that I fully grasped the extent of the ambitions of Gormlaith, and how ruthlessly she worked her way towards achieving them. I had led into the great hall my two wolfhounds, settled them near the king's chair and stood back to keep an eye on them. King Sigtryggr was jealous of his regal dignity, and the last thing I wanted was for one of the big grey dogs to leap up suddenly and snatch food from the royal hand while the king was eating.

'Are you sure that Sigurd is going to keep his word?' Gormlaith was asking him.

'Positive,' her son replied, worrying at a chicken leg with his teeth and trying to stop the grease dripping onto his brocaded shirt. 'He's one of the old breed, never happier than when he's got a war to plan and execute. Cunning too. He's got a bunch of hard men at his court, Icelanders, renegade Norwegians and so forth. He knows that a campaign in Ireland will keep them occupied so they don't start plotting against him in Orkney.'

'And how many men do you think he will be able to bring?'

'He claimed he could raise eight hundred to a thousand.'

'But you're doubtful?'

'Well, Mother, I wasn't there long enough to count them,' Sigtryggr answered petulantly, wiping his hands on a linen cloth that a page held out for him. Sigtryggr was a great one for aping foreign etiquette.

'My information is that the Earl of Orkney can probably raise five hundred men, possibly six hundred, no more – and that's not enough,' she said. It was evident that his mother already knew the answer to her own question.

Sigtryggr grunted. He had detected the stern tone in his mother's voice, and knew that an order was coming.

'We need more troops if we want to be sure of dealing with that dotard Brian,' Gormlaith continued firmly.

'And where do you expect to find them?'

'A merchant recently arrived from Man mentioned to me this morning that there's a sizeable vikingr fleet anchored there. They are operating under joint command. Two experienced leaders. One is called Brodir and the other is Ospak Slant-eye.'

Sigtryggr sighed. 'Yes, Mother. I know both men. I met Brodir two years ago. Fierce looking. Wears his hair so long that he has to tuck it into his belt. Old Believer, of course. Said to be a seidr master.'

'I think you should recruit the two of them and their men into our forces,' his mother said firmly.

Sigtryggr looked stubborn, then decided to concede the point. I suspected that he had long since given up trying to dissuade his mother from her schemes, and it was obvious what was coming next.

'Good,' she said. 'It's less than a day's journey to Man.'

For a moment I thought that the king would raise some sort of objection, but he hesitated only briefly, then petulantly threw the chicken bone at one of the two wolfhounds and, forgetting the page with the napkin, wiped his hands on his tunic and ostentatiously turned to open a conversation with his wife.

Gormlaith's wish was Ketil's command. He was terrified of her, and that evening the steward was fluttering around warning the palace staff. *Spindrifter*'s crew were to be aboard by dawn, ready to take Sigtryggr to Man. 'And you,' he said to me spitefully, 'you're going too. You can take the big dogs with you. The king thinks that they will make a handsome present for those two pirates. I expect he'll tell them that they are war dogs, trained to attack. But from what I've seen of them they're happier to lie on the rushes all day and scratch for fleas. At least we'll be rid of them.'

The voyage to Man was cold, wet and took twice as long as we had expected. My two charges were miserable. They scrabbled on the sloping deck, threw up and shivered, and after falling into the bilges for the twentieth time, just lay there and were still looking wretched when *Spindrifter* rounded the southern headland of Man and under oars crept slowly into the sheltered bay where the vikingr fleet lay at anchor. We approached warily, all our shields still hung on the gunnels, the crew trying to look submissive, and Sigtryggr and his bodyguard standing on the foredeck weaponless and without body armour, making it clear that they came in peace. *Spindrifter* was easily the largest vessel in the bay, but she would not have withstood a concerted attack from the vikingr. Ospak and Brodir had assembled thirty vessels in their war fleet.

Neither side trusted the other enough to hold a parlay on one of the ships, so the council was held on the beach in a tent. Naturally Sigtryggr wanted his two hounds to be on display. Dragging along the two seasick dogs, I felt almost as cold and wretched as they did when I took up my station in the entourage. Ospak and Brodir paid no attention to the cutting wind and the occasional bursts of rain, which slatted and battered the tent as they stood listening to Sigtryggr's proposal. By now I knew his methods well enough to know what was coming. He spoke at length about the extent and prosperity of the Irish High King's realm, and how Brian Boruma had grown too old really to protect the kingdom's wealth effectively. An example of his fading powers, Sigtryggr pointed out, was how he had mistreated his wife Gormlaith. He had locked her up for three months, recklessly disregarding that this would be an insult to her family, the royal house of Leinster. Brian Boruma was old and feeble and losing his touch. It would take only a well-managed attack to remove him from power and lay Ireland open to pillage.

The two Viking leaders listened impassively. Brodir was the more imposing of the two. Ospak was slender and ordinary-looking, apart from the odd angle of his left eye socket which gave him his nickname, Slant-eye. But Brodir was huge, taller by nearly a head. Everything about him was on a massive scale. He had a great rough face, legs like pillars, and he had the largest hands and feet that I had ever seen. His most distinctive feature, however, was his hair. As Sigtryggr had told his mother, Brodir grew his hair so long that it came to his waist and he was obliged to tuck it into his belt. Unusually for a Norseman, this tremendous cascade of hair was jet black.

The meeting ended without reaching any firm conclusion. Both Ospak and Brodir said they needed to consult with their chief men and would let Sigtryggr have a decision the following morning. But as we made our way back down the shingle beach to our small boats, Sigtryggr took Brodir on one side and invited him to continue the discussions privately. An hour later the viking giant was clambering aboard *Spindrifter* and ducking in under the striped awning of the tent, which we had rigged to protect ourselves from the miserable weather. Brodir stayed for nearly an hour, deep in conversation with Sigtryggr. In the confined space there was little privacy, and every word of the discussion could be heard by the men on the nearest oar benches. Brodir wanted to know more about the political situation in Ireland, who would be supporting the High King and what would be the division of spoils. In his answers Sigtryggr sweetened the terms of the proposed alliance. He promised Brodir first choice in the division of any booty, that he would receive a special bonus, and that his share was likely to be greater than Ospak's because Brodir commanded more ships and more men. Finally, as Brodir still sat, cautiously refusing to commit himself to the venture, Sigtryggr made the same grand gesture that he had made in Orkney: he promised that Gormlaith would marry Brodir if Brian Boruma was defeated and that would open the way to the throne of the High King. As he made this empty promise, I noticed several of our sailors turn away to hide their expressions.

Brodir was not fooled. 'I believe you made the same offer to the Earl of Orkney recently,' he rumbled.

Sigtryggr never faltered. 'Oh yes, but Gormlaith changed her mind when I got back to Dublin. She said she would much prefer you as her husband to Sigurd the Stout – though he too is a fine figure of a man – and we agreed that there was no reason for Sigurd to know of the change of plan.'

At that precise moment Sigtryggr noticed that I was within earshot. I was crouched against the side of the vessel, with one of the hounds despondently licking my hand. Belatedly it must have occurred to Sigtryggr that perhaps I was a spy for the Earl of Orkney. 'As a token of my regard,' he went on smoothly, 'I would like to leave you with these two magnificent Irish wolfhounds. They will remind you of the homeland of your future wife. Come now, let us make a bargain on it and seal it with this present.' He reached forward, clasped Brodir's brawny right arm, and they swore an oath of friendship. 'You must come to Dublin with your ships within the month, and try to persuade Ospak to come too.'

Brodir rose to his feet. He was such a colossus that he had to stoop to avoid brushing his black head on the wet tent cloth. As he turned to go, he said to me, 'Come on, you,' and I found myself once more dragging the unfortunate dogs out of the bilges and over the edge of the drakkar. When they refused to jump down into the little boat and paused, whimpering, on the edge of the gap between longship and tender, Brodir, who had already gone ahead, simply reached up and grabbed each dog by the scruff of the neck and hauled them down as if they had been puppies.

I awoke next morning, after an uncomfortable night curled up between the two hounds on the foredeck of Brodir's warship, and looked across to where *Spindrifter* had lain at anchor. The great drakkar had gone. Sigtryggr had decided that his mission was accomplished and had slipped away in the night, setting course for Dublin doubtless to report to his mother that she was now on offer to two ambitious war leaders.

In mid-afternoon Brodir beckoned to me to join him. He was sitting at the foot of the mast, a chunk of wind-dried sheepmeat in one hand and a knife in the other. He cut off slivers of meat and manoeuvred them into his mouth past his luxuriant beard as he cross-examined me. I think he suspected that I was a spy placed by Sigtryggr.

'What's your name and where are you from?' he enquired.

'Thorgils, sir. I was born in Orkney, but I grew up in Greenland and spent time in a place called Vinland.'

'Never heard of it,' he grunted.

'Most recently I've been living in Iceland, in the Westfjords.'

'And who was your master?'

'Well, I was in the service of Snorri Godi at first, but he sent me to live with one of his people, a man called Thrand.'

Brodir stopped eating, his knife blade halfway to his mouth.

'Thrand? What does he look like?'

'A big man, sir. Not as big as yourself. But tall and he's got a reputation as a warrior.'

'What sort of helmet does he wear?'

'An old-fashioned one, bowl-shaped with eye protectors, and there are runes inside which he showed me.'

'Did you know what the runes read?' Bordir asked.

'Yes, sir.'

Brodir had put aside the lamb shoulder and looked at me thoughtfully. 'I know Thrand,' he said quietly. 'We campaigned together in Scotland a few years ago. What else did he tell you about himself?'

'Not much about himself or his past, sir. But he did try to teach me some of the Old Ways.'

'So you're an apprentice of seidr?' Brodir said slowly.

'Well, sort of,' I replied. 'Thrand taught me a little, but I was with him for only a few months, and the rest of my knowledge I have picked up by chance.'

Brodir turned and peered out from under the longship's awning to look at the sky. He was checking the clouds to see if there would be a change in the weather. There was still a thick overcast. He turned back to face me.

'I was once a follower of the White Christ,' he said, 'for almost six years. But it never felt right. I was baptised by one of those wandering priests, yet from that moment on my luck seemed to falter. My eldest son – he must have been a little younger than you – was drowned in a boating accident, and my vikingr brought little reward. The places we raided were either too poor or the inhabitants were expecting us and had fled, taking all their property with them. That was when I met up with Thrand. He was on his way to visit his sister, who was married to a Dublin Ostman, and he joined my war band for a quick raid on one of the Scots settlements. Before we attacked, he made his sacrifices to Thor and cast lots, and he predicted that we would be successful and win a special reward. It was a hotter fight than we had anticipated because we did not know that the King of Scotland's tax collector happened to be staying in the village that night, and he had an escort with him. But we chased them off, and when we dug in the spot of churned earth, we found where they had hastily buried their tax chest containing twenty marks of hack silver. My men and I were delighted, and I noticed how Thrand took care to make an offering of part of the hoard to Thor. Since then I have done the same before and after every battle. I asked Thrand if he would stay on with me as my seidr master, but he said he had to get back home to Iceland. He had given his word.'

'That would be to Snorri Godi, sir,' I said. 'Snorri still consults Thrand for advice before any sort of conflict.'

'And you say that you studied seidr under Thrand?'

'Yes, but just for a few months.'

'Then we'll see if you can be more than a dog boy. Next time I make a sacrifice to Thor, you can assist me.'

Brodir and Ospak held their combined flotilla at Man for another ten days. There was much coming and going between the two men as Brodir tried to persuade Ospak to join him in King Sigtryggr's alliance. The two men were sworn brothers, but Ospak took umbrage at Brodir's grand plan to become Gormlaith's consort and felt that the new scheme had now replaced their own original agreement for a vikingr campaign. Ospak's ambitions were more down to earth than Brodir's. He wanted booty rather than glory, and the more enthusiastically that Brodir spoke about the wealth of King Sigtryggr and his potential as an ally, the more Ospak saw the assets of Dublin as something waiting to be plundered. So he prevaricated, repeatedly pointing out that an alliance with King Sigtryggr was dangerous. The High King Brian, Ospak noted, had the more impressive record as a warrior, and even if King Brian was now getting old, he had four strapping sons, all of whom had shown themselves as capable commanders on the battlefield.

Eventually Brodir became so exasperated with this hesitation that he suggested to Ospak they should take the omens and see which way the forthcoming campaign would turn out. Ospak was also an Old Believer, and he agreed to the idea at once, so a sweat cabin was set up on the beach. I have mentioned that the Norse are as clean a people as circumstances allow. Among their habits is to take baths in hot water, quite a regular occurrence in Iceland, where water already hot emerges from the ground; they also bathe in steam, though this is more complicated. It involves constructing a small and nearly airtight cabin, bringing very hot stones and then dashing fresh water on the stones so that steam fills the chamber. If the process is excessive, more and more steam fills the room until the occupants become giddy from heat and lack of air and sometimes lose their senses. In Iceland Thrand had told me how this could be done to induce a trance-like state and, if one is fortunate, bring on dreams or even spirit flying.

While the steam hut was being prepared on the beach, Brodir set up a small altar of beach stones very like the one I had seen Thorvall construct in Vinland, and asked me to cut invocation runes on several pieces of driftwood. When the heated steam stones were placed inside the steam hut with a bucket of water, Brodir took my rune sticks and, after approving the staves I had cut, added them to the embers. As the last wisps of grey smoke curled up from the little pyre, he removed all his clothes, coiled his hair around his head and squeezed his great bulk into the hut. I covered the doorway with a heavy blanket of cloth, reminded of the similar structure where I had met the Skraeling shaman.

Brodir stayed in the steam cabin for at least an hour. When he emerged he was looking dour and did not say a word, but dressed quickly and ordered his men to row him out to his ship. Seeing his expression, no one on board dared ask him whether he had seen visions and, if so, what they were. The following day he repeated the process with much the same result. If anything, he emerged from the ordeal looking even more solemn than before. Later that evening he called me over and told me that next day it was my turn. 'Thrand would not have wasted his knowledge on someone who has not the sight. Take my place in the steam cabin tomorrow and tell me what you see.'

I could have told him that there was no need. I already knew. On both nights after Brodir had undergone his ordeal in the steamhouse, I had violent dreams. By now I knew enough about my own powers of sight to realise that my own dreams were echoes of his earlier visions. In the first dream I was aboard an anchored ship when there was a roaring noise in my ears and the sky began to rain boiling blood. The crew around me tried to seek shelter from the downpour and many of them were scalded. One man was so badly burned that he died. The dream on the second night was similar except that after the shower of blood the men's weapons leapt from their sheaths and began to fight, one with the other, and again a sailor lost his life. So when the flap dropped down behind me in the steam cabin, and I poured the water on the stones and felt the steam sear my lips and nostrils and burn deep into my lungs, I had only to close my eyes and I was immediately back in my dream. Now the sky, instead of spewing bloody rain, disgorged flight after flight of angry ravens like fluttering black rags. The birds came cawing and swooping, their beaks and claws were made of iron, and they pecked and struck so viciously at us that we were obliged to shelter beneath our shields. And for the third time we lost a sailor. His eyes pecked out and his face a bloody mess, he stumbled blindly to the side of the vessel, tripped on the coaming and, falling into the water, drowned in the spreading pink tendrils of his own blood.

Brodir woke me. Apparently I had been lying in the steam hut for six hours and there had been no sound. He had broken in and found me insensible. Brodir did not question me but waited until I had recovered sufficiently, then sent for Ospak to come to the beach. The three of us withdrew to a quiet spot, out of earshot of the other men, and there Brodir described his visions in the sweat hut. As I suspected, they were almost exactly what I had seen in my own dreams. But only I had the nightmare of the iron-beaked ravens. When Brodir rumbled, 'The lad has the sight. We should listen to him as well,' I described how Odinn's crows had attacked my shipmates and caused such ruin and disaster.

Only a fool would have been blind to the omens and Ospak was no fool. When Brodir asked whether he would be joining with him in King Sigtryggr's alliance, Ospak asked only for time to think things over. 'I need to consult with my shipmasters,' he told Brodir. 'Let us meet again on the beach this evening after dusk, and I will give you my answer.'

When Ospak returned to the beach that evening, there was barely enough light to see by. He was accompanied by all his ship's captains. It was not a good sign. They were all armed and they looked wary. I realised that they were frightened of Brodir, who, besides being very burly, was also known to be quick-tempered. I reassured myself with the thought that there is a prohibition among the Old Believers – not always obeyed – that it is unwise to kill someone after dark because their ghost will come to haunt you. Even before Ospak started speaking, it was obvious what had been decided. 'The dreams are the worst possible omen,' he began. 'Blood from the sky, men dying, weapons fighting among themselves, war ravens flying. There can be no other explanation than that there will be death and war, and that brother will fight brother.' Brodir scowled. Right up to that moment, he had been hoping that Ospak and his men would join him, and that he would be able to keep the combined flotilla together. But Ospak's blunt interpretation of the dreams left no doubt: Ospak and his ships would not only leave the flotilla, but he and his men intended to throw in their lot with the Ostmen fighting for King Brian. With the High King, they thought, lay their best chance of victory and reward.

Brodir did lose his temper, though only for a moment. It was when Ospak referred to the ravens again, almost as an afterthought. 'Perhaps those ravens are the fiends from hell the Christians are always talking about. They are supposed to have a particular appetite for those who have once followed the White Christ and then turned away.' Brodir had been some sort of priest during his Christian phase, I later learned. Stung by this jibe, he took a step forward and moved to draw his sword. But Ospak had stepped quickly back out of blade range, and his captains closed up behind him. 'Steady,' he called, 'remember that no good will come of killing after dark.'

Killing a man after sunset might be forbidden, but departing in the dark is not. That same night Ospak and his captains quietly unmoored. Their vessels had been anchored in a group, close inshore, and their crews poled them out into the ebb tide so that they silently drifted past us as we slept. Later some of our men said that Ospak had practised some sort of magic so that none of us awoke. In truth several of our sailors did glimpse Ospak's squadron gliding past in the blackness, but they did not have the heart to wake their colleagues. All of us knew that, soon enough, we would meet again in battle.

FIFTEEN

'NONE OF US can escape the Norns' decision,' said Brodir heavily. He was fastening the buckles and straps of his mail shirt. 'We can only delay the hour and even then we need the help of the Gods.' Brodir's fingers were shaking as he did up the straps, and I thought to myself that he was not as trusting as Thrand. Brodir's mail shirt was famous. Like Thrand's helmet, it was reputed to have supernatural qualities. It was said that no sword or javelin could penetrate its links, rendering its wearer invulnerable. Yet I judged that Brodir did not believe in the magic qualities of his armour but wore it only as a talisman to bring good luck. Or perhaps there were few mail shirts large enough to fit the leader from Man.

Brodir's contingent, nearly seven hundred men, was getting ready for battle. Our position was on the extreme right of Sigtryggr's grand alliance of Dublin Ostmen, Sigurd's Orkneymen, King Mael Morda's Leinstermen and sundry Irish rebels who had taken this chance to challenge the domination of the Irish High King. Behind us, an arrow-shot away, was the landing beach of sand and shingle onto which the keels of our ships had slithered at first light that morning.

The plan had been to catch Brian Boruma off guard. For the past ten days the allies had been gathering in Dublin in response to King Sigtryggr's request that they arrive before the great Christian festival at the end of March. I thought this was an odd calendar to set for such staunch Old Believers as Sigurd the Stout and Brodir, but at the long, long war council in the king's hall which preceded our deployment Sigtryggr had explained there was a reason for this unusual deadline, a reason based on intelligence which Gormlaith had supplied. While married to Brian Boruma, she had detected that her ex-husband was becoming more and more obsessed with his religion as he grew older. Apparently the Irish High King had vowed to her that he would no longer fight on the high and holy days of the Christ calendar. It was blasphemy, he had said, to do battle on such sacred occasions and such days were ill-fated. When Sigtryggr mentioned this, some of the Norse captains exchanged nervous glances. Sigtryggr had come closer to the mark than he knew. Rumours of Brodir's raven dream had spread among the Norse and there were many who thought we had no business pursuing our campaign after such an ill-starred start. Brodir had not revealed the content of our visions on the beach at Man, nor had I – the source had been Ospak. From Man he had promptly sailed to Ireland and marched to Brian Boruma's camp to offer his services to the Irish High King. Ospak must have expected a vast haul of loot from Dublin because, that very day, he cheerfully submitted to being baptised by the Irish priests. On the other hand he put such little store by his conversion that he lost no time in spreading word about the raven dreams and how they foretold that Brodir and his men were doomed.

Gormlaith herself spoke at Sigtryggr's council of war and she was very persuasive. Brian Boruma's personal prestige had been vital to his previous military success, she told the hard-bitten war captains. His army rallied to him personally. That was the Irish habit. Their warriors flock to a clan chief considered to be lucky, and when it comes to a battle they like to see their leader at the forefront of the charge. So Sigtryggr's grand alliance would hold a crucial advantage if it brought the High King's army to battle when Boruma himself was unable to participate for his misguided religious reasons. The one day of the Christian calendar that Boruma was sure to refuse to carry weapons was the gloomy anniversary of the White Christ's death. Brian Boruma regarded it as the holiest day of the year, and there was no possibility that he could personally lead his men into battle on that day. Gormlaith had also pointed out that the morbid nature of such an anniversary would further dishearten the High King's forces. Some of his more devout troops might even follow their master's example in refusing to bear arms. Her logic impressed even the most sceptical of the council, and there was not a single voice raised in objection when Sigtryggr set Good Friday as the day most suitable for our attack. Sigtryggr also suggested that Earl Sigurd and Brodir might go back aboard their ships the previous evening and pretend to sail off. The hope was that Boruma's spies stationed on the hill overlooking the river would report that many of Sigtryggr's allies were deserting him, and the High King would be further lulled into inaction.

But such a commonplace deception had clearly failed. Already depressed by whispers about Odinn's ravens, our troops were further discouraged by the sight which greeted us as we came ashore. Drawn up on the hill facing us were the massed ranks of the High King's army and clearly they had been expecting us. Even more clearly, they had no compunction about spilling blood on the holy day. 'Would you look at that?' said one of Brodir's men who was standing next to me as we began to form up. He must have been a shiphandler rather than a fighting man as he was poorly equipped, carrying only a javelin and a light wooden shield, and had neither helmet nor mail shirt. 'I can see some of Ospak's men in the line right opposite us. That fellow with the long pike and the grey cloak is Wulf. He owes me half a mark of silver, which he never paid after our last dice game, and I didn't dare press him for the debt. He's got a foul temper, which is why everyone calls him Wulf the Quarrelsome. One way or another, that's a debt he and I are likely to settle today.' Like me, the shiphandler had been assigned to the rearmost of the five ranks in our swine array, the standard formation for a Norse brigade. It places the best armed and most experienced fighters in the front rank, shield to shield and no more than an arm's length apart. Youngsters like myself and the lightly armed auxiliaries fill up the rearmost ranks. The idea is that the shield wall bears the brunt of any charge and is too dense for the enemy to penetrate, while the lightly armed troops can make some minor contribution to the contest by hurling spears over the heads of their fighting colleagues. Quite what I was supposed to do, I had no idea. Brodir had told me to bring the two so-called 'fighting dogs' on shore, but there was no role for such fanciful creatures in the swine formation. Not that the the two hounds were in the least interested in biting enemy flesh. They were nervously darting from side to side and getting their leads in a tangle. As I hauled on the dogs' collars, I glanced across to my left, and with a sudden shock of surprise I recognised at least a dozen of the Burners among Earl Sigurd's Orkneymen. The Burners had sworn their oath to Sigurd the Stout and now they were obliged to do their duty. Just beyond their little group rose Earl Sigurd's famous battle standard with its symbol of the black raven. The sight caused me to have a sudden doubt. Had I misinterpreted my dream? I wondered. The iron-beaked birds who had swooped into the attack from far afield and torn men's flesh, were they Brodir's enemies? Or did they symbolise the arrival of Sigurd and his Orkneymen across the Irish Sea, following the raven banner to wreak havoc on Boruma's host?

My confusion was increased by this familiarity of friend and foe. Here I was fighting alongside men who would have counted me their enemy if they had known of my role in Kari's vengeance. And the sailor at my side was standing in the battle line facing a companion with whom, until a month ago, he had rolled dice. Nor was this mutual recognition restricted to the Norse warriors. 'Are you there, Maldred?' bellowed one of our front-rank men. He was a big, round-shouldered, grey-haired warrior, well armoured and carrying a heavy axe, and he was shouting his question across the gap that separated the two armies. 'Yes, of course I am, you arsehole!' came an answering cry from the High King's forces. From the opposing rank stepped a figure who, apart from his stature – he was slightly shorter – and the fact that he wore a patterned Irish cloak over his chain mail, was almost indistinguishable from our own man. 'No more farting about, now's the time to see who is the better man,' called our champion, and while the two armies looked on and waited as if they had all the time in the world, the adversaries ran forward until they came within axe swing, and each man let loose a mighty swipe at the other.

Each deflected the blow with his shield, and then the two men settled down to a bent-kneed crouch as they circled one another warily, occasionally leaping forward to deliver a huge blow with the axe, only for the other man to block the blow with his round shield and take a retaliatory swing which failed to connect because his enemy had jumped back out of range. When the two men lost patience with this alternate thud and leap, it seemed as if they reached some mutual pact of self-destruction, for in the instant that one man flung aside his shield so he could raise his axe with both hands his opponent did the same. Suddenly the contestants were charging at one another like a pair of mad bulls, each determined to deliver the mortal blow. It was the man with the cloak who struck first. He knew he had the shorter reach, so he let go of his axe as he swung. The weapon flew across the last two feet and struck the Norseman a terrific blow on the side of his face, laying bare the bone. The Norseman staggered, and blood sprayed from the wound, yet the surge of his charge and the momentum of his blow carried him forward so that the strike of his axe smashed down on the Irishman's left shoulder, cutting deep into the neck. It did not behead the victim, but it was a killer blow. The Irishman fell first to his knees, then slowly toppled forward face down on the mud. His conqueror, dazed and disorientated, with blood pouring down his face, lasted only a few moments longer. As the two armies looked on, the Norseman wandered in a circle, tripping and lurching, the side of his face smashed open by the axe, and he too fell and did not rise again.

'Can you see the High King anywhere?' I heard someone ask in front of me.

'I think I caught a glimpse of him earlier, on horseback, but he's not there now,' a voice replied. 'That's his son Murchad over there on the left. He seems to be in charge. And his grandson is that cocky youngster dressed in a red tunic and blue leggings.' I squinted in that direction and saw a lad, younger than myself, standing in front of one of the enemy divisions. He was turned to face his men, Irishmen to judge by their dress, and he was waving his arms as he declaimed some sort of encouraging speech.

'Dangerous puppy,' said a third voice, 'like all his family.'

'But no sign of the High King himself, are you sure? That's a bonus.' It was the same man who had asked the first question, and by the plaintive tone in his voice I guessed he was trying to find some courage to cheer himself up.

'Not much different from us then,' said a voice sourly. We all knew what he was talking about. King Sigtryggr had not expected to dupe the High King with the fake withdrawal of his Norse allies; he preferred to dupe his own allies. When the longships had withdrawn the previous evening, Sigtryggr had promised to be ready on the beach next morning to join forces with us. But we found waiting for us only Mael Morda's Leinstermen and several bands of bloodthirsty Irish volunteers from the northern province, Ui Neills they called themselves. From Dublin's garrison there was just a handful of troops, but the best of them, Sigtryggr's personal bodyguard, were entirely absent. They had stayed behind to protect Sigtryggr himself and Gormlaith, who had chosen to watch the outcome of the battle from their vantage point behind the safety of Dublin's walls. It was hardly a cheerful beginning for our own efforts, and I suspected that some of our men would have been happy if King Sigtryggr's face had been at the opposite end of the blows from their battleaxes.

I had little time to ponder King Sigtryggr's duplicity. At that moment the enemy line began to move. It came at us not in a single organised rush, but as a ragged, rolling charge, the Irish first letting loose a high keening scream, which overlaid the deeper roar of their Norse allies. They ran forward in a broken torrent, brandishing axes, swords, pikes, spears. A few tripped on the rough ground and went sprawling, vanishing under the feet of their companions, but the ones on top rushed on, determined to gather as much speed as possible before they hit the shield wall. When the collision came, there was a massive, shattering crash like oak trees falling in the forest, and into the air flew an eerie cloud of grey and white sprinkled with bright flecks. It was the dust and whitewash from several thousand shields that had been carefully cleaned and repainted before the battle.

The thunderous opening crash immediately gave way to a confused, indiscriminate chaos, the sound of axes thudding into timber and stretched cowhide, the ringing clash of steel on metal, shouts and curses, cries of pain, sobs of effort, the scuffling grunts of men fighting for their lives. Somewhere in the distance I heard the high, wild, urgent notes of a war horn. It must have come from the High King's army because we had no war trumpeters as far as I knew.

The two opposing battle lines lost all formation within moments. The conflict broke into swirling groups, and I noticed how the Norsemen tended to fight with Norsemen and the Irish with Irish. There was no cohesion, only larger clumps of fighters clustered around their own war leaders. Sigurd's raven banner was the centre of the largest and most unified group, and Brodir's contingent appeared to be the chosen target for the men who followed Ospak. My own role in the conflict was minimal. The two war hounds panicked at the sound of the initial collision between the armies and bolted. Foolishly I had tied their leads around my wrist and the dogs were so strong that I was plucked off my feet and dragged ignominiously over the ground, until the leather thongs snapped and the two dogs raced free. I never saw them again. I was scrambling back to my feet, rubbing my aching wrist to restore the circulation, when a light spear thudded into the ground beside me, and I looked up to see an Irish warrior not twenty paces away. He was one of their kerns – lightly armed skirmishers – and thankfully both his aim and courage were inadequate to the situation. Just as I was realising again that I was unarmed, apart from a small knife hanging inside my shirt, the Irishman must have thought he had ventured too far inside the enemy lines, and he turned and scampered away, his bare feet flying over the turf.

Already the opposing armies were growing exhausted. First the skirmishers disengaged and withdrew, and then the knots of hersirs, the Norse warriors, began to disentangle as both sides fell back to their previous positions, and paused to count the cost of this first engagement. The losses had been severe. Badly injured men sat on the ground, trying to staunch their wounds; those who were still on their feet were leaning over, propped on their spears and shields, as they gasped for breath like exhausted runners. Scattered here and there were dozens of corpses. Mud and blood were everywhere.

'Seems that we're not the only ones to have slippery allies,' said a tall, thin soldier who was trying to stop the blood running down into his eyes from a sword slash that had nicked his forehead just below the brow line of the helmet. He was looking across at a large Irish contingent of the High King's army, which now stood some distance away from the rest of his battle line. It was apparent from their fresh appearance that these cliathaires as the Irish call their fighters, had not joined in the charge, but had stood by, watching. 'That's Malachi's lot,' explained one of our Ostmen. 'He laid claim to be the High King before Brian Boruma pushed him off the throne, and he would dearly like to have it back. The moment Malachi joins in the battle, then we'll know who's winning. He'll throw in his troops to join whoever is about to be victorious.'

'Form shield wall!' bellowed Brodir, and his men moved into line and began to lock shields again. A concerted ripple of movement among the High King's troops farther up the gentle slope of the hill showed that our opponents were getting ready for a second charge.

This time they picked their targets. The elite of the Irish forces was Murchad's bodyguard. As the High King's eldest son, he was entitled to an escort of professional men-at-arms, many of them battle-hardened from years of fighting in his father's numerous campaigns. The most menacing among them were the Gall-Gael, the Irishmen known as the 'Sons of Death', who had been adopted into Ostmen familes as youths and trained in Norse fighting methods. They combined their weapons skill with the fanaticism of re-converts, and of course their Norse opponents regarded them as turncoats and traitors, and never gave them any quarter. The result was the Gall-Gael were as feared as any berserk. In their earlier charge Murchad's bodyguard had singled out Mael Morda's Leinstermen. Now they shifted their position along the Irish battle line to join forces with Ospak's raiders and strike at Brodir and the contingent from Man.

They came screaming and bellowing at us, running downhill with the advantage of the slope, and the shock of their charge broke our shield wall. I found myself being bundled here and there in a shouting, swearing mass of men as Murchad and his bodyguard erupted through the first and second ranks of the swine array, closely followed by chain-mail-clad troops from Ospak's division, who surged into the gap torn in our line. I thought I recognised the face of Wulf, the cantankerous card player, over the upper rim of a red and white shield when the tall, gangling warrior behind whom I was standing, took a direct hit in the chest from a spear. He gave a surprised grunt and fell backwards, knocking me to the ground. As I squirmed out from under his body, one of the Gall-Gael careering into the attack took a moment aside from the more serious fighting to glance down and casually club at me with the back of his battleaxe. Even in the hubbub of the battle he must have heard the loud snapping crack as the axehead struck my spine. I caught a glimpse of his teeth as he bared them in a grimace of satisfaction before turning away, satisfied that he had broken my back. The shocking thump of the blow sent a terrible pain searing through me and I let out a gasp of agony as I fell face forward into the earth. I was dizzy with pain and when I tried to move, I found I could only turn my face far enough to one side to breathe.

As I lay there semi-paralysed, I watched from ground level the fight raging above and around me. I recognised instantly the Irish leader, Murchad. He was armed with a long, heavy sword and using it two-handed to thrust and sweep as he carved his path through the disorganised swine formation. He had no need for a shield because fully armoured bodyguards kept pace with him on each side, blocking the counter-blows and leaving Murchad the glory of killing his opponents. I saw two of Brodir's best men go down before him, no more than five paces from where I lay, and then Murchad was called away by someone shouting urgently in a tongue which, even in the waves of pain coming from my spine and ribs, I could understand as Irish. Then someone trode heavily on my outflung arm, and the edge of a grey cloak passed across my field of vision. I closed my eyes, pretending to be dead, and after a moment's pause I opened them a slit and saw that it was Wulf the Quarrelsome who had tramped over me. He still held his long pike in his hand and was headed for the huge figure of Brodir, who was sweeping with his battleaxe to fend off a frontal attack from two more of Ospak's men. I was too tired and in a state of shock to shout a warning, even if I had thought to do so. It probably would have been the death of me, for Gall-Gael and Ostmen thought nothing of spearing a wounded man lying on the battlefield. Instead I watched Wulf come within pike thrust of Brodir and pause, waiting for his chance. As Brodir's axe swept down on one of his adversaries, Wulf lunged. He was aiming for the weakest spot in Brodir's famous mail shirt, the place in the armpit where even the most skilful armourer finds it impossible to make a flawless join between the metal rings which protect the shoulder and the torso. The point of the pike pierced the mail and carried into Brodir's side. The huge Manx leader staggered for a moment, then turning, pulled the weapon free. His face had gone deadly pale, though I could not tell whether it was from the pain of the stab or the shocking realisation that his talisman, the famous mail jacket, had failed him. Wulf had stepped back half a pace, still holding the pike, its point wet with Brodir's blood, and then stabbed again, hitting the same spot, probably more by good luck than judgement. I had expected Brodir to counter-attack, but to my dismay he began to retreat. He switched his battleaxe to his uninjured arm, and took several steps backwards, his body hunched over to protect his wounded side while still swinging his battleaxe to keep off his attackers. From his ungainly posture it was clear that he was hurt, and even more obvious that he was strongly right-handed and not at all accustomed to using a battleaxe with his left hand.

As Brodir backed away slowly from his attackers, it dawned on me that he should not have been fighting alone. Members of his war band should have been on hand to protect their leader's retreat, but no one was coming to his assistance. Cautiously I twisted my head around to see what was going on elsewhere. The sound of battle was ebbing, and I guessed that there would soon be another lull in the fighting to allow the two armies to pull back and regroup. Lying prone on the ground, I could not see what had happened on the rest of the battlefield, who had sustained the heaviest losses or who had gained the upper hand. But the fighting between Brodir's men and Ospak's followers must have been murderous. Beyond the body of the tall soldier whose collapse had knocked me down lay three dead men. Judging by their armour, they were from the front line of our swine array, and they had not given up their lives cheaply. In front of them were two enemy corpses and one casualty, whether he was friend or foe I could not tell, who was still alive. He was lying on his back and moaning with pain. He had lost an arm, chopped off at the elbow, and was trying to sit up, but was so unbalanced by his maiming, that he never managed to rise more than a few inches before falling with a small whimper. Soon he must bleed to death. Cautiously I began to check my own injuries. I stretched out one arm, then the other, and half-rolled onto my side. The pain from my back pierced deep into me, but I was encouraged to find that I could feel sensation in my right leg. My left leg was completely numb and then I saw that it was still trapped under the dead soldier. Cautiously I worked the leg free and, like a crab, pulled myself away from the corpse. After a pause to gather more strength, I struggled up onto my hands and knees, and reached back to feel the spot where the axe had struck me. Under my shirt my hand touched a hard, jagged edge and for one awful moment I thought I was touching the end of a broken rib emerging from my flesh. But I was imagining. What I was feeling was the broken haft of the small knife, which I usually wore out of sight, protected in a wooden sheath and hanging loosely from a thong around my neck. During the turmoil of the battle, the knife must have swung round behind my back, and it had taken the full force of the axe blow. The crack that the Gall-Gael thought was my spine breaking was the knife and wooden sheath snapping in two.

Slowly I rose to my feet as waves of dizziness swept over me, and set off at a hobbling run, weaving my way between the scatter of dead and wounded men and heading for the one symbol that I could recognise: the black raven banner of Earl Sigurd, which marked where the Orkneymen still rallied to their leader. There were not nearly as many of them as I had remembered, and at least half of those who were still on their feet appeared to be wounded. Sigurd himself was in the centre of the group and unharmed, so I guessed that his bodyguard had done their duty. Then I noticed that most of his surviving bodyguard were Burners. They must have stood together in the battle as fellow Icelanders and that is what had saved them. To my surprise, Sigurd the Stout noticed me at once. 'Here's Kari Solmundarson's young friend,' he called out cheerfully. 'You wanted to come to Ireland and find out what it is like. Now you know.' At the mention of Kari's name, several of the Burners glanced round and I was sure that the Burner who had been puzzling over my identity finally realised who I was and that he had seen me at the Althing. But there was nothing he could do, at least for the moment.

Sigurd was demanding everyone's attention. An overweight butterball of a man, he did not look as if his place was among the cut and thrust of the battlefield, but his courage matched his corpulence. Purple in the face and hoarse from shouting, he began to stamp up and down, exhorting his men to get ready for the next clash, to fight boldly and to maintain their honour. His mother's seidr spell on the black raven banner was holding true, he told them. The Orkneymen had been the most successful of Sigtryggr's allies on the battefield. They had withstood the enemy onslaught better than anyone else, and he praised the sacrifice of the three men who had been cut down while carrying the standard.

'Even now the Valkyries are escorting them to Valholl, where each man has rightly earned his place. Soon he will tell the tale of how he defended Odinn's raven though it meant his own certain death.' Few of the Orkneymen seemed impressed. They looked utterly exhausted and when Sigurd called for a volunteer to carry the banner at the next assault, there was no response. There was an awkward silence into which I stepped. Why I did this, I still cannot say for sure. Perhaps I was dizzy and disorientated from the battering I had received; perhaps I had decided that I had nothing to lose now that I had been recognised by the Burners. I only know that as I walked unsteadily to where the flagstaff was stuck in the ground I was feeling the same sensation of calm and inevitability that I had felt years earlier when, as a boy, I had crossed the clearing in the wood in Vinland and entered the hut of the Skraelings. My legs were acting on their own and my body was separate from my mind. I felt as if I was floating at a little distance outside and above my physical self and calmly looking down on a familiar stranger. I tugged the flagpole from the earth. For a moment Sigurd looked astonished. Then he gave a roar of approval. 'There you are,' he called to his men 'we've got our lucky bannerman! The lad's unarmed, yet he'll carry the black raven for us.'

My role as the earl's standard bearer was brief and inglorious. For a third time the High King's forces came swarming down the slope at us, and once again it was Murchad's shock troops who led the way. We had now been on the battlefield all morning and both sides were torn and weary, but somehow Murchad's people seemed to find the strength to smash down at us as fiercely as ever. Sigurd's raven banner was their supreme prize. First it was a half-crazed, kilted Irish clansman leaping down the hill determined to show his courage to his colleagues by seizing the standard. Then came a pair of grim-faced Norse mercenaries heavily chopping their way through the shield wall, concentrating at the spot nearest to the raven banner. For a short interval Fat Sigurd's Orkneymen held firm. They stood solid, shields locked together, resisting the onslaught and exchanging axe sweeps with the enemy. Two paces behind them, for I was in the second rank of the swine array now, I could do no more than use the banner staff as my crutch, leaning on it for support with my head bowed and one end of the pole resting on the ground. I was in agony from my damaged back and I tried desperately to think of a galdr spell chant that might help me, but my mind was in turmoil. I heard and felt the conflict rather than saw it. Once again there was the shouting of voices, much hoarser now, the clang of metal, the thump and thud of bodies meeting and falling, the press and jostle as our formation bent and buckled. I do not even know who struck – Gall-Gael, kern or Ostmen. But suddenly there was a terrible pain in the hand that held the staff and the banner was wrenched from my grasp as I doubled over, clasping my injured hand into my belly. Someone swore in Norse, and I was aware of a tussle as two men fought over the flag, each trying to wrench the shaft from the other. Neither won the contest. I looked up to see one of Sigurd's bodyguards, it was one of the Burners – Halldor Gudmundsson, receive a killing sword thrust in his left side, just as another of the Burners stepped behind the other man and crippled him with a downward blow behind the knee. The man fell sideways and was lost beneath the stamping feet.

'Rally to the Raven!' It was Sigurd's voice, shouting over the tumult, and the tubby earl himself pushed through the brawl and grabbed the banner staff. 'Here! Thorstein, you may carry our emblem,' and he held it out to a tall man standing nearby. It was another of the Burners.

'Don't touch it if you want to live,' warned a voice sharply. An

Icelander, Asmund the White, chose this moment to desert his lord.

Thorstein hesitated, then turned away. At that moment I understood that my first interpretation of my omen dream had been correct. We had spurned our own emblem of Odinn, and the war ravens were our enemies.

Overweight and out of breath, Sigurd might have been a poor foot soldier but he was not a coward. 'Right then,' he growled, 'if no one else will carry the banner, then I will do so even if it means my death. It is fit that the beggar bears the bag, and I would prefer to die with honour than to flee, but I will need both hands if this is to be my final fight.' He pulled the red and black banner from the staff, folded it lengthways, and wrapped it around his waist as a sash. Then, with a sword in one hand and a round shield on the other arm, he stumped forward, puffing and wheezing. Only a handful of men followed him, and at least half of them were Burners. Perhaps they too realised that their lives were over and that, forbidden to ever return to Iceland, they might as well die on the battlefield. The final encounter was very brief. Sigurd lumbered straight towards the nearest Irish chieftain. Once again it was Murchad, who seemed to be everywhere during the battle. There was little contest. Murchad took a spear from a solder nearby, levelled it and when Sigurd came within range thrust forward so the weapon took Sigurd in the throat. The Earl of Orkney fell, and the moment he went down those who remained of his contingent turned and began to retreat towards the ships. A moment later I heard a deep baying cry and the wilder rattle of light drums. It was Malachi committing his fresh troops on the side of Brian Boruma.

I ran. Hugging my injured hand to my chest, I fled for my life. Twice I tripped and fell sprawling, crying out with pain as my spine was wrenched. But each time I got back on my feet and blundered forward, hoping to reach the safety of the boats. My eyes were filled with tears of pain so I could barely see where I was going. I knew only to run in the same direction as my fellows, and try to keep up with them. I heard a choking cry as someone close to me received an arrow or javelin in the back. And suddenly I was splashing through water, the salty drops flying up in my face, and my headlong rush slowing so I almost pitched forward. I looked up and saw that I had reached the beach, but was far from safety. During the battle the tide had come in, and the sand flats to which we had brought the longships that dawn were now submerged. To get to the ships our defeated men would have to wade, then swim.

I laboured forward through the pluck of the water, my feet slipping on the unseen sand and mud. Not all the men around me were fugitives. Many were hunters. I saw Norsemen who had taken Brian Boruma's pay catch up with their countrymen who had fought for Sigtryggr and cut their throats as they floundered in the sea. Blood oozed across the tide. The retreat was becoming a massacre. I watched a young Irish chieftain – he was the same man who had been pointed out as the High King's grandson – come bounding out through the shallows, his hair flying and his face alight with battle craziness. He closed with two Orkneymen, each far bigger than himself, and without a weapon his hand, he grabbed and pulled them down underwater to drown. There was a terrible thrashing in the water, and the three contestants surfaced several times before all three grew weaker until the youth and one of the Norse failed to come back and gulp for air. Their two waterlogged corpses were floating face down even as the third man, now too tired to swim the final gap, threw up his arms and sank from view.

As I watched him drown, I knew that my injured arm and hand would prevent me from swimming to the waiting boats. Turning, I waded back to land and by some intervention of the Gods I was left alone. Soaking wet, shivering with cold and shock, I emerged on the beach and, like a wounded animal, looked around me to seek shelter from my enemies. Halfway up the slope of the hill I saw a thicket of bushes at the edge of the wood overlooking the battlefield. Aching with tiredness, I laboured up the hill towards this refuge. For the last hundred paces I was panting with exhaustion and dreading the shout of discovery. But nothing came and as I reached the bushes I did not stop, but blundered forward until the tearing of the thorns slowed me. I dropped to my knees and crawled forward, holding my injured hand to my chest as a fox with a wounded leg seeks shelter after the trap. Reaching deep into the thicket, I collapsed on the ground and lay panting for breath.

I must have lost consciousness for some time, before the sound of singing penetrated through my nausea, and I thought that my ears were deceiving me. I heard the words of a hymn that my grandmother, Erik the Red's wife, had sung in the White Rabbit Hutch back in Greenland. Then the sound came again, but not in a woman's voice. It was a male choir. I crawled a few feet forward to find that my refuge was not as deep and effective as I thought. The bushes made only a thin fringe on the edge of the woods. On the far side of the bushes began a forest of young oak trees. There were wide open spaces between the tree trunks, and at that moment the nearest trunks gave the impression of being the columns of a church because, set on the forest floor, was a large portable altar. The sound of singing came from half a dozen White Christ priests who were celebrating some sort of ceremony, holding up sacred symbols, a cross, a bowl and even several candles as they sang. One of the celebrants was about my age and he was carrying a large dish covered with a cloth. The leading figure standing beside the altar was an old man, perhaps in his early sixties, grey-haired and gaunt. He was the high priest, I thought, because all the other priests were treating him with great respect and, though he was bareheaded, he was richly dressed. Then I heard the whicker of a horse and to my left I saw a large tent, half hidden among the trees, placed where it had a commanding view of the battlefield I had just left. Loitering beside the tent were half a dozen Norsemen. My brain was fuzzily trying to work out the connection between the tent and the religious ceremony when there was a great crashing sound. Out from the bushes, like an enormous enraged bear, burst Brodir. He too must have been hiding from enemy pursuit. Now he came lumbering out of the bushes and I caught a glimpse of the crusted streak down his right side where blood had leaked from his wound. Brodir still had his battleaxe in his ungainly left hand, but why he had burst from cover in this suicidal manner did not occur to me at once. I watched as Brodir ambushed the priests, and the young man with the dish tried to block his charge. The boy stepped into Brodir's path and held up the metal dish like a shield, but Brodir swept him aside with a single awkward blow from the battleaxe, and I cringed in sympathy as the boy's right hand was cut off, leaving a stump which spurted blood. Brodir gave a curious low growl as with another ungainly left-handed sweep he swung his axe at the old man's neck, half-severing his head from his body. The old man seemed to shrivel to a bunch of rags as he collapsed to the ground even as the men-at-arms came running forward, too late. Some knelt to pick up the fallen priest, the others, awed by Brodir's immense size, cautiously formed a half-circle around him and began to close in. Brodir offered no resistance, but just stood there, swaying slightly on his feet, the battleaxe hanging straight down from his weak left hand. He threw back his head and shouted, 'Now let man tell man that it was Brodir who killed King Brian.' At that moment I knew that the seidr magic of the black raven banner had been a hoax worthy of Odinn the Deceiver. I, the last person to carry the banner on high, had survived, yet we had lost the battle. By contrast our enemy, who had won the victory, had sacrificed their leader. I had witnessed the victory of the High King but the death of Brian Boruma.

Brodir was pressed back slowly by his enemies. It seemed that the men-at-arms wanted to take the killer of the High King alive. They held their shields in front of them as they advanced deliberately and cautiously, forcing Brodir back towards the thicket in which I lay. More than ever Brodir seemed like a great wounded bear, but now it was a beast that has been cornered at the end of a forest hunt. Finally he could back away no farther. His retreat was blocked by the thicket and as he took one more step backwards, still facing his enemies, he caught his heel and fell. The hunters leapt forward, literally throwing themselves on their quarry, smothering Brodir in a crackling smash of branches and twigs. Overcome in the confusion, I lost consciousness once again and the final image in front of my eyes was of the iron-beaked ravens swarming in until the entire sky went black.

SIXTEEN

I AWOKE TO a jolt of excruciating pain in my arm. I thought at first that the source was my injured hand. But the pain was now coming from the other side. I opened my eyes to find a cliathaire leaning over me, clumsily hammering a rivet to close a fetter on my right wrist. He had missed his stroke and struck my arm with the hilt of his sword, which he was using as a makeshift mallet. I twisted my head to look around. I was lying on the muddy ground not far from the bush, out of which I had been dragged unconscious. About a dozen Irish and Norse soldiers were standing with their backs to me, staring at something which lay at the foot of one of the oak trees. It was Brodir's corpse. I recognised it from the lustrous long black hair. He had been disembowelled. Later I was told that this had been done at the request of the mercenaries in the High King's bodyguard. They claimed that Brodir's murderous ambush of the unarmed High King had been the mark of a coward and should be punished in the traditional way – his stomach slit and his guts pulled out while he was still alive. So his entrails had been nailed up to the oak tree. The truth, I suspected, was that the mercenaries were trying to divert attention from their own deficiency. They should never have left the High King unguarded.

The Irishman hoisted me to my feet, then tugged the fetter's chain to lead me away from the scene of Brian Boruma's death.

'Name?' he asked in dansk tong. He was a short, wiry man of about forty, dressed in the usual Irish costume of leggings bound with gaiters and a loose shirt, over which he wore a short brown and black cloak. He slung his small round shield onto his back by its strap so that he had one hand free to hold my leading chain. In his other hand he still held his sword.

'Thorgils Leifsson,' I replied. 'Where are you taking me?'

He looked up in surprise. I had spoken in Irish. 'Are you one of Sigtryggr's people, from Dublin?' he demanded.

'No, I came here with the ships from Man, but I didn't belong to Brodir's contingent.'

For some reason, the Irishman looked rather pleased with this news. 'Why were you fighting alongside them, then?' he asked.

It was too complicated to explain how I had come to be with Brodir's men, so I replied only, 'I was looking after a pair of wolf hounds for him, as their keeper.' And, unwittingly, with those words I sealed my fate.

After a short walk we reached the area where the remnants of the High King's army were gathering together the plunder of battle. The simple rule was that the first person to lay hands on a corpse got to keep his spoil provided he stripped the victim quickly and made it clear that he had established his claim to the booty. Many victors were already dressed in several layers of garments, a motley collection of captured finery worn one on top of another, with many of the outer layers blood-stained. Others were carrying four or five swords in their arms as if collecting sticks of firewood in the forest, while their colleagues were busy stuffing looted shoes into their sacks, together with belts and shirts, which they had stripped from the slaincluding the dead from their own side. One Irish fighter had assembled a gruesome collection of three severed heads, which he had thrown on the ground, their hair knotted together. Clusters of men were disputing the more valuable items – chain-mail shirts or body jewellery. These arguments were frequently between Malachi's fresh troops and Boruma's battle-stained soldiers, who had done most of the fighting. The latter usually won the argument because they had an ugly, tired gleam in their eyes which indicated that after so much slaughter they were fully prepared to keep their rewards even if it meant taking arms against their own side.

My captor led me to a small group of his colleagues who were clustered around a campfire, preparing a meal. A jumble of their booty lay on the ground beside them. It was rather meagre, mostly weaponry, a few helmets and some Ostman clothes. They looked up as he approached. 'Here,' he said, jerking on my chain, 'I've got the Man leader's aurchogad.' They looked impressed. An aurchogad, I was to learn, was a keeper of hounds. This is an official post among the Irish and found only in the retinue of a senior chief. By the Irish custom of war it meant that, as far as my captors were concerned, I had been a member of Brodir's personal retinue. Therefore I was a legitimate captive, an item of war booty, and thus I was now my captor's slave.

Our little group did not linger on the battlefield. Word quickly spread that Malachi, who was now effectively the leader of the victorious army, was already in negotiations with King Sigtryggr, still safe behind his city walls with Gormlaith, and that there would be no attack on the city, so no booty there. With Brian Boruma dead, Malachi had lost no time in laying claim to the title of High King, and Sigtryggr was promising to support his claim on condition that Malachi spared Dublin from being plundered. So the real victors of our momentous battle were the two leaders who had taken the least part in the fighting and, of course, Gormlaith. As matters turned out, she was to spend the next fifteen years in Dublin as the undisputed power behind the throne, telling King Sigtryggr what to do.

The losses among the real combatants had been horrific. Nearly every member of Boruma's family who took part in the battle had been killed, including two of his grandsons, and Murchad's reckless courage had finally brought about his own death. He had knocked one of Brodir's men to the ground and was leaning over him, about to finish him off when the Norseman thrust upward with his own dagger and gutted the Irish leader. One-third of the High King's fighters lay dead on the battlefield. and they had inflicted a similar level of damage on their opponents. Mael Morda's Leinstermen had been annihilated, and only a handful of the Norse troops from overseas survived the desperate scramble through the tidal shallows to get back to their ships. Earl Sigurd's Orkneymen suffered worst of all. Fewer than one man in ten managed to escape with his life, and Earl Sigurd's entire personal retinue had fallen, including fifteen of the Burners, though, for me, that was little consolation.

My owner, I learned as we marched into the interior of Ireland, went by the name of Donnachad Ua Dalaigh, and he was what the Irish call a ri or king. This does not mean a king as others might know it. Donnachad was no more than the leader of a small tuath or petty kingdom located somewhere in the centre of the country. By foreign standards he would have been considered little more than a sub-chieftain. But the Irish are a proud and fractious people and they cling to any level or mark of distinction, however modest. So they have several grades of kingship and Donnachad was of the lowest rank, being merely a ri tuathe, the headman of a small group who claim descent from a single ancestor of whose semi-legendary exploits they are, of course, extremely proud. Certainly Donnachad was much too unimportant to have rated an aurchogad of his own. Indeed, he was fortunate even to have the services of the single elderly attendant, who helped to carry his weapons and a dented cooking pot, as we travelled west with his war band of no more than twenty warriors. Donnachad himself proudly held the chain attached to his one and only slave.

I had never seen such a verdant country in all my life. Everywhere the vegetation was bursting from bud to leaf. There were great swathes of woodland, mostly oak and ash, and between the forests stretched open country that brimmed with green. Much of the ground was soggy, but our track followed a ridge of high ground that was better drained and on either hand I looked out across a gently rolling landscape with thorn trees so heavy with white blossoms that the sudden gusts of winds created little snowstorms of white petals that drifted down onto the path. The verges on each side of the track were speckled with small spring flowers in dark blue, pale yellow and purple, and every bush seemed to hold at least one pair of songbirds so intent on their calls that they ignored our approach until we were nearly close enough to touch them. Even then they only hopped a few feet into the upper branches to continue to announce their courting. The weather itself was utterly unpredictable. In the space of a single day we experienced all seasons of the year. A blustery grey morning brought an autumn gale that buffeted us so fiercely that we had to walk leaning into the blast, and the squall was succeeded by a spring-like interval of at least an hour when the wind suddenly dropped and we heard again the shouting of the small birds, only for a swollen black cloud to throw down on us a rattling attack of winter sleet and hail that had us pulling up the hoods of our cloaks and pausing for shelter under the largest and leafiest tree. Yet by mid-afternoon the clouds had cleared away entirely and the sunshine was so hot on our faces that we were rolling up our cloaks to tie them on top of our packs as we tramped, sweating, through the puddles left by the recent downpour.

After all, Donnachad proved to be a rather good-natured man and not the least vindictive. On the third day of the journey he abandoned the practice of holding my lead chain, and let me walk along with the rest of his band, though I still wore the fetters on each wrist. This was particularly painful for my left arm because the hand in which I had held the staff of the black raven banner when I was struck was puffed up and swollen and had turned an ugly purple-yellow. At first I had thought I would lose the use of the fingers entirely, for I could not bend them and I had no sense of touch. But gradually the swelling receded and my hand began to mend, though it would always ache before the onset of rain. The small bones, I suppose, had been fractured and never knitted together properly.

We passed a succession of small hamlets, usually set off at

some distance to one side of the road. They were prosperous-looking places, groups of thatched farms and outbuildings often protected by a palisade, but their vegetable patches and grazing pastures were outside the defensive perimeter so evidently the land was not entirely lawless. From time to time Donnachad and his men turned aside to tell the farmers about the outcome of the great battle and to purchase food, paying with minor items of their spoil, and I looked for the barns where the farmers stored the winter hay for feeding their cattle, but then realised that the Irish winters were so mild that the herders could allow the cattle to graze outside all year long. We were travelling along a well-used road, and frequently met other travellers coming towards us – farmers with cattle on their way to a local market, pedlars and itinerant craftsmen. Occasionally we met a ri tuathre, a chieftain one step up the hierarchy from Donnachad. These mid-ranking nobles ruled over several smaller tuaths, and whenever we met one on the road I noted how Donnachad and his people stood respectfully aside to allow the ri tuathre to trot past on his small horse, accompanied by at least twenty outriders.

After the fourth or fifth of these self-important little cavalcades had splashed past us, the hooves of their horses sprinkling us with muddy water from the puddles, I ventured to ask Donnachad why the ri tuathre travelled with such large escorts when the land seemed so peaceful.

'It would be very wrong for a ri tuathre to travel alone. It would diminish the price of his face,' Donnachad answered.

'The price of his face?' I enquired. Donnachad had said 'log n-enech', and I knew no other way to translate it.

'The price of his honour, his worth. Every man has a value whenever he is judged, either in front of the arbitrators or by his own people, and a ri' – and here he sucked in his breath and tried to look a little more regal, though that was difficult in his shabby and mud-spattered clothes – 'should always act in measure with the price of his face. Otherwise there would be anarchy and ruin in his tuath.'

'So what would be the price of Cormac's face?' I meant this as a joke. I had noted that the Irish have a quick sense of humour and Cormac, one of Donnachad's cliathaires, was particularly ugly. He had bulging eyes, broad flat nostrils, and an unfortunate birthmark running down the left side of his face from his ear to disappear under his shirt collar. But Donnachad took my question entirely seriously. 'Cormac is a cow-freeman of good standing – he has a half-share in a plough team – so his face price is two and a half milch cows, rather less than one cumal. He renders me the value of one milch cow in rent every year.'

I decided to take my luck a little further. A cumal is a female slave, and Donnachad's reply would have some bearing on my own future as his property. 'Forgive me if I am being impolite,' I said, 'but do you also have a face price? And how would other people know what it was?'

'Everyone knows the face price of every man, his wife and his family,' he answered without even a moment's pause for thought, 'from the ri tuathre whom we saw just now, whose honour is eight cumals, to a lad still living on his parent's land whose face would be valued at a yearling heifer.'

'Do I have a face price too?'

'No. You are doer, unfree, and therefore you have neither price nor honour. Unless, that is, you manage to obtain your freedom and then by hard work and thrift you accumulate enough wealth. But it is easier to lose face price than to gain it. A ri endangers his honour if he even lays his hand to any implement that has a handle, be it hammer, axe or spade.'

'Does that include using a sword hilt as a mallet?' I could not refrain from answering, and Donnachad gave me a cuff around the head.

It was on the fourth day of our walk that I had my most notable encounter with this strange Irish notion of face price. We came to a small village where normally we might have stopped and bought some food. Instead we marched straight forward even though, as I knew, our supplies were running low. The brisk pace made my back hurt. It was still sore from the blow received in the battle, but my companions merely told me to hurry up and not delay them and that I would soon have medicine to reduce the pain. They quickened their pace and looked distinctly cheerful as if anticipating some happy event. Shortly afterwards we came in sight of a building, larger than the usual farmhouse and set much closer to the road. I saw that it had a few small outhouses, but there were no cattle stalls nor any sign of farming activity around it. Nor did it have a defensive palisade. On the contrary, the building looked open to all and very welcoming. Without a moment's hesitation my companions veered from the track, approached the big main door and, barely pausing to knock, pushed their way inside. We were in a large, comfortable room arrayed with benches and seats. In the centre of the room a steaming cauldron hung over a fire pit. A man who was evidently the owner of this establishment came forward to greet Donnachad most warmly. Using several phrases of formal welcome, he invited him to sit down and take his ease after the weariness of the highway. He then turned to each of the cliathaires – ignoring me and Donnachad's servant, of course – and invited them likewise. Scarcely had our group found their seats than our host was providing them with flagons of mead and beer. These drinks were soon followed by loaves of bread, a small churn of butter and some dried meat. There was even some food for myself and Donnachad's elderly servant.

I ate quickly, expecting that we would soon be on our way. But to my puzzlement Donnachad and his cliathaires appeared to be settling in to enjoy themselves. Their host promised them a hot meal as soon as his cook had fired the oven. Then he served more drinks, followed by the meal itself, and afterwards made another liberal distribution of mead and beer. By then the cliathaires had settled down to story-telling, a favourite pastime among the Irish, where – as at Earl Sigurd's Jol feast in Orkney – each person at a gathering is expected to tell a tale to keep the others entertained. All this time more travellers had been entering the room, and they too were seated and fed. By nightfall the room was full to capacity, and it was obvious to me that our little party would be spending the night at this strange house.

'Who is the owner of the house? Is he a member of Donnachad's tuath?' I asked Donnachad's servant.

He was already drowsy with tiredness and strong drink. 'Doesn't even come from these parts originally. Set up here maybe four years ago, and is doing very well,' the old man replied with a gentle hiccup.

'You mean he sells food and drink to travellers, and is making his fortune?'

'No, not making his fortune, spending his fortune,' the old-timer answered. 'He's made his fortune already, cattle farming somewhere to the north, I think. Now he's earning a much higher face price and he well deserves it.' I thought the old fellow's wits were fuddled and gave up the questions. There would be a better time to solve the mystery in the morning.

In fact next morning was not the right time to ask questions either. Everyone had fierce headaches, and the sun was already high before we were ready to set out on the road again. I loitered, waiting for Donnachad to pay our host for all the food and drink we had consumed, but he made no move to do so, and our host seemed just as good-natured as when we first arrived. Donnachad muttered only a few gracious phrases of thanks and then we rejoined his men, who were trudging blearily forward. I sidled across to the elderly servant and asked him why we had left without paying. 'You never pay a briugu for hospitality,' he answered, mildly shocked. 'That would be an insult. Might even take you to court for looking to pay him.'

'In Iceland, where I come from,' I said, 'a farmer is expected to be hospitable and give shelter and food to travellers who come to his door, particularly if he is wealthy and can afford it. But I didn't see any farming near the house. I'm surprised that he doesn't move away to somewhere a bit more remote.'

'That's precisely why he's built his house beside the road,' explained the old man, 'so that as many people as possible can visit him. And the more hospitality he dispenses, the higher will rise his face price. That's how he can increase his honour, which is much more important to him than the amount of wealth he has accumulated.'

What the briugu would do when all his hoarded savings ran out, he did not explain. 'A briugu should possess only three things,' concluded the old man with one of those pithy sayings of which the Irish are fond, 'a never-dry cauldron, a dwelling on a public road and a welcome for every face.'

We arrived at Donnachad's tuath in the second week of Beltane, the month which in Iceland I had known as Lamb-fold-time. After trudging halfway across Ireland in the mud with Donnachad and his slightly shabby band, I was not expecting Donnachad's home to be very grand. Even so, its air of threadbare poverty was flagrant. His dwelling was merely a small circular building with walls of wattle and daub and a conical thatch roof, and the interior was more sparsely furnished than the briugu's roadside hostel. There were a few stools and benches, and the sleeping arrangements were thin mattresses stuffed with dried bracken, while the beaten-earth floor was covered with rushes. Outside were some cattle byres, a granary and a small smithy. There was also a short line of stables of which Donnachad was proud, though there were no horses in them at the present moment.

From the conversation of his cliathaires I gathered that Donnachad and his warriors had gone to fight alongside the Irish High King not from loyalty, but in the hope of bringing back enough booty to improve the hardship of their daily lives. The land on which their clan or fine lived was unproductive at the best of times, being waterlogged and boggy, and there had been so much rain during the last three summers that their ploughings had been flooded and the crops ruined. At the same time a recurring murrain had afflicted their cattle herds, and because petty kings like Donnachad and his chief farmers counted their wealth in cattle, this loss had brought them very low. The victory at the weir of

Clontarf, as the battle was now being called, had been the only cheerful event in the past five years.

Donnachad put me to work as a field labourer, and he treated me fairly, even though I was a slave. He allowed me rest time at noon and in the evening, and the food he provided – coarse bread, butter and cheese, and an occasional dish of meat – was not much different from his own diet. He had a wife and five children, and the homespun clothes they wore were a sign of their very reduced means. Yet I never saw Donnachad turn away any stranger who came to the farm – the Irish expectation of hospitality extended farther than the briugus – and twice during that summer I was called in as a house servant when Donnachad entertained his clansmen at the banquets which they expected from a man with his log n-enech. The food and mead, I knew, were almost everything that Donnachad held in his storerooms.

That summer in the open air, herding cattle, minding sheep and pigs, making and mending fences, changed me physically and mentally. I filled out and grew in strength, my back healed, and my command of the Irish improved rapidly. I found I had a gift for learning a language quickly. The only disappointment was that my injured hand still troubled me. Though I flexed and massaged it, the fingers remained stiff and awkward, and it was a particular handicap when I had to grip a spade handle to cut and stack turf for Donnachad's winter fire or grapple with boulders that we pulled from the rough fields and heaped into boundary walls.

The harvest was poor but not disastrous, and soon afterwards I began to notice that Donnachad was showing signs of gathering anxiety. His normally cheerful conversation dried up, and he would sit for an hour at a time, looking worried and distracted. In the night I woke occasionally to hear the low murmur of voices as he talked with his wife, Sinead, in the curtained-off section of the house they called their bed chamber. In the scraps of their conversation I often heard a word I did not know – manchuine – and when I asked its meaning from Marcan, the elderly servant, he grimaced. 'It's the tax Donnachad must pay to the monastery in the autumn. It's levied every year, and for the past five years Donnachad has not been able to pay. The monastery allowed him more time, but now the debt has grown so large that it will take years to clear, if ever.'

'Why does Donnachad owe money to a monastery?' I asked.

'A small tuath like ours must have an over-ruler,' Marcan replied. 'We are too small to survive on our own, and so we pledge allegiance to a king who can give us protection when we need it, in a local war or a dispute over boundary lands or something of the sort. We give the over-king our support, and he gains in honour if he is acknowledged as over-king to several tuaths. Also he supplies us with cattle which we look after for him. At the end of the farming year we give back an agreed amount of interest, in goods such as milk and cheese or calves, and we do some service for him.'

'But how does a monastery get involved in all this?'

'The arrangement seemed sensible when Donnachad's grandfather made it. He thought the abb would be a more considerate overlord than our previous ri tuathre, who was always asking us to provide him with soldiers for his endless squabbles with other ri tuathre, or he would suddenly show up with a band of his retainers and stay for two or three weeks, treating our houses as his own and generally reducing us to beggary. Donnachad's grandfather came up with the notion of transferring our loyalty to a monastery. The monks weren't going to ask for soldiers to join in their wars, and they wouldn't come visiting so often either.'

'So what went wrong?'

'The new arrangement worked well for nearly twenty years,' Marcan replied. 'But then the new abb got grand ideas. He and his advisers began claiming a special sanctity for their own saint. He must have precedence over other monasteries with their patron saints. The abb started bringing in stonemasons and labourers to build new chapels and erect imposing monuments, and he began to purchase expensive altar cloths and employ the best jewellers to design and make fancy church fittings. It all cost a great deal.'

More log n-enech, I thought.

'That was when the monastery treasurer began asking for increased returns on the cattle that had been loaned to us and, as you know, our cattle herding has not been lucky. Next, his successor came up with a new way of raising revenue. The monks now go on a circuit of their tuaths every autumn, bringing with them their holy relics to show the people. They expect the faithful to provide them with the manchuine, the monastery tax, so that the abb can continue the building programme. If you ask me, it will take another couple of generations for the job to be done. They're even asking for money to pay for missionaries whom the monks will send abroad to foreign countries.'

Marcan's remark about the missionaries reminded me of Thangbrand, King Olaf's belligerent missionary to Iceland, who had made such a nuisance of himself. But I wasn't sure of the old man's religious views so I kept silent.

'When are the priests due to make their next visit?'

'Ciaran is their special saint and the ninth day of September is his feast. So we'll probably see them in the next couple of weeks. But one thing's sure: Donnachad won't be able to settle the debt that the tuath owes.'

For some reason I expected St Ciaran's relics to be part of the saint – a thigh bone and a skull, perhaps. I had heard rumours that White Christ people revered these macabre remnants. But it turned out that the relics which the monks brought with them ten days later were much less personal. They were the crooked head of a bishop's staff and a leather satchel, which, they claimed, still held the Bible that their saint had studied. Certainly the crozier was proof of Marcan's assertion that the monastery had spent huge sums on glorifying their saint. The bent scrap of ancient wood was enshrined in a magnificent filigreed case of silver gilt, studded with precious stones and cleverly fashioned into the shape of a horse's head. This, the monks claimed, was the staff that Ciaran himself had used, and they held up the glittering ornament for all of us who gathered outside Donnachad's house to see and revere.

Strangely, they were even more reverential of the book. They affirmed that it was the very same miraculous volume that Ciaran had always carried with him, studying it at every available moment, rising at first light to begin reading, and poring over its pages far into the night, rarely setting it aside. And, unwittingly, they reminded me of the day my mother's hay had failed to dry after the downpour of rain at Frodriver, as they recounted the tale of how Ciaran had been sitting outside his cell one day when he was unexpectedly called away. Thoughtlessly he placed the book on the ground, lying open with its pages exposed to the sky. In his absence, a heavy shower had fallen; when he came back to collect the book all the ground was sodden wet, but the fragile pages were bone dry and not a line of the ink had run.

To prove it to us, the monks unfastened the satchel's leather thongs, solemnly withdrew the book and reverentially showed us the pristine pages.

Such tales made a great impression on Donnachad's people, even if they were not capable of reading and had no idea how to judge the age of the book. It made for an awkward interview as the little party of monks in their drab gowns stood in the centre the earth floor of Donnachad's home and asked for payment of their dues. The abb, or abbot, was represented by the treasurer, a tall, lugubrious man who exuded a sense of sad finality as he made his request. From where I was standing against the side wall with Marcan, I saw that Donnachad looked embarrassed and ashamed. I guessed that his log n-enech was at stake. Humbly Donnachad asked the monks to allow him and his people to pay off their obligation in small stages. He explained how the harvest had been a disappointment once again, but he would gather together as much produce as could be spared and deliver the food to the monastery throughout the coming winter. Then he delivered his pledge: as an earnest of his intention he would loan to the monastery his only slave, so the value of my work would be a surety to set against the annual debt.

The sad-looking treasurer looked at me where I stood against the far wall. I no longer wore a chain or manacles, but the scars on my wrists made my status obvious. 'Very well,' he said, 'we will accept the young man to come to work for us on loan, though it is not our custom to employ slaves in a monastery. However, the blessed Patrick himself was a slave once, so there is a precedent.' And with that I passed from the ownership of Donnachad, ri tuathe of the Ua Dalaigh, into the possession of the monks of St Ciaran's foundation.

SEVENTEEN

TO THIS DAY I look back on my time at St Ciaran's monastery with immense gratitude as well as heartfelt dislike. I do not know whether to thank or curse those who were my teachers there. I spent more than two years among them and had no inkling that the knowledge made available to me was such a privilege. My existence seemed pointless and confined and there were many days when, in my misery, I feared that Odinn had abandoned me. With hindsight I am now aware that my suffering was only a shadow of what the All-Father endured in his constant search for wisdom. Where he sacrificed an eye to drink at Mimir's well of wisdom, or hung in agony upon the world tree to learn the secret of the runes, I had only to bear loneliness, frustration, bouts of cold and hunger, and the repetition of dogma. And I was to emerge from St Ciaran's monastery equipped with knowledge that was to serve me well every day of my life.

Of course, it was not meant to be like that. I came to St Ciaran's monastery as a slave, a non-person, a nothing, a doer. My prospects were as bleak as the grey autumn day on which I arrived, with the air already holding the chill promise of winter. I was a down payment against a debt, and my only value was the manual work I was able to perform to reduce the arrears. So I was assigned to the stonemasons as a common labourer and I would have remained with them, hauling and cutting stone, sharpening chisels and heaving on pulley and tackle until I was too old and feeble to perform these simple manual tasks, if the Norns had not woven a different fate for me.

The monastery stands on the upper slope of a ridge facing west and overlooks a broad, slow-flowing river which is the chief river of Ireland. Just as Donnachad's royal home was not a palace in the accepted sense, so too St Ciaran's monastery is not the imposing edifice which might be imagined from its name. It is a cluster of small stone-built chapels on the hillside, interspersed with the humble buildings which house the monks and contain their books and workshops, and surrounded by an earth bank which the monks call their vallum. In physical size everything is on a modest scale, small rooms, low doors, simple dwellings. But in ambition and outlook the place is immense. At St Ciaran's I met monks who had travelled to the great courts of Europe and preached before kings and princes. Others were deeply familiar with the wisdom of the ancients; several were artists and craft workers and poets of real excellence, and many were genuine Ceili De, servants of God, as they called themselves. But inevitably there were also dullards in community, as well as hypocrites and sadists who wore the same habits and sported the same tonsures.

The abb in my time was Aidan. A tall, balding and colourless man with pale blue eyes and a fringe of curly blond hair, he looked as though all the blood had drained out of him. He had spent his entire adult life in the monastery, entering when little more than a child. In fact, it was rumoured that he was the son of an earlier abb, though it was more than a century since monks were allowed to have wives. Strict celibacy was now the outward show, but there were still monks who maintained regular liaisons with women in the extensive settlement which had grown up around the holy site. Here lived the lay people who provided casual labour for the monks – as their carters, ploughmen, thatchers and so forth. Whatever his origins, Abb Aidan was a cold fish, conservative yet ambitious. He ran the monastery along the same unwavering guidelines that he had inherited from his predecessors and he shunned innovation. His great strength, as he would have seen it, was his devotion to the long-term interests and continuity of the brotherhood. He intended to leave the monastery stronger and more secure than when he was first made abb, and if such a stiff figure recognised the frailty and impermanence of human existence, it was in order to concentrate his energy on longer-lasting material foundations. So Abb Aidan strove to increase the reputation of the monastery by adding to its material marvels rather than its sanctity.

He was fixated on finances. Brother Mariannus, the treasurer, saw the abb more than any other member of the community, and he was expected to render an almost daily account of the money that was owed, the taxes due, the current value of the possessions, the costs of administration. Abb Aidan was not avaricious for himself. He was interested only in enhancing the prestige of St Ciaran's, and he knew that this required a constant flow of income. Anyone who threatened that revenue was dealt with harshly. Most of the monastery's income came from renting out livestock, and in the year before I arrived a thief was caught stealing the monastery's sheep. He was hanged publicly on a gibbet just outside the holy ground. An even greater stir came in the second year of the abb's rule. A young novitiate absconded, taking with him a few articles of minor value – a pair of metal altar cups and some pages from an unfinished manuscript in the scriptorium. The young man disappeared in the night and managed to travel as far as the lands of his tuath. Abb Aidan guessed his destination and sent a search party after him, with orders that the stolen items be recovered and the miscreant brought back under guard. When I arrived at St Ciaran's, one of the first stories I was told in scandalised whispers was how the young monk had arrived on the end of a leading rope, his wrists bound, his back bloody from a beating. The other monks had expected that he would suffer a strict regime of mortification to atone for his sins, and they were puzzled when the young man was only held overnight at the monastery, then led away to an unknown destination across the river. A month later news filtered through that the young man had been placed in a deep pit and left to starve to death. Apparently it would have been profane to shed the blood of someone who had been about to promise himself to the Church, so the abb had revived a method of execution rarely used.

The yield from Abb Aidan's meticulous husbandry of the monastic finances was spectacular. The monastery had long been known for its scriptorium – the exquisite illumination of its manuscripts was famed throughout the land – but there was now a whole range of other skills devoted to the glorification of the monastery and the service of its God. Abb Aidan encouraged work in precious metals as well as in enamel and glass. Many of the craftsmen were the monks themselves. They created objects of extraordinary beauty, using techniques they sifted from the ancient texts or had learnt in foreign lands during their travels. And often they exchanged ideas with the craftsmen who came to the monastery, attracted by its reputation as a generous patron of the arts. I was put to work for one of these craftsmen, Saer Credine the master stonemason, because our abb believed that nothing could express immutable devotion better than monuments of massive stone.

Saer Credine was surprisingly frail-looking for someone whose life was spent carving huge blocks of stone with mallet and chisel. He came from a distant region to the south-west where the rocks break naturally into cubes and plates, and his tuath was a place where stoneworkers have been reared and respected for time out of mind. Any fool, he would say, could attack a lump of stone with brutish strength, but it took skill and imagination to see the finished shape and form within the rock and know how to coax that shape from the stone. That was the God-given gift. When he first made this remark, I thought he meant that the White Christ had endowed him with his skills.

Abb Aidan had commissioned him to produce an imposing new stone cross for the monastery, a cross to be the equal of any of the splendid crosses which already stood in the monastic grounds. The base was to show scenes from the New Testament and the shaft would be incised with the most renowned of St Ciaran's many miracles. The senior monks had provided the stonemason with rough sketches of the scenes – the resurrection of the White Christ from his tomb, of course, and the wild boar bringing branches in its jaws to make St Ciaran's first hut – and they checked that the tableaux had transferred correctly to the face of the stone before Saer Credine gouged the first groove. But from that moment onward there was little that the monks could do, and everything depended on Saer Credine's competence. Only the master stonemason knew how the stone would work, and by subtle distinction how to lead and instruct the eye of the beholder. And, of course, once the carver's blow had been struck there was no going back, no rubbing out, starting again and altering the moment.

By the time I joined his labour force, Saer Credine had the massive rectangular base nearly complete. It had taken him five months of work. On the front panel a shrouded Christ was emerging from his coffin watched by two helmeted soldiers; on the rear panel Peter and Christ shared a net while fishing for the souls of men. The two smaller end panels were simple interlace carved by Saer Credine's senior assistant because the master craftsman was already working on the great vertical shaft. It was of a hard granite, brought by raft down the great river and laboriously hauled up the hill to the shed where we worked. When I arrived, the stone lay on its side, sheltered by a roof. It was supported on huge blocks of wood so as to be at a convenient height for Saer Credine to strike the surface. My first task was no more than to pick up the stone chips that dropped into the muddy ground, and at dusk my duty was to cover the half-completed work with a layer of straw against the frost. I was also, by default, the nightwatchman because no one had assigned me a sleeping place and I slept curled up on the straw bales. At breakfast time I went to stand in line with the other servants and indigents who came to the monastery kitchens to seek charity of milk and porridge, then I carried the food back to eat as I squatted beside the great block of stone that rapidly became the fixed point of my slave's existence. After a few days of gathering stone chips it was a short step to being given the task of brushing clean the worked face of the stone whenever the master craftsman stepped back to view his work or take a break from his labour. Saer Credine never made any comment on how he thought his work was progressing, and his face was expressionless.

Within a month I had graduated to the task of sharpening Saer Credine's chisels as well as wielding the sweeper's brush, and he even let me strike a few blows on the really rough work, where there was not the slightest chance that I could do any harm. Despite my stiffened left hand, I found that I was fairly deft and could cut a true facet. I also discovered that Saer Credine, like many craftsmen, was a kindly man beneath his taciturn exterior, and extremely observant. He noted that I took a more than usual interest in my surroundings, wandering round the monastery enclosure whenever possible to see what was going on, examining the other stone crosses that already stood with their instructional scenes. But, typically, he said nothing. After all, he was a master craftsman, and I was a doer, nothing.

Late one evening, when the butt of the shaft was finished, neatly flattened across the base and precisely squared on each of its corners ready to be dropped into its socket on the base, Saer Credine cut some marks which puzzled me – they looked like scratches, twenty or thirty of them. He made them after the other workmen had left, and he must have thought himself unobserved when he took his chisel and lightly chipped the lines across one of the corners. He made the marks so delicately that they could hardly be seen. Indeed, once the shaft was set into its socket hole the lines would be buried. Had I not observed him doing the work, I would not have known where to look, but I glimpsed him stooping over the stone, fine chisel in hand. When he had gone home I went to where he had been working and tried to puzzle out what he had been doing. The lines were certainly nothing that the abb and his monks had ordered. At first I thought they might be rune writing, but they were not. The lines were much simpler than the runes with which I was familiar. They were straight scratches, some long, some short, some in small clusters and several at a slant. They had been cut so that some were on one face of the squared-off stone, others on the adjacent face, and a few actually straddled both faces. I was completely baffled. After gazing at them for some time, I wondered if I was missing any hidden details. I tried running my fingertips over the scratches and could feel the marks, but they still made no sense. From the ashes of the midday cooking fire, I took a lump of charcoal and, laying a strip of cloth over the corner of the shaft, I rubbed the charcoal on the cloth to reproduce the pattern on the material. I had peeled the cloth away from the stone and laid it out flat on the ground so that I could kneel down and study it, when I became aware of someone watching me. Standing in the shelter of one of the monks' huts was Saer Credine. He had not gone back to his house, which was his usual custom, but must have returned to check on the final details for the stone shaft which was to be erected next day.

'What are you doing?' he demanded as he walked towards me. I had never heard him so gruff before. It was too late to hide the marked strip of cloth as I scrambled to my feet.

'I was trying to understand the marks on the cross shaft,' I stammered. I could feel my face going bright red.

'What do you mean "understand"?' the stonemason growled.

'I thought it was some sort of rune writing,' I confessed.

Saer Credine seemed surprised as well as doubtful. 'You know rune writing?' he asked. I nodded. 'Come with me,' he stated bluntly and set off at a brisk walk, crossing the slope of the hill to the site where many of the monks had been buried, as well as visitors who had died on pilgrimage to the holy place. The hillside was dotted with their memorial stones. But it was not a monk's last resting place that interested Saer Credine. He stopped in front of a low, flat, marker stone, set deep in the ground. Its upper surface had been carved with symbols.

'What does that say?' he demanded. I did not hesitate with my reply. The inscription was uncomplicated and whoever had cut it used a simple, plain form of the futhark. 'In the memory of Ingjald,' I replied and then ventured an opinion, 'he was probably a Norseman or a Gael who died while he was visiting the monastery.'

'Most of the Norse who came to visit this place didn't get a memorial stone,' the stonemason grunted. 'They came upriver in their longships to plunder the place and usually burned it to the ground, except for the stone buildings, that is.'

I said nothing, but stood waiting to see what my master would do next. It was in Saer Credine's power to have me severely punished for touching the cross shaft. A mere slave, and a heathen at that, who touched the abb's precious monument could merit a whipping.

'So where did you learn the runes?' Saer Credine asked.

'In Iceland and before that in Greenland and in a place called Vinland,' I replied. 'I had good teachers, so I learned several forms, old and new, and some of the variant letters.'

'So I have an assistant who can read and write, at least in his own way,' said the stonemason wonderingly. He seemed satisfied with my explanation, and walked back with me to where his great cross shaft lay on its trestles. Picking up the nub of charcoal I had left behind, he searched for a flat piece of wood, then shaved a straight edge with his chisel.

'I know a few of the rune signs, and I've often wondered whether the runes and my own writing are related. But I've never had a chance to compare them.' He made a series of charcoal marks along its edge. 'Now you,' he said, handing me the wooden stick and the charcoal. 'Those are the letters I and my forebears have used through the generations. You write your letters, your futhark or whatever you call it.'

Directly above my master's marks I scratched out the futhark that Tyrkir had taught me so long ago. As the letters formed I could see that they bore no resemblance to the stonemason's writing. The shapes of my runes were much more complicated, cut at angles and sometimes turning back on themselves. Also there were several more of them than the number of Saer Credine's letters. When I had finished copying, I handed the stick back to Saer Credine and he shook his head.

'Ogmius himself could not read that,' he said.

'Ogmius?' It was a name I had not heard before.

'He's also called Honey Mouth or Sun Face. Depends who you are talking to. He's got several names, but he's always the God of writing,' he said, 'He taught mankind how to write. Which is why we call our script the ogham.'

'It was Odinn who acquired the secret of writing, according to my instructors, so perhaps that is why the two systems are different,' I ventured. 'Two different Gods, two different scripts.' Our conversation made me feel bolder. 'What is it that you wrote on the cross shaft?' I asked.

'My name and the name of my father and my grandfather,' he replied. 'It has always been the custom of my family. We carve the scenes that men like Abb Aidan decide for us, and we take pride in such work and we do it as well as our gifts allow. But in the end our loyalty goes back much farther, to those who gave the skill to our hands and who would take away that skill if we did not pay proper respect. So that is why we leave our mark as Ogmius taught. The day that this cross is set in the foundation stone I will leave him a small offering beneath the shaft in thanks.'

Saer Credine gave me no hint of what he must have decided that evening when he learned that I could read and write the runes.

Three days later I received word that Brother Senesach wanted to speak with me. I knew Brother Senesach by sight and reputation. He was a genial and vigorous man, perhaps in his fifties. I had seen him frequently, striding around the monastery grounds, ruddy-faced and always with an air of unhurried purpose. I knew that he was in charge of the education of the younger monks, and that he was popular with them on account of his good nature and his obvious concern for their well-being.

'Come in,' Senesach called out as I paused nervously at the doorway of his little cell. He lived in a small hut made of wattle and daub and furnished with a desk, a writing stool and a palliasse.

'Our master stonemason tells me that you can read and write, and that you take an interest in your surroundings.' He looked at me keenly, noting my ragged shift and the marks left on my wrists by the manacles from Clontarf. 'He also says that you are hard-working and good with your hands, and suggested that you might one day become a valuable member of our community. What do you think?'

I was so surprised that I could scarcely think what to reply.

'It's not only the sons of the well-to-do who join us,' Senesach went on. 'In fact we have a tradition of encouraging young men of talent. With their skills they often contribute more to our community than the material gifts which the richer recruits bring.'

'I'm very grateful for your thoughtfulness and to Saer Credine for his kind words,' I replied, seeking to gain a moment's thinking space. 'I have never even imagined such a life. I suppose my first worry is that I am not worthy to devote my life to the service of Christ.'

'Few newcomers to our community are completely certain of their calling when they first arrive, and if they are, that is something of which I personally would be rather wary,' he answered gently. 'Anyhow, humility is a good place to start from. Besides, no one would expect you to become a fully observant monk for years. You would begin as a trainee and under my instruction learn the ways of our brotherhood, as scores have done before you.'

It was a suggestion which no slave could possibly have turned down. I had no one to pay a ransom for me, I was far from the places where I had grown up, and until a moment ago I had no prospects. Suddenly I was being offered an identity, a home and a defined future.

'I've already talked to the abb about your case,' Senesach continued, 'and although he was not very enthusiastic to begin with, he agreed that you should have a chance to prove your worth. He did say, however, that you might find that being a servant of God was more demanding than being slave to a stone-cutter.'

It occurred to me that perhaps Odinn had at last observed my plight and arranged this sudden opportunity. 'Of course I shall be happy to join the monastery in whatever capacity you think fit,' I said.

'Excellent. According to Saer Credine your name was Thorgils or Thorgeis, something like that. Much too heathen sounding. You had better have a new name, a Christian one. Any suggestions?'

I thought for a moment before replying, and then – silently acknowledging Odinn the Deceiver – I said, 'I would like to be called Thangbrand, if that is possible. It is the name of the first missionary to bring the White Christ's teachings to Iceland, which is where my people came from.'

'Well, no one else here has got a name like that. So Thangbrand it will be from now on, and we'll try to make it appropriate. Maybe you will be able to go back one day to Iceland to preach there.'

'Yes, sir,' I mumbled.

'Yes, Brother. Not sir. And we don't talk of the White Christ here, it is simply Christ or Jesus Christ, or Our Lord and Saviour,' he answered, with such sincerity that I felt a little ashamed. I hoped he would never discover that Thangbrand had failed completely in his battle against the Old Ways.

As the abb had warned, the physical life of a young novitiate at St Ciaran's monastery was little different from my days working for Saer Credine. I found that my previous chores as a slave were mirrored in my duties as a trainee monk. Instead of sweeping up the stonemason's chippings, I swept out the senior monks' cells and emptied their slops. In place of hammer and chisel, I grasped a hoe and spent hours stooped and hacking away at the rocky soil in the fields which my brethren and I prepared for planting. Even my clothing was much the same: previously I had worn a loose tunic of poor stuff held in at the waist with a bit of string. Now I had a slightly better tunic of unbleached linen with a waist cord, and a grey woollen cloak with a hood to go over it. Only my feet felt different. Previously barefoot, now I wore sandals. The major change was in discipline and for the worse. As a slave I was expected to rise at dawn and work all day, with a break for a midday meal if I was lucky, then curl up for a good night's rest so that I would be fit and strong for the next day's labour. A monk, I found, got far less rest. He had to rise before dawn to say his prayers, work in the fields or at his desk, repeat his prayers at regular intervals, and often went to bed far more exhausted than a slave. Even his diet was little consolation. A slave might be inadequately fed, but the monk ate coarse food that was little better. Worse than that, he often had to fast and go hungry. Wednesdays and Fridays were both fast days at St Ciaran's, and the younger ones among us ate double portions of food on Thursday, if we could.

But none of this mattered. Senesach's benevolence threw open the door of learning, and I walked in and revelled in the experience. As a slave I had been credited with the mind of a slave and offered only the knowledge that was relevant to my work – how best to scour a cooking pot with sand, stack a pile of turf, straighten a warped plough handle by soaking it in hot water. Now as a monk in preparation I was offered schooling in an extraordinary range of skills. It began, of course, with the requirement to learn to read and write the Roman script. Senesach produced a practice book, two wax tablets held in a small wooden folder, and he drew for me the letters, scratching them with a metal stylus. I think that even Senesach was astonished that it took me less than three days to learn the entire alphabet, and that I was writing coherent and reasonably well-spelt sentences within the same week. Perhaps my mind was like a muscle already exercised and well developed when I learned the rune writing and the rune lore – of which I said nothing – and had gone slack from disuse. Now all it needed was sharp stimulus and practice. My fellow students, as well as my teachers, soon came to consider me something of a prodigy when it came to the written or the spoken word. Maybe my combination of Norse and Irish ancestry, both peoples who relish the rhythms of language, also accounted for my fluency. In less than six months I was reading and writing Church Latin and was halfway to a working knowledge of French, which I was learning from a brother who had lived in Gaul for several years. Both the German tongue and the language of the English posed little difficulty, for they were close enough in pronunciation and vocabulary to my own donsk tong for me to understand what was said. By my second year I was also reading Greek.

My talent with words kept me on the right side of Abb Aidan. I had the feeling that he was waiting for me to falter and disgrace myself, but he could only acknowledge that I was among the star pupils of the community when it came to that prime requirement of memory – the learning of the psalter. There were some one hundred and fifty psalms and they were our chief form of prayer, chanted at holy service. Normally it took years for a monk to have the entire psalter word-perfect, and most of my contemporaries knew only the most popular psalms, those that we repeated again and again. But for some reason I found that I could remember almost every word and line more or less at the first hearing, so I found myself singing out the verses, line by line, while most of my colleagues were mumbling or merely joining in the refrain. My memory for the psalms was uncanny, though, as someone remarked, it was closer to the devil's work because, although I could remember the words, my singing of them was discordant and grating and offended the ears.

My new-found mastery of the Roman script meant that I was able to soak up all manner of information from the written page, though at first it was difficult to gain access to the monastic library because Brother Ailbe, the librarian, believed that books were more valuable than the people who read them, and he discouraged readers. In a way he was justified, as I came to appreciate when I was assigned to labour in the scriptorium. The manuscripts in his care were the glory of St Ciaran's and exceedingly valuable, even in the physical sense. The skins of more than a hundred calves were required to make sufficient vellum for a single large volume, and in a land where wealth is counted in cattle this is a prodigious investment. Eventually Brother Ailbe did come to trust me enough to let me browse the shelves where the books were stored and I found most of the volumes were Holy Scripture, mainly copies of the Gospels with their canon tables, breves causae and argumenta and paschal texts. But there were also writings from classical authors such as Virgil, Horace and Ovid, and works of Christian poetry by writers such as Prudentius and Ausonius. My favourite was a book of geography written by a Spanish monk named Isidore, and I spent hours dreaming of the exotic lands he described, little knowing that one day I would have the chance to see many of them for myself. I had a magpie's facility to select and carry away bright scraps of unrelated information in my head, and my erratic robbery from these solemn texts quickly irritated my teachers, the older and more learned monks who were assigned to give the novices their classes in such subjects as history, law and mathematics.

As novices, we were expected not just to acquire knowledge, but also to preserve and transmit its most precious elements, namely the Holy Scripture. That meant copying. We were issued once again with the wax tablets from which we had learned the alphabet, and shown how to form our letter with the help of a metal stylus and ruler. Over and over again, we practised, until we were deemed fit to mark the surface of reused vellum, over-writing the faint and faded lines left by earlier scribes until we had the gist of it. At that stage we were mixing our own ink from lamp black or chimney soot. Only when we could write a perfect diminuendo, starting with a large initial letter and then progressively writing smaller and smaller along the line, until the eye could scarcely distinguish the individual letters, were the most deft of us permitted to work on fresh vellum. It was then I appreciated why the monastery needed a never-ending supply of younger monks for the famed scriptorium just as much as it needed flocks of calves and lambs to produce the vellum skins. Young animals provided unblemished skin, and young monks provided sharper eyes. Our finest copyists were men of early to middle age, deft, clear-eyed and with remarkable artistic imaginations.

Strangely, the materials designed to please the eye remain in my memory according to their smells. The raw calfskins had been steeped in a fetid concoction of animal dung and water to loosen the hairs so they could be scraped off easily, and they gave off a pulpy, fleshy odour while stabilising in a wash of lime. Oak galls had a bitter stink when crushed to provide our best red ink, and as for greens and blues I still smell the sea whenever I see those colours. They were made by squeezing out the juice from certain shellfish found on the rocks. We then left the liquid to fester in the sun, which made the extract alter from green, to blue, to purple, all the while giving off the pungent smell of rotting bladderwrack. It complemented the fishy odour of the fish oil we employed to bind the ink.

The transformation of these reeking originals to such beauty on the page was a miracle in itself. I was never an outstanding copyist or illustrator, but I acquired enough of the techniques to appreciate the skill involved. Observing one of our finest illuminators decorate the initial letter of a Gospel would make me hold my breath in sympathy in case he made a slip. He required a steady hand as well as the finest brush – the hair from the inside of a squirrel's ear was favoured for the most delicate work – and a rare combination of imagination and geometric skill to interweave the lacing patterns that twined and curved like tendrils of some unearthly plant. Curiously, I was reminded of the patterns that I had seen – it seemed so long ago – carved on the curling stem post of King Sigtryggr's royal ship when he sailed from Orkney. How or why the patterns, Christian initial and Viking prow, were so similar I did not know. What was even stranger was that so many of the bookish trellis patterns ended in a snarling figurehead. That I could understand on the high bow of a ship of war, designed to frighten the enemy, but how the motif was found in a book of Holy Scripture was beyond my understanding. Still, it was not a topic on which I dwelt. The extent of my contribution in penmanship was to write the occasional line in black, using the tiny script which Abb Aidan favoured because it meant more words could be squeezed on each expensive square inch of vellum, and I was delegated to fill in the red dots and lozenges which were liberally scattered across the page as decoration. This kept me occupied for hours as they could number in the hundreds on a single page.

It would be wrong if I gave the impression that my life as a novice monk was spent in the fields, the schoolroom or the scriptorium. Religious instruction was severe and unfortunately was the responsibility of Brother Eoghan, who was at the opposite remove from the kindly Brother Senesach. Brother Eoghan's appearance was deceptive. He looked benign. Rotund and jovial-seeming, he had dark hair and very dark eyes that seemed to gleam with a humorous twinkle. He even had a booming, cheerful-sounding voice. But any of his pupils who presumed upon his good nature were quickly disillusioned. Brother Eoghan had a vicious temper and a grinding sense of self-righteousness. He taught not through reason, but strictly by rote. We were required to memorise page after page of the Gospels and the writings of the Church Fathers, and he tested us on our acquisition of the texts. His favoured technique was to pick out an individual in his class, demand a recitation, and when the victim stammered or erred, to suddenly turn to another student and shout at him to continue. Terrified, the second performer was sure to make a mistake, and then Brother Eoghan would swoop. Seizing the two novices, each by his hair, our tutor would complete the quotation himself, grinding out the words through gritted teeth, his face set grimly, and punctuating each phrase by banging together the two heads with a steady thump.

Every novice, and there were about thirty of us, reacted in his own way to the unyielding world in which we found ourselves. Most were meekly acquiescent and followed the rules and routines laid down. Only a handful were genuinely enthusiastic for the monkish life. One young man – his name was Enda and he was a little simple – sought to model himself on the Desert Fathers. Without informing anyone, he climbed to the top of the round tower. This was St Ciaran's most spectacular edifice, a slim spike of stone which had been a lookout in the days of the Viking raids, but now mostly used as a bell tower. Enda clambered to the very top, where, naturally, he was out of sight from the ground, and sat there for four days and four nights while the rest of us searched for him uselessly. It was only when we heard his weak calls for a supply of bread and water and saw the end of a rope he had lowered down – he had misjudged the height and his rope was dangling far too short – that we knew where he was. Brother Senesach organised a rescue party, and we clambered up and retrieved Enda, who by then was too feeble to move. He was taken to the infirmary and left there to recover, but the experience seemed to have left him even weaker in the head. I never knew what finally became of him, but in all likelihood he became a monk.

EIGHTEEN

I MADE ONLY one real friend among my fellow novices in the two years I spent at St Ciaran's. Colman had been sent there by his father, a prosperous farmer. Apparently the farmer had prayed to St Ciaran for relief when a severe cattle murrain had affected his herd. As a remedy he had smeared his sick animals with a paste made from earth scraped from the floor of the saint's oratory. When the cattle all recovered, the farmer was so grateful that he enrolled the lad – the least promising of his six sons – with the monks as a thank offering for the saint's beneficial intervention. Solid and reliable, Colman stood by me when the other novices, jealous that I outshone them in the classroom, ganged up to bully me about my own alien origins. I repaid Coleman's loyalty by helping him with his studies – he was something of a plodder when it came to book learning – and the two of us made an effective team when it came to breaking the bounds of monastic discipline.

Our dormitory huts were situated on the northern side of the monastery grounds, and at night the bolder ones among us would sometimes scramble over the monastery bank to see what the outside world was like. Slinking among the houses that had grown up around St Ciaran's, we watched from the shadows how ordinary people lived, eavesdropped on quarrels and conversations heard through the thin walls of their dwellings, listened to the cries of babies, the drinking songs and the snores. We were discreet because there were townsfolk who would report our presence to the abb if they saw us. When that happened the punishment was harsh. Spending three or four hours flat on your face on the earth floor reciting penances was the least of it. Worse was to be made to stand with your arms outstretched as a living cross until the joints creaked with pain, supervised by one of the more callous senior brothers, while reciting, over and over again, 'I beseech pardon of God,' 'I believe in the Trinity,' 'May I receive mercy.' Little mercy was available. One of the novices, reported for the second time for a nocturnal excursion, received two hundred lashes with a scourge.

A short walk from the monastery was a small stone-built chapel, sheltering in a wood. No one knew who had built it there or why. The monks at St Ciaran's denied any knowledge of its origins. The place was nothing to do with them, and they never went there. The little chapel was abandoned and falling into disrepair and housed, as we discovered, a hidden attraction. Which novice first found the lewd sculpture, I do not know. It must have been someone with remarkably sharp eyesight, for the carved stone was tucked away among the stones forming the entry to the chapel, and under normal circumstances it would have been invisible. Whoever found the carving mentioned it to his friends and they in turn passed on the knowledge to other students, so that it became a sort of talisman. We called the stone the Sex Hag, and most of us, at some stage, crept down to the chapel to gaze at it. The carving was as grotesque as any of the strange and leering beasts which appeared in our illuminations. It showed a older and naked woman, with three pendulous breasts sagging from a rugged rib-cage. She was seated with her legs apart and knees open, facing the observer. With her hands she was pulling apart the lips of her private entry and on her face was a seraphic smile. The effect was both erotic and demonic.

Of course, there was a good deal of salacious talk inspired by the Sex Hag's revelations, but for the most part it was ignorant speculation as we had few occasions to meet any women. Indeed the frightening posture of the Sex Hag acted as a deterrent. Several of the novices were so disturbed and repelled by the graphic quality of the carving that I doubt they ever touched a woman thereafter.

The same cannot be said for me. I was intensely curious about the opposite sex and spent a good deal of time trying to devise a way of striking up an acquaintance with a female of my own age. This was well-nigh impossible. Our community was all male, and our only regular women visitors were those who came from the nearby settlement to visit the infirmary or to offer prayers at the various oratories. Unfortunately they seldom included anyone who was youthful and nubile. Sometimes a young and unmarried woman was glimpsed among the pilgrims who came to St Ciaran's shrine, and we younger monks would gaze in fascination, telling ourselves there was nothing wrong in our curiosity because the temptation was only momentary as the pilgrims would linger just a few hours, then vanish out of our lives for ever.

It was Brother Ailbe the librarian who, unwittingly, provided me with the long-desired chance to meet a female of my own age. Our keeper of books was so solicitous about the well-being of the precious volumes that he wrapped all the important books in lengths of linen, then stored them in individual leather satchels to protect them from harm. One day he decided that the satchel which contained St Ciaran's own copy of the Bible – the same book which had been paraded before Donnachad on the day I was handed over to the monastery as a slave – needed attention. For any other book in his library Brother Ailbe would have ordered a replacement satchel from the best leather-worker in the town, sending a note with the necessary dimensions of the volume and waiting for the finished satchel to be delivered. But in this case the existing satchel was something very special. It was claimed that St Ciaran himself had sewn the satchel. So there was no question of throwing it away and ordering a new one. Yet the existing satchel was so shabby that it did no honour to the saint's memory, and there was an ugly rip in the leather that cut right across the faint marks which, it was said, were the fingerprints of the saint himself.

Brother Ailbe decided to entrust the repair to a craftsman living in the town, a man by the name of Bladnach, who was a master of the long blind stitch. In this technique the needle, instead of passing straight through the leather, is turned and runs along within the thickness of the skin to emerge some distance away from where it entered so that the thread itself is invisible. But using a long blind stitch on old and brittle leather is a risk. There is only one opportunity to run the needle in. There can be no second chance, no withdrawing the point and trying again, as this destroys the original substance. Yet this is how Brother Ailbe wanted St Ciaran's satchel to be mended so that it would appear to the uneducated eye that the satchel had never been damaged. Bladnach was the only craftsman capable of the work.

Bladnach was a cripple. Born without the full use of his legs, he moved about his workroom on his knuckles, though with remarkable agility. This way of motion had, of course, developed the strength and thickness of his arms and shoulders to an extraordinary degree, and this was no disadvantage for a man who needs all his power to drive a needle through heavy, stiff leather. But Bladnach's disability also meant that it was more logical for Brother Ailbe to bring the damaged book satchel to Bladnach's workshop than for Bladnach to be carried to the monastery each day to make the repairs. Yet St Ciaran's bible satchel was so precious that Ailbe could not possibly leave it unguarded. The librarian's solution was to ask Abb Aidan for permission for someone from the monastery to accompany the satchel to Bladnach's workshop and stay with it until the repair was done. By that time I was a familiar figure in the library, reading my texts, and Brother Ailbe suggested that I would make a suitable envoy. Abb Aidan agreed and stipulated that I was not to live in the leather-worker's house but to live, eat and sleep within the workshop itself, not allowing the satchel out of my sight.

Neither our abb nor our librarian were aware that when it comes to the sewing of the very finest leather, the most elegant stitching of delicate lambskin or the threading of a single twist of flax so fine that you cannot use a needle to insert it but make the merest pinprick of a hole, the work is almost invariably done by a woman. In the case of Bladnach the work was done by his daughter, Orlaith.

How can I describe Orlaith? Even after all these years I feel a slight tightening sensation in my throat as I remember her. She was sixteen and as fine-boned and delicately formed as any woman I have ever seen. Her face was of the most exquisite shape, where delicate cheekbones emphasised the slight hollows of the cheeks themselves and the gentle sweep of her jaw led to a small and perfect chin. She had a short, straight nose, a flawless mouth and the most enormous dark brown eyes. Her hair was chestnut, yet you could mistake it for being black, and it made an almost unreal contrast with her pale skin. By any standards she was a truly beautiful woman, and she took meticulous care with her appearance. I never saw her with a hair out of place or wearing a garment that was not perfectly cleaned and pressed and selected for its colours. But the strangest thing of all is that, when I first laid eyes on her, I did not think her beautiful. I was shown into her father's workshop, where she sat at her bench stitching a woman's belt, and I barely gave her a second glance. I utterly failed to appreciate her stunning beauty. She seemed almost ordinary. Yet within a day I was captivated by her. There was something about the fragile grace in the curve of her forearm as she leaned forward to take up a thread of flax, or the flowing subtlety of her body as she rose to her feet and walked across the room, which had me in thrall. She stepped as delicately as a fawn.

She was in the early bloom of her womanhood and responsive to my admiration. She was also, as I later understood, in despair for a private reason and that made her all the more alert to the chance of happiness. There was little that either of us could do during those first few days to progress our feelings. It took her father a week to mend the precious satchel, most of the time being spent applying coat after coat of warmed wool grease to soften and restore the desiccated leather. There was nothing for me to do but sit in the workroom, watching father and daughter at their work, trying to make myself useful in small ways. When Orlaith left the room for any reason, the room seemed to lose its colour and turn lifeless, and I would ache for her return just to be close to her, sensing her presence so powerfully that it was almost as if we were in physical contact. Two or three times we managed to speak to one another, awkward, shy words, each of us stumbling and mumbling, sentences fading away and left unfinished, both of us fearful of making a mistake. But these stilted conversations were only possible when Bladnach was out of the room, which happened rarely as it was a great effort for him to swing on his knuckles, hauling his useless lower limbs as he left the workshop to go to relieve himself. All three of us took our meals together, Orlaith fetching the food from her mother's cooking fire. We would sit in the workroom, eating in quiet, shared company, and I am sure that Bladnach was alert to what was happening between his daughter and myself, but he chose to ignore it. I suspect that he too wanted his daughter to have some happiness in her life. With his own disability he knew how to value any small chance that occurred.

When the satchel was repaired, Bladnach sent word to the monastery, and our librarian came down to collect the precious relic. As Brother Ailbe and I walked back to the monastery, my heart was close to bursting. On that last morning Orlaith had whispered a suggestion that we try to meet a week later. She had grown up around St Ciaran's, where all the sharp-eyed children knew about the novice monks and how they came out at nights to spy on the community. So she proposed that we meet at a certain spot outside the monastery vallum a week later, soon after nightfall. She thought that she could slip quietly out of the house and she would be free for an hour or two, if I could meet her there. This first tryst was to become a defining moment in my lifetime's memories. It was a night in early spring and there were a few stars and enough light from a sliver of new moon for me to see her standing in the darker pool of shadow cast by an ash tree. I approached, trembling slightly, aware even of the scent given off by her clothing. She reached out and touched my hand in the darkness and gently drew me towards her. It was the most natural, most marvellous and most tender moment that I could ever have imagined. To hold her, to feel her warmth, the yielding softness of her flesh and the wondrous life and structure of her fine bones within my arms was a sensation that made me dizzy with elation.

For the next weeks I felt as if I was sleep-walking through my daily routines of prayer and lessons, the sessions in the scriptorium and the hours spent labouring in the fields. My thoughts dwelt constantly on Orlaith. She was everywhere. I placed her in a thousand imaginary situations, speculating on her gestures, her words, her presence. And when I came back to reality, it was only to calculate where she was at that particular moment, what she was doing, and how long it might be before I held her in my arms again. My trust in Odinn, which had begun to falter among so much Christian fervour, came surging back. I asked myself who else but Odinn could have arranged such a wondrous development in my life. Odinn, among all the Gods, understood the yearnings of the human heart. He it was who rewarded those who fell in battle with the company of beautiful women in Valholl.

I should have been more wary. Odinn's gifts, as I knew full well, often conceal a bitter core.

Our love affair lasted nearly four months before catastrophe arrived. Every one of our clandestine meetings produced intoxicating happiness. They were preceded by a giddy sense of anticipation, then followed by a numbing glow of fulfilment. Our meetings became all we lived for. Nothing else mattered. Sometimes, returning through the darkness from the tryst, I found it difficult to keep walking in a straight line. It was not the darkness which confused me, but the physical sense of being so happy. Of course, the three companion novices who shared our sleeping hut noticed my night-time excursions. At first they said nothing, but after a couple of weeks there were some approving and slightly wistful comments, and I knew there was little risk of betrayal from that direction. My friend Colman stood by me one night, when an older monk noticed

I was missing. It was Colman who made some plausible excuse for my absence. As spring passed into summer – it was now the second year of my time as a novice – I grew bolder. My nocturnal meetings with Orlaith were not enough. I thirsted to see her by day, and I managed to persuade Brother Ailbe that two more satchels might need the leather-worker's attention. They were humdrum items of little value, and I offered to take them to Bladnach's workshop for his inspection, to which the librarian agreed.

My reception when I arrived at Bladnach's workshop was deeply unsettling. There was an awkward atmosphere in the workshop, a sense of strain. It showed on the face of Orlaith's mother as she greeted me at the door, and it was repeated in Orlaith's response to my arrival. She turned away when I entered the workshop and I saw that she had been crying. Her father, normally so quiet, treated me with unaccustomed coldness. I handed over the two satchels, explained what needed to be done and left the house, puzzled and distressed.

At the next meeting by the ash tree I asked Orlaith about the reason for the strange atmosphere in the house. For several harrowing moments she would not tell me why she had been crying, nor why her parents had been in such evident discomfort, and I came close to despair, faced with some unimaginable dread. I continued to press her for an answer, and eventually she blurted out the truth. It seemed that for many years both her parents had needed regular medical treatment. Her father's deformity racked his joints, and her mother's hands had been damaged by years of helping her husband at the leather-worker's bench. The smallest finger on each of her hands was permanently curved inward from the strain of tugging on thread to pull it tight, and her hands had become little more than painful claws. Initially they had used home-made remedies, gathering herbs and preparing simples. But as they aged these medicines had less and less effect. Eventually they had presented themselves at the monastery's infirmary, where Domnall, the elderly brother who worked as a physician, had been very helpful. He had made up draughts and ointments which had worked what seemed a genuine miracle, and the leather-worker and his wife were deeply grateful. In the years that followed, they began to made regular visits, every two or three months in summer and more frequently in winter when the pains were worse. Bladnach would be carried to the monastery on a plank, and it was on one of his early visits that he first came to Brother Ailbe's attention and received his initial commission to work on the library satchels.

But Brother Domnall had paid for his selfless work at the infirmary with his life. A yellow plague had swept through the district, and the physician had been infected by the invalids who came to him for help. Willingly he made the final sacrifice, and the running of the infirmary had passed to his assistant, Brother Cainnech.

When Orlaith mentioned the yellow plague and Cainnech's name, my heart plummeted. I knew all about the yellow plague. It had struck in the late winter, and to my sorrow it had carried off the stoneworker Saer Credine. His commission from the abb, the grand cross, still stood half finished as there was no one skilled enough to complete the carving. The yellow plague had left Brother Cainnech as our new physician in its wake, and there were many in the monastery who considered that he was a reminder of the pestilence. Brother Cainnech was a clumsy, coarse boor who seemed to enjoy hurting people under the pretext of helping them. Among the novices it was generally considered preferable to endure a minor broken bone or a deep gash than let Cainnech near it. He seemed to enjoy causing pain as he reset the bone or cleaned out the wound. Often we thought that he was under the influence of alcohol, for he had the blotched skin and stinking breath of a man who drank heavily. Yet no one doubted his medical knowledge. He had read the medical texts in Brother Ailbe's library, spent his apprenticeship as Domnall's assistant, and stepped naturally into the chief physician's role. After the outbreak of the yellow fever it was Cainnech who insisted that every scrap of our bedding, blankets and clothes were thrown on a bonfire, leading me to wonder if this is what my mother had intended at Frodriver when she had insisted that her bedding be burned.

One day, Orlaith told me, she had accompanied her father and mother on their regular visit to the infirmary for their treatment and she had come to Cainnech's attention. The following month Cainnech informed her parents that it was no longer necessary for them to come to the infirmary. Instead he would call at their house, to bring a fresh supply of medicines and administer any treatment. It would save Bladnach the difficult trip to the monastery. Cainnech's decision seemed a selfless act, worthy of his predecessor. But the motive for it soon became clear. On the very first visit to Bladnach's home, Cainnech began to make approaches to Orlaith. He was shamelessly confident. He presumed on the complicity of her parents, making it clear to them that if they thwarted his visits or hindered his behaviour while in their home, they would not be welcome back at the infirmary for treatment. He also emphasised to Bladnach that if he complained to the abb, there would be no further work from the library. Cainnech's visits quickly became a frightening combination of good and harm. He always remained the conscientious physician. He would arrive at the house punctually, examine his two patients, provide their medicaments, make careful notes of their condition, give them sound medical advice. Under his care both Bladnach and his wife found their health improving. But as soon as the medical consultation was over, Cainnech would dismiss the parents from the workshop and insist that he be left alone with their daughter. It was hardly surprising that Orlaith felt she could not divulge to me what went on during the sessions when she was shut up with the monk; she had never told her parents. What made the nightmare even worse, for both Orlaith and her parents, was Cainnech's absolute certainty that he could repeat his predatory behaviour for as long as he liked. As he left the house, leaving an abused Orlaith weeping in the workshop, he would pause solicitously beside Bladnach and assure him that he would return within the month to see how his patient was progressing.

Orlaith's wretched story made me all the more passionate about her. For the rest of that dreadful rendezvous, I held her close to me, feeling both protective and helpless. On the one hand I was outraged, on the other I was numbed by an acute sense of shared hurt.

Worse followed. Even more anxious to see Orlaith, I risked visiting the leather-worker's house in broad daylight, pretending that I was on an errand for the library. No one stopped me. The following week I repeated my foolhardy mission and found Orlaith by herself at her workbench. For an hour we sat side by side, mutely holding hands, until I knew I had to leave and get back to the monastery before my absence was noticed. I was aware that my luck would eventually run out, but I felt powerless to do anything else. I was so desperate to find a solution, I even suggested to Orlaith that we should run away together, but she dismissed the idea out of hand. She would not leave her parents, particularly her invalid father, who depended on her skill with the fine needle now that her mother was unable to work.

So it was an irony that her mother, unintentionally, caused the calamity. She came with a group of her friends to the monastery to pray at the oratory of St Ciaran. As she was leaving the oratory, she chanced to meet Brother Ailbe and mentioned to him how much she appreciated his continuing to send me to her house to assist her husband. Of course, Brother Ailbe was puzzled by this remark, and that evening sent for me to come to the library. He was standing beside his reading desk as I entered, and I thought he was looking slightly pompous and full of his own authority.

'Were you at the house of Bladnach the leather-worker last week?' he asked in a flat tone.

'Yes, Brother Ailbe,' I answered. I knew that I had been seen by the townsfolk on my way there and that the librarian could easily check.

'What were you doing? Did you have permission from anyone to go there, away from the monastery?'

'No, Brother Ailbe,' I replied. 'I went on my own initiative. I wanted to ask the leather-worker if he could teach me some of his craft. In that way I thought I could learn how to repair our leather Bible satchels here in the monastery, and then there would be no need to pay someone for outside skills.' My answer was a good one. I saw from Ailbe's expression that he anticipated a favourable response if he put the same proposal to the abb. Anything which saved the monastery money was a welcome suggestion to our abb.

'Very well,' he said, 'The idea has merit. But you broke our rule by leaving the monastery without authorisation. In future you are not to visit the town without first asking permission from me or from one of the other senior monks. You are to make amends by going to the chapel and reciting psalm one hundred and nineteen in its entirety, kneeling and cross figel.'

He made a gesture dismissing me. But I stood my ground. It was not because the punishment was severe, though the hundred and nineteenth psalm is notoriously long and would make the cross figel – kneeling with arms outstretched – very painful. I faced down the librarian because a strange and wild spirit of rebellion and superiority was welling up within me. I was overcome with scorn for Brother Ailbe for being so gullible. It had been so easy to dupe him. 'I just told you a lie,' I said and I did not bother to hide the contempt in my voice. 'I did not go to the leather-worker's house to ask to be his apprentice. I went there to be with his daughter.' Brother Ailbe, who had been looking rather smug, gaped with surprise, his mouth open and closed without making a sound, and I turned on my heel and left the room. As I did so, I knew that I had irreversibly destroyed my own life. There was no going back on what I had said.

Months later I realised that the spirit of defiance which had overwhelmed me had came from Odinn. It was his odr, the frenzy which throws aside caution and pays no heed to sense or prudence.

As I walked away from the library, I knew that I would be severely punished for breaking monastery discipline, above all for consorting with a female. That was the worst offence of all as far as the senior monks were concerned. But I found some consolation in the thought that at least I had brought Bladnach and his family to the attention of Abb Aidan, and it would be unlikely that Cainnech would risk continuing his abuse of their daughter until the scandal of my behaviour had died down. Maybe he would be warned off for ever.

I underestimated Cainnech's viciousness. He must have realised that, through Orlaith, I knew about his degenerate behaviour, and he decided that I should be put out of the way for good. That evening Abb Aidan called a conclave of the senior monks to discuss my fate. The meeting was held in the abb's cell and lasted for several hours. Rather to my surprise, there was no immediate decision on my punishment, nor was I called to give an explanation for my actions. Very late in the evening my friend Colman whispered to me that Senesach wanted to see me, and I was to go, not to his cell, but to the small, newly built oratory on the south side of the monastery. When I arrived, Senesach was waiting for me. He looked so despondent that I felt wretched. I owed so much to him. Yet I had failed to live up to his hopes for me. It was Senesach – it seemed so long ago – who had persuaded the abb that I should be released from slavery as the stonemason's assistant and given a chance to train as a monk, and Senesach had always been a fair and reasonable teacher. I was sure that if anyone had argued my case for me during the discussion of my transgressions, it would have been Senesach.

'Thangbrand,' he began, 'I don't have time to discuss with you why you chose to do what you did. But it is evident that you are not suited for life within the community of St Ciaran's. For that I am heartily sorry. I hope one day you will regain your original humility enough to pray for forgiveness for what you have done. I have asked you here for another reason. During the discussion of your misbehaviour, Brother Ailbe spoke up to say that he believed you may be a thief as well as a fornicator. He claimed that several pages are missing from the library copy of Galen's *De Usum Partium*, which you were studying as an exercise to improve your Greek. Did you steal those pages?'

'No, I did not,' I replied. 'I looked at the manuscript, but the pages were already missing when I consulted the text.' I had a shrewd suspicion who would have stolen them: Galen's writings were the standard authority for our medical work, and I wondered if Cainnech had taken the missing pages – as monastery physician he had regular and unquestioned access to the volume – and then drawn the librarian's attention to their absence.

Senesach went on, 'There was another complaint, a more serious one. Brother Cainnech' – and here my heart sank as usual – 'has raised the possibility that you have a Satanic possession. He pointed out that your association with the leather-worker's daughter has a precedent. When you first came to us you said your name was Thorgils, and we have learned that you were captured at the great battle at Clontarf against the Norsemen. Another Thorgils defiled this monastery in the time of our forefathers. He too came from the north lands. He arrived with his great fleet of warships and terrorised our people. He was an outright heathen and he brought with him his woman, a harlot by the name of Ota. After Thorgils's troops captured the monastery, this Ota seated herself on the altar and before an audience she uttered prophesies and disported herself lewdly.'

Despite the seriousness of my situation, an image of the Sex Hag sprang into my mind and I could not help smiling,

'Why do you have that stupid grin on your face?' Senesach said angrily. His disappointment in me came boiling to the surface. 'Don't you understand the gravity of your situation? If either of these accusations is found to be true, you will suffer the same fate as that stupid fool who ran off with the relics a couple of years ago. You can be sure of that. I've never told anyone this before, but when our abb condemned that youngster to death, I broke my vow of unquestioning obedience to my abb's wishes, and asked him to reduce the penalty. You know what he replied? He said that St Colm Cille himself was banished from this country by his abb because he was found guilty of copying a book without the owner's permission. Stealing the pages themselves, our abb told me, was a far worse crime because the misdeed permanently deprived the owner. So he insisted that the culprit had to suffer the greater penalty.'

'I am truly sorry that I have distressed you,' I answered. 'Neither accusation has any truth in it, and I will await the judgement of Abb Aidan. You have always been kind to me and, whatever happens, I will always remember that fact.'

The finality in my tone must have caught Senesach's attention, for he looked at me closely and said nothing for several seconds. 'I will pray for you,' he said and, after genuflecting to the altar, he turned and strode out of the chapel. I heard the brisk footfalls of his sandals as he marched away, the last memory of the man who had given me the chance of bettering myself. That chance I had taken, but it had led me onto a different path.

NINETEEN

I WAS CERTAIN that the conclave would find me guilty. And, as I had no wish to be left to starve in a pit like my predecessor, that night I gathered together my few belongings – my monk's travelling cloak, a workmanlike knife that Saer Credine had given me, and a sturdy leather travelling pouch that I had made for myself while sitting in Bladnach's workshop. I clasped Colman's hand in farewell, then crept out of our dormitory hut and found my way to the library. I forced the door, and took down the largest of the bible satchels from where it hung on its peg. I knew that it contained a ponderous copy of the Gospel of St Matthew. Sliding the great book out of the case, I took out my knife and with the point I prised out several of the stones which had been inset as decoration into the heavy cover. They were four large rock crystals as large as walnuts, and a red-coloured stone about the size of a pigeon's egg. The stones were of little value in themselves. I just wanted to hurt the monastery in the only way I knew, by stealing something which would cause Abb Aidan a moment of financial pain. I wrapped my booty in a strip of linen rag torn from the Gospel's slip cover, and dropped it into my satchel. Then I made my way to the earth vallum that marked the monastery boundary, and clambered over it, as I had so many times before on my way to meet Orlaith.

In my flight I had one single advantage over the wretched runaway novice who had been starved to death in a pit. He had been caught because he had fled back to his tuath, and Abb Aidan had easily guessed his destination. This was the natural course for any fugitive. Among the native Irish the only place that an ordinary man or woman has any security is on the territory of their own tuath, among their own kinsfolk, or on the land of an allied tuath which has agreed mutual recognition of rights. But such rights are worthless when confronted with the power of an important abb capable of making his own laws and regulations. So the fugitive had been handed over meekly by his own people and led away to his death. But I had no tuath. I was a foreigner. I had neither clan nor family nor home. So while everyone's hand was against me, my lack of roots also meant that the abb and his council would have no idea where to send their people to look for me.

For one stupid moment, as I dropped down on the ground on the outer side of the vallum, I thought that I might make a brief visit to Bladnach's house to say goodbye to Orlaith. But I quickly put the idea out of my mind. It would only make matters worse for her. The monks would surely interrogate her and her family about where I might have gone. It was better that they remained ignorant of any details of my departure, even the hour when I had disappeared. Besides, any time spent visiting Orlaith reduced my chances of getting away cleanly. I had already decided that my best route lay to the west and that meant I had to get across the great river before dawn.

St Ciaran's stands on the east bank, on the flank of the hill where the great road follows the line of the ridge then dips down to the river crossing. Here the monks had built a bridge, famous for its length and design. It stood on massive tree trunks driven deep into the soft mud as pilings, and approached by a long causeway laid across the marshy ground. Stout cross-pieces of timber held the main structure together, and the surface was made of layers of planks interleaved with brushwood and laid with rammed earth. Everyone used the bridge. The river was so broad, its banks so soft and treacherous and the currents so unpredictable, especially in the winter and spring floods, that the bridge was the natural choice for any traveller. For this reason the monks maintained a toll keeper on the bridge to collect money for the upkeep of the structure, which needed constant maintenance. Few people travelled at night, but the monastery profited from any surplus income, so Abb Aidan insisted that the toll keeper stayed on duty during the hours of darkness. He lived in a small hut on the eastern side of the bridge.

The events on the beach after the battle at Clontarf had taught me that very few of the Irish know how to swim. Those of our men who had escaped the defeat that day did so by swimming out to the longships, and I had seen how few of the Irish fighters had been able to follow them. Even Brian Boruma's grandson had drowned in the shallows because he was a poor swimmer. By contrast there is hardly a single Norseman who is not taught to swim when he is a boy. It is not just as a matter of survival for a seafaring people. At home in Iceland we considered swimming a sport. Besides the usual swimming races, a favourite game was water wrestling, when the two contestants struggled to hold one another underwater until a victory was declared. Though I was a rather indifferent swimmer by Norse standards, I was positively a human otter when compared to the Irish. Yet my ability to swim was something the monks could not possibly have known. So the bridge, which ought to have proved an obstacle, in fact served me as a friend.

I crept cautiously down to the river bank. A half moon gave enough light for me to select a path. Unfortunately the moonlight was also strong enough for the nightwatchman on the bridge to see me if I attracted his attention. With each step the ground grew softer until I was ankle-deep in the boggy ground. The stagnant water gave off a rich, peaty smell as I gently pulled my feet from the ooze. There was insufficient wind to cover any noise if I blundered so I moved very, very gently, dreading that I would startle a night-nesting bird in the reeds. Very soon I was half walking, half wading. The water was quite warm, and when I was almost out of my depth, I rolled up my travelling cloak and tied it in a bundle with my leather satchel and strapped them both on my back. Then I launched out into the river. I was too cautious to risk swimming the entire width of the river in a single attempt. I knew that my cloak and satchel would soon become a soggy burden, and hamper me. So I swam from piling to piling of the bridge, keeping in the shadow. Each time I reached a piling I hung on quietly, listening for any sounds, feeling the pluck of the current sucking at my body. When I had almost reached the far bank, where the causeway began again, I paused.

This was the riskiest part of the crossing. The west bank of the river was open ground and there was no question of leaving the river here. In the moonlight I would have been in full view. I took a deep breath, submerged, then released my grip. Immediately the current swept me downstream. I lost all sense of direction as I was spun in the eddies. A dozen times I came to the surface for a gulp of air, then let myself sink again. I did not even try to swim. I only surfaced, sucked in air, then used my arms to push myself back underwater. Gradually my strength faded. I knew that I would have to begin to swim again if I was not to drown. The next time I came back to the surface, I glanced up at the moon to find my direction and struck out for the shore. The diving had tired me more than I had anticipated. My arms began to ache, and I wondered if I had left it too late. Cloak and satchel were weighing me down badly. I kept lowering my feet to try to find the ground, only to be disappointed and I was so tired that each time I took a swallow of muddy water. Finally my feet did touch bottom, though it was so soft that I could not support myself, but floundered, lurching and flailing with my arms, for I was too tired to care any longer about keeping silent. I only wanted to reach safety. With a final effort I staggered through the shallows until I could grasp at a clump of sedge grass. I lay there for at least five minutes until I felt strong enough to slither forward on my stomach and pull myself onto firmer ground.

Next morning I must have looked like some ghoul of the marsh. My clothing was slimed with mud, my face and hands scratched and bloody where I had hauled myself face down through the swamp. Occasionally I gave a retching cough to try to dislodge the foul residues in my throat from all the muddy water I had swallowed. Yet I was confident that my crossing of the river had gone undetected. When the abb of St Ciaran's sent out word that I was to be stopped and brought back to the monastery, his messengers would first go to check with the keeper of the bridge if I had been seen, and then alert the people living on the east side of the river. By the time the news spread to the west bank, I should have put some distance between myself and any pursuit. Equally, I had to admit that my long-term chances of evasion were slim. A single, desperate-looking youth, wandering through the countryside, skulking past villages and hamlets, would be the object of immediate suspicion. If caught, I would be treated as a fugitive thief or an escaped slave and I still had the faint scars of the manacles that had been hammered on my wrists by Donnachad after Clontarf.

An image came to my mind from my childhood in Greenland. It was the memory of my father's two runners, the Scots slaves Haki and Hekja, and how the two of them would set off each spring and travel up into the moors, barefoot and with no more than a satchel of food between them, and live off the land all summer. And there was the tale, too, of how Karlsefni had set them ashore when he first arrived in Vinland with instructions to scout out the land. They had gone loping off into the wilderness, as if nothing could have been more normal, and returned safely. If Haki and Hekja could survive in unknown Vinland, then I could do the same in Ireland. I had no idea what lay beyond the great river, but I was determined to do as well as my father's own slaves. I got up and, bending double, began picking my way through the tussocks of grass towards a line of willow bushes that would provide cover for the first few steps of my flight to the west.

The next five days blur together so I have no way of knowing the order of the events, or what took place on which day. There was the morning when I tripped over a tree root and twisted my ankle so painfully that I thought I was crippled. There was the lake that I came across unexpectedly, forcing a wide detour. I remember standing for at least an hour on the edge of the woods, gazing at the water and wondering whether I should circle around to my left or my right and, having made my decision and started walking, how I spent the next few hours wondering whether I was going in the right direction or doubling back on my path. Then there was the night when I was asleep on the ground as usual, wrapped in my cloak and with my back to a tree trunk, and I was startled awake by what I thought was the howling of wolves. I sat up for the rest of the night, ready to climb the tree, but nothing came closer. At dawn I was so drowsy that I set out carelessly. I had walked for an hour before I noticed that my knife was not in its sheath. Alarmed by the howling, I had pulled the knife out and laid it on the ground beside me. I turned back and retraced my steps. Luckily I found the knife within moments, lying where I had left it.

I never lit a fire. Even if I had carried a flint and steel to make a spark, I would not have risked the telltale smell of wood smoke. The autumn weather was mild so I did not need a fire for warmth, and I had no food which required cooking. I lived off wild fruit. This was the season for all manner of nuts and berries to ripen – hazelnuts, cranberries, blackberries, whortleberries, rowan berries, plums, sloes, wild apples. Of course, I still went hungry and sometimes my gut ached from eating only acid fruit. But I made no attempt to catch the occasional deer or hare that crossed my path. I was as shy as the animals themselves. I crouched back into the undergrowth when I observed them, fearful that the alarmed flight of game would attract hunters who might then find me by accident.

I was never far from human settlement, at least during the first part of my journey. The countryside was a mixture of woodland, cleared fields, pasture and bogland. There were frequent villages and hamlets, and twice I came across crannogs, places where a ri tuath had built himself a well-protected home on an artificial island in the middle of a lake. The village guard dogs were my chief worry. From time to time they detected my presence and raised a furious barking of alarm, forcing me to retreat hurriedly and then make a wider circuit round them. Once or twice gangs of children playing at the edge of the forest nearly discovered me, but in general their presence was useful. Their shouts and cries during their games often alerted me to the existence of a village before I blundered into it.

I had no idea how far to the west I was progressing. I noted, however, that the landscape was slowly changing. The forest was not nearly so dense and there were many stretches of open, scrubby ground. Increasingly the hills showed bald caps of rock, and there were broad expanses of barren moorland. It was a more harsh and unforgiving land so there were fewer settlements, yet the lack of forest cover made me more vulnerable to detection. After five days I had become so accustomed to slinking across the countryside that I began to think of myself as almost invisible. Perhaps made light-headed by lack of food, I found myself again recalling the fantasies of my Greenlandic childhood and how I had fancied myself in the role of Odinn the Invisible, travelling the world without being seen.

So my discovery on the sixth day of my flight was all the more shocking. I had spent the previous night in a little shelter that I made by laying branches to form a roof over a cleft between two large rocks on a stretch of open moorland. Soon after daybreak I emerged from my lair and began to descend the valley that sloped down from the edge of the moor. Ahead I could see a grove of trees on the bank of the little stream which ran through the dale. The trees would give me some cover, I thought, and if I was lucky I might also find some which were fruiting. I entered the wood and penetrated far enough to come to the bank of the stream itself. The water was clear and shallow, rippling prettily over brown and black pebbles, and overhung with vegetation. Shafts of sunlight speckled the greenery of the undergrowth, and I could hear birdsong from several directions. The place seemed as innocent as if no human had ever stepped there. I pushed aside the bushes, placed my satchel on the ground beside me on the bank and lay down flat on the earth so that I could submerge my face in the water and feel it run cool against my skin. Then I drank, sucking in the water. Finally I got back on my knees, reached down to scoop up a palmful of water and splashed it on the back of my neck. As I wiped away the drops, I looked up. On the far side of the stream, no more than ten feet away from me, stood a man. He was absolutely motionless. With a shock I realised that he must have been standing there even when I first arrived and that I had failed utterly to notice him. He had made no attempt to conceal himself. It was only his stillness which had deceived me, and the fact that the wood was full of the natural sounds of birds singing, insects chirping and rustling, the ripple of the stream. As I looked directly into the man's face, his expression did not change. He stood there, considering me calmly. I felt no alarm because he seemed so relaxed and self-contained.

The stranger was wearing a long cloak rather like my own, of grey wool, and he carried no weapon that I could see, though he did have a plain wooden staff. I guessed his age at about fifty, and his face was clean-shaven with weatherbeaten skin and regular features that included a pair of grey eyes now regarding me steadily. What made me gaze at him in complete astonishment was his hair. From ear to ear the man had shaved his head. From the back of his head the hair hung right down to his shoulders, but the front half of his scalp was bald except for some stubble. It was a hairstyle that I had read about while browsing in the monastery library, but had never expected to see in real life. The monks at St Ciaran's – those who still had any hair – used the Roman tonsure, shaving the central patch. The man in front of me still wore his hair as a monk would have done if the style had not been outmoded and forbidden by the Church for nearly two hundred years past.

TWENTY

'IF YOU ARE hungry as well as thirsty, I can offer you some food,' said this apparition.

Feeling foolish, I got to my feet. The stranger barely glanced back at me as he walked away through the undergrowth. There was no path that I could see, but I meekly splashed across the stream and followed him. Before long we came to a clearing in the wood which was obviously where he had set up his home. A small hut, neatly made of wattle and thatched with heather, had been built between the trunks of two large oak trees. Firewood was stacked beside the hut, and streaks of soot up the face of a large boulder and a nearby blackened pot showed where he did his cooking. A water bladder hung from the branch of a thorn tree. The stranger ducked into his hut and reappeared with a small sack in one hand and a shallow wooden bowl containing a large knob of something soft and yellow in the other. He tipped some of the contents of the sack into the bowl, stirred it with a wooden spoon, and handed the bowl and spoon to me. I took a mouthful. It proved to be a mix of butter, dried fruit and grains of toasted barley. The butter was rancid. I was not aware until then just how hungry I was. I ate everything.

The stranger still said nothing. Looking at him over the edge of the wooden bowl, I guessed he must be a hermit of some kind.

The monks at St Ciaran's had occasionally spoken of these deeply devout individuals who set themselves up in some isolated spot, far away from other humans. They wanted to live alone and commune in solitude with their God. St Anthony was the inspiration for many of them, and they tried to follow the customs of the Desert Fathers, even to the point of calling their refuges 'diserts'. They were not far removed in their behaviour from the pillar dwellers whom poor Enda had tried to emulate at St Ciaran's. What was odd was that this half-shaven hermit was so hospitable. True hermits did not welcome intruders. I could see no sign of an altar or a cross, nor had he blessed the food before passing it to me.

'Thank you for the meal,' I said, handing back the bowl. 'Please accept my apologies if I am trespassing on your disert. I am a stranger to these regions.'

'I can see that,' he said calmly. 'This is not a hermitage, though I have been a monk in my time as, I suspect, you have been.' He must have recognised my stolen travelling cloak, and maybe I had a monkish way about me, perhaps in my speech or in the way I had held the bowl of food.

'My name is—'. I paused for a moment, not knowing whether to give him my real name or my monastery name, for fear that he had heard about the fugitive novice called Thangbrand. Yet there was something in the man's shrewd gaze which prompted me to test him. 'My name is Adamnan.'

The corners of his eyes crinkled as he took in the implication of my reply. Adamnan means 'the timid one'.

'I would have thought that Cu Glas might be more appropriate,' he replied. It was if we were speaking in code. In the Irish tongue cu glas means literally a 'grey hound' but it also signifies someone fleeing from the law or an exile from overseas, possibly both. Whoever he was, this quiet stranger was extremely observant and very erudite.

I decided to tell him the truth. Beginning with my capture at Clontarf, I sketched in the story of my slavery, how I had come to be a novice monk at St Ciaran's and the events that had culminated in my flight from the monastery. I did not mention my theft of the stones from the Gospel. 'I may be a fugitive from the monks and a stranger in this land,' I concluded, 'but I originally came to Ireland hoping to track down my mother's people.' He listened quietly and when I had finished said, 'You would be wise to give up any hope of tracing your mother's family. It would mean travelling from tuath to tuath all across the country, asking questions. People don't like being cross-examined, particularly by strangers. Also, if you do manage to trace your mother's people, you may be disappointed in what you hear, and your curiosity will certainly have aroused suspicion. Sooner or later you would come to the attention of the abb of St Ciaran's, and he will not have forgotten the unfinished business between you and the monastery. You will be brought back to the monastery to stand punishment. Frankly, I don't think you would find much pity from him. The Christian idea of justice is not so charitable.'

I must have looked doubtful. 'Believe me,' he added. 'I know something about the way the law works.' This was, as I learned later, an extreme understatement.

The man I had mistaken for a hermit was, in fact, was one of the most respected brithemain in the land. His given name was Eochaid, but the country people who encountered him in the course of his work often referred to him as Morand, and this was a great compliment. The original Morand, being legendary as one of their earliest brithemain, was renowned as a man who never gave a flawed verdict.

My teachers at St Ciaran's had warned us about the brithemain, and with good reason. The brithemain are learned men – judges is not quite the right word – who trace their authority to a time long before any of the Irish had even heard of the White Christ. Many Irish – perhaps the majority – in the remoter parts still retain a profound respect for a brithem, and their deference galls the monks because the brithem lineage goes back to those early physicians, lawgivers and sages commonly known among the Irish as drui, a name the monkish scholars have been at pains to blacken. Yet the nearest word in their clerkly Latin that the monks could find to describe the drui was to call them magi.

I can write about these matters with some familiarity because, as it turned out, I was to spend almost as long in the company of Eochaid as I did with the brothers of St Ciaran's and, truth be told, I learned as much from him as I did from all the more erudite brothers put together. The difference was that in the monastery I had access to books, and the books provided me with most of my monastic education. Eochaid, by contrast, looked on book learning almost as a weakness. The brithemain did not write down the laws and customs – they remembered them. This required prodigious feats of memory, and I recall Eochaid saying to me one day that it needed at least twenty years of study to learn brithem law, and that was just the basics.

I would be proud to claim that Eochaid took me on as his apprentice, but that would not be true. I stayed with Eochaid because he invited me to remain for as long as I wished, and I found sanctuary in his company. For the next two years I served him in the capacity of an assistant or orderly, and at times as a companion. He had no ambitions for me as his student. He probably thought my memory was already too weak for that. The brithemain begin their studies when they are very, very young. Formerly there were official schools for the brithemain but they are nearly all gone and now the knowledge passes from father to son, and to daughters as well, for there are female brithemain of distinction.

I was lucky to stumble on him. Each year he spent only a few months in his forest retreat. The rest of the time he was a wanderer, travelling the country. But retreat to the forest was essential to him, and as a result he could identify the tune of every songbird, recognise the tracks left by deer or wolf or otter or hare or squirrel, name each shrub and herb and flower, and knew the medicinal properties of each of them. He was a herb doctor as well as a brithem, and as well as dispensing justice to the people we visited he also gave out medical advice. In his forest hut he was so calm and peaceable that the wild animals seemed to sense little danger near him. The deer would wander into the clearing by our hut to nose about the cooking fire, looking for grains that had dropped from our plates, and a tame badger lumbered unafraid around our feet and became a pet. But Eochaid was not sentimental about these animals. My second winter with him was bitterly harsh. Snow lay on the ground for a week – a most unusual event – and the ponds turned to ice. It was freezing cold in the hut and we came close to starving. The badger saved us – as a stew.

'The wilderness is where the inspiration for the first brithem laws arose,' he once told me, and 'natural justice' was a phrase he often used. 'It is a heavy responsibility to interpret the Fenechas, the laws of freemen. False judgements ruin men's lives and the evil consequences live on for generations. So I need to return regularly to the ultimate source, to the rhythms and mysteries of Nature.' He smiled his self-deprecating smile and mocked himself. 'How much easier if I could wear one of those heavy iron collars which the first brithemain had around their necks. If they made a poor judgement the collar tightened until they could scarcely breathe. When they amended the judgement to make it fair, the collar loosened.'

'But how could the early brithemain make false judgements?' I asked him. 'The monks at St. Ciaran's told me that the brithemain were really drui in secret, and communed with evil spirits and, besides being able to fly through the air, made profane prophecies. So they must have been able to foresee the future and would have known if they were in error.'

'It is true that in the earlier days some drui were trained as seers and soothsayers,' he answered. 'But those days are gone, and much of what appeared to be their prophesy was really only a prolonged observation. For example, by watching the animals in the forest I can foretell the coming weather. Those who study the movement of the stars learn how they behave. From that knowledge they can predict events like the eclipses of the sun or moon.

Such predictions impress people who fail to notice the signs or who do not understand the value of accumulated wisdom. Six hundred and thirty years is the length of time our star watchers use when measuring a single cycle of star movements in the sky. You can imagine the power of so much stored wisdom.'

Eochaid's journeys were determined by his own celestial calendar. The first occasion he left the forest after my arrival was shortly before the start of the thirteenth month of his year. A thirteenth month, of course, has no equivalent in the White Christ calendar, but for those who measure time by the waxing and waning of the moon it obviously does exist and occurs three or four times every decade. Eochaid called it the elder month, and he invited me to accompany him on his journey. It would be a tiring walk, he warned, but he had a duty to perform for a confederation of four tuaths some distance to the north-west. The people of this region were so respectful of the Old Ways that they had named their territory Cairpre, to commemorate one of the greatest drui, reputedly the son of the God Ogmius.

It was indeed a long walk, six days' striding across an increasingly bleak countryside of moorland and rock to our destination, a substantial crannog. At Eochaid's suggestion I took along my battered leather satchel with a spare change of clothes for myself, a white gown belonging to Eochaid, and a small supply of dried nuts and grain for food. Eochaid himself carried nothing of value, no symbols of his profession. He had only a small cloth bag slung over his shoulder and a sharp sickle, which he used to clear a space in the undergrowth when we slept out in the open or to cut medicinal herbs that he noticed growing by the wayside. Plants which heal, he explained, are available at all times of the year if you know where to look. Some are best gathered in the spring when their sap is full, others when they show their summer flowers, and several when their roots are dormant or they are bearing autumn fruit. On that journey he was collecting the roots of burdock thistles for making an infusion to treat skin diseases and boils, and with the point of his sickle he dug up the roots of something he said was a cure for ringworm. He called it cuckoo plant.

'That broken hand of yours,' he commented to me one day, 'would have healed much quicker if you had known how to treat it.'

'What should I have done?'

'Found the root which people call boneset or knitbone – it's very common – then made a paste and applied it to the wound as a poultice. It would have reduced the swelling and the pain. The same paste, dissolved in water, can be used as a treatment for diseases of the stomach or even given as medicine to children who have whooping cough.'

With his medical skill Eochaid was welcome at every settlement we passed. He seemed to be able to produce a remedy for any malady, even if it was severe. He gave an invalid, who was coughing as if to burst his lungs, an oily drink made from the fruit of water fennel, and an unfortunate who suffered from fits was calmed with an extract of all-heal root. 'Valerian is another name for it,' Eochaid said to me as he prepared the fetid-smelling drug, 'which comes from the Latin "to be in health". But you want to be careful with it. Too big a dose and you'll put a person to sleep for good.' I was about to ask Eochaid how he came to know Latin, when we were interrupted. A distraught mother arrived to say her child was suffering from a very sore throat, and Eochaid despatched me to fetch haws from a whitethorn bush we had seen not far back down the road so she could make hawthorn broth for the youngster.

The inhabitants of the hamlets and villages treated Eochaid with a deference bordering on awe. If we needed shelter, we were always given a place of honour in the home of the leader of the community, and no one ever asked where we were going or what our business was. I commented on this to Eochaid, and the fact that he carried no weapon and did not ask permission of any of the tuath people to cross their lands, though this would have been a dangerous act of folly for any stranger. He answered me that the brithemain were privileged. They could walk the trackways and be certain that they would not be impeded or molested, even by brigands. This immunity, he explained, arose from a belief among the country people that to harm a brithem would result in terrible misfortune. 'It's one of the beliefs which date back to the early days of the drui, and which the Christian priests, though they complain that the drui were sent by the devil, have been shrewd enough to turn to their advantage. They now say that harming a priest will also bring a curse on the evildoer, and they sometimes carry and display holy relics to strengthen the aura of their protection. Mind you,' he added, 'if the relic is too valuable, that doesn't always prevent thieves from robbing them.' Thinking of the ornamental stones that I had prised from the big Gospel book and still carried, I said nothing.

The chieftains of the four allied tuaths were waiting for Eochaid to decide their backlog of legal cases. Having seen how the Icelanders dispensed justice at their Althing, I was interested to observe how the Irish applied their laws. The lawsuits were heard in the crannog's council hall, where Eochaid sat on a low stool flanked by the chieftains. They listened to what the plaintiffs had to say, then called on the defendants for their versions of events. Sometimes a chieftain would ask a question or add a piece of corroborating detail, but Eochaid himself said very little. Yet, when the moment for a judgement arrived, the entire assembly would wait for the brithem to pronounce. Invariably Eochaid began his remarks with a reference to earlier custom in a similar case. He would quote 'the natural law', often using archaic words and phrases that few of his listeners could comprehend. Yet, such was their esteem for brithem law that they stood respectfully and they never disputed his decision. Eochaid rarely imposed a sentence of imprisonment or physical punishment. He dealt mainly in compensation. When he found a genuine offence had been committed, he explained its gravity and then suggested the correct compensation that should be paid.

The first cases he heard were fairly trivial. People complained of horses and oxen that had broken into neighbouring pastures, pigs trespassing on a vegetable patch, and even the case of a pack of hounds, not properly restrained, which had entered a yard and defiled it with their droppings. Patiently Eochaid listened to the details, and decided who was at fault – the landowner for not fencing his property more securely, or the animals' owner for allowing the creatures to stray. Then he would deliver his judgement. The pigs' owner was obliged to pay a double fine because his animals had not only eaten the vegetables but had rooted up the earth with their snouts and this would make the garden more difficult to restore. The man complaining about a neighbour's cattle in his field lost his case because he had failed to build his fence to the approved height and strength to stop the oxen pushing through it. In the case of the errant dogs, Eochaid found for the plaintiff. He recommended that the dogs' owner pick up the droppings, and then produce restitution in the form of the same amount of butter and dough as the quantity of dog turds retrieved. This particular arbitration raised broad smiles of approval from his audience.

As the day wore on, the cases before the brithem became more serious. There were two divorce cases. In the first a woman sought a formal separation from her husband on the grounds that he had become so fat that he was impotent because he was no longer capable of intercourse. One look at the obesity of the husband made that an easy case to settle. Eochaid also awarded the woman most of the joint property on the grounds that the fat man was also lazy and had clearly contributed little to the income of the household. The second case was more finely balanced. The husband claimed that his wife had brought shame on his honour by flirting with a neighbour, and she counter-claimed that he had done likewise by gossiping to his friends about the intimate details of their own sexual relationship. The pair became increasingly strident until Eochaid cut short their quarrelling by announcing that neither side was at fault, but it was obvious that the marriage was over. He recommended that they separate, each taking back whatever property they had originally brought into it. The woman, however, was to retain the family home as she had children to rear.

'How do you know that your judgements will be obeyed?' I asked Eochaid that evening. 'There is no one to enforce your decisions. Once you leave this place, who will oblige the guilty party to carry out the terms you have laid down?'

'Everything depends on the respect that the people have for the brithem law,' he answered. 'I cannot oblige people to do what I say. But you will have noticed that I try to produce a settlement that both parties can accept. My intention is to restore equilibrium within the community. Even in the extreme case of a murder I would not suggest a death sentence. Executing the murderer will not bring the dead victim back to life. It is surely more sensible that the killer and his kinsfolk pay restitution to the family of the deceased. In that way people will think before committing murder, knowing that their own kinsfolk will have to suffer consequences.'

'And what if the compensation is so severe that the kinsfolk cannot find the money to pay?' I asked.

'That is part of the brithem's proper training,' he replied. 'It is our responsibility to know the face price of every person and the value of every misdeed, and how to vary the compensation according to a myriad of circumstances. A ri, for example, has a greater face price than an aithech, a commoner. So if the ri receives an injury, then the compensation awarded to him is higher. But at the same time if it is the ri who is at fault then he must pay a greater amount of compensation than I would award against an aithech.'

While Eochaid was hearing the cases, more and more people kept arriving at the crannog, until the latecomers were so numerous that they were obliged to camp on the surrounding lands. To add to the congestion the cowherds and shepherds brought in their animals from the outlying pastures in preparation for the forthcoming winter season. Surplus animals were slaughtered, and any meat which was not preserved was being cooked over open fires. A holiday atmosphere developed as the people gorged themselves and drank copious amounts of mead and beer. A number of market stalls appeared. Though the gathering was far smaller than the Althing I had witnessed in Iceland when I first met the Burners, I was struck by the similarity. There was a difference, though: among the Irish I became aware of a certain underlying nervousness. It was the eve of their Samhain, the Festival of the Dead.

On the last day of Eochaid's law court a great crowd gathered at the causeway leading to the crannog. Many of the people were carrying bundles of firewood and there was a strange mixture of jubilation and apprehension. Eochaid emerged from the gate of the crannog wearing a plain white surcoat over his normal tunic. He held a long staff in one hand and his small sickle in the other. Behind him came the chieftains of the allied tuaths. The little group crossed the causeway and headed off across the fields with the crowd following them. In the distance stood a clump of trees. I had noticed the trees earlier because all the surrounding land had been cleared for farming, but this small copse had been left untouched. It was primeval woodland.

I fell into step behind Eochaid as he entered the wood, which was composed almost entirely of hazel trees. In the middle was a small lake, scarcely more than a pond. Behind us the crowd spread out among the trees and laid down their burdens. A dozen of the chieftain's servants began cutting back the undergrowth at the edge of the pond, clearing a space for Eochaid. He stood there calmly, sickle in hand, watching the preparations. Then, as dusk fell, he moved to the edge of the little lake. Soon it was so dark that it was only just possible to make out the dim shapes of the watching crowd amid the darker shadows of the trees. The whole copse was silent except for the occasional crying of a baby. Eochaid turned towards the lake and began to declaim. He spoke sentence after sentence in a language that I did not understand. His voice rose and fell as if reciting poetry, his words producing a flat, dull echo from the surrounding trees. The entire crowd seemed to be holding their breath as they listened. The water in the pond was inky black and an occasional whisper of breeze ruffled the surface, dissolving the reflected circle of the moon. As the clouds slid by, the moon's image appeared and disappeared randomly.

After about half an hour Eochaid stopped speaking and leaned forward. The white overgown he was wearing made it possible to see his movements clearly, and I glimpsed the glint of the sickle in his right hand. He reached forward and cut a wisp of dried reeds from the edge of the pond. A moment later, by a process I could not detect, a flicker of flame danced in his grasp as the wisp began to burn. As the flames grew brighter, they reflected off the white cloth of his gown and illuminated Eochaid's face so that his eyes seemed in deep shadow. He walked over to a pile of hazel twigs and thrust the burning tinder among them. At once the twigs burst into flame. Within moments the fire was burning so vigorously that orange tongues of flame were twisting and wavering to head height. As the fire took increasing hold, the chieftains of the tuaths stepped forward with their bundles of wood and threw them on the fire. I heard the rapid crackle of blazing timber and sparks began to fly upwards in the hot air currents. Soon there was so much heat radiating from the fire that my face was scorching, and I put up an arm to shield my eyes. There was a low appreciative murmuring from the crowd, and looking across the flames I could see that someone had come forward out of each family group. Each face was lit by the blazing fire and had an expression so intent that it seemed as if the person was enraptured by the swirling of the flames. Several stepped so close to the fire that I thought they would be burned. They all cast small items onto the fire – I could make out a tiny rag doll, a child's shoe, a handful of seeds, a ripe apple. They were offerings from those who sought to have children and bountiful crops in the coming year, or making thanks for their past blessings. The fire burned down quickly. One moment it was a high blaze, then next moment it collapsed on itself in a cascade of sparks. That was when the heads of families each thrust a brand into the flames. As soon as the brand had caught alight, they turned and, gathering up their families, began to walk away, heading back to their homes and tents, each carrying a burning flare. They would guard the brand through the night, and use it to relight their hearth fires, which they had extinguished to mark the passing of summer. The flares being carried out across the countryside made a remarkable spectacle, a sprinkle of bobbing light in the darkness. A hand touched my elbow. I looked round and recognised the steward of one of the tuath chieftains. He nodded for me to follow him, and we began to walk back to the crannog. Halfway there I paused and turned to look at the hazel copse. I could see the glow of the embers, and standing beside them the white-clad figure of Eochaid. He had his back towards us and was looking out at the lake. He had both arms outstretched to the sky, and I fancied that I saw the arcing glint of his sickle as he threw it into the pond.

These were mysteries to which I could not be privy, and the steward kept hold of my arm to make sure that I did not double back to rejoin Eochaid. Instead my guide led me to where his own people were waiting. They were from the farthest of the federate tuaths and had set up their camp at a little distance from the crannog. My escort brought me into the circle where the families had gathered to celebrate the successful conclusion of the ceremony. They had lit a central bonfire with their sacred flame and were seated on the ground, eating and drinking and enjoying themselves. I was greeted with nods and smiles. Someone put a wooden cup of mead in my hand, someone else handed me a rib of roasted sheep, and space was made for me in the circle to sit down and join the feast. I started to gnaw at the tendrils of mutton and looked around at the ring of faces. This was the first time that I had been exposed to the society of the true Irish, the ordinary people from the remotest fringes of their island, at a time when they were most relaxed. Now I was a guest, not a war captive, or a slave, or a novice. I savoured the mood of the gathering. Abruptly I felt a shocking lurch of recognition. Seated about a third of the way around the circle was Thorvall the Hunter. I knew it was impossible. The last time I had seen Thorvall had been when he had left our Vinland settlement, angry with Karlsefni and Gudrid, and sailed off in our small boat with five companions to explore farther along the coast. We had never heard anything more of him, and presumed he had been killed by the Skraelings or drowned, though someone did say that Thor would never let someone drown at sea who was so robust in his belief in the Old Ways.

I stared at the wraith. Not since I had seen the fetch of Gardi the overseer in Greenland eleven years before had I seen a dead man come back among the living. Thorvall looked older than when I had last seen him. His beard and hair were shot with grey, his face was deeply lined and his massive shoulders had acquired a slight stoop of age. But the lid of his left eye drooped as it had always done, and I could still see the mark, much fainter now in the creases and folds of his ageing face, where the bear claws had left the hunting scar that had made such an impression on me as a child. A leather skullcap was pulled down on his head and pressed his hair over his ears so I could not see whether, like the Thorvall I knew from Vinland, he had also lost the top of his left ear. He was dressed in the clothing of an Irish cliathaire, laced leggings and a heavy jerkin of sheepskin over a rough linen shirt. Laid on the ground in front of him was an expensive-looking heavy sword. I tried to remain calm. I had taken to heart what Snorri Godi had warned me about: that when you experience second sight it is wiser to pretend that all is entirely normal, even though you are seeing something invisible to others. I continued to chew on my meat, occasionally glancing across at Thorvall and wondering if his ghost would recognise me. Then I noticed the man seated on Thorvall's right turn towards him and say something. My flesh tingled. I was not alone in seeing the wraith. Others were aware of his presence. Then it occurred to me that perhaps I had let my imagination run away with me. The man seated on the other side of the fire was not Thorvall, but someone who looked very like him.

Getting to my feet, I backed away from the circle, then walked round to where I could approach the seated stranger from one side. As I came closer, the more certain I was that it really was Thorvall. He had the same big-knuckled, gnarled hands that I remembered, and I glimpsed around his neck a necklace of bear claws. It had to be him. Yet how did he come to be seated among Irish clansmen, dressed like a veteran Irish warrior?

'Thorvall?' I enquired nervously, standing a little behind his right shoulder.

He did not respond.

'Thorvall?' I repeated more loudly, and this time he did turn round and looked up at me with a questioning expression on his face. He had the same pale blue eyes that I remembered staring at me in the stable all those years ago when I was first interrogated about my second sight. But the eyes looking at me had no sense of recognition.

'Thorvall,' I said for the third time and then, speaking in Norse, 'I am Thorgils, don't you recognise me? It's me, Leif's son from Brattahlid in Greenland.'

Thorvall continued to stare at me with no reaction except for a slightly puzzled frown. He had not understood a word I said. People were starting to take notice of my behaviour and glancing curiously at me. I began to lose my nerve.

'Thorvall?'

My voice trailed away in confusion. The man gave a grunt and turned back to face the fire, ignoring me.

I crept back to my place by the fire, thoroughly embarrassed. Luckily the tide of mead was rising and my strange actions were forgotten in the general merriment. I kept glancing across at Thorvall, or whoever he was, trying to resolve my confusion.

'Who's that man over there, the one with the big sword on the ground in front of him?' I asked my neighbour.

He looked across to the man with the scar on his face. 'That's Ardal, the ri's champion, though he's had very little to do ever since we allied with the other tuaths,' he replied, 'Just as well. He's getting a bit long in the tooth to do much duelling.'

I remembered Eochaid's warning about not asking too many questions and decided that it would be better to wait till next day to consult the brithem about the mysterious clansman.

'King's champion?' Eochaid replied next morning. 'That's an

old title, not used much today. He's usually the best warrior in the tuath, who acts as the ri's chief bodyguard. He also represents the ri if there is a quarrel between two tuaths which is to be decided by single combat between two picked fighters. Why do you want to know?'

'I saw a man yesterday evening who I thought was someone I knew long ago when I was living in the Norse lands. I was told his name was Ardal and that he is, or was, the king's champion. But I was sure he was someone else. Yet that seems impossible.'

'I can't say I know him. Who did you say he was with?' Eochaid asked.

'He was seated among the people who came from the farthest tuath, the one near the coast.'

'That'll be the Ua Cannannain.' Eochaid and I were standing in the mead hall of the crannog, waiting to say a formal farewell to the ri. Eochaid turned to the ri's steward. 'Do you know this man called Ardal?'

'Only by reputation,' he replied. 'A man of very few words. Not surprising. He was half dead when he was washed ashore and it was thought that he would never live. But he was nursed back to health in the ri's own house and became a servant there. Then it turned out that he was so good with weapons that he eventually became the king's champion. Quite an advancement for someone who was fuidir cinad o muir.'

It was a phrase I had never heard before. A fuidir is someone half-free or ransomed, and cinad o muir is 'a crime of the sea'. I was about to ask the steward what he meant, when the man added, 'If you want to meet Ardal, it will have to wait till next year. Early this morning most of the Ua Cannannain set out to return to their own tuath.'

Eochaid looked at me. 'What makes you think that you knew this man Ardal previously?'

'He and his friend, a smith named Tyrkir, were my first tutors in the Old Ways,' I replied, 'but I thought he was dead.'

'He may well be dead,' Eochaid observed. 'We are now in

Samhain, the season when the veil between the living and the dead is at its thinnest, and those who are no longer with us can pass most easily through the veil. What you saw may have been your friend who has returned briefly to this world.'

'But the steward said that he had been in this land for several years, not just at this season.'

'Then perhaps you were imagining your friend in the form of this man Ardal. It seems an appropriate name for the king's champion. It means someone who has the courage of a bear.'

A berserker, I thought. or was it because of the bear-claw necklace? And this thought distracted me from asking what the steward meant by a fuidir cinad o muir.

I never solved the mystery of Ardal because on the next celebration of Samhain I fell sick during the six-day walk to Cairpre. I developed a shivering fever, probably caught from too many damp days spent in Eochaid's forest retreat during what was a very wet summer, even by Irish standards. Eochaid left me in the care of a roadside hospitaller, whose wife fed me – as he had instructed – on a monotonous diet of celery, raw and in watery broth. The cure worked, but it gave me a lasting dislike for the taste of that stringy vegetable.

TWENTY-ONE

I WAS NOW in my nineteenth year, and my situation in the company of a forest-dwelling brithem, offered little opportunity for contact with the opposite sex. My heartbreak over Orlaith had left its mark, and I often wondered what had become of her. A sense of guilt for what had happened made me question whether I would ever achieve a satisfactory relationship with a woman, and Eochaid's attitude towards women only served to increase my confusion.

Eochaid regarded women as subject to their own particular standards. There was the day when two women appeared before him for judgement after one had stabbed the other with a kitchen knife, causing a deep gash. They were both wives of a minor ri, who had exercised his right to have more than one wife. When the two women were brought before Eochaid, he was told that the wounded woman was the first wife and that she had initiated the affray. She had attacked the new wife a few days after her husband had married for the second time.

'How many days afterwards?' Eochaid asked gently.

'Two days later, when the new and younger wife first came into the home,' came the reply.

'Then culpability is shared equally,' the brithem stated. 'Custom states that a first wife has the right to inflict an injury on a new wife provided it is non-fatal and it is done in the first three days. Equally, the second wife has the right to retaliate, but she must limit herself to scratching with her nails, pulling the hair, or abusive language.'

An assault with words was, in brithem law, as serious as an attack with a weapon of metal or wood. 'Language,' Eochaid once said to me, 'can be lethal. A tongue can have a sharper edge than the best-honed dagger. You can do more damage by inventing a clever and hurtful nickname for your enemy than by burning his house or destroying his crops.' He then cited a whole catalogue of verbal offences, ranging from the spoken spells of witchcraft uttered in secret, through hurtful satire, to the jibes and insults which flew in a quarrel. Each and every one had its own value when it came to arbitration. 'If the monks ever told you that the drui used spells and curses,' he said to me on another occasion, 'they were confusing it with the power of language. A drui who aspired to be a fili ollam, a master of words, was striving for the highest and most difficult discipline, to deploy words for praise or poetry, irony or ridicule.'

That was the day he told me about his own time as a monk. We were seated on a log outside his forest hut after returning from an expedition to net small fish in the stream, when a blackbird burst into full-throated song from somewhere in the bushes. Eochaid leaned back, closed his eyes for a moment to listen to the birdsong and then began to quote poetry,

> 'I have a hut in the wood, none knows it but my Lord;
> an ash tree this side, a hazel on the other,
> a great tree on a mound encloses it.
> The size of my hut, small yet not small, a place of familiar paths;
> the she-bird in its dress of blackbird colour sings a melodious strain from its gable.'

He stopped, opened his eyes, and looked at me. 'Do you know who composed those lines?' he asked.

'No,' I answered. 'Are they yours?'

'I wish they were,' he said. 'They were spoken to me by a Christian hermit in his disert. He was living here, on this very same spot, when I first came across these woods. It is his hut which we now occupy. He was already an old man when I found him, old, but at peace with himself and the world. He had lived here for as long as he could remember, and he knew that his time would soon be over. I met him twice, for I came back a couple of years later to see how he was getting on and to bring him some store of food. He thanked me and rewarded me with the poem. The next time I came back he was dead. I found his corpse and buried him as he would have wished. But the poetry stayed echoing in my head, and I decided that I should go to the monastery where he had been trained, to visit the place where the power of such words is nurtured.'

Eochaid had enrolled at the monastery as a novice and within months was its star pupil. No one knew his brithem background. He had shaved his head completely to remove his distinctive tonsure, telling the monks he had suffered from a case of ringworm. With his phenomenal trained memory, book learning came easily to him and he quickly absorbed the writings of the early Christian authors. 'Jerome, Cyprian, Origen and Gregory the Great . . . they were men of acute perception,' he said. 'Their scholarship and conviction impressed me profoundly. Yet, I came to the conclusion that much of what they wrote was a retelling of the far earlier truths, the ones in which I had already been schooled. So in the end I decided that I would prefer to stay with the Old Ways and left the monastery. But at least I had learned why the Christianity has taken hold so easily among our people.'

'Why is that?' I asked.

'The priests and monks build cleverly on well-laid foundations,' he answered, 'Samhain, our Festival of the Dead, becomes the eve of their All Saints' Day; Beltane, which for us is the reawakening of life and celebrated with new fire, is turned into Easter even with the lighting of their Paschal Fire; our Brigid the exalted one, of whom I am a particular adherent, for she brings healing, poetry and learning, has been transmuted into a Christian saint. The list goes on and on. Sometimes I wonder if this means that the Old Ways are really still flourishing beneath the surface, and I could have stayed a monk and still worshipped the Gods in a different guise.'

'Didn't anyone at the monastery ask after the hermit who lived here? After all, he had been one of them.'

'As I warned you, the monks can be harsh towards people who abandon their way of life. They had a nickname for him. They called him Suibhne Geilt, after the "Mad Sweeney" who was driven insane by a curse from a Christian priest. He spent the rest of his life living among the trees and composing poetry until he was killed by a swineherd. Yet, such is the power of words that I have a suspicion that Mad Sweeney's verses will be remembered longer than the men who mocked him.'

On the eve of my third Samhain in Eochaid's company he announced that, instead of going to Cairpre that year, he would travel east to the burial place of Tlachtga, daughter of the famed drui Mog Ruth. A distinguished drui in her own right, Tlachtga had been renowned for the subtlety of her judgements, and it was custom that those brithemain who were adepts in arbitration should assemble at her tomb every fifth year to discuss the more intricate cases they had heard since their last conclave and agree on common judgements for the future. The hill of Tlachtga lies only a half-day's travel from the seat of the High King at Tara, so it is here that the High King of Ireland also comes to celebrate the Samhain feast. 'It is one of the great gatherings in the land,' Eochaid told me, 'so perhaps Adamnan the Timid might be better advised to stay away. Equally, it might be a chance for you to learn whether you should begin using Diarmid as your alias.' It was an old joke of his. With his usual keen observation he had noted how I kept glancing at the younger women whenever we went to the settlements. In legend Diarmid carried on his forehead a 'love spot', a mark placed there by a mysterious maiden which caused women to fall madly and instantly in love with the handsome young man.

The great gathering at the foot of the hill of Tlachtga was a spectacle that surpassed anything I had anticipated. The bustle and flamboyance of the Irish who came to the High King's festivities made a lively impression. There were several thousand participants, and they arrived in their kin groups, with each chieftain trying to impress his equals. Their retinues swaggered through the crowds, flaunting the expensive finger rings, torcs and brooches which their leaders had awarded them. By regulation long-bladed and long-handled weapons had to be set aside during the festivities, but daggers were permitted and were worn to show off their workmanship or decoration. There were displays of horses and hounds, and even a few chariots came bouncing and swaying in behind their teams of shaggy war ponies; the wheels of these old-fashioned contraptions were brightly painted in contrasting colours so as they spun they looked like children's toys. In the presence of the Irish, wherever there are horses and dogs in any number, there will be racing and contests and gaming. By the time Eochaid and I arrived, a wide circle of wooden posts had been driven in the ground to create a race track, where crowds of spectators jostled each morning and afternoon to watch the contests.

Sometimes just two riders settled a personal challenge by racing their mounts. More often it was a general match with an honour prize to the winner, a wild stampede of a score of lathered, sweating horses thundering round the course, urged on by the shouts of the crowd and the flailing whips of their riders, usually skinny young lads. On my second day at Tlachtga I also came across an event which, to an outsider, might have seemed like a mock battle. Two squads of wild-looking men were milling together and striking at one another with flat clubs. Occasionally a man fell to the ground, bleeding from a head blow, and it seemed that the fighters were hitting out with unrestrained viciousness. Yet, the object of their attention was only a small hard ball which each side was trying to propel into the opponents' territory and then through an open mark. The blows to the head were accidental, or allegedly so. The reason for my fascination was that I had seen a similar sport being played – though with less riot and fervour – by my youthful companions in Iceland and I had once played it myself.

I was standing on the sidelines, watching the contest closely and trying to detect the differences from the Icelandic version of the game, when I received a shattering blow on the back of my own head. It must have been a harder stroke than anything being dealt on the games field because everything went dark.

I awoke to the familiar sensation of lying on the ground with my wrists tied together. This time the pain was not as bad as it had been after the battle of Clontarf because my bonds were leather straps, not iron manacles. But the other difference was more serious. When I opened my eyes, I knew my captor: I found myself looking up into the face of the treasurer of St Ciaran's.

Brother Mariannus was gazing down at me with an expression in which distaste matched satisfaction. 'What made you think you would get away with it?' he asked. I shook my head groggily. I had a violent headache and could feel the large bruise swelling up where someone had struck me with a weapon. I wondered if I had been hit with a games stick. A clout on the head with a heavy crozier would have done the job just as well. Then I remembered Eochaid. While I was watching the Irish at their sports, he had gone in search of other brithemain and he probably did not know what had happened to me. He had important business to attend to and when I failed to show up would probably surmise that I had departed in search of strong drink or female diversion. I had left my cloak and travelling satchel in the hut where we were staying, but he might even think that I had taken the chance to part company with him altogether.

'You'll discover that it's both a sin and a crime to steal Church property,' the treasurer was saying grimly, 'I doubt you have any respect for the moral consequences of the sin, but the criminal repercussions will have more impact on someone of your base character.'

We were in a tent, and two of the monastery servants were standing over me. I wondered which of them had hit me on the head. The younger man had the stolid gaze of an underling who would do unquestioningly as he was told, but the older servant looked as if he was positively enjoying seeing me in trouble.

'My men will take you back to the monastery, where you will be tried and receive punishment. You'll start out tomorrow,' Brother Mariannus went on. 'I presume that you have disposed of the property you stole, so you can expect the maximum penalty. Would you not agree, Abb?'

I turned my head to see who else was in the tent, and there, standing with his hands clasped behind his back and looking out of the tent flap as if he wished to have nothing to do with this sordid matter of theft and absconding from his rule, was Abb Aidan. The sight of him brought to mind something that Eochaid had once explained to me about the laws of the Christians. The monastery abbs, he said, had created most of their statutes and regulations as ways of raising money locally. Shrewdly they had adopted the brithem principle that whenever a rule was broken, then the transgressors had to pay a fine. So their cana, as they called their laws, were only valid within the territories the abbs controlled. Farther afield, Eochaid had stated, it was not monastery law which applied, but the king's law.

'I claim my right to trial before the king's marshal,' I said. 'Here at Tlachtga I am not subject to the cana of St Ciaran's. I am outside the monastery's jurisdiction. More than that, I have the right to protection from the king's law because I am a foreigner, a fact acknowledged when I was first interviewed for admission into the community at St Ciaran's.'

Brother Mariannus glowered at me. 'Who taught you anything about the law, you impudent puppy . . .' he began.

'No, he's right,' Abb Aidan interrupted. 'Under the law he is entitled to a hearing before the king's marshal, though that will not make any difference to the verdict.' I felt a faint stir of satisfaction. I had judged the abb correctly. He was such a stickler for custom and correctness that I had avoided being transported back to St Ciaran's and within range of Brother Cainnech, whom I knew was my real foe.

'Take him outside and tie him up securely, feet as well as hands, to make sure he doesn't disappear a second time,' Abb Aidan ordered and then, addressing the treasurer, 'Brother Mariannus, I would be obliged if you would contact the officials of the royal household and ask if the case of Thorgils or Thurgeis, known sometimes as Thangbrand, can be heard at the first opportunity, on a charge of theft of Church property.'

So, late the next day, I found myself at a legal hearing once again. But this time I was not an observer. I was the accused. The trial was held in the mead hall of the local ri, a modest building that could scarcely hold more than a hundred spectators, and which that afternoon was far from full. Of course, the High King himself was not there. He was represented by his marshal, a bored-looking man in late middle age, with a sleek, round face, straggling moustache and large brown eyes. He reminded me of a tired seal. He had not expected an extra case to be brought before him so late in the day and wanted it to be dealt with quickly. I was pushed into the centre of the hall and made to stand facing the marshal. He sat at a plain wooden table and on his right was a scribe, a priest, making notes on a wax tablet. Farther around the circle from the penman were about a dozen men, some seated, others standing. They were clearly clerics, though I could not tell whether they were there as advisers, jury, prosecutors, or merely onlookers. Opposite to them, and fewer in number, were a group of brithemain. Among them, to my relief, I could see Eochaid. He was standing in the rear of the group and made no sign that he knew me.

The proceedings went briskly. The treasurer recounted the charges against me, how I had joined the monastery, how I had betrayed their trust and generosity, how I had disappeared one night, and the next day the library was found broken into and several holy and precious ornaments to a Gospel book had been torn from their mountings. Earlier some pages had gone missing from an important manuscript, and I was suspected of being responsible for that theft as well.

'Has any of the stolen material been recovered?' the marshal asked without much interest.

'No, none of it. The culprit disappeared without trace, though we looked for him widely and carefully. It was only yesterday, after an interval of two years, that he was seen here at the festival by one of our people and recognised.'

'What penalty are you seeking?' the marshall enquired.

'The just penalty – the penalty for aggravated theft. A death penalty.'

'Would you consider some sort of arbitration and a payment of compensation if that could be arranged?' The question came from the marshal's left, from one of the brithemain. The question had been addressed to the treasurer and I saw several of the Christians stir and come alert. Their hostility was obvious.

'No,' replied the treasurer crisply. 'How could the wretch possibly pay compensation? He has no family to stand surety for him, he is a foreigner, and he is obviously destitute. In his entire life he could never repay the sum that the loss represents to the monastery.'

'If he is so destitute, would it not be appropriate to forgive a pauper for his crime? Isn't that what you preach – forgiveness of sins?'

The treasurer glared at the brithem. 'Our Holy Bible teaches us that he who absolves a crime is himself a wrongdoer,' he retorted. To the marshal's left I saw the churchmen nod their agreement. They looked thoroughly pleased with the treasurer's response. No one asked me a single question. Indeed they barely glanced at me. I knew why. The word of a runaway novice counted for nothing against the word of a senior monk, particularly someone with the status of the treasurer. Under both Church law and brithem custom, the value of testimony depends on the individual's rank, so whatever I said was of no import. If the treasurer stated I was the culprit, then it was useless for me to deny it. For my defence to be effective, I needed someone of equal or superior status to the treasurer to speak for me, and there was no one there who appeared willing to act on my behalf. As I had known from the beginning, it was not a question of whether I was innocent or guilty, but of what my sentence would be.

'I find the culprit guilty of theft of Church property,' the marshal announced without any hesitation, 'and order that he should suffer the penalty as sought by the plaintiff.' He began to rise from his chair, clearly eager to close the day's hearings and leave for his supper.

'On a matter of law . . .' a voice interjected quietly. I could recognise Eochaid's voice anywhere. He was addressing the marshal directly and, like everyone else, ignored me completely. The marshal gave an exasperated grimace, and sat back down again, waiting to hear what Eochaid had to say. 'It has been stated by the plaintiff that the accused is a foreigner and that he has no family or kin in this land, and therefore there is no possibility of compensation or restitution for the theft. The same criteria must surely apply to the court's sentence: namely, any individual without family nor kin to guide or instruct him in what is right and what is wrong, must – by those circumstances – be regarded as having committed his or her crime out of a natural deficiency. In that case, the crime is cinad o muir and must be punished accordingly.'

I had no idea what Eochaid was talking about.

But Brother Mariannus clearly did know what the brithem had in mind because the Treasurer was looking wary. 'The young man has been found guilty of a major felony. His offence was against the monastery of St Ciaran, and the monastery has the right to carry out the appropriate sentence,' he said.

'If it is the monastery which is the injured party,' Eochaid replied calmly, 'then punishment should be carried out in accordance with monastic custom, should it not? And what could be more appropriate than allowing your own God to decide this young man's fate. Is this not how your own saints were willing to demonstrate their faith?'

The treasurer was clearly irritated. There was a short silence as he searched for a retort, when the marshal intervened. He was getting bored with the continuing discussion. 'The felon is judged to have committed a cinad o muir,' he announced, 'He is to be taken from here to the nearest beach and the sentence to be carried out.'

I thought I was to be drowned like an unwanted cur, with a stone about my neck. However, the following day, when I was brought to the beach, the boat drawn up on the shingle was so small that I could not imagine how I would fit into it as well as the person who was to throw me overboard. The tiny craft was barely more than a large basket. It was made of light withies lashed together with thongs to form an open framework and then covered over with a skin sewn of cowhides. The boat, if such a flimsy vessel could be called that, was in very poor condition. The stitching was broken in several places, there were cracks and splits in the leather cover, and the thongs of the basketwork were so slack that the structure sagged at the edge. It looked as if its owner had abandoned the craft on the beach as being totally unfit for the sea and that, I gathered, was precisely why it had been selected.

'We'll have to wait for the wind,' said the senior of the two monastery servants who had escorted me. 'The locals say that it usually gets up strongly in the afternoon and blows hard for several hours. Enough to see you on your way for a final voyage.' He was relishing his role. On the half-day's walk to the beach he had lost no chance to make my journey unpleasant, tripping me up from time to time, then jerking viciously on the leading halter as I struggled to get back on my feet. Neither Abb Aidan nor the treasurer had thought it worth their while to come to the beach to witness my sentence being carried out. They had sent the servants to do the work, and there was a minor official from the marshal's court to report back when the punishment had been completed.

Apart from the three of them, there was just a handful of curious bystanders, mostly children and old men from the local fishing families. One of the old men kept handing a few small coins from one gnarled paw to the other, his lips moving as he counted them again and again. I guessed he was the previous owner of the semi-derelict little boat, which, like me, had been condemned.

'Are you from the settlement outside St Ciaran's?' I asked the older servant.

'What's that to you?' he grunted disagreeably.

'I thought you might know Bladnach the leather-worker.'

'And so what? If you think he'll show up here by some holy miracle and sew up the boat before you set sail in her, you must be even more optimistic than Maelduine sailing for the Blessed Islands. Without his legs, Bladnach would really need a marvel to get here so briskly.' He laughed bitterly. 'You would have thought he had suffered enough without losing his daughter as well.'

'What do you mean, losing his daughter?'

He shot me a glance of pure loathing. 'Don't think your antics with Orlaith didn't get noticed by her neighbours. Orlaith got pregnant, thanks to you, and there were complications. She ended up by having to go to the monastery for treatment, but the hospital couldn't help her. Both she and the baby died. Brother Cainnech said there was nothing he could do.'

His words sickened me. Now I knew why the servant had been so vicious to me. It was no good protesting that I could not have been the father of her child.

'I'm sorry,' I said feebly.

'You'll be more than sorry when the wind changes. I hope you die at sea so slowly that you wish you had drowned; and, if your wreck of a boat does float long enough for you to come ashore, that you fall into the hands of savages who make your life as a fuidir unbearable,' he retorted, and kicked my feet from under me so that I fell heavily on the shingle.

Now I knew what Ardal had been when he was described as fuidir cinad o muir. He had been a castaway, found in a rudderless boat which had drifted onto the coast. The tribesmen of Cairpre had presumed that he was a criminal deliberately set adrift as punishment. If such a person came back to land, then whoever found him could treat him as his personal property, whether to kill or enslave him. That was what it meant to be fuidir cinad o muir – human flotsam washed up by the waves, destined for a life of servitude.

As predicted, the wind changed in the early hours of the afternoon and began to blow strongly from the west, away from the land. The two monastery servants roused themselves and, picking up the battered little boat with ease, carried it down the beach and set it afloat. One man held the boat steady, and the other came back to where I sat, kicked me hard in the ribs and told me to get down to the water's edge and climb into the boat. The tiny coracle tipped and swivelled alarmingly as I got aboard, and water began to seep in through the leather hull. Within moments there were several inches of water in the bilge. The older servant, whose name I gather was Jarlath, leaned forward to cut the leather thong binding my wrists, and handed me a single paddle.

'I hope God does not grant you any more mercy than he gave Orlaith,' he said. 'I'm personally going to give your boat such a shove that I hope it carries you to Hell. Certainly you cannot paddle back to land against this wind, and in a few hours it may even raise waves big enough to swamp your vessel if you have not already capsized. Think about it and suffer!'

He was about to send the boat into deeper water when someone cried, 'Wait!' It was the court official, the man deputed to report on the conduct of my punishment. He waded out to where I sat rocking on the waves.

'The law allows only a single oar, a sail and no rudder, so that you cannot row to shore but are dependent on the weather that God sends. However, you are also permitted one bag of food . . . here . . .'

He handed me a well-worn leather satchel filled with a thin

gruel of grain and nuts blended with water. I recognised Eochaid's favourite diet, the produce of what he called the briugu caille, the hospitaller trees of the forest. I also identified the leather satchel. It was the same one that I had carried away with me from the monastery when I fled from St Ciaran's. Old and stained and battered, it had been repaired many times because the original leather was thick and stout enough to take the needle. I clutched it to me as Jarlath and his colleague began to push the little cockleshell of a boat out into deeper water, and my fingers slid down the fat seams of the satchel so I could feel the hard lumps. They were the stones I had stolen from St Ciaran's. My time spent sitting in Bladnach's workshop waiting for him to blind stitch the book satchels had not been wasted. I had practised how to slit and close leather so neatly that the stitches could not be seen, and that is where I had hidden my loot. Now, belatedly, I understood that Eochaid must have known all along about my hidden hoard.

Jarlath was so determined that I never come back to land that he kept on wading after his colleague had turned back, until he was chest deep in the sea and the larger waves were threatening to break over his head. He gave the boat a final shove, then I was adrift and the wind was rapidly carrying me clear. Still clasping the satchel, I slid myself down to sit in the bilge of the coracle and make her more stable. There was no point in looking back because the man who had helped me was not there. Without Eochaid's intervention at my trial before the king's marshal, I knew I would have finished up like the unfortunate sheepstealer at St Ciaran's, hanging from a gibbet in front of the monastery gate. I found myself wishing that somehow there had been a moment when I had thanked Eochaid for all he had done for me, ever since that morning on the day we first met when he had stood silently regarding me drink water from the woodland stream. Yet, probably I would not have found the right words. Eochaid remained an enigma. I had never penetrated his inner thoughts, or learned why he had chosen to be a brithem, or what sustained him along that demanding path. He had kept himself to himself. His Gods were different from mine and he had never discussed them with me, though I knew they were complex and ancient. His studies of their mysteries made him wise and practical and gave him a remarkable insight into human nature. Had he been an Old Believer, I would have taken him for another Odinn, but without the darker, cruel side. My silent homage to him as I drifted out to sea was to admit that if there was one man on whom I wished to pattern my life it would be Eochaid.

At first I clung fiercely to the sides of the little coracle as it lurched and swivelled crazily in the waves, then tilted and hung at a steep angle, so that it seemed on the point of capsizing at any moment and throwing me into the sea. With each gyration I braced myself in the bottom of the little vessel, and tried to counterbalance the sudden movement. But soon I discovered it was better to relax, to lie limp and let the coracle flex and float naturally to the waves. My real worry was the constant intake of water. It was seeping through the cracks and splits in the leather and splashing over the rim of the little vessel with each wave crest. Unless I did something, the coracle would swamp and founder. I gulped down the gruel in the satchel and began to use the empty leather bag as a scoop, steadily tipping the bilge water back into the sea. It was this action, repeated again and again and again, which distracted me from my fear of capsize and death. As I bailed, I found myself thinking back to my fellow fuidir cinad o muir – Ardal, the mysterious clansman who had been found adrift on the western coast. The more I thought of Ardal, and how closely he had resembled Thorvall the Hunter, the more I convinced myself that they were one and the same man. If so, I told myself as I carefully poured another satchelful of water back into the sea, then Thorvall had drifted across the ocean from Vinland in an open boat, a voyage of many weeks riding the wind and current. The terrible ordeal must have destroyed his memory so he no longer knew his own identity or recognised who I was, but he had survived. And if Thorvall could live through such a nightmare, then so could I.

It was impossible to tell when the sun went down. The sky was so overcast that the light merely faded until I could no longer make out the distant line of the coast far astern. My horizon was reduced to a close circle of dark, restless sea, out of which appeared the white flashes of wave crests. I kept bailing steadily, my arms aching, my skimpy gown soaked against my skin, and the beginnings of a thirst brought on by licking away the spray which struck my face. It must have been nearly midnight when the cloud cover began to break up and the first stars appeared. By then I was so tired that I scarcely noticed that the waves were diminishing. They broke less frequently into the coracle. I found myself setting aside the satchel and relaxing until the rise of bilge water from the leaks obliged me to go to work again.

In these intervals, resting from the labour of bailing, I thought back to the eerie coincidences that had occurred in my life. From the time that my mother had sent me away as an infant, it seemed that there had been a pattern. I had been brought into contact, repeatedly, with people who possessed abnormal qualities – my foster mother Gudrid with her volva's powers could see draugar and fetches; Thrand knew the galdrastafir spells; Brodir had shared with me the vision of Odinn's ravens on the battlefield; Eochaid had spoken of his mystic inheritance from the ancient Irish drui; and there had been the brief encounter with the Skraeling shaman in the Vinland forest. The more I thought upon these coincidences, the more calm I became. My life had been so strange, so disconnected from the humdrum progress of other men, that it must have a deeper purpose. The All-Father, I concluded, had not watched over me through so many vicissitudes only to let me drown in the cold, grey waters of the sea of Ireland. He had other plans for me. Otherwise, why had he shown me so many wonders in such far-flung places, or let me learn so much? I sat in the water swilling in the bottom of the coracle and tried to determine what that design might be. As I brooded on my past, I scarcely noticed the wind was dying away. A stillness settled on the water until even the swell was barely felt. In that tiny coracle, motionless save for a very gentle rocking motion, I was suspended on the surface of black sea, the darkness of the night around me, the inky depths below. I began to feel that I was leaving my own body, that I was spirit flying. From exhaustion, from exposure, or because it was Odinn's will, I went into a trancelike stupor.

A hand grasping my shoulder broke the spell.

'Sea luck!' said a voice. I looked up into a heavily bearded Norse face.

It was broad daylight, my coracle was nuzzling against the side of a small longship, and a sailor was leaning down to grab me out of the coracle.

'Look what we've got here,' said the sailor, 'a gift from Njord himself.'

'Pretty miserable gift, I would say,' commented his companion, helping drag me aboard still clutching my satchel, then sending the coracle on its way with a contemptuous kick so that the little vessel tilted and sank.

'May Odinn Farmatyr, God of Cargoes, reward you,' I managed to blurt out.

'Well, at least he speaks good Norse,' said a third voice.

My rescuers were savages. Or that is what the monks of St Ciaran's would have called them, though my word for them was different – they were vikingr, homeward bound after a season on the coast of what I later knew as Breton land. Their luck had been fair, a couple of small monasteries surprised and looted, some profitable trading for wine and pottery in the small ports farther south and now they were headed north again in their ship. They were proper seamen, so the lookout with the dawn light behind him had spotted the tiny black speck of the coracle appearing and disappearing on the gentle swells. They had rowed across to check what they had found and as they approached they had seen me sitting there, so motionless that they thought I was a corpse.

The Norse consider it propitious to rescue someone from the sea, as much for the rescuer as the rescued. So I received a kindly welcome. I was shivering with cold and they wrapped me in a spare sea cloak and gave me chunks of dried whale blubber to chew, their diet for someone who has been exposed to the cold and wet. After I was recovered, they asked me for my story and discovered that I had abundant tales to tell. This made me popular. My stories helped to pass the long hours of the homeward trip and Norsemen love a good yarn. I found myself telling my tales again and again. With each repetition I became more fluent, more able to pace the run of my narrative, to know which details caught the attention of my hearers. In short, I began to understand how satisfying it is to be a saga teller, particularly when the content of your tales has an appreciative audience. I learned that I was one of only a handful of Norse survivors from the great battle at Clontarf, so I was asked repeatedly to describe the progress of the great battle, where each man fought in the line, how each warrior had dressed for the combat, what weapons had proved best, who had said what and to whom, whether such-and-such had died with honour. And always when I came to describe how Brodir of Man had ambushed the High King and slain him in the open, though he knew it would mean his own certain death, my audience would fall silent and, as often as not, greet the conclusion of my story with a sigh of approval.

As I told the story for perhaps the twentieth time, the thought occurred to me that this might be what Odinn was intending – that I should be an honest chronicler of the Old Ways and the truth about the far-flung world of the Norsemen. Was it really Eochaid who had told me that words hold greater power than weapons? Did Senesach at St Ciaran's encourage me to learn to read the Roman and Greek scripts and write with the pen and stylus? Was it Tyrkir who showed me the cutting of runes in Greenland and taught me so much of the Elder Lore. Or were all of them really Odinn in his many disguises equipping me for my life's path?

If it was Odinn, then I am keeping his faith by writing this account, and I will describe how I travelled even farther afield in the next phase of my life and took part in events that were even more remarkable.

AUTHOR'S NOTE

THORGILS, SON OF Leif the Lucky and Thorgunna, did exist. According to the Saga of Erik the Red, 'The boy . . . arrived in Greenland, and Leif acknowledged him as his son. According to some people this Thorgils came to Iceland the summer before the Frodriver Marvels. Thorgils then went to Greenland, and there seemed to be something uncanny about him all his life.'

The events of Thorgils's life imagined here derive mostly from the Icelandic sagas, one of the great collections of world literature and widely translated, notably in the Penguin Classics. Eochaid's poem of the hermit's hut is taken from Kenneth Hurlston, *A Celtic Miscellany*, first published by Routledge & Kegan Paul, 1951; revised edition published by Penguin Books, 1971, reprinted 1973, 1975.